FADE THE HEAT

"RITA finalist Thompson takes the reader on a roller-coaster ride full of surprising twists and turns in this exceptional novel of romantic suspense."
—*Publishers Weekly* (Starred Review)

"The precise details of Thompson's novel give it a rich, edgy texture that's enthralling…. For keen characters, emotional richness and a satisfying story that doesn't fade away, read Thompson's latest."
—*RT BOOKclub*

"I highly recommend this novel to any reader who loves a spicy and sensual romance that has some mystery thrown in for fun. A true pleasure to read! Look out, romance world, Thompson is on her way to the top!"
—*A Romance Review*

"*Fade the Heat* starts off hot and never lets up. Ms. Thompson does a superb job of weaving a tale wrought with danger, secrets, murder, and love."
—*Romance Reviews Today*

"This is a remarkable and marvelous suspense thriller… A great storyline, strong characterization and a sizzling romance make *Fade the Heat* a real winner. I'm searching for more books by Colleen Thompson because this one is so great."
—*Fresh Fiction*

"[An] outstanding, fast-moving, romantic thriller…*Fade the Heat* is a riveting, highly emotional page-turner, full of twists and shocks. This is one story you won't soon forget."
—*Affaire de Coeur*

WHATEVER IT TAKES

"Go ahead and take the pistol," Spence told Claire. "Hold it if you want to, or slip it in your pocket. Do whatever it takes so you'll feel safe enough to listen to me."

"Spence," she breathed, as jumbled waves of emotion crashed into each other. Terror, love, regret…and beneath them all, a sickening awareness of the heavy scent of blood.

"Do it, please." Fatigue underscored his blue eyes, but still, they looked straight at her. "Because that's all I ask, for you to listen."

Trembling with revulsion, she picked up the weapon by its still-warm barrel, then dropped it into her pocket as quickly as if she were holding a live coal. Even so, she felt some of her equilibrium returning. She met his gaze head-on. "Give me one reason why I should."

Other books by Colleen Thompson:

FADE THE HEAT
FATAL ERROR

The
DEADLIEST
Denial

Colleen Thompson

LOVE SPELL NEW YORK CITY

To three friends I couldn't do without:
Patricia Kay, Barbara Taylor Sissel, and Jo Anne Banker.
You rank among the finest women I have ever known.

LOVE SPELL®

May 2006

Published by

Dorchester Publishing Co., Inc.
200 Madison Avenue
New York, NY 10016

ISBN 0-505-52670-0

The name "Love Spell" and its logo are trademarks of Dorchester Publishing Co., Inc.

Printed in the United States of America.

Visit us on the web at www.dorchesterpub.com.

ACKNOWLEDGMENTS

I'd like to express my appreciation to those who offered the support and expertise that helped take *The Deadliest Denial* from rough idea to finished book. To my husband, Mike, and son, Andrew, thanks, as always, for your help and understanding on the home front. I absolutely couldn't do without it. Thank you to the dear friends who faithfully read, critiqued, and reread this work: Patricia Kay, Barbara Taylor Sissel, Jo Anne Banker, Betty Joffrion, Linda Helman, and Wanda Dionne. I want also to mention my friends in both the Northwest and West Houston RWA, whose support means so much to me.

Special thanks to Houston Fire Department Paramedic Jesus Villanueva for sharing his expertise on the realities of addiction.

I owe a debt as well to the wonderful professionals I've been privileged to work with, including agent Meredith Bernstein, editor Alicia Condon, and the fabulous sales and support staff of Dorchester Publishing. Thanks for always putting forth your finest. I appreciate you.

ACKNOWLEDGMENTS

ONE

Hardly a day goes by that we don't hear it. On the news and in the papers or from stories passed along by friends or family members. How someone, usually a woman, has been destroyed by a man she loved and trusted. Beaten, sometimes. Humiliated, violated, ripped off, betrayed.

And then there are the times it comes to murder.

But as we chew these stories over, we think of all the ways it might have been, could have been, probably was her fault. Overwhelmed by the sheer volume of examples, we make ourselves feel safer by pointing out the signs the woman missed—or stubbornly refused to recognize. Telling ourselves we would know better and we would be bold enough to face the truth, unlike the foolish creature whose sad fate made the news.

Afterwards, we turn back to our own lives, to the same bad habits, poor decisions, and fractured resolutions we stumble over almost daily. But that's all right, we think, feeling superior in the knowledge that we may have our human foibles, but we didn't fall victim to the worst. . . .

As of this day, this moment, we have not yet partaken of the deadliest denial.

The worst day of Claire Winslow's life started early, with a banging at the front door that began at five a.m.

Predictably, the three-legged sheltie Spence had brought home last year barked her fool head off, so Claire's first impulse was to chase the brown-and-white hairball to the condo's living room and stop the noise before it woke the neighbors.

Her second was to stare in horror at the door as a wave of dizziness broke over her and her body trembled like the most damaged of her patients at the rehabilitation center.

Spence was due home from his shift this morning. But her husband would never bother knocking. Instead he would try to steal in silently—a real feat, considering Pogo's joyful histrionics whenever she spotted her master returning to the fold. On those occasions when he managed to slip past their sleeping pet, he would remove his badge and holster, then rouse his wife of five years with kisses . . . and often something more. Or at least he'd done that up until his friend Dave Creighton's death back in October.

When the hammering was repeated, she let go of the wriggling sheltie and switched on the nearest lamp against the predawn gloom. Bursting into motion, Claire hurried back into her bedroom and grabbed her robe, her mind stumbling through the thought: If Spence's dead, I'm not letting them tell me while I stand there in one of his old T-shirts.

If Spence's dead . . . God, no.

She pulled the robe tighter around her and told

Pogo, "If your dad's just forgotten his keys, I'm going to chew his ears off."

It would serve her husband right, too, for scaring her to death. Every cop knew his wife worried, even if it was the proverbial elephant in the living room they both tip-toed around, the big dread neither dared to speak of.

And now it's gone and happened anyway, she thought as her feet, seemingly detached from her free will, carried her to the door and her traitorous hand fingered the dead bolt.

Pogo quieted, then crouched expectantly on her single foreleg, her body quivering with the need to either bark or wag, depending on who stood behind the still-closed door.

A memory tumbled through Claire's mind: her husband's reminder only last week that this was San Antonio and not her goddamned wide-spot-in-the-road-of-a-hometown and she'd end up dead as Dave if she didn't watch herself. He'd been furious at that moment, but it was the absolute terror shining in his blue eyes that made her hesitate now, leaning forward to peer through the peephole, her lips moving in a silent prayer: *Be Spence, be Spence, be Spence.*

It wasn't. With a cry, she fumbled through unlatching the chain and releasing the locks, then threw open the door and asked the two uniformed men, "Is he dead? Or in the hospital? Has someone shot my husband? Why are you here—tell me."

Pogo lowered her crouch and whined plaintively at the pair. Though mismatched in terms of both uniform and appearance, the men stood shoulder to shoulder, their backs as straight as steel spikes and their hats held in their hands.

Claire's gaze bored into the smaller and darker of the two, the newly divorced sergeant she and Spence had had over for dinner just last Sunday. Claire had invited him out of sympathy, but she'd gotten the impression he had accepted to see how Spence was behaving around her. To make sure what was happening at work hadn't leached into their home life.

Now Raul Contreras shook his head before releasing a long breath through his nose. He looked hard at her, his deep-set brown gaze so sorrowful that she was reminded of the doctor who had told her, years before, that her sister Karen's cancer had spread to the brain.

Claire's pulse thumped wildly. She was going to die, she thought. Her heart was exploding in her chest. She wished for a split second that it would hurry up and take her.

"No," Sergeant Contreras told her. "Spencer hasn't been killed, and he's not hurt either."

At first she simply stared, unable to move or speak or draw breath. Had she heard him right, or had her mind manufactured the words that she most needed?

Hoping for some clue, she looked at the taller man, whose tan uniform stood out in contrast to the dark blue of the San Antonio PD. His hair was thick and golden brown and long for law enforcement; his features were strong, his shoulders wide and heavily muscled, as if he'd spent his youth alternating between football fields and weight rooms.

But he hadn't. Claire knew that because she knew him—a fact that shocked her. What was Joel Shepherd from her hometown doing here, at her front door?

"Spence isn't dead?" she asked both men. She needed that confirmation more than she needed answers—or even air to breathe.

"He's not dead," Joel answered, his voice deeper than she remembered, his eyes a golder shade of green. But his expression remained as grim as the day they'd buried Karen—the girl he should have married instead of Lori Beth Walters, one of her sister's class-mates. "I swear it."

Closing her eyes, Claire whispered, "Thank God. Thank God. Thank God."

Anything else she could handle. Anything else she could survive.

But she didn't understand that there were worse things. Possibilities too dark to fathom. Possibilities she first heard in the raw emotion of Sergeant Contreras's and Joel Shepherd's questions.

"May—may we come in?" her husband's supervisor asked.

"Can we call someone to be with you?" Joel added, and for the first time she noticed he wore a sheriff's badge now. "How 'bout your daddy, maybe, or a friend?"

He was laying on the good old boy a little thicker, playing up the country lawman comfort in a way that jolted forks of fear through her midsection.

Shaking her head, Claire backed up, pausing only to snatch up the fifteen-pound dog and press the lower part of her face into the thick warmth of Pogo's fur.

All the better not to scream, Claire thought as the two men entered her living room. Joel closed the door softly, but he didn't lock it. Perhaps he felt safe with his gun in its holster, or perhaps he realized, as Claire was beginning to, that the worst had come already.

"Why don't you sit down?" Contreras asked her.

Lifting her chin from the dog's warmth, Claire felt her temper boil to the surface. "And why don't you quit patronizing me and tell me right out—where the hell is Spencer? Why are you two here instead of him?"

The sergeant took another deep breath. "Last night, your husband was arrested."

"He's bein' held in Little Bee Creek, in the Buck County Jail," Joel added. "My jail."

Claire's knees loosened, and the miniature collie yelped in surprise as she was dropped. Pogo tucked her tail between her legs and hop-bounced to escape into the bedroom. Before Claire understood what was happening, the two men grabbed her arms and steered her to an armchair, where they planted her.

Shrugging off their hands, she cried, "That's a lie. Why would you say such—such—Spence can't be in Little BC. He was on patrol last night down by the River Walk. Right here in San Antonio."

She saw the two men's glances touch, saw how troubled both looked. When neither answered, she said, "Damn you. Damn you both—did my husband put you up to this? If this is some sick joke, it's not funny."

Joel sat on the sofa's edge and angled his long legs in her direction. Those green-gold eyes skewered her, reminding her of the cougars rumored to have come back to Buck County. "This is serious, Claire, and so am I. You're going to need somebody with you. Tell me now so I can call. And then we'll explain it to you."

She flipped her red-brown hair free of her robe's collar. "All of it?"

When both men nodded solemnly, Claire relented. "Call my father. Please. He's number two on my speed dial."

Number one was the entry she really wanted. Spence's number. If she could talk to him, he'd clear up this mistake in no time.

But Joel got up to call her father, then took the telephone into her bedroom and closed the door behind him. She tried to listen, but a buzzing in her ears overwhelmed the distant murmur of his voice.

"My dad's a criminal attorney, and he lives in Little BC," she told Sergeant Contreras. "He'll know how to fix this. He'll probably drive over to the jail and call us right back, tell us it's not Spence in there. You've told me yourself, Spence is a really good cop. He wouldn't be arrested."

The sergeant took the spot where Joel had been seated and looked at her from beneath the shaggy overhang of his brows. Like his hair and his thick mustache, they were salted with white strands, the only clue the man had recently celebrated his fiftieth birthday.

"I know this is hard," he said. "It's damned hard for me, too, first losing Dave and now . . . The truth is, Claire, Spencer hasn't been himself lately. You know that as well as I do."

"He saw a twelve-year-old shoot down a fellow cop." Claire heard the strain in her own voice, the bitterness that bubbled through her words, but there was nothing she could do to stop the torrent. "My husband watched his best friend die over a forty-nine-dollar video game."

Mall security, who had called the police once they caught the shoplifter, had brought him to their office, but they hadn't searched his clothes for weapons. When the two uniforms came in, the kid had panicked, whipping a little .38 out from under his untucked shirt, killing Dave and wounding the store detective before Spence shot the boy dead.

"How can you expect him to snap right back like it was nothing?" Claire demanded. "Aside from losing a close friend, Spence loves kids. And now he's killed one."

There had been knee-jerk outrage in the Hispanic community, since the boy was Mexican and Dave, Spence, and the store detective were all white, but the store's video surveillance tape had cleared her husband of wrongdoing. Still, he'd asked Claire over and over—sometimes waking her up in the middle of the night—if there was anything, anything, he could have done to save either his friend or the kid. Every time, she'd told him no, then wrapped her arms around a body made unfamiliar by its tension.

"Spencer said he'd had enough time off, enough of counseling," Contreras told her. "And I was keeping a careful eye on him, believe me."

"Not careful enough, it sounds like. Not if he really did leave his patrol to drive over an hour to Buck County last night. I still don't buy it." She expected her husband's big frame to fill the doorway any moment, expected to hear Pogo's cheerful barking at seeing her master—the man who had once lifted her from a busy street where he had found her matted and bone-thin, with one front leg mangled from a run-in with a car.

"He didn't work last night, Claire. He called in sick before his shift."

The shock of it went through her, and she wanted to scream, Impossible. Would have screamed, if she could speak. Because she'd kissed Spence good-bye last night and watched him leave wearing his uniform, his badge . . . his gun.

His gun.

"What did he do, Sergeant?" she asked in a small voice.

"We believe he killed a man in Little BC."

8

She blinked in surprise at Joel Shepherd, who was standing in the bedroom doorway. Sheriff Shepherd. She hadn't noticed him come back from calling her dad. But it was his words, not his presence, that made her mouth go dry.

"No," she told him, shaking her head. "Of course he didn't do that. Why would Spence kill anyone up there? I mean, that's where we have our—"

She clamped down on the thought. This couldn't have anything to do with the Little BC property she and Spence had just purchased, and the horse therapy center she had been planning, organizing, and raising funds for over the past two years. This had nothing to do with her dream—

The dream that Spence had asked her to put on hold in the days following Dave's shooting.

She'd told him no, she couldn't. She'd tried to make him understand that it was then or never, that if they didn't close on the acreage before Mrs. Hajek moved into the nursing home, her heir would be sure to stop the sale. Already, her realtor nephew—who hadn't bothered visiting his aunt in years—had accused Claire of taking advantage of a dying woman. If Mrs. Hajek herself hadn't rallied and threatened to disinherit the grasping little snot, Claire was sure the whole thing would have ended up in court. And if the woman's long-missing daughter, Gloria, had finally turned up . . .

"We aren't sure what this is about," Joel said as he crossed the room to stand beside her. "But we do know this. Adam Strickland wasn't the only person—"

"Adam . . . Adam who?" The name struck her as familiar, but Claire couldn't seem to place it.

"Adam Strickland," Joel answered, pausing only to

clear his throat, "wasn't the only person your husband wanted dead. There was someone else, too."

"Someone else?" She was still trying to make sense of this—or find the key that would unlock this awful nightmare and let her wake up in her bed.

From the bedroom, she heard her alarm go off, an alarm meant to begin her last day at the rehabilitation center, where she had worked for the past five years as an occupational therapist.

This is no dream, she told herself as Joel Shepherd knelt before her. No dream, the thought echoed as he took her ice-cold hand in his.

"It was you," Joel told her. "Your husband, Spencer Winslow, was planning to kill you."

TWO

This tiny cell might be cut off from the night sky, but all the same, its tarry blackness leached into Spence Winslow's thoughts.

Your third night, he told himself. This is your third night on the wrong side of the bars. All you have to do is breathe your way straight through it. Suck it in; puff it out. You remember how.

All the same, he kept up his pacing, stalking back and forth with the hopeless determination of tigers in close confines. He remembered reading somewhere how it drove the big cats crazy, how the path wore itself so deeply into their psyches that even if the animals were moved to spacious preserves, they would forever continue walking the same pattern—their behavior molded irrevocably.

But in spite of his exhaustion, Spence couldn't make himself lie down. For one thing, he couldn't get past the suspicion that pacing was the only way to pump the bellows of his lungs, the only sure way to survive until this nightmare ended—until he could convince

Joel Shepherd and the judge they had the wrong man in this cage.

Yeah, right, something whispered. Something that had wormed its way into his marrow. Something squirming and voracious that was eating at the core of him. Doubt maybe, or its kissing cousin, terror.

You're just another criminal inside the cage, Spence. Another lame excuse in a universe that teems with lame excuses.

In his ten years with the San Antonio PD, Spence had arrested his fair share of suspects. He'd jailed Hispanics, blacks, and whites alike: from the well dressed to the naked, the perfumed to those who reeked of sweat and vomit, from men to women to more juvies than he could shake a stick at. Losers with nothing more in common than big trouble—and an even more universal factor: their immutable denial.

As he stalked the dusk-dark cell, Spence kept hearing their voices. "I didn't do it, mofo. It was another brother, looked like me." "My ex-wife told my girls to say I touched them. It was probably that goddamn sleaze she's screwing." "How was I supposed to know that car was stole? One of the *vatos*, he drove up in it and offered me a sweet deal. Hell no, he didn't write no bill of sale."

After so many bullshit stories, told with such conviction, a cop learned to tune them out in self defense. On those infrequent occasions someone punched through his barriers, he'd been disappointed time and again to uncover the kind of slam-dunk evidence that warmed the cockles of the prosecutors' cold steel hearts. After a time, he could only rarely consider that the person he'd arrested might be innocent. And after

Dave's death, Spence closed down completely to that possibility.

Yet here he was, in the Buck County lockup, an ancient, crumbling jailhouse that imprisoned the memory of an especially wet Hill Country winter in its damp stone walls. He coughed like a TB case because the constant dampness had settled thick as fog inside his lungs.

They had put him in his own cell—one of only a half dozen—because cops didn't last long among chronic lawbreakers, not even in a podunk burg like Little Bee Creek. Still, he was close enough to see and smell the inmates beside him and across the narrow corridor. Close enough that the drunk-and-disorderly and assault prisoners behind the opposite set of bars were enjoying the late-night entertainment of screaming threats in his direction.

"You like it up the ass, cop?" Drunk-and-Disorderly sneered and pushed his flabby face against his cell's bars, where it was ghoulishly spotlighted by the security light shining straight down from the ceiling. His ruddy features marked him as a longtime alcoholic, and his shapeless nose and swollen eyes bespoke a brawl gone bad. " 'Cause that's what you'll get where you're going. I'll tell you what. You come over here now and I'll break you in real easy."

Emboldened by his cellmate, the weasel-like Assault One—a greasy-haired twenty-year-old who had supposedly belted his own grandma—crowded close to D&D to put in his two cents. "They gonna shove a shiv in your gut, bleed you out, and have themselves a little pig roast—that's what those boys in the state pen's gonna do."

From his bunk in the cell to Spence's right, Criminal Mischief—the jail's only other prisoner—screamed at both of them to shut up and let him get some sleep. Spence said nothing, but he almost hoped the two would hang in there with the verbal jabs. Ugly as their threats were, at least they were keeping him awake.

And keeping him from dreaming about Claire again, from seeing her tear-streaked face each time he closed his eyes and imagined the absolute hell she must be suffering—all because of him.

His body began shaking, for even with his eyes wide, he saw her dropping to her knees before him, sobbing into Pogo's thick fur—both the woman and the dog so real and solid that he couldn't keep himself from reaching for them.

Reaching out to bang his hands into the rough chill of a stone wall. He turned away from the hallucination, his breathing quicker and more ragged and his pacing more agitated than ever. He glanced wildly around the tiny cell, but rough as they'd been with him, Sheriff Shepherd and the deputies had left him nothing he could hurl, nothing he could kick or smash or use to hurt anyone. Not even himself.

Breaking his long silence, Spence swore until the jail's walls echoed with his anguish, drowning out the voices of the other prisoners. But not even the harshness of his words could stop the images from tumbling through his mind: his pretty young wife, smiling as she swung into the saddle, her red-brown hair fluttering around her shoulders as her mount galloped away from him into a meadow filled with bluebonnets.

Spence hadn't broken down through his arrest or his arraignment, hadn't buckled when the judge set his bail at a cool million or his attorney informed him the department was taking steps to fire him. He hadn't even flinched when Claire's father glared at him across the courtroom. Though on some level, Spence figured he deserved every bit of it. Behind the thick wall of unreality that iced his vision, none of it seemed possible; none of it seemed real.

He continued pacing, ignoring the catcalls of the prisoners across from him and warning himself he couldn't fall apart now—not if he wanted to live to take Claire into his arms again, to make her understand that he'd been wrong, dead wrong, to turn away from her in his pain. That he'd been a lot of things, a lot of bad things, but aside from that horrible, hellish moment in the security office of the department store, he had never been a killer.

Even if some sonofabitch had gone through one hell of a lot of trouble to make him look like one.

Three weeks later

Peering over the saddled back of the new horse, Claire felt fear jolt through her, filling her mouth with the sour-sharp taste of electricity.

What was her father doing here now, when he'd told her today he was driving to San Antonio to show a realtor the condo she had shared with Spence? Claire hadn't been back since the morning Raul Contreras and Joel Shepherd dropped the bomb on her. She would still be wearing the same clothes she'd put on that morning if Janine, her friend from the rehab center, hadn't taken pity and packed up and delivered several boxes of what she'd deemed necessities.

Because Claire couldn't face her father now, she swung aboard the horse Coyote. Because she couldn't bear more bad news, she pretended she hadn't glanced up the hill and spotted his brand-new long white Cadillac pulling in behind her dark green pickup. Instead she bent low in the saddle to unhook the loop of rope that closed the practice ring's gate. Once clear, she nudged the gray gelding's sides until he trotted briskly through the opening and in between two pastures, where six other horses looked up from their grazing.

Though he was blind in one eye and nearly white with age, old Coyote rose to the occasion, his gait lengthening before shifting into a glass-smooth lope. As the west pasture's tenants raced along the fence line and whinnied after them, Claire told herself she'd needed to try out Coyote anyway. So what if Ellen Martin, the program's expert trainer, had assured her the old schooling horse was calm and patient enough to handle their clientele? If they wanted to get therapy sessions started next month on schedule, it was her responsibility, her obligation to—

That's a damned lie, her conscience interrupted, forcing her to face the fact that her real goal was no loftier than disappearing behind a mixed stand of gnarled cedar and mesquite trees. But if it was, so be it, for in the past three weeks, she had choked down more bad news than most people had to swallow in a lifetime. And every bit of it, from the deleted e-mails recovered from their laptop computer's hard drive to the audiotape Joel Shepherd had grimly played for her, had gone down like a spoonful of rusted tacks.

Still, it wasn't so much the news her father might be bringing that had Claire riding toward the taller trees clustered near the bluffs. It was what she needed to tell him that had her scared and confused enough to make a clicking sound at the old Arabian to hurry him along.

Put it out of your mind, she told herself as they meandered through the fringe of wildflowers and mountain laurels that bloomed an ode to April. Less than a minute later, she paused beneath the overarching branches of a live oak to watch the morning sunlight filter through its leaves, and to feel the cooler, moister air against her skin.

Stay here in this place, this moment, and think about how beautiful it is. Think about how peaceful.

From the moment her father's eighty-six-year-old neighbor, Mrs. Hajek, offered her the west section of the old family compound, Claire had known it would be the perfect place for healing. But the past fall when she and Spence had bought it, she'd had no idea she would need the eighty acres to heal her broken heart.

"I know it's sentimental—that your old neighbor wants you to have it because you remind her of her long-lost daughter. And I know it's the bargain of a lifetime, too, but you don't want this place," Spencer had insisted as the two of them rustled through dried grasses, then walked beneath the sheltering arms of the oak grove. Though deep olive leaves clung to the mid-October trees, the couple's hiking boots crunched acorns so thick that both the deer and feral hogs had tired of them. "It's too far from town, for one thing. Besides, your father's sure to stop by every day. Maybe more than once a day, now that he's closed his San Antonio office."

"It's not such a bad drive. I commuted before I met you, and Dad did it for years." Though he represented the occasional local client out of his home office, her father liked to joke that Little BC didn't have enough sin to keep a criminal attorney, a Baptist preacher, or a part-time prostitute in business. San Antonio, on the other hand, had earned him more than enough to buy back and meticulously restore the stone-and-cypress ranch house his father had been forced to sell back in the fifties.

As she thought of how much he enjoyed showing off his pride and joy, Claire smiled and added, "Besides, I'm always glad to see him."

But she felt guilty almost as soon as she had said it, for she knew this hadn't been her husband's point.

Her father had never liked Spence, partly because, as a criminal defense attorney, Will Meador distrusted cops on principle, and partly because his daughter's new relationship had cemented her desire to move to San Antonio, a city he associated with the criminals—or "suspects," as he would certainly correct her—he'd spent decades representing. But mainly, Claire realized, because no man on earth could measure up to her father's hopes for his sole surviving child.

Claire had led her husband past a stand of possumhaw holly drooping beneath the weight of jewel-bright red berries. Moving beyond the screen of shrubs, they stepped out onto a limestone bluff that overlooked Little Bee Creek, some thirty feet below. Upstream, rust-colored cypress trees guarded the opposite shoreline like a line of ancient sentries, their straight gray trunks so thick that she and Spence together could not wrap their arms around them. But here, where the creek curved away from them, its flow had undermined the bluff—and carved out a swimming hole. Its deep waters were so clear they could make out the shapes of fish darting among the rocks that lined the bottom—or perhaps they were the spirits of the ancient Indians whose arrowheads occasionally turned up along the stony shore.

At his first sight of it, she heard her husband's sharp intake of breath.

"Gorgeous, isn't it?" she had prompted.

He wouldn't say so aloud, for the weeks-old wounds from the shooting were still so raw and ragged that such an admission was beyond him. But his blue eyes widened as he craned his neck to take in the wooded swells of low hills just beyond them, and the view that stretched out so far, the green along its edges faded into silver. It was a vista unbroken by roads, power lines, or any sign of other humans. The only noises were the light breeze as it shivered through the tree-tops and Little Bee Creek's chatter as it washed over a bend dotted with worn-smooth rounded rocks.

Unwilling to disturb the sacred stillness, she circled around her husband and murmured into his ear.

"When I was a little girl, the Hajeks let me have the run of the place. Their daughter, Gloria, had disappeared years before, and you could tell how much they missed having kids around.

"I camped in the hunting cabin they used to rent out," she continued, "and climbed down the bluff to fish the creek for little bass and trout." Her father would have had a fit if he had known it. Unlike her sister Karen, however, Claire let nothing deter her—not even the distant memory of their mother's tragic death. To Claire, who was only two when it had happened, the story seemed apocryphal, a boogie-monster legend meant to keep her from having fun.

That October day with Spence, she wasn't thinking about what her father still referred to as The Accident. She was more intent on spinning out a tale of her own choosing—more intent on erasing the memories of the bad dreams he had had the night before.

"Sometimes, when the sun got too hot," she'd breathed into the shell-like curve of Spence's ear, "I'd peel my clothes right off and splash around that deep hole—"

He turned his head to look at her, and at long last, a little of the sadness lifted from his eyes. A weak grin slanted across his face, a ghost of the smile that had attracted Claire when she first met him. It had happened at a birthday barbecue for Janine, a mutual friend and rehab co-worker who had grown up in Spence's San Antonio neighborhood. Alive with mischief, that smile had turned his ordinary features into something that set Claire's bones vibrating like a wellstruck tuning fork.

"Are you trying to seduce me into agreeing with you on this?" he asked, then followed up with a selfdeprecating shrug. "Because I'm telling you now, I'm a man who can be bought."

She understood that he was trying for her sake, so she tickled his neck with soft kisses and ran her hands beneath his shirt. Since Spence was such a geology nut, she tried to sweeten the deal by whispering, "This bluff we're standing on is mostly limestone. Beneath our feet, it's honeycombed with caves—you can get inside them if you swing off the edge here with a rope. That's why they call it Little Bee Creek—it looked like a hive to the first—"

He'd turned to pull her close and answered in a low growl that sounded almost like the old Spence, a voice that made the fine hairs rise behind her neck. "Enough about the history. Let's hear some more about your naked, nubile little body splashing around in that

20

swimming hole. Or maybe one of those caves that's big enough to spread out a sleeping bag. Or how about that old cabin? It looks in pretty decent shape."

Claire slowed the old horse and shook her head in an attempt to dispel the painful memories. It didn't work. Lately her mind succeeded at nothing but replaying every aspect of her life with Spence, the memories repeating as stubbornly as a snatch of song stuck in the brain.

I charmed him into this place, she realized, still thinking of their purchase. I knew how badly he was hurting, how ambivalent he felt, but I seduced him with these trees, this land, with Little Bee Creek and my body. And in the wake of their lovemaking, she had sealed the deal with the one promise she knew he could not resist: "We'll own all this, you and I. And someday we'll pass this place on to our kids."

At the thought, she circled around a clump of prickly pear cacti, but she barely noticed their dazzling yellow blooms. Instead she turned Coyote's head toward home, her throat clogging with tears. For suddenly, to her mind, the threat of dealing with her father, even of telling him her news, was less painful than the sight of Little Bee Creek—and more memories of the time she had spent there with her husband . . . her best friend . . . her lover. . . .

The same lover who had paid a man ten thousand dollars to put a bullet through her brain.

As she rode past the stock pond and up the hill to the newly built paddock, Claire caught a glimpse of the gleaming white Caddy before she spotted her dad in the shade of a pecan tree. He was involved in a predictably one-sided chat with the horse trainer's daughter, Megan Martin, a sprightly seventeen-year-old volunteer who had come today to muck out stalls—and possibly sneak in a little riding. Meg, whose long, straight locks were this week dyed an in-your-face blond, was talking at her usual breakneck speed, using her hands to dramatize whatever she was saying, while Claire's dad squatted down on expensive, hand-tooled Western boots and rubbed Pogo's belly. Now and again he nodded for Meg's benefit, but even from this distance, Claire got the distinct impression that he wasn't really listening.

Not that Meg would allow such a thing to deter her. The girl needed to talk the way most people needed oxygen; an attentive listener was only the icing on the cake.

Though he was close to seventy and had had angioplasty to open a blocked blood vessel two years earlier, Claire's father looked as lean as ever in his boot-cut jeans. His eyes were still as deep a brown as hers and his face looked more weathered by the elements than by age. His friends—a cadre of socially prominent Little BC citizens ranging from the owner of On the Hoof Feed and Seed to a retired judge who had presided over a number of Will Meador's cases—often kidded him about his ageless appearance. But in the terrible weeks since Spence's arrest, Claire had noticed more silver in his thick, dark hair, more of a stoop to his proud bearing—enough so that she had nagged him only yesterday to make an appointment with his doctor for a checkup.

When he glanced up at her, his grave expression struck raw fear in Claire. Swallowing hard, she threw her leg over the Western saddle and slid down in the dust some ten feet short of him.

"Want me to take care of Coyote?" Meg asked, her slender hand already reaching for the reins.

"Thanks," Claire managed before adding, "Could you walk him cool, please, and give him a good rubdown? But don't put him back with the other horses. I don't want him in there until someone can watch them interact. Let's keep him in the little pen for now."

No matter how small a herd or how well mannered under saddle, the horses spent a few days sorting out their pecking order with each new addition. One of the mares, a pretty palomino, was recovering from a nasty kick to her hock, and the program didn't need any more expensive vet bills.

"Sure thing, Claire. Then I'll poop-scoop the east pasture." Meg lingered, though, clearly waiting for the words that were her only paycheck.

Claire was wiping her sweaty palms on her jeans when she finally noticed. Mentally kicking herself in gear, she added, "I don't know what we'd do without you, Meg. Feel free to take out Bushwhack once you're finished."

Heaven only knew the big bay could use the exercise. Before they had purchased Bushwhack for the program—their very first therapy mount—Spence had ridden some to please her, but horses had never been his thing. Yet somehow Bushwhack had been drawn to her husband in the dark days following the shooting. Whenever Spence came to help dig postholes—or whatever excuse Claire used to lure him out-of-doors—the young gelding had followed him like an outsized dog, making a game of pilfering the leftover Christmas candy canes her husband kept in his shirt pocket. Even, on one memorable occasion, eliciting laughter from a man who had forgotten how to smile.

23

Since Spence's arrest, Claire hadn't been able to bring herself to give Bushwhack the extra attention that he craved. Swallowing the sour taste that filled her mouth, she reminded Meg, "Don't forget to wear your helmet. I don't want you getting hurt."

Claire unclipped the chin strap of her own riding helmet and removed it. It was a precaution she insisted on for everyone who rode at Monarch Ranch, not only for insurance reasons, but because she had worked with far too many brain-injured children and adults to take any chances.

The girl beamed and thanked her, flashing a hundred-kilowatt smile before leading Coyote away. As the pair walked off, Claire could hear Meg chattering happily to the old horse, saying, "Oh my God, Coyote. You'll never believe who called me for help with his geometry homework last night. . . ."

Smiling, Claire shook her head and told her father, "I hope she didn't wear out your eardrums."

He smiled weakly and gave Pogo a last pat. "Oh, you know I enjoy young people."

Though she did—for years, he'd mentored kids from the consolidated high school's debate team, whose framed graduation photos hung on the wall of his home office—the pain in his dark eyes sent fresh fear shafting through her. He was already so upset about her situation, so outraged that someone she had loved and trusted had arranged to have his "little girl" shot, he could barely eat or sleep. How could she add to his grief—or the strain on his health?

"Dad?" she asked, hating the tremor in the question, the way the strength and confidence had faded from her voice.

You've got to toughen up, she told herself, as she did

at least a dozen times a day. You have to do what needs to be done, or that shit might as well have killed you. And right now, you have to tell Dad. Tell him everything.

Her father rose slowly, his knees crackling and popping as they did so often. Moving closer, he hugged her to him. So hard, so fiercely, that she wondered if he had somehow learned her news.

"I'm so sorry, Claire," he said into her hair. "I did everything I could to stop it, but I couldn't—"

She pulled back far enough to stare into his face. "What's going on, Dad? What now? Has—has something happened to him?"

She could not bear to say her husband's name aloud, but her mind was full of Spencer. Had he found a way to take his life, or had the other prisoners hurt him? As horrible, as painful and inexplicable as his meltdown had proved, somehow his death or injury would make her feel worse. She told herself she was a sap for feeling that way, yet her raw, bruised heart remained unmoved.

It loved him still, no matter what her better judgment told her or her friends advised. *What the hell is wrong with me?*

Her father's brown eyes darkened. "Spence is fine. Too fine for my taste. He's going to be released."

"What? Released? How could they let him go? I know they never found that biologist's body—Adam Strickland, I mean." After Spence's arrest, she had remembered where she'd heard the name. The twenty-six-year-old, a gangly-looking man with tousled reddish hair, had come by the property to request access to the creekside area not long after they'd been hit by heavy rains. He was testing the water for some environmental study he was doing for his doctoral thesis, something about the impact of runoff on an obscure endangered salamander. With his boundless enthusiasm for his project, his mustard-colored hip waders, and a pair of glasses so mud-flecked she couldn't imagine how he saw, she had figured him as some kind of eco-nerd—until he had asked her to dinner. She had laughed about it afterward, telling Spence that only the condition of Strickland's glasses—and possibly a head cold—could account for the fact that he'd hit on a woman who had just spent the morning mucking out stalls. Days after he'd disappeared, Joel Shepherd—exhausted from tromping along the tributaries of the flood-stage creek—had come up with the harebrained theory that Spence had been insanely jealous. Supposedly he had mentioned to some friend of his how he intended to run off the biologist if the man came "sniffing around again"—but Claire didn't buy it for a minute.

"Maybe that man just wandered off on his own, but Spe—Spen—my husband tried to have me murdered." Because she could not quite wrap her brain around that part either, even now, she added, "At least that's what everyone keeps saying."

"Everybody's right," her father insisted. "But that doesn't mean he can't make bail."

"How could he do that? He doesn't have a million dollars. He doesn't even have the ten percent he needs to get the bond." Every penny they could scrape together had gone into the down payment for this land. Though the Monarch Ranch Foundation had built the combination office/stable, the paddock, and the rings, the property belonged to her.

And Spence.

"They didn't let him use the land, did they? They wouldn't let him make it his collateral?" She had cashed in her retirement fund, eight years' worth, to make the purchase happen. Aside from what little she expected to get out of the condo's sale, this property represented everything she had—as well as the future of her dream. She remembered her father talking about trying to get Spence to sign some papers turning over the property to her, but she had been too shell-shocked these past weeks to ask if he had signed it.

Her father shook his head. "No, they wouldn't do that. Not unless you gave permission."

She snorted. "Not in this lifetime." She might be a total sap, but she still had a handful of working brain cells.

A smile ghosted across her father's features, but it quickly disappeared. "There was a bail reduction hearing. His friend, Sergeant Contreras, swore he'd keep Spence straight, make sure he'd adhere to the conditions—"

"What conditions?"

"His bail will be revoked if he has any contact with you. He can't call or come to see you. He can't set foot on my property as long as you're staying at the house, and he's not allowed here either. He can't possess or be around a firearm, nor can he use a computer."

She shivered with a sick chill, both at the thought of Spence holding a weapon and at the memory of the e-mail he had sent to a so-far-untraceable address.

"It's an impossible situation," he had written. "I don't know how much longer I can take being in the same room with her, sleeping in that bed, listening to her rattle on about her Mary-fricking-Sunshine farm for crippled kiddies. God, I'm sick to death of hearing all that

27

bullshit. It makes me wish she would just go away—disappear forever. It makes me wish someone would fix her, that someone would shut her up for good."

There had been other e-mails, worse ones, but no one would let her see them. Joel and her father had only let her look at one because she'd refused to accept their explanations until she recognized her husband's words.

As she had, God help her. During the investigation of the department store shooting, in the wake of Dave's death, she'd done her damnedest to be patient and supportive. Still, they'd fought about her project several times, about the money they'd sunk into it and about the demands her newly fledged foundation was making on her time. On their worst day—Spence's worst day—he had used those same words, calling her dream the "Mary-fricking-Sunshine farm for crippled kiddies."

At the ugly sneer in his voice, she'd flown into a white-hot rage. She'd be damned if she would let his cynicism ruin something that meant so much to her—and not only to her, but to the volunteers who'd banded together to give of their time, the parents and trainers and therapeutic professionals who had come on board, the businesses both large and small that had signed on as program sponsors, and especially to the kids whose lives they all hoped to transform. She knew things were hard for Spence—knew he had no other family to support him—but that day, for the first time in her marriage, she had stormed out of the condo and driven to her dad's place on the property next door to this one. And she had stayed there for two nights before her husband came to get her—to tell her how sorry he felt, and how deeply shamed.

Brushing away tears, she thrust aside the memory of their bittersweet reunion . . . and the lovemaking that had followed.

"Is he—is he out of jail now?" she asked her father.

He sighed deeply. "If he isn't, he soon will be."

Claire pinched her lower lip beneath her teeth, then swallowed, though her throat had suddenly grown sore. "Do you think—do you think I'll be safe?"

Her father reached behind himself and pulled out something small and dark. He held it with exaggerated care, his fingers caging it as if it were a pet bird that might take flight at any moment.

But it wasn't. As his hand unfurled, she saw that it was a pistol. Small and gleaming. Hideous.

Reverently, he lifted it, then offered it to her.

Claire took a full step backward, raising empty palms.

"What?" Her throat had gone so tight, she could barely force the words free. "What the hell do you think I'm going to do with that?"

"You're going to take it from me, Claire." Tears trembled in her father's eyes, tears all too close to spilling. "You're going to keep it with you at all times. And when that bastard comes for you, you're going to shoot your loving husband right between the eyes."

THREE

Sergeant Raul Contreras read Spence the riot act as they jounced along in a little lime green Datsun that looked old enough to vote, and then some. Every time Raul put his foot on the gas pedal, the thing shuddered before coughing out more ominous black smoke.

"If you even think about making some dumb-ass move, think about this piece of shit I'm driving," Raul snarled as they wound along one of Buck County's more infamous rural roads. Rough with broken asphalt—and the occasional patch of weeds thriving in its potholes—this one wended its way among increasingly rocky wooded hills and played tag with a clear, rain-swollen creek. "This is what I've got, since the divorce. Carla's driving my new Honda, and I'm in a shitball apartment on the wrong side of town, thinking about taking my retirement so I can start a second career in the private-frigging-security business—well, what I'm saying is the ten grand I scraped together to bail you out was a very big deal to me."

"So why did you?" Spence knew he should be grateful, but the sight of the hills and the spring foliage was making him morose. If the prosecutor had his way, he would be locked up so long, he would forget what green leaves looked like, forget the way the breeze could pile tall clouds one atop another. Forget the smell of freedom and the soft warmth of fresh air.

Raul struggled to jam the Datsun into fourth gear. "You've worked with me for, what, six years? You and Dave both. And after what happened last fall, I couldn't help thinking—"

Spence shivered with a sudden chill, then cranked up his open window. "Don't bring up last fall again. This has nothing to do with that day. This is someone setting me up. Or don't you believe me? Haven't you even bothered checking out how that arrest went down? How someone sent a message to draw me out to Buck County—where I got arrested and knocked down with a stun gun before I ever got a word in edgewise."

The transmission ground a protest, and Raul darted a glance his way. In that instant of eye contact, Spence had his answer—even before his sergeant spoke.

"I think," Raul said carefully, "I think things started going south after Dave died. You lost your way, Spence, and I partly blame myself for that. I should have seen it coming."

Spence popped the plastic dash so hard it hurt his hand. "Goddamm it, Raul. This is Claire we're talking about—my Claire. I may be a little screwed up, but there's one thing I sure as hell know. She's been the best thing in my life, the single shining island in this cesspool."

"Elegantly put as always, Winslow." The tension in Raul's face belied his levity. "Somebody ought to write that down and put it in a love song."

The squad room–style banter did nothing to ease Spence's anxiety, though before Dave's death, he had been as quick to make a joke as he was to laugh at those at his expense.

"I swear I didn't do it," he repeated, more aware than ever of the way countless suspects before him had worn away the words' meaning with their myriad denials. Before finances forced him to drop out a semester short of his degree, Spence had studied geology in college. He still loved poking among rock formations, imagining how time shaped them—so it came to him that each suspect's repetition cast a grain of sand into the wind. Over the years and decades, perhaps millennia, the resulting sandstorm had chipped and weathered and finally carved to slivers the monolith of human trust.

Even his own friend's. He could tell from Raul's long silence that his subordinate's guilt or innocence was irrelevant. The sergeant had stuck his neck out for Spence out of loyalty—and nothing more. Well, screw Contreras, then. Let him draw his pension and become a freaking rent-a-cop, if he couldn't even believe in—

A loud crack made Spence duck instinctively in anticipation of a bullet. But the rattling bumps that followed, the small car's sudden swerve, and Raul's struggle to guide it to the rocky shoulder all pointed to a blowout.

"Goddammit, how do you like that?" Raul asked. "Those tires were the newest things on this heap. Spent a hundred thirty bucks on them last month."

Spence wondered what kind of tires someone could get for that price—although the blowout pointed to the answer. Climbing from the car, he saw that the right front tire had disintegrated into black ribbons, which were strewn like so many dead snakes across the broken surface of the road.

"Got a spare?" he asked. Figuring he owed Raul a change—at the very least—he rolled up his shirtsleeves.

"Sure thing." Contreras went around to the trunk, popped it, and swore fiercely. "The damned thing's flat, too. Guess I should've replaced it when I did the others."

He looked up and down the road, which curved past a rock-strewn pasture populated by a scruffy-looking collection of big gray goats. "Maybe somebody will be along soon. If I hold out my badge, maybe they'll—"

"How many cars have we passed?" Spence asked. "I can't remember seeing any. Like I told you earlier, this road's a little more direct, but most people opt for the state highway. We could wait here for a couple hours, and even then there's no guarantee anyone would stop."

"Son of a—"

"Our best bet is to hike over to the ranch road that intersects with this one in, oh, about a mile and a half. Then hang a right and walk about three miles to the intersection with the state highway. There's an old-style service station on the corner. They still have 'em in Buck County."

"So maybe four, five miles?" Raul glanced upward at the silver bellies of the clouds. "Doesn't look too threatening, and we still have hours of light. I even have my running shoes here in the trunk."

"Never knew you were such an optimist," Spence said as Raul leaned against the bumper and changed from Western boots into a surprisingly expensive-looking pair of white shoes. Spence had on the jeans, faded chambray shirt, and beat-up tennis shoes he'd changed into before heading to Joe Reno's place on the night of his arrest. The same night he'd been handed a message that lured him to Buck County like a lamb to sacrifice. His stomach spasmed around the memory's icy core.

Raul started down the road, then glanced back at Spence. "You aren't coming? Would've thought you'd be glad enough for a chance to walk, after a few weeks in a cage. Especially the way you like to hike."

Spence, Claire, Dave and his girlfriend, Marissa, had hiked together in the Grand Canyon last year on their vacation. All that gorgeous rock, all those epochs of geology . . . the memory of it was almost enough to make Spence smile.

Almost, but not quite.

"I was just thinking of Gus Patton, the guy who runs the service station," Spence explained. "His family's lived in these parts since roughly the last ice age. Like Claire's family, the Meadors. There's a good chance Patton's not going to want my business."

"You really think . . ." Raul smoothed his mustache, and his thick brows drew together. "Close as it is to the city, I keep forgetting we're in Bumfuck. You probably ought to wait here, maybe lay low if you hear someone coming. I'm going to try to talk the guy into a ride back with the tire, and I'd hate to piss him off by having you along."

Spence nodded. "Might be a good idea if you happen to flash your department ID when you take out your wallet, too."

"Why's that?"

"Old Man Patton doesn't like Hispanics. Thinks nothing about rattling off about lazy jigaboos, sisterhumpin' white trash, and thievin' Mezkins. Somehow he gets away with it, maybe because he's an equal-opportunity hater. But he'll think twice about cheating a guy who could arrest him."

Contreras scowled. "Sounds like a charming individual. Thanks for the heads-up. I'll bring you along a Coke when I come back."

As Spence watched him go, his imagination conjured the bubbly cola sweetness of an ice-cold soft drink. Damn, he was sorry he would miss it. And sorry, too, to take advantage of Raul's trust. But he had no intention of being here by the time his sergeant made his way back.

By then, he intended to be well on his way to seeing Claire for the first time since his arrest. And more than likely, for the last time ever.

"Oh my God—oh my God, Ms. Winslow." Megan Martin's voice squeaked in her excitement. "You have to come right away."

"Not now, Meg." Standing at the lone desk in the small and still-spare office built on one end of the stable, Claire raised two fingers in a wait-a-minute signal. With her other hand, she deftly slipped the pistol into the pocket of her jacket and prayed the girl hadn't spotted the weapon.

After the strange conversation with her father, Claire had retreated here, ostensibly to brew a pot of coffee. But really she'd needed time to regroup, to decide what to do about the gun he'd given her. And to figure out how she felt about her husband making bail. She wished now she'd locked the door and turned the lights off, because the last thing she wanted at the moment was Megan drowning her in chatter.

"I mean it, Ms. Winslow. You—you really need to come."

This time Claire whipped around, recognizing that it was fear squeezing the girl's voice higher. Alarm jolted up Claire's spine as she thought of Spence—and her father's insistence that, judge's orders or not, her husband would come for her. "What's happened?"

Tears slicked Meg's reddened face, and her lips trembled as she spoke. "It's Coyote. He's down—You have to hurry, please. He looks—he looks real bad. His eyes were rolling, and he's flailing his legs, struggling to get up. He wouldn't let me—I tried, but I couldn't get near him."

All thoughts of Spence forgotten, Claire instantly went into action, grabbing a halter and a rope from the tack room. Megan whirled around her like a blond comet orbiting the sun, her thin legs working overtime to keep up with Claire's longer strides.

"I was riding past Coyote's pen when I saw he wasn't there. At first I thought I might not have chained the gate right," Meg explained as she followed Claire outside. "Then I saw the fence was down in back."

At the hitching post, where Meg had tied the sturdy bay Bushwhack, Claire paused long enough to shoot the girl a sharp look. "Again? That's the third break we've had in the past week. And don't tell me another dead tree fell across it."

Meg shook her head. "It looked like someone cut it—then I heard poor Coyote from that little ravine back behind the trees. I guess he must have fallen, and he was—God, he was making the most horrible sounds—I've never heard a horse scream. I didn't even know they could. I hated to leave him, but I had no idea what to do."

Claire spared another moment to lay her hand on Meg's arm.

"You did the right thing, coming for me. Coyote wouldn't mean to, but he could really hurt you with that thrashing. Right now I need you to stay calm. I'll take Bushwhack and find Coyote. I want you to stay here in the office and call your mother right away." In spite of her tough-talking, never-say-die attitude, the program's trainer had gone home earlier, miserable with spring allergies. But Ellen would reappear in a flash as soon as she learned of the emergency. And unlike her daughter, she would know exactly what should be done.

"Get a hold of Dr. Brummell, too," Claire added. "We're sure to need a vet."

Meg nodded, relief in her blue eyes. From the looks of her, the girl wasn't eager to witness the old Arabian's suffering again, and that was just as well. Claire's cell phone never worked out here—they were too far from a tower—so she needed Meg to man the phone. And if Coyote's injury was as devastating as it sounded, it would be best to keep her out of range.

At the thought, Claire felt herself begin to tremble. She would give anything—anything she owned—to have someone else to turn to, someone to put in charge. Someone emotionally equipped, who wasn't coping with a traitorous husband, not to mention her own pathetic inability to quit caring what happened to the bastard. Even her father, who didn't really know squat about horses, would have been a welcome sight, except that, at her insistence, he'd gone ahead and driven to San Antonio to meet the realtor.

But Claire was already untying the bay horse from the hitching post and looking downhill toward the pasture, her jaw tightening with grim resolve.

There was no one else to do this. And nothing but her courage standing between an injured animal and a world of pain.

A short time later, it was the rain that brought Claire to herself: light rain that chilled her as she sat among the rocks, dead leaves, and broken branches that lined the deeply veed ravine.

She used one hand to wipe the mix of salt tears and fresh water from her face. The other, moving of its own volition, stroked the cooling silver neck.

At first she had imagined that the sharp crack of the shot she'd fired had ruptured both her eardrums. But as her jeans wicked up the dampness, she heard sound come back into the world: raindrops tapping lightly at the mountain laurel's green leaves, small frogs peeping out their lusty declarations, and a pair of cardinals singing to each other. Life, abundant and oblivious to the death around it. And always, always moving forward, as if in defiance of the doom that lay in wait.

At the thought, Claire's hand moved from Coyote's neck onto her belly. And then her gaze flew upward, toward a louder sound—a foot cracking a branch?

She sucked in a breath to call out, but then it came to her that either Ellen Martin or the vet would have shouted her name in an attempt to find her, or come running if either had been close enough to hear the blast. Whomever she heard was moving slowly and, for the most part, quietly; she had to strain her ears to catch the sound of someone coming nearer.

Or something, she thought nervously, recalling the reports of a cougar spotted hunting in the area, a mountain lion large enough to take a deer—or maybe a grown woman.

Don't be stupid. Who had ever heard of a cougar attacking anyone around here? Reaching for the pistol she had laid beside the dead horse, Claire's heart pounded an off-kilter rhythm.

Spence, then? Had he come here for her, as her father had warned he would? Her stomach squeezed itself up toward her throat.

At a crunching near the ravine's edge some twelve feet above, Claire raised the pistol, aimed it toward the sound . . .

And nearly had a heart attack when Sheriff Joel Shepherd crested the rim, his own gun drawn—and pointed straight down at her head.

With a scalded-cat cry, she let go of her weapon and lifted her palms. At the same moment, Joel gave a deeper shout and jerked his gun's barrel toward the low, gray sky.

"Jesus, Claire." He was breathing hard, sweat dripping from the damp hair beneath his broad-brimmed hat. "I nearly shot you. . . ."

His head turned slightly, and she saw his eyes widen at the awful sight: the gray gelding lying dead beside her in the ravine's bottom; a tiny bullet hole dribbling blood onto the white star on his forehead; the horse's horribly twisted foreleg and the rocks kicked over all around his body, where his struggling had dislodged them.

Joel's gun hand shook visibly. "Meg was telling me you were out here when I heard that shot and came running. What the hell happened?"

"You can put that thing away," she said, her gaze

glued to his weapon. Her voice sounded small and hollow, as if its owner had plummeted down a deep and distant well. "The shot you heard was—it was just me, doing what needed to be done."

Though the day had warmed to the midsixties, Claire's teeth chattered, clacking together painfully. She felt strange, outside herself, so hyperaware that she saw Joel's green-gold eyes dilate as they adjusted to the dimness beneath the canopy of trees.

Holstering his weapon, he asked, "Are you hurt?"

Her head shook of its own volition. Like the hand that stroked the coarse mane, it didn't feel as if it were a part of her.

"I had to do it." The explanation loosed a fresh onslaught of tears, but now it didn't matter. She had been strong for the few minutes when it counted and didn't give a damn what Joel thought about her crying. "I could see—hell, anyone could see—that broken femur."

She kept her eyes averted from Coyote. She had to, to keep from vomiting. "And the way he kicked and struggled, all he was doing was hurting himself more. And the screaming. Dear God. I could hear him halfway from the office. I couldn't stand to let him go on suffering like that. Couldn't make him wait for the vet to come and end it."

After scrambling down the ravine's steep side, Joel took her by the elbow. He pulled her to her feet and into his strong arms.

"You did right, Claire." As he spoke, he stroked her back. "You did right. I would have done the same thing. No horse could survive a break like that."

She pulled away, partly to see if he meant what he said and partly because of the perverse thought that kept roaring through her head. *I want Spence, only Spence. Spence's arms around me. Spence's voice telling me whether it was right.*

When Joel reached for her again, she saw the gold flash of his ring. The reminder of a wedding band, which was totally at odds with what was flickering in his expression.

"You took ten years off my life," he said. "You know that?"

"Hasn't done me much good either."

Glancing at the horse's body, he asked, "How did he get down here?"

Claire chewed her lower lip as a possible scenario came together in her mind. "We've had three fences down this week, two with dead trees laid across them, but this one looks like someone cut the wire. I'd say a vandal did it, and then the horse spooked—or was spooked intentionally, and he shot right out the opening. Hit this drop-off at a gallop and fell hard against that big rock. When I get my hands on the idiot delinquent who caused this, I'm going to strangle—"

"Come on, collect your gun there and let's walk back toward the office. You look cold, and you've been through a hard thing. The vet got held up, but Meg said your trainer and a volunteer are on the way. They'll be here soon to help with the arrangements."

For the burial, he meant. They would have to hire a backhoe and some men with ropes and . . . Claire couldn't bear to think about it.

Nodding woodenly, she forced herself to pocket the pistol once more, then let Joel help her up the rocky slope and onto level ground. She saw that Bushwhack was gone; terrified by Coyote's screams, the smell of blood, and the loud crack of the gunshot, he'd proba-

41

bly broken free, then bolted for the safety of his pasture. She would have to ask someone to find him and give him the TLC he'd need. She couldn't bear to see another good horse ruined.

Joel paused to look at the break in the fence as they walked past it. "I think you're right about it bein' cut," he said, "but what makes you think it was a kid?"

She shrugged, "Who else would do something like—"

"Your husband. I figured Spence had found you. That's why I ran so fast. He bailed out a few hours ago."

Claire jerked away, as if she had been struck. "Why is everyone so sure he'll come for me? He's not an idiot. He knows he'll go back to jail if he does something so stupid."

"He's been asking to see you or to call you. Pleading, actually—demanding. Every single day—hell, ten times every day—since he was arrested. He seemed awful single-minded on the issue." Joel shook his head and looked disgusted. "Unfortunately, Judge Ahern wasn't concerned. He figured Sergeant Contreras can keep Spence in line."

"I'm sure he will," Claire murmured, too miserable to worry about it at the moment.

"I'm glad you're taking precautions, anyway. It's only sensible," Joel said.

"What?" Shaking her head, she stared a question. "I don't know what you mean."

"The gun," he answered. "You were carrying a pistol."

Grimacing, she nodded, feeling its weight like an anvil in her pocket. "My father insisted."

Joel darted a glance her way. "Your daddy's got good instincts. You know, I'm supposed to ask if you've got a permit to carry concealed."

She shook her head once more, but he raised a hand, as if to ward off the sight.

"I only said that I'm supposed to," he told her. "Not that I would. After all, this is your property and this is still Buck County. Where men are men, wildlife's ornery, and even good folks are armed to the teeth."

His strained smile reminded her of how he'd tried to cheer her up at Karen's funeral. At twenty to her sixteen, he'd seemed like an adult to her then. But today, in spite of whatever life had thrown at him in the past fourteen years, he seemed far younger than she was.

But then, to her, everyone seemed innocent, naïve, untempered as they were by the worst of all betrayals. When Joel slept beside his wife, Lori Beth, it probably never occurred to him that she might want him dead, that she might pay big bucks to make it happen. Claire decided that such knowledge was the apple in the garden, the taste that first made Eve aware of sin . . . for all time, irrevocably, right down through her descendants.

"I'm not planning to shoot Spe—" Claire balked, then forced herself to say it. It was only a name, damn it, not some mantra that would make the man materialize before her. "I'm not shooting Spencer Winslow. I just took the gun to appease my dad. He's been pretty nervous lately. Hovering even more than usual. And once he hears about poor Coyote and that cut fence, he's really going to freak. I'll be lucky if I can restrain him from coming here to stand guard while I work."

"Maybe that wouldn't be such a bad idea." Joel's voice was grave, the kind well suited to delivering bad news.

The kind of voice well suited to a lawman. Like Spence. Shivering, Claire used her free hand to rub her arm.

"You have to understand, Claire. You're all the man has left. Your daddy lost his wife in a horrible accident, and then his—and then Karen." Joel shook his head, but he couldn't shake off the haunted look that had come over him. "She was such a special girl, your sister. Such a gentle spirit. Every now and then these past few weeks, I'll catch a sideways glimpse of you, with that same pretty hair and big brown eyes, and for just a minute, it's like I'm seein' her again. And my heart starts galloping like a herd of—"

"I'm *not* her," Claire murmured, something she'd been saying for the fourteen years since Karen died. From her high school teachers to her mother's myriad relatives, all of them had at one time or another wondered aloud why she couldn't be as sweet, as generous, and well-groomed as the sister she had lost. Everyone except her father, who had gone out of his way to let her know he loved her as a person: stubborn streak, skinned knees, grubby fingernails, and all.

Joel cleared his throat and blinked, as if coming out of a trance. "Of course you aren't Karen. But you are a woman who's at risk, Claire."

"I don't think that's right," she said. "Assuming Spence wasn't just talking, blowing off steam in those messages, I think if he ever really wanted me dead, it had to be a passing thing. He'd been super down, too—probably clinically depressed—after the shooting incident, and it must have clouded his judgment. Surely now that he's had time to think about it—"

"Do you hear yourself?" Anger flushed Joel's handsome face once more. " 'Assuming he wasn't just talking,' 'if he ever really wanted me dead.' You sound exactly like every single battered woman who's ever called the jail and begged me to let her husband come back home. Every single woman I've gone back to find hurt later. Including the one I found shot to death in her kitchen with her little baby crawlin' all around her, leavin' smeary blood trails on the new linoleum."

Claire blinked away the nightmare image that rose before her. Shaking her head furiously, she told him, "I didn't say I wanted Spence back. I don't—I could never."

"Yet you're making excuses for this bastard, the same man we caught trying to pay off what he thought was a hit man."

"I'm not excusing him, Joel. I've already spoken with a family law attorney about divorce, for heaven's sake. But I'm still trying to make sense of it, for my own sake—my own sanity. You'd get it if you really knew Spence, if you'd seen our marriage. We were always going places, doing things together. Camping and canoeing. Riding, of course, and lots of hiking. A few days before the shooting, he even surprised me with a weekend trip to Chaleston for our anniversary.

"My friends at the rehab center teased me about it all the time," she went on, "how our honeymoon went on forever, how Spence must be some sort of Stepford husband. But it was never like that. He's never been a wimp or a pushover. He's just been . . . the best friend I've ever known, with a side order of great lovemaking."

It was her turn to blush this time; she felt the heat of it rising to her face as she looked away. But it was important to her to make Joel understand that Spence hadn't always been the man who had written those damning e-mails and said those horrible things. That she hadn't been an idiot to love him.

Joel frowned, and for several moments, he seemed lost in thought. Finally he managed, "Well, the honeymoon is over—your 'for better' just got worse. That man tried to have you murdered, darlin'. And it wasn't any momentary lapse or so-called depression, either. It all boiled down to one of the Big Two, same way it always does."

As they walked up the hill leading to the office, she spotted Ellen Martin and the volunteer who chaired the Monarch Ranch Foundation's board. But Claire stopped dead in her tracks and raised a tight fist to her temple.

"The Big Two?" she echoed, struggling to focus her attention and sensing that whatever he was going to tell her would be the verbal equivalent of an ice pick through the eye. "What are you talking about, Joel?"

He shrugged, "Crimes of this sort—not that we have very many of 'em here in Little BC—usually boil down to one of two things: money or a third party in the marriage."

"I don't give a damn about 'crimes of this sort.' I only want to know about this one. There was no other woman, and there's no way I'm buying that Spence was worried about Adam Strickland moving in on me. So why would—"

"Spencer had another problem besides Strickland. A three-hundred-twenty-thousand-dollar problem."

Ellen and Mrs. Briggs-Hadley were shouting to her, but Claire could make no sense of the words. Her pulse thundering in her ears, she kept her gaze riveted on Joel's face.

"Three hundred twenty . . ." Her stomach roiled, and out of the corner of her eye, she saw Ellen charging toward her, her wedge of yellow hair flapping at her shoulders and her short legs pumping furiously. An impeccably dressed petite woman in shades of lilac followed, wobbling on a dangerous-looking—and undoubtedly expensive—pair of heels.

"What are you talking about?" Claire demanded. "Spence didn't—"

"He was gambling heavily." Joel lowered his voice so the approaching women couldn't hear. "According to my best deputy, Spence dug himself into a deep hole, and the sides were cavin' in fast—about to bury him."

Claire wanted to stop him, but she couldn't find her voice.

Joel's gaze bored into hers—hard, relentless, but at the same time mournful. Delivering this news for the same reason she'd delivered the bullet to the suffering horse's brain. Because he had to, and there was no one else to do it.

"There was only one way out of this fix for him," he told her. "And that way out was through you."

FOUR

As cool droplets funneled down his turned-up collar, Spence wondered whether Raul had made it to Gus Patton's station before the drizzle turned into a light but steady rain. And whether the old son of a bitch would give the sergeant a lift back to his Datsun.

Not without a twinge of guilt, Spence hoped Gus wouldn't, and that Raul would be forced to roll the replacement tire all the way back to his car. It would buy more time, at any rate. More time for Spence to make his way along Little Bee Creek.

In case Raul ratted him out, Spence carefully left a southbound scent trail before he braced himself for the chill, then hopped into the water and started wading upstream toward Monarch Ranch.

The trail toward San Antonio wouldn't fool the searchers long; both Raul Contreras and Joel Shepherd would have to be first-class morons not to guess where he was really heading. But Spence didn't care if they figured it out. All that mattered was getting enough of a jump on his pursuers to let his wife know that in spite of all his screw-ups, he had never for one minute contemplated killing her. Himself, sure, on the worst days, the days he couldn't get past the fact that he'd lived when Dave hadn't—and the memory of how that damned kid's chest had exploded when Spence's bullets tore it open. On more than a few such days, the only way he could keep himself from eating his revolver was to slip into the back room of Joe Reno's place for four or five solid hours of video poker, or over to Retama Park, where he'd bet the simulcast horse and greyhound races when the hometown ponies weren't sufficient. Yet he could never quite get numb enough, and he always went home hating himself more.

As he trudged upstream, his legs ached with bone-deep cold, and his body shivered from the rain that soaked his shirt. Uselessly, he wished for his Mustang, but his lawyer had informed him that the car had been impounded by one of the agencies looking into Adam Strickland's disappearance. Spence had almost laughed off the idea, until he realized that evidence could just as well be trumped up in two cases as one.

He grimaced, then broke into a sloshing trot and refocused on his goal. Keeping an image of Claire firmly in mind, he barely slowed after he slipped on an algae-slick stone and soaked himself up to the shoulders.

Find her. He repeated the two words like a mantra, stubbornly forcing them out through jaws that chattered painfully.

He had to see her one more time, had to convince her how much he admired the skilled and patient work she did retraining broken people and helping them move toward independence. He needed her to know how he treasured the way her equine rehab dream had lit her up from the inside with the bright flame of a lantern—and the way she shared its spark with everyone she met. And, especially, he had to tell her how she cleansed his spirit after a workday spent swimming upstream in the city's sewage, the way her sweet face represented all that was good and right about the world.

He had to tell her all that, and even more important, had to tell her how damned sorry he was, before he hunted down the bastard who had set him up. Then and only then could he do the right thing, the honorable thing.

The thing he should have done six months before.

As thunder vibrated the timbers of the office, Pogo whined and ducked, shivering, beneath the lone desk.

"Are you freaking nuts?" Ellen Martin demanded through a wad of tissue before she leaned forward in her folding chair and blew her nose again. Beneath the lemony sheaf of the woman's dripping bangs, her bright blue irises looked like a pair of buttons tossed onto fresh-ground hamburger. Every time Claire looked at her, her own eyes watered in sympathy.

"No way . . . you're going out . . . in that again. Not after . . . hell you've been through." A strong-willed woman in her midfifties, the trainer fought to make herself heard over the rain pelting the metal roof. Still, her gravelly voice kept splintering into silence.

Claire winced, thinking it must hurt, then shrugged on the green jacket her father had given her the past Christmas. Made of a space-age, camouflage-patterned material, the jacket was advertised to shed moisture like a duck's back. She was about to find out if it lived up to the hype. "Don't try to talk, Ellen. We both know you'll be down with bronchitis again if you don't take your antihistamines and get to bed. And don't send your daughter back here. Meg's a great kid, but she is still a kid. She's been through enough for one day."

Meg had been so upset to learn Coyote had been put down, and so close to launching into full-blown hysterics, that her mother had talked Joel into dropping the girl off at home, where her brothers could look after her.

Mindful of Mrs. Briggs-Hadley, who was washing out the scorched coffeepot in the office restroom, Claire lowered her voice. "As far as the others go, we both know that, nice as they are, Mrs. Briggs-Hadley and any volunteers I could call aren't up to traipsing around the property. It has to be someone who really knows this place."

Ellen frowned, but didn't argue the point. "Bushwhack's probably . . . in the shelter of some trees, munching . . . grass and laughing his ass off at us. He'll be fine 'til morning. You shouldn't . . . do this, you of all people."

The trainer dropped her gaze, and uneasiness arced from the older woman to the younger. Claire froze in the act of putting on her dark blue riding helmet.

Had her former riding instructor, a woman Claire had known since she had gone to her as a ten-year-old for riding lessons, guessed? Had she somehow intuited what Claire hadn't gotten up the nerve to tell a single person? A widowed mother to both Megan and two teenaged sons, Ellen Martin had developed a knack for ferreting out secrets.

"It's not just a knack," she'd once explained. "Around my house, it's self-preservation."

Claire willed her to come out with it, to bring the

subject into the open so she could get the older woman's take on things. God only knew, Claire had turned it over in her mind so often these past few days, she'd lost all perspective.

An icy frisson skated along her nerve endings, and she nearly blurted it herself to relieve the stress.

"Your father . . ." Ellen added before her voice disintegrated into a fit of coughing. "He'd have my ass if I let you—"

"My father?" Claire asked, and suddenly she got it. The two of them must have been talking, conspiring these past weeks to keep her from flying apart at the seams.

Ellen shrugged. "He's been sick with worry for you. Under the circumstances, can you blame him?"

When Claire didn't say anything, Ellen added, "If you had—had kids of your own, you'd understand. You never stop being their parent, no matter how grown up they . . . seem to the outside world."

Claire released a breath she hadn't realized she'd been holding. "You're right. I don't have kids. But I do have horses in my care, depending on me to make sure they're all right. Don't argue this with me, El. You know as well as I do that horses run to their stalls when the world gets scary. Since Bushwhack didn't, something's wrong. He could be stuck—a stirrup hung up on a tree branch or a rein caught between rocks."

A vision flashed through her mind: Bushwhack trotting after Spence; Spence's laughter when the big brown head reached over his shoulder and lifted free the candy cane. *"You flea-bitten thief, I'd slap my cuffs on you if I thought they'd fit."*

52

Tears welled in Claire's eyes. "Or he might be hurt. Really hurt. Like poor Coyote."

A silence stretched between the women, broken only when Lenore Briggs-Hadley came out of the restroom, a water-filled and sparkling coffee pot held aloft like a trophy. She smiled pleasantly, her makeup perfect and every short, highlighted hair in place. Her orchid-colored, lightweight sweater, matching slacks, and diamond earrings looked better suited to lunch in an Alamo Heights tearoom than traipsing around a rain-soaked Little BC ranch. But, then, Claire had never seen the volunteer dressed in anything that didn't look classy and expensive.

"Taa-daa," she sang, a sound that made Pogo poke her head out briefly from beneath the desk. "I thought I'd never get the baked-on sludge out of this thing."

"You'll ask Mrs. Briggs-Hadley if she'll stay?" Ellen never took her watery gaze from Claire.

Still smiling, Mrs. Briggs-Hadley turned from where she was pouring water into the coffeemaker for a fresh pot. "I keep telling y'all, it's Lenore, please. My husband will be in London on business for another week yet, and there's nothing pressing on my calendar. So I'm here to help for as long as Claire will have me."

The rain had suddenly diminished, leaving the woman's overly loud words hanging in the air. Even when they faded, something of their sadness lingered.

"Thanks, Lenore," Claire managed, though it felt strange calling the woman by her given name. Mrs. Briggs-Hadley might be no older than her late thirties, but everything about her, from her multimillion-dollar, African game–stocked ranch to her decked-out black Land Rover and her frequent appearances in the society column of the *San Antonio Express-News*, elevated her light years above Claire's circle.

Or at least it would have but for the tragedy that marred the woman's fairy-tale life. After Lenore's three-year-old son's near-drowning in a hot tub, she and her husband had brought the boy to Claire's rehab center for two years in the hopes that the various therapists could reteach little Jamie to talk and walk again . . . or at least to hold his head up and swallow on his own.

But none of them had been able to do a thing to stop the pneumonia that ravaged the boy's already weakened system, finally taking him to a place Claire prayed he would once more run and play. In the eighteen months since her only son's death, Lenore Briggs-Hadley had poured all that remained of her battered heart into the fund-raising to make Monarch Ranch a reality—and to forget how often her husband now left her alone.

Now that the evil rain had lessened, Pogo crept out of her hiding place and leaned against Claire's leg.

"And you'll damn—I mean darn—well call me if there's anything"—more coughing interrupted Ellen's words—"anything at all you need. Right?"

Lenore shooed her toward her hooded yellow raincoat, which hung on one of several hooks beside the door. "If it's happy news, we'll let you know. Otherwise we'll contact Dr. Brummell or one of the volunteers with horse experience. Now go home, Ellen, before we have to call out the volunteer rescue squad for you."

Since Claire knew the county's two decrepit ambulances were mainly driven by teenagers, she added, "You know how their mamas worry when they have to go out after dark—and on these wet roads, no less."

Ellen's lips cinched up, making a wrinkled star of

her unpainted mouth. But apparently appealing to her maternal instincts worked, for she slipped on her raincoat, grabbed her purse out of a locker, then stared meaningfully at Claire.

"All right, all right. I'm going home now. But if you get your ass killed out there, don't come crying to me."

Spence had long ago learned that the margin of survival could be thinner than a gnat's wing. He'd seen the evidence of a drive-by shooter's bullet missing a woman's head after a sneeze made her bob forward. He'd been on the scene after a construction site accident had driven a steel spike straight through the skull of a worker—who remained conscious, though none too comfortable, and lived to tell the tale. Last October, Spence had made it—and Dave hadn't—only because a left-handed twelve-year-old had shot first to his dominant side.

And today he might survive—or fail to— depending on his ability to find and balance on a spine of jagged rock.

Between the miles of slogging through the chilly creek and the steadily increasing rain, Spence was soaked and bruised and bleeding from dozens of scratches where he'd clambered over cattle fencing, fallen trees, and old snarls of barbed wire cast off by the early spring floodwaters.

If he made it out of here, he would worry about tetanus. But if he planned on making it through these next few hours, he'd damned well better worry about drying off and getting warm.

His teeth clacking violently, Spence clambered from the creek bank toward the overhanging bluffs, his eyes peeled for the odd spine of jutting rock that Claire had dubbed The Staircase. It wasn't much of one, not really, though his wife scampered up and down the widely spaced and dangerous-looking footholds as nimbly as a mountain goat—mostly, she claimed, because she'd been doing it since she was a child.

But now he couldn't find the damned rocks, though he was almost certain he was in the right spot. He looked this way and that, thinking that the bluffs looked wrong—until he found the spot where the creek turned and deepened and, high above, the caves he had begun exploring less than a week before his life went totally to hell. He thought about the climbing equipment he'd brought out here on the exciting day he'd found the mortar holes where Indian women had once ground seeds and nuts into meal. But staring upward and wishing neither brought him back his rope and harness nor carried him to one of the ancient shelters.

Finally snapping out of his daze, he caught sight of the rocky ridge. He realized that he had at first looked past it because a small section to its right had collapsed, forming a steep drop-off beside The Staircase. And making it even more dangerous than usual—a bad thing, in his present state.

He began picking his way along his only avenue up the thirty-foot-tall bluff. Sloshing along in sodden shoes, he moved with the exaggerated care of the very old. His mind tempted him to hurry, recasting the old hunting shack, with its cobwebs and its leaky roof, as a palace of unimagined splendors, but he knew that one misstep would leave him with a broken leg—or worse.

As if sensing its chance, the rain picked up, and a chill breeze increased his torment. This is hell, he thought. I only thought I was there after the shooting.

Heaven would be Claire, soft and warm as she nestled beneath the covers close beside him. With that thought in mind, he made the last step—a jump, really—and finally landed on the limestone top of the bluff.

Where his survival would balance on an even thinner margin: the memory of a candy cane in the mind of a sodden—and extremely traumatized—bay horse.

By the time Claire rode out on a red-brown mare named Cinnamon, the pewter clouds had leached most of the remaining light from the spring sky. The rain had intensified once again, and a distant rumble warned of more to come.

First she checked the pasture, with its three-sided shelter, where the remaining horses comfortably munched on wisps of hay from their last feeding. But Bushwhack hadn't figured out a way in, nor did she find him lingering hopefully around the fence perimeter.

Bad sign. Horses hated to miss meals, and Bushwhack was even more gluttonous than most. With this in mind, Claire had brought along a bucket with enough sweet feed to rattle enticingly.

And now she breathed a prayer that the bay remained alive to hear it. And that—God help her—she would not be forced again to use the pistol she had quietly moved to the pocket of her rain jacket.

"Bushwhack," she called again and again as she shook the feed—an act that was causing Cinnamon to prance and nicker in frustrated greed.

As Claire rode in ever-widening circles, the normally placid mare grew increasingly restless, flinching when the breezes flipped up the silvery undersides of leaves and squealing when the sky flashed. Thunder pealed overhead, and Cinnamon fought to drop her head; only two decades of riding experience kept Claire from sailing over the mare's withers.

"It's all right, girl. It's all right," she said in her most soothing voice, though all the while she was thinking, Great. I'm going to get tossed any second. The perfect ending to a perfect day.

But Cinnamon had another trick in mind. As the strobe-lit sky shook, the mare jerked her head forward, tearing the reins loose from Claire's hands—

And sending them swinging into the grip of a man who burst out of a stand of mountain laurel.

The next seconds fragmented into mirrored shards, each reflecting more terror than the last: the mare whinnying and struggling to bolt; Claire screaming, kicking at the dark shape, then flying through the air and landing hard as Cinnamon finally dislodged her; the man's shouting, calling out her name in a voice that slammed into her heart with the force of a sledgehammer.

Claire's hand reaching, grabbing for the pistol in her pocket . . .

And firing, for the second time that day.

FIVE

A sharp cry brought home the difference between this afternoon's shot and this one. At the man's shout of pain, Claire's body stiffened, comprehending even before her mind grasped the meaning of the form sprawled in wet leaf litter not six feet from where she'd landed on her side.

Spence.

Instead of putting down an animal doomed to suffer, she had shot the man she'd stood beside before an altar, where they had taken vows that bound the two of them forever.

No, not quite forever, a voice whispered through her shell-shocked mind.

"Until death do you part . . ."

The minister's words echoed across the years, merging with the rattle of raindrops in the leaves and the watery tap against her riding helmet. And an instant later, with the sound of Spence's voice as he rolled out of range of Cinnamon's prancing hooves and tossing head. With one of her reins still clutched in his hand, he stood and tried to quiet the mare with shushing noises.

But Claire's attention was riveted to the darkness blossoming on the sleeve of his upper left arm. Blood, she realized, as it mingled with rainwater to run down toward his elbow.

In spite of the wound, he managed to grasp both of the mare's reins in his left hand. As the horse calmed, he clamped the right over his wound to stanch the flow. "Are you all right? Are you hurt, Claire?"

Even in the weak light, she saw how crimson squeezed its way between his fingers. She noticed, too, that his clothes were soaked with rain and his light blue shirt torn in places. Deep scratches marked his too-pale face, and his teeth chattered uncontrollably.

Yet he had calmed the frightened horse and asked if she was hurt.

Disentangling her fingers from the pistol, Claire dropped it before pushing herself into a squat. "You're shot." Her voice sounded childlike, amazed, as if she'd had not a thing to do with his condition.

"Yeah," he said. "Hurts like hell, too. Proving once and for all that 'only a flesh wound' is pretty much a load of made-for-TV bullshit. God, Claire, I'm so sorry."

She heard his words, but in her mind they weren't adding up to anything like sense. She'd shot her husband. Shot him. "You're sorry? That I—that I hurt you?"

He barked a laugh that sounded so like him, her hot tears welled to mingle with the cooler raindrops.

"Of course I am," he said. "This is going to be damned inconvenient. But mostly I'm sorry I scared you into doing it. I know better than most people what a burden it can be, dealing with the fact you've put a bullet in another human being."

Claire's thoughts strayed to the moment that had changed their lives forever: the shooting that had taken place last fall. Her gaze dropped, falling on the pistol she had left lying on the ground. Would the ripples from the shot she'd fired spread out and swell the same way? Would they build like a tsunami to come crashing down on unsuspecting lives?

The questions were so big, so frightening, that her mind bolted back to practicalities. She shouldn't allow the mud and water to run inside the pistol, couldn't leave it there where Spence might pick it up—but how could she touch the thing when even looking at it made her want to vomit?

"Go ahead," Spence told her. "Take it. Hold it if you want to, or slip it in your pocket. Do whatever it takes so you'll feel safe enough to listen."

"Spence," she breathed, as jumbled waves of emotion crashed into each other. Terror, love, regret . . .

"Do it, please." Fatigue underscored his blue eyes, but still they looked straight at her. "Because that's all I ask, for you to listen."

Trembling with revulsion, she picked up the weapon by its still-warm barrel, then dropped it into her pocket as quickly as if she were holding a live coal. Even so, she felt some of her equilibrium returning. She met his gaze head-on. "Give me one reason why I should."

"So I can make you understand how much I love you. And that no matter how I've screwed things up, I would never, ever hurt you."

No, the wounded part of her raged, you'd pay off someone else to do the job instead. But she couldn't shake the words loose. Instead she stood and edged just close enough to take Cinnamon's reins from his hand. Backing away, she said, "I have to go find Bush-whack. That's why I came out here."

"Bushwhack's fine. He's safe. But what about you, Claire? You didn't answer me before. Did you hurt your-self when Cinnamon threw you?"

She paused, considering, but no pain soaked through the tightly knit fabric of her shock. Shaking her head, she asked, "You caught Bushwhack and tied him somewhere, didn't you? Because you knew I would come looking."

Spence's head shook, flinging droplets, before his sodden, seal-brown bangs fell across his eyes. "I found him saddled near the creek. At first I thought he was running free, but then I saw he'd gotten tangled—a branch ran up under the headstall on his bridle. Didn't hurt him any, but he wasn't going anywhere."

It could have been the dusk leaching away all color, but Spence's face looked ashen, and his lips were turning blue. Was he going into shock? She still didn't trust him, but it scared the hell out of her to think he might die.

"Let's go get him, and then we'll take you some-place warm and dry. You're going to need a hospital—"

His head shaking harder, he spoke over the dark muttering of thunder. "No. God, no. They'll throw me right back into jail—"

"It's better than a coffin."

His gaze pleaded with her, his whole body shaking visibly. "That's debatable. Please, Claire. I'm begging you. Just come back to the cabin with me—that's where I left the horse tied anyway, under some thick limbs for shelter. We can go inside, and then I'll tell you. I'll tell you everything, I swear it."

The whole time he was speaking, her head shook back and forth. "Why should I believe you? Why should I even listen?"

"You—you can keep the gun on me the whole time, point it right in my face." His chattering was making it harder for him to speak now. "And afterward, if you don't buy it, I don't care—shoot me if you want to. But if you ever loved me, even for an instant, please do this for me, Claire. Just this."

She swallowed hard, her vision blurring with tears. In all the years she'd known him, he'd never begged for anything, except maybe for God to tell him why a twelve-year-old shoplifter had to pull a .38.

As a wild wind hurtled through the wet leaves, fat raindrops stung Claire's face. But she barely noticed for the mix of love and pity that welled in her soul's wounds. In its wake, she found a nightmare vision of herself in the future, living with the knowledge that she had killed this man. No matter what the rest of her life held in store, her regret would be so poisonous, she knew she would never wash its bitter taste away.

She found herself nodding, knowing she couldn't leave him out here. "All right, Spence. All right. We're going to the cabin. Can you climb up on Cinnamon? I'll lead you."

His teeth chattering, he shook his head. "We'll both ride."

"No way. She's wound up so tight, she'll come unglued and spill both of us without someone to hold her head. And that someone needs to be the one of us who doesn't stink of blood." When she recognized his stubborn look, she added, "Don't even think of going all macho on me, or I swear I'll leave your ass here while I run back home and call the cavalry."

His exhausted-looking smile struck straight to her core.

"That's my girl," he told her with what sounded for all the world like pride.

It was a measure of his desperation that he acquiesced so easily, a measure of his failing strength that she had to help him mount the mare after retrieving the bucket she had dropped when she was thrown. With Claire's gentle guidance and soft words, Cinnamon did her part, carrying Spence to the spot where the interlacing boughs of huge live oaks blocked most of the rain and Bushwhack stood unsaddled. As they approached, the tethered bay horse raised his head from grazing and neighed a welcome, and Claire released a breath she hadn't known she had been holding. As Spence had promised, the gelding looked perfectly fine.

After an awkward dismount, Spence stood with his feet far apart, one hand clamped over his upper left arm. Claire watched him sway as she tied Cinnamon and loosened the cinch on the mare's saddle. She fed each horse half of the soggy sweet feed remaining in her bucket, then stepped to Spence's right side and slipped her arm around his waist.

She'd meant to steady him for the short walk to the cabin, but recognition jolted through her system. She was holding him again, though she had spent these past weeks listening to well-intentioned people tell her this part of her life was over, though she had tried time and again to convince herself that the only feeling she had left for him was rage.

So why then did it scare her so, feeling the cadaverous chill that had settled on his flesh? Why did her heart skip a beat each time he stumbled as they left the little copse?

No matter how hard she fought to hold onto her fury, she felt nothing but relief at the sight of the small cypress cabin nestled among tall trees, its tin roof nearly hidden by a thick accumulation of dead leaves. The place still looked as homely and weather-beaten as it had last fall, when the two of them had pried open the door, then startled the mice with their lovemaking. Yet though decades of neglect had faded the wood and grimed the windows, the split logs remained sturdy and the small building's frame so straight that she imagined it would easily stand for decades more.

Claire threw open the door and helped her husband inside, where he recovered enough to flip the switch of an old electric lantern. The moment her eyes adjusted to the brightness, she surveyed the boxlike structure.

It was clear Spence had been here earlier, that he had broken into a padlocked cabinet where supplies were stored for those who had once leased the place during hunting seasons throughout the seventies. Though she was too young to remember, she'd been told the Hajeks had put a stop to the practice after that terrible day a hunter had mistaken Claire's mother for a deer down by the creek . . . the accident that had forever changed her family.

Aside from the lantern the two of them had brought here the past fall, nothing had been changed, from the four camp-style wooden bunks to the thick swags of cobwebs that hung from every surface. The contents of the locker, several pilled and holey dark blue blankets along with a cracked white plastic first aid box, lay atop a bunk. As she started toward them, Claire sneezed at the dust.

"Bless you," Spence mumbled, and she glanced over, struck by his reflexive courtesy.

He stood dripping in the center of the small space, still holding his hurt arm and shaking with chill. Behind his mask of scratches, his blue eyes had grown vacant and his face even grayer than before. When she tossed him a blanket, he didn't catch it. Instead he let it slide down all six feet of his body.

He's slipping into shock, she realized. If she wanted him to live, she had to do something.

Crossing the room, she picked up the blanket, then draped it over his shoulders and led him like a child to the bunk.

She used her booted foot to knock an inch-long scorpion to the floor, then stepped on it. The last thing Spence needed was a painful sting to add to his discomfort.

"Lie here," she ordered, but not unkindly. When he complied, she covered him with a second blanket and then wadded the last beneath his feet to elevate them.

A tiny spark came back to his eyes. "Claire."

Carefully, she uncovered his left arm. "I'll need to look at this."

He let her push aside his stained and sticky right hand, and her stomach clutched at her first sight of the bloody wound. She closed her eyes until a swarm of black dots vanished, then sucked in a deep breath to clear her head. Feeling somewhat better, she forced herself to look again, to find the place the bullet had pierced his bicep. But look as she might, she couldn't locate an exit wound. Which meant that, contrary to Spence's earlier statement, the bullet had either lodged in bone or been deflected off it, then traveled somewhere else inside the body. Almost anywhere.

Panic hollowed out her belly. She was in way over her head, with nothing but an ancient tube of antibiotic ointment and a roll of white gauze that crumbled into powder at her touch. And even if she were equipped, occupational therapy was a world away from the practice of emergency medicine.

"Damn it." She removed her helmet and peeled off her rain jacket. As good as its advertising, the space-age material had kept her body warm and her long-sleeved cotton shirt dry. And what she needed now was dry cloth, even if it wasn't as sterile as she might like.

She stripped off her violet T-shirt, then noticed Spence looking at her body, a little of the color returning to his cheeks. More than the cabin's chill, it was his naked longing that had her reaching for her jacket to put it on again.

"Don't." His word came rough, almost a growl, and he continued staring as if he meant to memorize her contours.

She might have laughed and reminded him of a day when he had sworn her body could make him rise from the grave—or at least one portion of him. But in that cabin, at that moment, she could neither recall the sound of laughter nor think of how to form it. Instead she shook her head and finished pulling on the damp sleeves, her attention distracted by the tug of the gun's weight inside the jacket's pocket.

Grabbing up two handfuls of her T-shirt, she began to tear it into strips. The ripping sounded like pure anger, coloring her thoughts. How could he have brought them to this? What in God's name had possessed him to ruin what they'd had?

"I'm so damned mad at you," she said, suddenly shaking with her outrage. "I ought to leave you right here."

He shrugged on his good side. "It's no more than I deserve. I was gambling, Claire, gambling away our future."

"So I heard." Despite the coldness of her voice, she rubbed her hands to warm them before helping him remove what was left of his shirt. "Mind telling me why?"

He winced as the sleeve caught on his injured arm, then closed his eyes as she pulled away the sodden fabric. Afterward, she used it to wipe away what blood she could.

When she finished, he hissed out a long breath before he finally answered. "I don't even know myself, not really. After Dave—the shooting—I just liked sitting in the dark, letting my mind shut down. I could do it there, at Joe Reno's—it's a video poker joint down on the South Side. Pushing those buttons, watching the cards float up on the screen . . . it was the nearest I could come to turning off the pictures of that dead kid, the pictures of Dave and the injured guard. And then I found the horses over at Retama Park. They've got a simulcast lounge. They keep it pretty dark there, too."

"If you'd stayed home, I would have turned the lights off. I would have broken every fucking bulb." The uncharacteristic curse rebounded off the empty walls, filling the cabin with her pain.

To give her hands something to do, she tried to break open the ointment. But the cap was crusted on, and she realized that the contents had hardened into uselessness.

"I know you would have, baby." His eyes shone with unshed tears. "I know that, but I couldn't stay. I could—

I know this sounds so crazy, but I could feel your dis-appointment. I kept thinking how disgusted, how ashamed you must be, living with a loser, how you'd probably leave me—"

"So you arranged to have me killed? I saw the e-mail, Spence. You can't deny it."

"What e-mail? That trumped-up bullshit they gave my attorney?"

It hurt like hell for her to think of what she'd been shown, let alone repeat the cruel words, yet each one came back to her, as if the message had been carved into her heart.

" 'I don't know how much longer I can take being in the same room with her, sleeping in that bed, listening to her rattle on about her Mary-fricking-Sunshine farm for crippled kiddies,' " she quoted, then skipped straight to the deepest cut of all. " 'It makes me wish she would just go away—disappear forever. It makes me wish someone would fix her, that someone would shut her up for good.' "

Looking away from her, he pressed both hands to his temples, as if his guilt might burst the confines of his skull.

Seeing him, she thought he must really have done it, no matter what denial had whispered in her ear, no matter what scenarios it had cooked up during the darkest hours of her sleepless nights. Claire wound a cotton strip around his still-bleeding arm, then yanked it tight to hear him yelp. She didn't want him dying, but she needed him to feel a fraction of her pain.

"I was half out of my mind when I typed that, e-mail-ing an old friend and blaming you for everything screwed up inside me." Spence looked up, his blue eyes serious. "But I never wrote that last part, about wishing someone would—would 'fix you.' I swear it on my life, Claire. I never wrote that part. This has got to be some kind of setup."

"So you're expecting me to believe . . . what? That al Qaeda sneaked onto your laptop and added a few lines to your e-mail?"

He looked away, disgust and pain written in the set of his jaw. "I know I deserve that, but hell no, it wasn't anything so random."

"Then who?" She hated the way her hope sprang toward his lame excuses. Of course he would claim he hadn't done it. But what if that was truth she heard in his voice? "Who would want to hurt you?"

"I owed a lot of money, a whole lot, to a bookie." He paused, his breathing labored, as if the effort of speaking was exhausting him. "When I couldn't pay it, he sold my marker to someone else. Someone far more dangerous."

She stared into his face. "Who?"

He gritted his teeth, then shook his head. His eyelids sagged and he blinked, as if to keep himself awake. "It's better that you don't know. You'll be safer that way."

Her gaze dropped to his arm, where fresh blood was staining the violet bandages. Her wretched effort at first aid wouldn't do at all. "I'm taking back Bushwhack and sending Mrs. Briggs-Hadley home. If I don't show up at the office soon, she's sure to call for help.

"As soon as I can finish there," she added, "I'll run back to my dad's house. You're going to need real bandages, and I've got some antiseptic. I'll bring back aspirin, too, and coffee."

"Please don't go, Claire."

She squeezed his hand to reassure him. His skin felt warmer now, and his color had improved some. "I'll come back. I promise. And when I do, you're going to tell me the whole story. Every bit of it. No bullshit, no mysterious holes, and not one made-up bad guy whose name you can't tell me. You're going to tell me why and how, because you owe it to me."

"You won't call the sheriff?"

If she had any sense, she would do exactly that. Though his pulse proved steady when she checked it and the look of shock had passed, her stomach balled into a knot of nerves. Spence had been shot—she had pulled the trigger—and aside from whatever havoc his condition would play with her emotions, she was legally responsible for what had happened to him.

Yet her instincts screamed that if she lost this opportunity, it would never come again—that she would never get the chance to ask Spence in person the questions that were eating her alive. So she would return to him with her sterile dressings and her medicines—and the gun in her pocket. She would hear him out this one time, not so much because he'd asked it, but for her own sake.

Her own sake and the future that she must face all too soon.

SIX

Rumor has it that a rising tide floats all boats, but when the spring rains raise the water level of the creeks that drain the Central Texas Hill Country, all manner of things float to the surface. Some even break free of their moorings to travel miles downstream, until their progress is blocked by craggy rocks or fallen timber. . . .

Or until a recently submerged fence post snags a pair of mustard-colored waders, anchoring the unfortunate occupant as well.

In the wild country that makes up Buck County, such an event could go long undetected, except, perhaps, by a wandering coyote or a feral hog. But when such a thing takes place within sight of a bridge across a county road, it is only a matter of time before some driver or passenger happens to glance in the correct direction.

Only a matter of time.

Just as she had predicted, by the time Claire reached the office, Lenore Briggs-Hadley was preparing to call the sheriff's department to send out someone to find her.

"I'm really sorry it took me so long to bring Bush-whack," Claire told her as the sheltie danced a greeting near her feet. "I didn't mean to worry you."

Lenore sighed. "It's all right. It's just that I didn't have anything to do except talk to Pogo and drink coffee. And the more coffee I drink, the more jittery I get."

Mrs. Briggs-Hadley raised a hand so Claire could see it shaking. She could definitely relate, nervous as she was about her encounter with Spence. Anxiety flipped around her stomach, reminding her of the need to get back to him quickly with medical supplies.

Still, she forced a smile. "That reminds me, next time I go to the store, I'll pick up some decaf. You like the vanilla hazelnut, right?"

Lenore waved off the peace offering, flashing perfectly-manicured nails that complemented her orchid-colored outfit. The sight reminded Claire of the loss of her own slightly darker T-shirt. Beneath her dripping jacket, she wore nothing but a flesh-colored lace bra.

"I'm so glad you and both the horses are all right," Lenore said. "Would you like me to help you with them?"

Bless her heart, the woman looked as though she meant it, though up until now she had steered clear of the dirty work. Claire appreciated those skills she did offer—especially the donations the Monarch Ranch board president had brought in by organizing an elegant benefit attended by many of San Antonio's leading lights. But at the moment, Claire needed to get Mrs. Briggs-Hadley out of here as quickly as possible.

"Thanks, but that's all right," Claire told her as she

reached down to rub the silken spot at the base of Pogo's ears. The sheltie grinned, tongue lolling and eyelids at half-mast. "They're both muddy, and it would be a shame to ruin your pretty outfit. Besides, it wouldn't be safe in those heels."

"I can at least let Ellen know you're all right—"

"Why don't you call from your place? It's a miserable night," Claire interrupted. "Hard as it's raining, the creeks will be up. I really appreciate your waiting for me, but I think maybe you'd better get home. Remember how that little bridge near your house washed out last fall?"

Though everything she'd said was true, she felt guilty as uncertainty flickered in the socialite's blue eyes.

"I'll call Ellen when I get home, then. But what about you?" Lenore asked.

"As soon as I put up the horses and give them a good feeding, I'm heading to Dad's for a hot shower, a grilled cheese sandwich, and a can of tomato soup."

Mrs. Briggs-Hadley smiled, probably at the quaint notion of eating anything that had come in contact with a can. "Are you sure, Claire? You look, well, you don't look like yourself this evening."

Claire's heart thumped, and she groped mentally for a better explanation than *I'm a little shaken up because I just shot my husband.* "I'll be fine," she said. "It's just—it was pretty tough today, what happened with Coyote."

Lenore laid a hand on Claire's damp shoulder. "Putting that poor horse out of his misery was the right thing, and you were brave to do it. If it had been me, I don't believe there's any way I could have pulled that trigger. You're a strong woman, Claire, and I admire you."

Mrs. Briggs-Hadley soon left, taking her umbrella with her. And leaving Claire to wonder why people—even a woman who had faced tragedy herself—believed that surviving the unthinkable conferred extraordinary courage. She'd been scared, so damned scared every hour since that awful morning Raul Contreras and Joel Shepherd had come to her front door. She had been shaking like a leaf when she'd put down Coyote and terrified out of her wits when she had fired that wild shot at Spence.

She was still scared while she hurried through the steps of caring for the horses and climbed, with Pogo at her side, into her pickup for the short drive—not quite a quarter mile—to her father's place next door. As she pulled up to the closed garage doors, she searched the house's windows, then released a pent-up breath. It was dark inside, so her father must not yet be back from San Antonio. If the weather was as nasty there as here, she wouldn't be surprised if he called to say he planned to spend the night in town.

With Pogo at her heels, Claire unlocked the side door and stepped into the mudroom, an addition her father had had built onto the eighty-year-old native-stone-and-cypress ranch house. While the dog danced near her empty food bowl, Claire pulled off her muddy boots. Afterwards, she fed Pogo before grabbing a handful of plastic grocery sacks out of the recycling bin. If her father would only stay away a while longer, she could gather what she needed and borrow the four-wheel ATV he had bought the year before to keep tabs on his thirty acres. He boasted that the thing was far more economical than a horse—as if he couldn't afford to keep a stableful of fine ones—but Claire hadn't seen him ride his toy since he'd banged up his left side in a bad spill the past September.

She only hoped the ATV would start for her today so she wouldn't have to catch and saddle a fresh mount. She would have tried taking her truck back there, but trees had largely overgrown the rutted dirt track, making it impassible in spite of the Chevy's four-wheel-drive.

Claire grabbed a Thermos bottle for the half pot of coffee still on the warmer at her office, then moved to the master bathroom medicine cabinet, where her family stored first aid supplies. There she found a new tube of antibiotic gel and a bottle containing a couple of leftover pain pills from her father's ATV mishap. She rooted around the narrow bathroom closet until she came up with a box of small adhesive bandages that lay hidden behind a stack of towels and washcloths, but no gauze.

"Not enough," she muttered before her gaze fell on her father's neatly folded bed linens.

Thinking she might make bandages, she laid her hand on a white flat sheet, then decided to look for some her father wouldn't miss. She moved into Karen's old room, which had been turned into an extra guest room, with antique furnishings and a blue-and-ivory handmade quilt. But despite the fussy perfection of the redecorated space—she remembered Spence rolling his eyes when her dad had shown it off—the cupboard remained a catchall.

Its door opened with a creak to the faint odor of mothballs. She dug way in the back until she found a set of old but clean cream-colored sheets.

"Perfect," she said, assuming that anything buried this deep would not be missed. She stuffed the sheets into her grocery sack, then paused as something slapped against her socked foot.

She stared down at the ring of interlocking silver links without realizing what she was seeing. As she stooped to grab it, she decided it must have been tucked among the old linens, lost there for heaven only knew how many years.

A bracelet, she realized as she heard the metallic tinkle of perhaps a dozen tarnished heart-shaped charms. Smiling, she decided it must have been her sister's—she couldn't remember having one like that herself, and it looked to her like something a young girl or a teenager would wear.

For some reason, she found it lifted her spirits, as if Karen had offered her a blessing from beyond. Claire dropped it into her jacket's pocket, thinking she would look at it when she had more time.

A thumping sound caught her attention, the muffled *thwap-thwap* of Pogo's bushy tail against the wall to her left.

"Hang on, girl," she muttered, figuring the dog wanted to go out after finishing her meal.

At the sheltie's whine, Claire looked over—and saw that Pogo was dancing at her father's feet as he stood in the bedroom doorway. Though he had always had a soft spot for the three-legged dog, his back was ramrod-straight, his gaze fixed on Claire's face. In his hand he held a plastic bag clutched like a lunch sack, and he looked distinctly irritated.

Startled, Claire gasped and thumped her free hand against her chest. "Dad, you scared the fool out of me. I didn't see any lights on, so I thought you were still in San Antonio."

Only then did she notice that, like her, her father had removed his boots, and his hair was damp.

"I was out behind the well house, cleaning up a

mess. Some damned animal or other knocked over one of the cans, and there was trash everywhere, floating in the puddles," he said. "And I hadn't gotten halfway to the city when the realtor called my cell phone. She had some kind of family situation and needed to reschedule."

That did a lot to explain his irritation, but still . . . His expression darkened, growing even grimmer than when he had handed her the .38.

"Is something wrong—with you, I mean?" she asked. Had someone told him she had used his pistol on Coyote?

"Why don't you take off that wet coat, Claire? Then we'll sit down and talk about it."

Her breath froze in her lungs, and her gaze dropped to the drugstore sack in his hands. In a moment of horrifying comprehension, she realized what it was he had found back by the trash can.

She started to unzip her jacket before she remembered that she didn't have a shirt beneath it. Her hand stopped, her fingers locked on the tab. Looking into her father's face, she said, "I never meant for you to find out this way."

Claire winced as he pulled the box out of the bag. Though it was sodden and crumpled, she could easily read the lettering that marked it as a home pregnancy test kit.

"From the looks of you, I guess I don't have to ask how it came out," he said. "I thought— I thought you had some kind of female problems—that you decided to put a family on hold."

Some kind of female problems. That was as close as he would come to mentioning the ectopic pregnancy Claire had suffered almost a year before. The pain had been excruciating, and she might have bled to death had Spence not gotten her to the hospital quickly. With only one tube left—and a higher than average risk of a repeat—Claire had been afraid to try again, until the day she'd made her promise to Spence by Little Bee Creek.

"I'm pregnant," she said, and the words seemed to echo down the hallway. "I know the timing isn't good, but—"

"Isn't good?" Her father shook his head, his expression incredulous. "This is beyond not good. Way past it. This is crazy."

"I didn't know it at the time, but I was already pregnant when I found out about my husband." Claire's pulse thrummed loudly in her ears, and she felt her temper rising. "It's not as if I had a crystal ball, Dad. It's not as if he took out goddamned ad space in the paper."

"Don't raise your voice to me, Claire, and you'd better watch your language. I'm not accusing you of anything." His expression softened, and moisture glimmered along the rims of his brown eyes. He opened his arms, offering his embrace. "I just want to help you."

Claire fought the impulse to throw herself against him, to let her father hug her tears away. An image rose before her of Spence lying on that hard wooden bunk, his arm bleeding through its wrapping. But she couldn't leave quite yet, not with her father's kindness still hanging in the space between them.

"I'll be fine, Dad." She thought she would, too. For one thing, if it had been another tubal pregnancy, she was almost certain she would have known by now. "There are lots of single mothers. I'm sure I'll—"

"Do you realize what you're saying? Think about it. If you have this child, you'll be tying yourself forever to a man who tried to have you killed. And how will you explain it? Will you tell your little one why his daddy's locked away in prison? Will you take him there to visit, or let Spence's relatives—"

"I haven't thought that far ahead yet," Claire said, fighting off the image of herself passing a tiny infant to one of Spence's hairy uncles. His parents had died from a cracked radiator's carbon monoxide fumes one night when he was staying over at a friend's house— something he'd confessed still gave him nightmares. The hairy uncles had gone through the motions of getting their surviving nephew through his final year of high school and off to college. Other than that, their contact had been limited to Christmas cards, which often included photos of their Harleys or their latest girlfriends, most of whom wore black leather and prominent tattoos. Spence had more than once joked that by becoming a cop, he had sealed his reputation as the black sheep of the family.

He and Claire used to laugh about it, in the days when they'd known laughter. So much laughter, so much love . . . it seemed like a memory from another lifetime.

"You're still so young, only thirty. You'll have other chances if you—Claire? Are you listening to me?" her dad asked. "Come on into the family room. Let's sit down and talk."

"Let me change, at least. I'm filthy." She gestured toward her clothing, which was splotched with mud and—to her horror—bloodstains. Had her father noticed? She thought of bringing up Coyote's accident to cover but decided that unless he said something, she would let him get past one shock before springing the next.

Her father nodded. "I'll be waiting for you."

After grabbing fresh clothes from the wardrobe in her reclaimed bedroom, Claire ducked into the bathroom and dirtied a perfectly good washcloth. She felt better for her quick wash and dry jeans, but her stomach was in knots. She had to make short work of this conversation so she could return to Spence. But how could she get away with a bag of first aid supplies without her father guessing?

She didn't find him in the family room, but instead of looking elsewhere, Claire hesitated in front of the fireplace, her gaze drifting while her mind scrambled for some excuse to leave.

Comfortably rustic, the room was dominated by both the native stone hearth and oversized leather furnishings. The rugs were made from tanned skins—all dating from before her mother's accident, when her father had hunted avidly—and an antique Kentucky rifle hung above the mantel. Paintings of rural landscapes and rough-hewn side tables offered further evidence of the time and money her dad had spent polishing and perfecting his boyhood memories. Hidden from view was a very modern flat-screen TV and a small, but fine sound system.

After taking a deep breath, she followed the clink of bottles from the kitchen. There she found her father grabbing a bottle of his favorite root beer from a vintage white refrigerator.

Immediately she launched into the lie she'd chosen. "I can't stay long, Dad. One of the horses has a nasty cut, and there's another fence down in the back. I thought I'd pick up a few supplies before I run back out there."

Turning, he offered her a bottle. "Want one?"

She shook her head and poured herself a glass of milk instead. Like the rest of the house, the kitchen was a stylized version of her father's childhood. Concessions to convenience were cleverly camouflaged behind the woods of yesteryear, while antique implements held sway. Spence thought it weird that a man would care so much about such details. But, then, before they'd married, Spence's idea of décor had involved old beer signs and interesting rocks he'd found while caving with his college buddies.

Instead of moving to the family room, Claire's father broke out some raisin-walnut oatmeal cookies—a heart-healthy brand she had chosen—from the Hoosier cabinet. Once he'd opened the new package, the two of them sat down on opposite benches at the old oak table, where they had talked so many times before.

Her gaze touched on the outside door, and she noticed that, for once, he'd locked it. Clearly Spence's release had him worried.

When her father shoved the cookies her way, Claire's stomach growled loudly. She hadn't realized she was starving, but come to think of it, she hadn't had a bite since breakfast. Back in the dusty cabin, was Spence hungry, too?

She'd wolfed down three cookies—they tasted good, for low fat—and was going for more milk when her father finally broke the silence. "There's a doctor I know. He could take care of you in private."

Her gaze snapped to meet his, nausea fisting deep inside her.

"Claire? Honey?"

The spell broken, she glanced down to see that the milk she had been pouring had overflowed the glass's sides. A white puddle was spreading across the counter.

After putting down the carton, she grabbed a sponge and wiped away the mess.

Which was exactly what her father was suggesting . . .

"You think I should have an abortion." It was a statement, not a question, a statement that had cold sweat breaking out on her forehead. The hand that held the sponge shook.

"It's the wrong time, that's all." His brown eyes searched hers for understanding. "No one could blame you. Hell, no one else will even have to know. You haven't—you haven't said anything to anyone yet, have you?"

She shook her head. Under the circumstances, she had been afraid to talk about her pregnancy. Afraid her friends would give the same advice that had just come from this unlikely quarter. An abortion.

"I'm not getting rid of it," she told her father flatly.

"If it's the Church," he said, "I know you'd be forgiven. Jesus, Claire . . . Spence Winslow paid a man to have you murdered—"

She threw the sponge into the sink, where it hit with a satisfying splat. "Don't you think I know that? I don't need you to keep drumming what he did into my head. But this—this baby—didn't do it. This child is innocent."

"You're not thinking straight now. We can talk about it later."

She knew what he was thinking: that he could wear her down, make her see sense. But she wasn't a little girl anymore, and she resented his attempt to "handle" her the way he would one of his clients. As if he knew far better than she did.

"You're not changing my mind on this," she snapped. "I've thought about it all week, and I've made my decision."

"Claire—"

"I'm taking the stuff I borrowed for my barn first-aid kit and I'm leaving now," she told him. "And before you ask, I don't want company."

He glanced at the pitch-black window, which overlooked what Claire and her sister had grown up calling the Deer Meadow. "But it's dark out, and he's free now. You need someone with you."

"I'll have the gun you gave me. It's going to have to be enough."

SEVEN

By all rights, the body shouldn't have been spotted before morning, but Lenore Briggs-Hadley had heard one too many accounts of drownings in the area. During the previous year's rains, an entire family had been lost when the mother blindly turned her minivan onto the little bridge separating her home from the road. She must have driven over it a thousand times before, must have taken for granted the tiny stream it spanned. But that wild and windy night during the coldest February in a decade, the tiny stream had swollen to a rushing torrent, carrying the center of the private bridge downstream.

It had taken days to find the bodies of the twenty-eight-year-old woman and her two small children.

Lenore was thinking of that tragedy this night, though the winds were calm and the rain had dwindled to a trickle. But Claire's warning nagged at her, so she braked the black Range Rover in front of the bridge leading to an empty house that most would call a mansion and few—including Lenore—would ever think of as a home. Flipping on the high beams, she scanned the water carefully. . . .

Until her gaze snagged on a color that did not belong.

Before she consciously recognized what she was seeing, Lenore's stomach knotted and her jaw dropped. By the time it finally registered, her hand was snaking into her purse and her lips were murmuring a prayer that this time, this time please, God, her cell phone would pick up a signal so she could call for help.

Spence jolted awake, the velvety darkness around him so complete it offered no clues as to his location. In jail, there were always lights—had the storm brought on a blackout?

When he attempted to sit up, the pain hit, rocketing up his arm into his shoulder. He sucked a breath between clenched teeth, and memory filled him the way the chill air filled his lungs.

He coughed, which detonated more pain. Steeling himself against it, he fumbled for the electric lantern Claire had left beside the bunk.

He knew a moment's panic when he couldn't find it. But as he swung his feet down to the floor, he accidentally kicked it over. Cursing, he groped until he first located, then righted it and flipped the switch.

A halo of soft yellow light touched the other bunks, a pair of wooden stools, and the edges of the locker. His heartbeat slowed a little as he realized he hadn't dreamt his release from custody. Then he glanced down at his watch—a well-worn digital—and saw that it was a few minutes after nine p.m.

Could Claire have had some trouble with the horses, or had she changed her mind about returning? Right after she had left him, he had been so sure of her. . . .

Was it possible that her presence, after three weeks of longing, prayers, and pleas to see her, had sparked groundless optimism? Or had shock and blood loss clouded his thinking?

Reluctantly, he peeked at the cloth strips that bound his wound. Though they had quickly soaked through after Claire wrapped his arm, the stain hadn't grown much larger in the hour or so since. His head felt clearer, too, since he had slept—clear enough to wonder if he'd been a fool to trust a woman who would shoot him.

Though he had encouraged her to keep her weapon, did Claire still fear him enough to call the sheriff instead of coming back herself? He was well aware that years ago Joel Shepherd had been her sister's fiancé. Because of his history with her family, she would tend to trust him, wouldn't she?

The cabin might be chilly, but Spence felt hot sweat erupt above his upper lip. Why wouldn't Claire turn to the sheriff instead of the man arrested for scheming to have her killed?

"Damn it." Though anxiety was digging its sharp claws into him, Spence forced himself to get up slowly. Even so, a wave of dizziness broke over him, and sweat poured down his face. Rain or not, he had to get the hell away from here before it was too late.

At the thrumming of an engine—a sheriff's department motorcycle or an ATV?—panic set his heart pounding a tattoo against his chest wall. His gaze jerked to one of the two grimy windows. Could he squeeze through the narrow frame and slip out into the darkness? One thing was for damned sure: He couldn't let them catch him here and lock him up again.

The door handle rattled. It was already too late. For better or for worse, he was about to find out if his trust had been misplaced.

"Spence?"

At the sound of Claire's voice, relief flowed through him, warm and sweet as honey in his veins.

"Claire," he breathed, even as she stepped inside the ring of light. Tension was written in the stiffness of her shoulders, but she was here, at least, a silver thermos in one hand and a black flashlight in the other. A couple of white grocery sacks were looped over her arm. Beneath her rain jacket, she wore a fresh set of clothes, though the ride out here had already spattered them with mud. With her helmet apparently forgotten, her hair was an untidy mass of chestnut waves that fell just past her shoulders.

She had never looked more beautiful to him. He fought an impulse to reach out to her, to pull her into his arms and kiss her until she couldn't speak.

That time in their lives had passed, no matter how often the memories overwhelmed him.

"I—uh—I've brought coffee." Her brown eyes warmed a little, and some of the strain left her mouth. "And something to take the edge off the pain, too."

"You're a goddess," he rasped, and he felt a grin pull at his lips. Lord, but it felt good to smile.

"You should sit." She nodded in the direction of the bunk. "Can't have you falling over before we talk."

Even more than her words, the firmness of her voice reminded him of her earlier demand. She wanted the whole story, wanted all her questions answered.

She certainly deserved that much, after the hell he'd put her through. But still, Spence's gut clenched at the idea of revealing the dangerous people who had involved themselves in his life. No, strike that, he thought fiercely, and make it the dangerous people he had invited into their lives, his and Claire's. Maybe not consciously, but he'd worked in law enforcement long enough to know the sort of shit that went down when people got involved with big-time gambling. He'd understood he was getting in over his head, even realized on some level that when it all came crashing down, he would not be the only one crushed.

And still he'd kept right on screwing things up—hoping, he supposed, that whatever came would put his lights out, so he wouldn't have to feel. Now that he realized what he'd thrown away, it made him so furious with himself, he could spit.

But self-loathing wouldn't change a thing, no matter how warranted.

He sat on the bunk, his thoughts morose, as Claire explained how she'd put up the horses and then gone to fetch supplies and her father's four-wheeler.

"At least it's quit raining," she said before she frowned down at his arm. "Let's take another look at that."

He noticed that, though she wore no makeup, her long lashes were clumped. From crying, he supposed. Because of him.

She fumbled with the now-bloody fabric she'd wrapped earlier around his arm. "I knotted this end too darned tight. I think it would be easier if I cut through it."

With that, she pulled a wicked-looking utility blade out of her jeans.

For her sake, he tried on a smart-ass smirk as he glanced at the knife's tip. "What is it today with you and weapons?"

She managed a half smile. "Wait'll you get a load of the flamethrower stashed in my other pocket."

He snorted, and she warned him, "This could hurt a little."

"Then how about a little of that coffee first, and aspirin? I could stand some fortifying."

Nodding, she poured the steaming liquid into the caplike cup of the Thermos and shook a tablet from a bottle into his good hand. "No aspirin, Spence. It would keep you bleeding. Besides, this is a little stronger."

"Any old port in a storm." He gulped down the pill with a mouthful of the brew. Too fast—the bitter coffee burned him. He sucked in a quick breath to cool his tongue.

"I brought you another shirt for later," she said as she pulled one of the cabin's two stools near the bunk. "I swiped one of my dad's. Raided the kitchen on my way out, too. It was slim pickings—grocery day's tomorrow—but I found cheese and crackers and a couple of apples."

His eyes stung at the thought that after everything, she'd considered his comfort. He hadn't even given food a thought. "Thank you."

A minute later, he was clamping his teeth, thinking only of riding out the pain as she sawed through the fabric of the bandage. After it was off, she gently wiped away the bloody mess, using half a pack of moist towelettes.

At the fresh blood welling in the wound, she grimaced. "Sorry I got it bleeding again, but it needed cleaning before we put on the antibiotic."

"Seriously," he asked her, "did you buy that gun because of me?"

Her head shook, but she kept her gaze latched on his arm. "Dad said you'd come after me. Joel was worried, too."

"Your father gave it to you?" Spence guessed. With both the sheriff and her dad warning her, no wondered she'd been so quick to pull the trigger. Spence blamed himself, though, for badgering everyone who'd listen to let him see his wife.

Claire nodded, her expression darkening. "He's taking this whole thing really hard, Spence. If he figures out you're here, I don't know—I can't imagine what he'd do."

Spence could, easily. Will Meador would come after him. From the first time the two of them had met, at a Mexican restaurant outside San Antonio, the criminal attorney had made himself clear, returning Spence's handshake with a bruising grip and saying, "She's all the family I have left. You hurt her, and I'll make you regret you ever heard my name."

"Dad," Claire had burst out, blushing to the roots of her hair and making Spence wonder exactly how many previous boyfriends the old man had run off.

Slapping at his arm, she had begged her father, "Don't kid around like that. He'll think you're serious."

Meador grinned and slapped his back, and Spence returned another handshake, but all three of them knew the attorney wasn't joking. Since his wife's and elder daughter's deaths, Claire was everything to him. But Spence had figured there were worse qualities a guy could have than loving his kid too much. Besides, Spence was so far gone on Claire by that time, he wouldn't have turned back if she'd had a basketful of rattlers for relations.

"I'm sorry he was hurt. When this is over, you tell

him that for me." His own sincerity surprised Spence. Her dad could be an interfering pain in the ass upon occasion, but Spence knew how *he'd* react if he learned someone had tried to have Claire murdered. And if it had been someone he had trusted, he'd want to kill the bastard with his own two hands.

"You tell him yourself," she said, and squeezed some of the ointment on her fingers. "I imagine this will hurt, too."

Looking away from his arm, Spence gritted his teeth and counted silently while Claire rubbed on the ointment. His vision grayed, but before he lost it completely, she was finished.

She took out an ivory-colored sheet and used her knife to nick the border. As she tore it into strips, she said, "You need a hospital. I didn't have real bandages, and you could still get an infection."

"I'll be fine for now."

"We don't even know where the bullet's gone. Sometimes they can bounce around inside a person." Her gaze pleaded. "I don't want you dying, Spence. I don't want to have killed you."

"That makes two of us." With his good hand, he touched her wrist—and fought not to react when she jerked away as if she had been prodded by a red-hot poker. It hurt, though; God, how it hurt. Far worse than his arm.

"Come on, Claire." He had a struggle on his hands to keep his tone light. "Look at me. I'm doing okay. If the bullet clipped an artery, we'd know it by now. I'll get it looked at later. I know a doc in San Antonio who can't afford to ask too many questions."

After a brief silence, she rebandaged his arm. Once she had secured it with some first aid tape, she looked up at him. "Who else do you know? What other criminals?"

When he hesitated, she stood. "When you wanted me to come back, I gave you my price. The truth, Spence, or I'm out of here."

He looked at her, trying to weigh the threat in her words, but he saw nothing to indicate she might be bluffing. And he didn't want her walking out on him, not before he made her understand.

"All right," he said. "All right. Let's back up to that bookie. He said something to a guy who said something to a guy about my trouble paying. And sooner or later, it got to the wrong guy that a street cop who patrolled his turf was having money problems."

"So this 'wrong guy,' " she ventured, "saw a way to take advantage?"

Spence nodded, and she sat again, perching on the stool beside him. He wanted desperately to touch her, to smooth the worry from her face, to kiss away her grief. But her earlier reaction to his touch reminded him that he had lost that privilege. Irrevocably. The thought lodged in his throat, making it impossible to swallow.

"Yes," he told her. "That's exactly it. He wanted certain favors. Phone calls warning him of raids on his dope labs and crackdowns on his dealers or his ladies. A blind eye—not to everything, but to those busts that would cost his gang too much time and money."

"So it's one of the gangs, then. Which one?"

Fear came ripping through him, cold as a fevered chill. "They'll come after you, Claire. They'll kill you if they think you know. You remember that reporter, don't you? The one they ambushed because he mentioned too much in his article? And then there was that six-year-old girl they kidnapped and executed because her uncle dissed somebody's mama, and God knows how many drive-by shootings. Hell, they've even had throats slashed inside prisons when they think one of their own *vatos* might roll for a lighter sentence. These are scary people, Claire."

She looked directly into his face. "I'm not an idiot. I don't plan on telling anybody. But I have to know, Spence. It's my price."

When he named the group, she blinked and ran her fingers quickly beneath her damp eyes. He knew she'd worked with a number of victims of gang violence at the hospital. Teaching them to sit up, feed themselves, or use the toilet. She would have come across the tattoos, learned which ones "protected" the members of the group in prison—and which ones celebrated various crimes, including murder.

"I've seen the things they do in the name of their so-called *familia*," she said, her lip curling in a sneer. "I've seen the utter waste, the kids who'll never have a chance at any different life, the innocents whose only crime was being in the way of trouble. Tell me, did you help them? Did you do as you were asked?"

He shook his head. "Hell, no. Why do you think they set me up?"

She pinched the bridge of her nose, turning on the stool until her back was to him. When he saw her shoulders shaking, he slid to the bunk's edge—close enough to hear soft snuffling.

"Claire . . . honey." He ached with the need to pull her to him.

She swung around her knees, then went rigid when they bumped his. Yet instead of backing up this time, she stared into his face. "How am I supposed to get through—to get through all of this?" she asked him. "What am I supposed to feel?"

"I'm sorry," he whispered. He slid onto his knees, then gave in to desire and encircled her waist with his arms. Leaning his head against her hip, he closed his eyes, repeating, "I'm so sorry, Claire."

Once again she stiffened, but she did not push him away. He counted that as a victory.

They remained like that for several minutes, until Claire finally drew a noisy breath. "I was already pretty freaked out when I went out on Cinnamon. Coyote died today, Spence. I—I used the gun—the same gun that hurt you—to put him down, and Bushwhack spooked and ran off."

He hugged her again, then shifted back onto the bunk to give her more space. Their knees, though, remained touching. "Tell me about what happened."

She did, in a jumbled story full of false starts, back-tracking, and various asides. It took Spence a while to figure that it had begun with Megan Martin rushing into the office and ended with Joel Shepherd nearly shooting Claire over Coyote's cooling corpse.

The horror of it sank down to his marrow.

"You could have died." Spence felt as if he would be sick at any moment. "You could have been the one shot."

She smiled weakly, though her light freckles stood out against her pallor. "Or I could have shot the sheriff, too. The way my day's been going, it would've been par for the course, right? Who knew I'd need to ask my dad for extra bullets straight off?"

Spence laughed, mostly from relief at her attempt to joke about it—and out of relief that both of them were here, together and alive. Their gazes caught, and this time he didn't hesitate to drag her into his embrace.

Taking care with his wounded arm, he stroked the silken hair behind her neck. "One thing I didn't get," he said. "How did Coyote get out in the first place?"

"I think it was a vandal," Claire said. "We've been having a lot of trouble with our fences. At first, when dead trees fell across a couple, I chalked it up to bad luck. But this time, the wire had clearly been cut. I can't help wondering if whoever did it deliberately spooked Coyote and sent him galloping into the ravine."

"You have any ideas about who would—?"

"Joel thought it might be you."

Irritation needled him at the way she kept calling the man by his first name. "Well, *Joel's* dead wrong—but what should I expect? Sheriff Sherlock's been off the mark on me on every other count these past three weeks."

She pulled away to look him in the face. "Not on every one, Spence. He told me about the gambling."

"So score one for the big-hat."

Her forehead crinkled, and her gaze intensified. "You're jealous of him? With your whole life—both our lives—going down the tubes, you're worried about a ridiculous thing like that?"

He shook his head. "Not really, not in that way. I'm just scared you'll start believing him instead of me."

She looked down at her knees, where she had braced her hands. A silence swelled between them, so painful that Spence couldn't bear it.

"You know, Randall could've done it," he said, overwhelmed by the need to change the subject. "Knocked down the fences, I mean."

The more he thought of it, the more likely it seemed. He remembered Claire telling him how in his teen years, Randall had invited a group of friends to party at his aunt's house while she and her husband had been out of town. The young guests had gotten out of hand, breaking into a locked liquor cabinet and laughing like hyenas as they smashed Mrs. Hajek's collection of stoneware garden gnomes. It might have gone much further, except Claire's father had gotten suspicious of the noise and called the sheriff.

She looked up. "Randall Hajek? Mrs. Hajek's nephew?"

Spence shrugged. "Why not? He was plenty hacked off when she sold us the place. What with him threatening to sue, I figured he was banking on inheriting the whole piece. And at Mrs. Hajek's funeral—what was it—in January, didn't we hear he was planning to relocate his business and move into his aunt's place?"

"Yeah, I guess he's living in the house now. I've seen his SUV pull into the driveway a few times. A spanking-new Suburban with one of those big brush guards on the front grill. I waved hello to him one day, but the little turd and his blond friend—the same guy from the funeral—kept right on driving."

Spence remembered that on the occasion he had seen the man, Randall had been in the company of a young Adonis with a sleek European haircut, a store-bought tan, and a silk collar unbuttoned to give a hint of naked chest. The boy toy had been twitchy, and his big brown eyes looked vacant, but it was plain enough that Randall didn't keep him around to mine insightful nuggets from his conversation.

"Randall must still be pissed, then," Spence said, thinking that out here in the Hill Country, a man could be an alcoholic, a wife beater, or a petty thief, but everyone responded to the traditional two-finger, over-the-steering-wheel howdy, especially on the back roads. To do any less was a serious breach of Buck County etiquette. "Maybe pissed enough to cut those fences."

"I don't see it," Claire said. "I have a hard time imagining him summoning the nerve to wrap the mailbox with toilet paper, much less sneak around the property with a pair of wire cutters. I think something like a lawsuit's more his speed, where he could sic a pack of nasty lawyers on us like he threatened."

She did have a point. The smallish realtor, with his carefully trimmed goatee and a balding pate that flared red at the slightest provocation, didn't exactly have the market cornered on testosterone. But the guy had bought a macho truck . . . Next thing you knew, he'd be trading in his Gucci loafers for a pair of hand-tooled boots and covering that shiny head of his with a big Stetson. There was something about moving to the Hill Country that gave a lot of city types—Randall had spent the past few years selling fancy lofts in downtown Houston—the need to cowboy up with high-priced accessories.

The question was, did a Texas-sized vendetta fit into the picture? Could a little guy like Hajek, who was rumored to collect movie memorabilia and pricey wines, possibly have the sort of malice and connections needed to take down a San Antonio cop?

Spence couldn't credit the thought, but even so, he couldn't discount the possibility that Randall had been skulking about the property exacting petty vengeance.

"I don't want you taking any chances," he told

Claire. "For the time being, you shouldn't go out on the back acreage alone."

She lifted her chin in a clear challenge. "Like I did tonight for you?"

"I'm not Randall Hajek, and I'm not the man the sheriff and your father think I am. You know who I am, Claire, or you never would have come here for me."

She looked down at her hands. "Maybe I'm just crazy. The more I think about it, the more it sounds like that to me. You're suggesting Randall's out to get me—and some gang banger's come up with this complicated plot to frame you. It's a lot, Spence, a whole lot to swallow."

"He's not just any gangbanger. He's the coldest little son of a bitch anyone in SAPD's ever seen. He clawed his way to the top two years ago, at only twenty-three. Kid grew up on the streets, but he's got this savage kind of brilliance—hell, he offed his own brother, then used the life insurance payout to put himself through business school. The asshole's got himself an MBA and some legitimate business interests to launder the money he takes in on his criminal enterprises."

"You never told me, who is he?"

Spence had been hoping that after hearing the gang's name, she would understand how dangerous it was for her to know more. But giving her a name would make no difference; she had already heard enough to get her killed. If he wanted her to trust him, he had to tell her something.

"He goes by Beto Chavez," Spence said. "And that's not a name it would be healthy to go bandying about."

"Why isn't he in jail," she asked, "if SAPD knows about the brother and the illegal businesses?"

Spence shook his head. "You've heard me talk

about it more than once, how there's a hell of a big gap between common knowledge and legal proof, especially for a man with a whole pack of crack attorneys on retainer."

"So we'll find it. Proof. It's the only way we're going to get you out of this."

He shook his head. "I wanted you to understand, Claire. But there is no 'we' in this. Only me."

One of the hands braced on her knees balled into a fist. "So you expect me to believe all this, to buy all the stuff about a criminal organization capable of tampering with e-mails and faking tapes as well. You risk your freedom to convince me, but you're saying that we're finished? That I'm just supposed to stand by on the sidelines, content to be the helpless victim?"

Her face formed a montage of emotion. Skepticism. Anger. Fierce determination. "That's garbage, Spence. Pure bullshit. Either you're lying through your teeth, in which case I'm glad I shot you and I'll see you in divorce court, or we're fighting for a chance. Because this Beto stole my life, too. This isn't just your cross to bear."

Fear churned in Spence's gut. He'd been so desperate to get to her, he hadn't taken her stubbornness into account—or imagined she might claim the right to stand by him in this.

"I want you to divorce me." Every word throbbed in his throat. "I want you clear of this—and me. I've signed the quitclaim, so the land's yours—"

She shook her head. "I don't give a damn about it. We'll sell it if we have to, give the money back to Beto. Pay the bastard off so he'll leave us alone."

Spence huffed out a sigh. "It's not about the money,

even if we could raise enough. If he was mad enough to do this, it's about sending a message that nobody can cross him—not even a cop."

"But what about your fellow cops? What about Sergeant Contreras? Can't they—"

"This isn't your fight, and it's not theirs, either. The department's washed its hands of me—as far as it's concerned, I went over the edge after the shooting last fall." He folded his arms across his chest, though he was careful to avoid aggravating his wound. "Even Raul thinks I'm a total screwup. And they're right, Claire. They're all right. The gambling and the lying. I—I didn't come to drag you into this. I came—I came to say goodbye."

She laid both palms on his forearm and leaned close to his face. Her gaze bored into him, looking not so much at him as inside him. "I can see you going down, Spence, down for the last time. And I'll be damned it I sit by and watch it without throwing you a line."

The one who had been left behind breathed deeply, yet he struggled against the panic crowding tight inside his chest. After so long, things were moving far too quickly, spinning into shapes he neither recognized nor fully understood.

How was it that things so well and deeply hidden could still exert such influence? How was it a man's plans, his intentions could go so horribly awry?

The answer rose like a dead sun, to cast not light but the ink-black stain of shadow on the answer.

Woman. Woman was the trouble, with her unfathomable reactions, her resistance to the flow of logic.

The way her heart leapt from emotion to emotion arranged like stepping stones across the torrent he'd unleashed.

Nothing left to do but raise the floodgates once more. Wash away the damned rocks, or submerge them beneath a flood so deep and furious that she would have no choice except to swim or drown.

EIGHT

Claire wanted so much to believe him, to imagine that the two of them could conspire to turn back time. But Joel Shepherd's words flooded her memory, an icy current flowing beneath the fragile common ground where she and Spence now stood.

"You sound exactly like every single battered woman who's ever called the jail and begged me to let her husband come back home. Every single woman I've gone back to find hurt later."

An image formed in her mind of the woman he'd described: her beaten body on the kitchen floor, her baby crying, crawling through congealing scarlet puddles.

And yet Claire knew her husband, knew that no matter how bad things had gotten for him, he had never lashed out at her physically. Understood that even now he intended to distance himself from her to save her from more pain.

"So he's sorry," Joel's voice warned. "They're always sorry afterwards."

If the dead wife in the kitchen had not been banished to a silent plane, would she have heard her husband break down and beg for her forgiveness? Would she have heard him say he'd always loved her, though the bloody spatters on his clothes had not yet dried? Had he told her all those things as he had turned to leave?

The murdered woman was transfigured in Claire's imagination, the staring blue eyes darkening, the splayed hair on the floor turning red-brown, the facial features morphing into a semblance of her own. Though her heart lay still, the child's wails cut straight to it until her dead arms ached to lift him from the gore, to take him far from pain and hatred to a place of love and peace.

A place where she had no choice except to go on alone, leaving him all by himself in hell . . .

Banishing the nightmare image, Claire sucked in a deep breath and thought about their child, hers and Spence's, the child she must protect above all else. The child whose existence she must not speak of to her husband.

Still, her hands were powerless to stop stroking Spence's forearms. And she was helpless to climb free of the bottomless blue wells of his eyes.

He was part of her, too, and had been for such a long time. How could she turn away from their shared history and from the need so clearly written in his face?

A prescient warning overwhelmed her, whispering in her ear, *If you leave him now, it's over. You'll never see this man alive again.*

Unable to bear the thought, Claire leaned forward, her eyes closing as their lips met in a kiss as tenuous and tender as the first kiss they had shared—had it been five years ago? She felt his callused fingertips feather strokes along her jaw, her neckline. Felt the tingling of her nipples and the yawning ache beneath her navel.

The ache of an emptiness she feared would stretch into forever.

Her mouth opened to his tongue, and as their kiss deepened, a moan rose from deep inside her, rushing to the surface like a spirit loosed from the abyss. Her misgivings flickered and then vanished, leaving behind not so much as a single puff of smoke.

As he pulled her onto the bunk and into his embrace, her body cried out in recognition of the solid warmth of his bare chest. She reclaimed him with her hands, running her palms along his back, his sides, over his broad shoulders, and a sob caught in her throat. God, how she had missed this. She felt like a refugee from this territory, returning home to the hard planes and the muscled hillocks she had come to know so well. She splayed her fingers above his heart just to feel its pounding, and a hot tear trickled from the corner of her eye.

Spence's kisses dropped to her neck, his lips trailing and teeth nipping until his tongue flicked warm and wet inside her ear. He reached beneath her shirt and unhooked her bra in one deft move, then scooped one of her breasts to thumb the nipple. At the rumbling murmur of his hunger, bright electric flashes throbbed behind her eyelids—unheeded warning lights.

Her clothes had grown unbearably confining, so when he tugged at her jacket's sleeve, she was quick to help him strip it off her. Her shirt came next, and before she knew it, all her clothes were sailing to the dusty floor, with the lone exception, her bra, landing on the lantern to throw weird shadows across the tiny room.

She wriggled around the nest of blankets to trail hot kisses down his chest and run her fingers through the coarse hair. She drank in the smell of his heat, tasted the salt of sweat, the tang of musk. And pushed aside the fear that each sensation, every rush of pleasure, was sure to be the last for them. That the white heat of their bodies was about to crack the ice and plunge them both into the deadly currents rushing just below.

Spence knew this was the wrong thing, that in taking what she offered, he was ripping away the still-bloody strips of flesh that held her heart together. If he were any sort of man, he would stop this right now—stop and walk away from her forever.

Yet with each kiss and every touch, desire roared to the surface, drowning out all else but the memory of his desperation in the jail cell. Greedily, he plied her breasts with kisses, marveling at how much fuller, how much riper they seemed than he recalled. He lingered for a long time, tasting each, then suckling—his body hardening painfully at the hoarse sound of her groans.

He knew her every weakness, knew what drove her wild better than she knew herself. And as the last strains of conscience faded, he put that knowledge to wicked use, his fingers plunging deep inside her wetness, his thumb rubbing at the spot that made her back arch and her lips murmur his name. Her muscles tightened, quivered, but when he was certain she must come, she rolled away from him.

The spell shimmered before his eyes, like the rainbow iridescence of a drop of oil on a puddle. He couldn't bear to lose its beauty—couldn't stand the thought of gazing down into the ugliness that lay beneath the surface.

"Help me," Claire whispered as she fumbled with the button of his jeans.

Relieved beyond speech, Spence shuddered out a breath and felt the throbbing pressure heighten as tooth by tooth the zipper parted. Her short nails catching his waist, she raked down everything he wore to expose his straining cock.

He kicked free of the pants legs a moment before flipping her beneath him and kissing her with all the desperation in his soul. He meant to make it last forever, to pleasure her with hands and tongue, to brand every inch of her with the memory of his passion. But when Claire pulled his hips so that he was pressed into her dampness, what was left of his control was shattered. . . .

Until he tried to push himself above her and raw pain ripped through his left arm. The pain of the bullet he had somehow managed to put out of his mind.

He jerked back, sucking air through his clenched teeth.

Claire sat up, staring into his face. "Oh, Spence. You're hurting. You poor—"

His gaze met hers and held it. "I don't want your pity, Claire. I want you, more than anything I've ever wanted in my life. I need you."

One more time, he thought, as she pushed him back and climbed astride him. He pulled her mouth down where he could take it, and she slid over his erection, her body sheathing his. The old bunk creaked with their rocking, slow at first as they savored each sensa-

tion, then faster, faster, until the world of Spence's
darkness splintered into blinding light.

Mere seconds before a different sort of flickering
captured his attention—a gleam that tracked across
the pair of filmy windows. A ray that looked precisely
like the beam from a flashlight.

NINE

Once her shuddering subsided, Claire floated cloud-like in the wake of pleasure, her body limp but for the smile tugging at the corners of her mouth. A sensation of well-being swamped her, a high so fine drug addicts sold their souls in vain attempts to come near it.

It lasted only seconds before Spence shook her.

"There's someone here," he whispered frantically. "Someone outside with a light."

Just that quickly, her bliss fractured and fear rushed in to take its place. Climbing off him, she grabbed for her jeans and jammed a foot into one leg. "Oh, shit, if that's my father—Spence, you have to hide."

From outside, the hitch and rumble of a gas engine made her eyes flare wide. "The ATV," she warned, recognizing the roughness of its motor. "Someone's starting it."

Spence stood stark naked beside a window, his head canted to peek carefully out into the darkness. "Some son of a bitch is stealing it!"

Her jeans now on, Claire grabbed for her jacket and

plunged her hand into a pocket. The wrong one, she realized, then fished for the other—the one that held her gun.

Spence clamped down on her wrist. "Let me, Claire."

She didn't try to stop him. After all, he'd spent the past ten years chasing criminals.

Pistol in hand, he jerked open the door—in time to see a red flash from the four-wheeler's brake light before it disappeared from view.

Claire eased into the doorway just behind him. "We'll never catch him on foot."

He turned to look at her. "Your vandal?"

She nodded. "I suppose. I can't imagine a run-of-the-mill thief coming way back here at night, probably on foot, too."

Spence went for his own pants and sat down on the bunk to dress. "You're saying 'he.' Are you thinking Randall, or is there somebody else?"

She shook her head. "I don't know—I can't worry about that now. I'm too scared. What if he does something to the horses? What if he's riding to the paddock right now to hurt them?"

"Slow down, Claire. You were right when you said we can't catch him, and running off half-cocked could get you hurt."

After hooking her bra behind her, she snatched her shirt off the floor. She didn't appreciate Spence's attempts to calm her down—and the fact that he was right only aggravated her more.

"I have to keep them safe." The words spilled like a broken strand of beads. "What happened earlier today—I let those animals down."

"You can't blame yourself for what some nutcase did, some criminal—"

"Isn't that what you did?" she demanded, anxiety and frustration exploding into words. "Blaming yourself for that boy? Isn't that what ruined everything for us?"

She saw him flinch, saw the pain flash over his face, but she couldn't stop herself. "Isn't that the reason we're sneaking around out here, you bleeding from a gunshot, me wondering how the hell I'm going to raise a—"

She froze, appalled by the next words on her lips. She had promised herself she wouldn't tell Spence she was pregnant. Not now, with so much already in the balance. And certainly not while someone was riding around on her dad's ATV, doing God only knew what to her horses.

"How you're going to *what?*" Spence asked.

Her hesitation lasted only a split second. "How I'll raise interest in a new investigation. To get you cleared of the charges."

She sat to pull on socks, then jammed her feet into her mud-caked boots.

His head shook. "No way. That's not for you to do. I told you earlier, I want you to—"

She went to the bags she'd brought and tossed him the faded denim work shirt she had liberated from her dad's collection. "That was before we—before we made love. Or was that just an old reflex, Spence? One last time for the road?"

He pulled the shirt on, his attention focused on getting the sleeve over his injured arm. He didn't—or wouldn't—look at her. "This isn't your fight anymore, Claire. It can't be."

She blinked back tears. "I won't give up on you."

"If you won't file for divorce, I'll do it. You aren't about to change my mind on this."

Gritting her teeth, she pulled on her jacket and grabbed the lantern. She headed for the door, then paused to look at him. "So I'm supposed to say good-bye now. I'm supposed to let you run off and handle this yourself."

Or die trying, she added mentally, realizing that was what he meant to do. Get himself killed to free her of the mess he'd made. Most likely by confronting Beto Chavez . . .

She would rather see her husband locked up, thrown in jail forever, than let him do such a thing.

Spence looked away from her, into a dark corner. "Just remember that I loved you."

"Damn you, Spencer Winslow. Damn you."

Still carrying the lantern, she threw open the door. She hesitated briefly, ears straining for the sound of the ATV's rough growl. When she didn't hear it, she scrambled off into the darkness as quickly as her feet would take her. Tears sliding down her face, she never looked behind her, though she heard Spence breathing heavily, his passage snapping sticks and crunching old leaves.

Even with her light, Claire's headlong rush was costly. Branches snatched at her sleeve and a noose-like loop of thorny vine gouged the tender flesh around her neck. After a time, she could no longer hear Spence moving.

But it wasn't until she reached the quiet paddock that Claire realized she had lost him. And not only her husband. In her hurry to get back to the horses, she had also left the gun behind with Spence.

Sprawling across the broken stump that had tripped him, Spence grabbed at his ankle. He was heaving, struggling for breath as pain exploded in both his left foot and his injured arm. Water soaked into his clothing, and the ground sloshed when he moved.

But none of it held a candle to the agony of losing Claire.

By the time he had recovered enough to call out to her, he had long since lost sight of her light. He shouted anyway, shouted in the darkness until his throat was raw, but if she heard him, she gave no sign.

Too winded to continue, Spence struggled to his feet and braced himself against a slender tree trunk. With clouds blotting out the stars, he couldn't make out anything except the throbbing strobe of distant lightning.

He strained his ears, desperate to hear Claire's voice calling out his name. But all that came back to him was the faint murmur of thunder and the sound of water dripping through the leaves above him. He thought he recognized the distant music of more water rushing through the swollen creek. But no Claire and no motor—what the hell had happened to the ATV?

He prayed whoever took it was long gone. For one thing, he had never given her the gun back. Yet even if she had it, he hated the idea of her rushing toward a confrontation. Claire normally had good sense, far too much to confront a thief out here alone, but something warned him that tonight all bets were off. Between the horrors she'd been through with him and the trauma of having to put down one of the horses, she had been stressed to the breaking point. From hard experience, he knew it was no place to be when making life-and-death decisions.

Something rustled in the leaf litter at his right. Spence jerked toward it, bringing up his fists to fend off whatever came next. Then laughing at the realization that it couldn't have been much larger than a foraging armadillo or a hungry possum.

Lowering his hands, he started feeling his way back to the cabin. Claire had had a flashlight with her earlier; maybe he could find it now. He would need it if he was going to find his way through this pitch-black night.

Which was exactly what he must do, not only to keep Claire safe from a possible vandal, but to protect her from the suspicions descending on him like a host of vultures, their dark wings pumping terror through his soul.

TEN

Stone dead, that was how Joel Shepherd found him, facedown in an unnamed tributary off Little Bee Creek.

As sheriff, he might be a long way from an official identification, but from the moment Deputy Frank Ashford had called him at home with the description, Joel figured they had at last found Adam Strickland. Along with the Spencer Winslow case, the mystery of the biologist's disappearance had consumed scores of man-hours, keeping Joel working late so often that Lori Beth was pretending not to recognize him. Once the medical examiner got a look-see at the corpse, Joel hoped he'd be on the fast track to convincing the prosecutor the same man was responsible for both crimes—and to finally getting his marriage back on track.

The younger of Joel's two deputies, his second cousin Earl Branson, stripped off shoes and socks and waded into the swiftly moving stream. "Jesus, this is cold," he griped, a toadlike grimace bisecting his round face.

Though he kept his flashlight on his twenty-four-year-old deputy, Joel didn't pay too much attention. Earl had always been the kind of titty-baby who would cry if you hung him with a new rope.

Earl edged to within six feet of the body, his sausage-like arm already stretching toward the fence post that had hooked the yellow waders. Knocked sideways by the rushing current, he yelped as the flow surged past his thighs.

"Christ, that's cold. Goddamn! My balls are climbin' up around my throat."

"Careful, there." Joel wasn't referring to Earl's safety, which he had assured by means of a stout rope tied at one end around his deputy's soft middle and the big Ford SUV's bumper at the other. Joel's immediate concern was Mrs. Briggs-Hadley, who stood not ten feet away with her arms twined around her waist and her eyes carefully averted. Frank, who had first responded to the call, was holding an umbrella over her head against the occasional drip and trying to convince her to go ahead inside, where it was dry. So far she'd resisted, leaving Joel to suspect she didn't want to be alone inside that museum of hers, with its tall white columns and its marble floors. Impressive as it was, the one time Joel had been invited there, the house had echoed eerily, giving him the creeps.

When dealing with a lady of her standing, it was important for all the men to watch their language and extend every courtesy. Especially in light of her husband's generous contributions to Joel's recent campaign. With eighteen years in Buck County law enforcement under his belt—several more, in fact, than Joel—the sallow-faced Frank understood Buck

County's political realities as well as Joel, but Earl . . . well, some days Earl could screw up a two-car funeral.

As if to prove the point, he called up, "God, but this thing stinks, and it don't look so solid, either. If I tie him off to haul him out, cuz, we're likely to lose a few hunks."

Goddamned idiot redneck—if he weren't a "special project" of Joel's mama, he'd be out on his ass for saying such a thing within hearing of a lady. And especially for calling Joel "cuz" on the job.

Keeping his voice low, Joel half whispered, "Quiet down, jackass, and let me help you out of there. We'd better call the fire department for some backup. We can't afford to lose any evidence."

Even from this distance, some twenty feet away, Joel could see that Earl was right about the condition of the body. The limbs fluttered like boiling noodles in the current, and the pale and swollen flesh hung loosely, billowing out where the flow tugged it. In places chunks were missing, either torn by rocks and branches during the unfortunate's rough passage or by the feasting of turtles and whatever other critters had got to it. With the help of the volunteer firefighters, they could string a net downstream from the body, then wrap it in a tarp before they tried to move the thing.

Earl grunted as he used the rope to pull himself onto the bank. "Hell, cuz. Any evidence on this ol' boy's already twenty miles downstream. Don't need no coroner to tell me he's been dead for days—or probably longer. More'n likely since Winslow nailed him about three weeks ago."

Though Joel suspected Earl was watching more *CSI*

than was good for him, the rookie deputy was more than likely right about the way this looked. In his mind, Joel ran through how he would sell it to the prosecutor, how Claire Meador's—make that Claire *Winslow's*—husband, who was already halfway around the bend over his fellow cop's death in San Antonio, had seen or imagined something that convinced him Strickland was a threat. Spencer had then murdered the biologist and hidden his body in or near the creek a couple of miles west of here, close to Monarch Ranch. Maybe he'd thought of killing Claire then, too, but he couldn't stomach it himself. Or more likely, the longtime cop had known a spouse would be looked at carefully as a suspect. Unlike the theory involving Claire's life insurance policy and Winslow's gambling debts, this one explained both killings.

But something bothered Joel about this latest scenario, no matter how strongly he defended it when hashing things out with the prosecutor. Maybe Claire's reluctance to believe was shaking him, or maybe he had a problem with going after a fellow lawman, one who, by all accounts, had been a damned good cop.

That had to be it, he decided. In the back of the mind of every law enforcement man, Joel suspected the same fear festered—the fear that all the darkness he dealt with would consume him. And now Joel was working on a case where it had happened, a case that made him wonder if he could ever be a danger to Lori Beth and their two kids.

After he gave Earl a hand untying the rope around his waist, Joel turned toward his department SUV and said, "I'm going to call for the volunteers now. See that you keep a civil tongue in your head, Earl."

The wind changed direction, filling their nostrils with a dank and fetid stench.

"You smellin' that shit, cuz?" the antinepotism poster child asked him. "God help the lot of us if that thing splits open when we haul him up the bank."

Embarrassed, Joel glanced at Mrs. Briggs-Hadley, only to find her staring at them, horror written on her pale face.

"Sorry, ma'am," he muttered, and touched the broad brim of his hat before he grabbed his second cousin by the arm and hauled him to the Expedition.

In that instant, Joel knew he was as capable as any man alive of murdering a family member. Only Lori Beth had nothing to fret about as long as Earl remained around to tempt fate every time the dumb-ass moved his lips.

By the time Spence found the flashlight, he had added a few more bruises to his burgeoning collection. After grabbing the food and everything that looked useful, he stuffed the items in one of the plastic grocery bags, then hurried to the door.

He paused when something sparkled in the beam of light. Something metallic that was lying on the dusty floor. Thinking Claire had dropped her keys, Spence scooped up the item—only to find that it was a bracelet.

A bracelet he had found a month ago at the edge of Little Bee Creek. How the hell had the damned thing gotten out here? The last time he had seen it—

He jammed the bracelet into his pocket. There would be time enough to think about it later, after he found Claire.

* * *

Claire found several of the horses dozing, dark shapes in the pasture, standing with their heads down. Cinnamon and Bushwhack, who had been confined to those stalls closest to the office to recover from their ordeals, nickered hungrily at her approach, their ears pricked forward in anticipation of a midnight snack.

Claire gusted out a sigh and lowered the lantern she was holding. Whoever had taken the ATV must have ridden elsewhere, or the animals would be restless. With her heart still pounding and her lungs raw from her dash here, she felt like huddling against the warm and solid creatures and soaking in the peace she so often felt with horses.

But even if she had time, they would soon pick up on her anxiety and reflect it back at her tenfold. Once she murmured good-bye to them, Claire switched off her lantern and backed out into the night.

She felt as if she'd fallen into a vat of ink. Moving through the darkness made her more aware than ever of her isolation, and more aware that either Spencer or the thief could be hiding close enough to make a grab.

She wasn't certain which possibility scared her most, but, then, her thoughts were so disordered, she had fallen back on instinct. She had listened when it warned that her lantern would draw trouble like a beacon. She was listening now when it told to get her ass inside the office and lock the door behind her fast.

A fingernail tore when she plunged her hand into her pocket to pull out her keys. She groaned—not with pain but with the realization that she'd slipped the ring onto the ATV's key. In her hurry to get back to Spence, she had left it in the ignition.

Which had clearly proved convenient for whoever

had been prowling about the property—or whoever had followed her out to the cabin. Nausea fluttered at the thought—and at the fear that someone could have seen Spence, could have watched through the window as the two of them made love.

Anyone from the vandal to a deputy to one of Beto Chavez's lieutenants, or whatever it was gang leaders called their trusted thugs. Panic jabbed through her at the thought. If the thief hadn't been the vandal, but one of the other possibilities, maybe he had taken the four-wheeler to go for reinforcements.

And maybe they were coming back to capture Spence—or to kill him. The blood inside her veins froze at the thought. As horrible as it was to imagine Spence back in jail, the possibility that he could be murdered here tonight was even worse.

Instinct once more came to her rescue, and before she understood what she was doing, she was stooping near the rocky border of the flower bed, snatching up a stone larger than her two fists, and smashing out the window.

She didn't care about the noise, and she had forgotten her own safety. The only thing she knew for sure was that she had to call Joel Shepherd. She had to tell him that Spence was here and hurt and that they must find him quickly.

They simply had to find her husband and lock him somewhere safe.

ELEVEN

It was the sound of breaking glass that drew him. But it took Claire's words to slice Spence to the bone.

"He's here," he heard her saying, presumably into the telephone. "He's on the property—and injured. Please come right away, Joel. Bring your deputies and put him back in jail where he belongs."

"Jesus . . ." The word came low, more prayer than oath. A prayer that he had heard wrong. A prayer that pain and hunger and exhaustion had drawn the words from his imagination.

But he only had to listen a few moments longer to understand that it was true. Claire had betrayed him in the worst way, in spite of all that had passed between them earlier.

Spence wanted to fall down on his knees, to retch and retch until his body emptied itself of emotion. But pain and fury rose like blood in a fresh wound, followed by a rush of shame. For he understood that he had earned this—and that if he wanted the chance to absolve himself, even to a small degree, he was going to have to find some secret place to hole up and rest awhile.

He knew the spot—knew for certain it would shelter him in safety through the night. What he didn't know was if he had enough left in him to make it there.

Enough strength.

Enough will.

Enough heart.

When Joel Shepherd pulled into his driveway a little after two a.m., the Subaru wagon Lori Beth drove was missing from the carport.

Apprehension squeezed the breath out of him. She had to get to the preschool where she taught early in the morning, so there was no way she would be out this late . . . unless Tyler had the croup again, or maybe four-year-old Kylie. Each of them had required trips to the ER in the dead of night during the past year.

He tried to remember whether either of the kids had been sick. Lately, by the time he got home, his family had been sleeping. He frowned in concentration. Had Lori Beth said anything about it on the phone?

But his mind could only delude him with this line of thought for so long. Things had been going downhill for weeks, since she had found the engagement ring— the ring he once had given Karen Meador—in the pocket of his work pants in the laundry. He still remembered the shock and hurt in his wife's eyes. She'd had no idea he'd been keeping the ring, with the tiny diamond he'd once been so proud of, in their safe deposit box all these years—and she'd been even less understanding about why, in recent weeks, he'd felt the need to carry it with him. He'd put off Lori Beth's pleas for a "serious discussion," put them off so long that he understood she had left him. She had packed up the kids and probably their kitten, too, and gone back to her parents' place in Comfort.

"I can't compete with a dead woman, Joel. And right now I can't remember why I ever cared to try."

The echo of his wife's words didn't stop him from racing through the house, his heart pounding out its splintered hope while his feet took him from room to empty room.

Claire hadn't imagined she would sleep, hadn't believed it possible, after last night's calls to Joel and the tense conversation that followed with her father. But when the phone rang, the sound woke her, even though her father answered after the first ring.

Raising herself from the sofa cushion on one elbow, Claire looked toward the wall-mounted kitchen telephone. Her father's back was to her, but she recognized raw tension in the stiffness of his neck, the nervous jiggling of his left wrist. It flashed through her mind to double-check to see if he'd called for that appointment with his cardiologist.

"You got him yet, Joel?" her father asked.

Seeing her mistress awake, Pogo bounded into the family room, planted her paws on the edge of the burgundy leather sofa, and started licking Claire's face. Gently fending off the kisses, Claire straightened. She was still wearing the clothes she had put on last night, but the morning light streaming through the picture window illuminated a host of stains and small tears in the fabric.

"Well, why the hell not?" Her father's words snapped like flags before a gale-force wind. "You find yourself some dogs, then, Sheriff—and if you catch sight of that bastard, you shoot first and ask questions la—"

"Dad." Claire shot to her feet and closed in on him, her hand already outstretched. "Give me that phone this instant."

Excited by the movement, Pogo leapt and barked as Will Meador first glanced at his daughter, then shifted the receiver to keep it out of her reach.

"I have to deal with Claire now," he said gruffly. "You call me when you have some answers—and make it goddamned soon."

Before Claire could snatch the phone away, he banged it down in its cradle and muttered, "Hasn't found my ATV, hasn't found your husband. What the hell good is—"

"Damn it, Dad. You can't go telling him to shoot Spence. I only called Joel in the first place to keep Spence from getting—"

"He paid to have you—to have you killed, Claire." Her father's voice cracked like an old man's. "And then, the minute he could do it, he came straight here to see you. I won't let him hurt you. I can't let him hurt us anymore."

Claire opened her mouth to argue, but the anger drained out of her like hot water through a colander. For Spence had wounded her father, in some ways even worse than he had her. And no matter what the truth was, whether Spence had been set up in retaliation or the whole scenario had been some kind of terrible misunderstanding, her father would never forgive him. Nor would he stop trying to protect her.

"Don't you see?" His voice dropped to a whisper. "If Spence is . . . gone—if he's finished—then you can have this baby. It'll be hard, hard enough that my offer from last night still stands. But if you insist on going through with this, I'll help you raise—"

She captured one of his hands, big and bony and spotted with age, between both of hers. Looked into the dark eyes so very like her own.

"I love him," she said quietly. "I know it doesn't make sense, and I know you don't understand. I hardly understand myself. But that's the way it is, Dad. That's just the way it is."

Something hardened in his face, and he jerked his hand away. Turning from her, he poured himself black coffee from the pot sitting on the counter. "I've always loved you, Claire. And always done my damnedest to respect all your decisions. When you've made mistakes, I've tried to keep back and let you learn from them—even when you set your heart on marrying a street cop brought up by a pack of no-good motorcycle toughs."

"So they're a little rough around the edges," she argued for the hundredth time. "Spence's uncles are harmless—actually, they're kind of sweet in their own way."

"I'm a criminal attorney. I know what they are: shifty-eyed defendants who'll steal anything that's not nailed down. And I knew what your husband was, even before he paid to have you—"

She stepped around him neatly and picked up the receiver. "Stop it, Dad, before you make yourself sick. I'm calling Joel back right now. And I'm going to tell him again that there's no way Spence tried to hurt me. I'm going to say whatever I can think of, whatever it takes to convince him and his deputies not to shoot my husband."

This time she turned her back to her father. But she could hear his boot heels strike the tile floor as he stormed out of the kitchen. As she spoke with Joel, the back door slammed shut. Less than a minute later, the white Caddy's powerful engine roared to life.

She looked out the window to see her father leaving, his jaw set and his expression grim. As he turned the wheel, the morning sunlight glinted off his windshield so brightly that she looked away in self-defense.

"You hear me?" Joel was saying on the telephone. "I said I'm almost positive it's Strickland's body your friend Mrs. Briggs-Hadley found in the creek last night."

Caught up in the conversation—and her urgent need to mitigate her father's harsh words—Claire didn't watch which way his car turned. Nor did she think about him until later, when she walked past his study on her way to use the bathroom.

Without understanding what had caught her eye, she froze in place until she realized what was amiss. It was the gun cabinet, unlocked and standing open.

When she looked inside it, she saw the empty space where his favorite shotgun always lay. And knew in one terrible instant what her father meant to do.

A cuckoo clock hung in the kitchen, a reminder of Claire's mother, who had bought it on her only trip to Europe. But Claire, who remembered nothing of the woman save a frozen image from the photo on her nightstand of the beautiful brunette, was overcome with the desire to hammer the memento into wood pulp when it mocked her with the passing hours.

Though she had turned her back to the timepiece, she counted out the grotesquely comic chirrups:

nine . . . ten . . . now eleven before the damned thing shut up. A glance over her shoulder confirmed the thought that the morning was slipping away with no news of either Spence's or her father's whereabouts.

"Don't you worry about the time," Ellen scolded as she shoved a pale blond lock behind one ear. "All you need to think about is chewing and swallowing your next bite of omelet."

Ellen had shown up within a half hour of Claire's father's disappearance. Claire wasn't certain who had drafted the horse trainer, but she suspected Joel had done it as soon as the two of them got off the phone.

However she came to be here, Ellen had launched into full-fledged mother mode. Judging from the clarity of her blue eyes, even her allergies didn't stand a chance against her mission to take Claire's care in hand. Already the older woman had half coaxed and half bullied her into showering and changing into fresh jeans and a soft green T-shirt. While Claire was occupied, Ellen had commandeered the kitchen to whip up a breakfast fit for her football player sons and the always-hungry Megan.

The trouble was, Claire didn't feel like being coddled—or doing anything but hunting down her dad before he got himself into huge trouble. Or somehow managed to find Spence before Joel and his searchers did.

Her fork clattered against the plate as it slipped out of her fingers. The egg, cheese, pepper, and onion mixture swam before her eyes, and Claire's stomach roiled. "I can't do this."

Grasping the table's edge, she planted her feet and began to stand. But froze halfway when Ellen fisted one hand against the flare of her hip.

The other pointed at the nearly full plate. "Sit your ass down right this minute, Claire."

Too surprised to argue, Claire dropped back into the seat and glowered. "I'm not one of your kids."

"Damn straight. They'd be cooking their own omelets—and washing them down with Tabasco."

Claire tried to smile, but the thought of the hot sauce made her nausea even worse. Wincing at the image, she eyed the untouched slice of whole-wheat toast. "How about I try that? My stomach's really not up to—"

"Your stomach's just out of the habit. You think I haven't noticed how much weight you've dropped and how exhausted you've looked since this thing started? Now eat, Claire." Her voice softening, she added, "Please."

Claire picked up the toast, now cold, and chewed off a corner. Her mouth was so dry, the food clotted in her throat like sawdust, but she washed it down with a swallow from her glass of milk. After waiting a moment to be sure it stayed down, she locked her gaze on her plate. "I've never been so scared and worried in my life. But it's not all stress . . . I—I'm pregnant."

As Claire looked up, she braced herself for another argument like the one she'd had with her father the night before. But instead of the disapproval she expected, Ellen's jaw dropped and she blinked hard as comprehension slapped her.

"Wow," she finally managed. "You do have a few things on your mind. The timing's—Well, the timing's what it is. So tell me, what can I do to help?"

Claire loosed a pent-up breath, and her heart slowed its wild thumping. Ellen's offer struck her as sincere.

"I don't know yet," Claire said. "My dad's all up in

arms—he found out about it last night. He keeps telling me what a bad idea this is, bringing a child into this mess."

"But what do *you* think?" Again, there was no hint of judgment.

Against all reason, Claire felt a smile tugging the corners of her mouth. She gave in to it. "I think it's the best possible reason I have to go on. I'm having this baby, Ellen, and I'm not letting anyone or anything talk me out of it."

Ellen's broad smile counteracted the wrinkles around her mouth. "Stubborn as you are, I believe it—and I'm real glad for you, Claire. You're going to make a great mama."

"But my dad—"

"Your dad'll come around. You see if he doesn't. When I see him, I'll start talking up the grandpa angle. Something tells me you'll have your work cut out to keep him from spoiling that little one to pieces."

Her eyes dampened. "Do you really think so?"

"Are you kidding?" Ellen asked. "My parents thought I'd gone loco, marrying a fellow twenty-two years my senior and finally jumping on the baby train in my late thirties. But as soon as they saw those little peepers, man, it was love at first sight. The uncomplicated kind that comes without the two a.m. colic and the need to keep 'em in line. They're still crazy over the whole darn pack of brats."

Claire steepled her elbows on the table and cradled her head in her hands. "But my dad's out there with a shotgun. Probably looking for my husband."

"First of all, Will Meador's a smart man, an attorney. Anybody around here could tell you he has more sense than to go around shooting anybody. Besides, the sheriff and his men are looking out for him. More than likely, your father saw them and is holing up somewhere nursing his hurt pride."

"Pride? What does pride have to do with anything?"

Ellen waved off the question. "With men, especially men from Texas, it's always about pride. And your father in particular's got more than his share. Everybody in Buck County knows he worked like a dog to buy back that ranch when you and Karen were still tiny, and everybody knows he's turned himself inside out to put it back the way it should be—even after what happened to your mother. And he's respected for it, no matter what his daddy did."

Claire was surprised to hear her late grandfather's alcoholism mentioned, however obliquely. Though her father had warned her people in Little BC had long memories, she couldn't recall anyone ever mentioning the way he had grown up after his mother ran off with the local doctor.

But Ellen wasn't finished. "That pride of his was hurt when he was snookered by Spence's actions in the first place. And this morning it must've been hurting even worse at the thought of waiting on the sidelines, sitting on his hands. I'm sure he feels like he needs to do something."

Claire cocked her head. "You've been talking a lot to my dad lately, haven't you?"

Ellen shrugged and smiled sheepishly. "Fred's been gone four years now, and I always was a sucker for a handsome older man. Besides, your father and I have a common interest. You."

It was Claire's turn to blink as she let the information soak in. Could her dad be interested in Ellen, too? Claire couldn't remember the last time he had gone out with anyone but his friends. And was his heart really strong enough to— She cut short the thought, unwilling to let her imagination stray behind his bedroom door.

"Well, when he shows up again," she vowed, "I'm borrowing a pair of Joel Shepherd's handcuffs and chaining that man somewhere he can't scare me half to death."

"You go, girl." Ellen punched the air, sounding like her daughter in her enthusiasm. "Now hurry up and eat, and I'll take you next door. Some of the volunteers and board members came out this morning, and they've got a surprise."

"Ellen, I'm not up to facing a whole crowd of people."

"They aren't just people. They're your friends, Claire, the folks who've worked their butts off to make your dream a reality. And they're the ones who'll help you through this next stage of your life."

Claire went through the motions, her body mechanically downing nearly half of the huge breakfast; then she returned to the bathroom to brush her teeth and hair. But her mind would not stop worrying over how she could possibly survive a stage of her life that did not include Spence Winslow.

At the thought, a heavy coldness shifted uncomfortably inside her. She tried to banish it with a memory from the night before, of her husband's hands on her breasts, his tongue thrusting into her mouth, her hips flexing against his. But the echo of his words snuffed out the fleeting memory of flame: *If you won't file for divorce, I'll do it. You aren't about to change my mind on this.*

If she believed for a moment that he had wanted her dead, she could let it go at that. Or even if she thought he'd fallen out of love with her or found another woman. But she knew to her core that he wanted her out of the picture because he still loved her. Loved her in the present, not just in the past.

When the phone rang in the kitchen, her heart jolted.

Spence.

Her feet flew toward the kitchen, but she wasn't fast enough. Ellen had the receiver pressed to her ear, and she was nodding, her lips pressed together in an unreadable line.

"Good, Sheriff. She'll be glad to hear it."

"Let me—let me talk to him." Without waiting for an answer, Claire all but tore the phone from Ellen's grip. "What is it, Joel? Did you find Spence?"

"Sorry, Claire. We don't have a lot of manpower, but we trailered over some horses and checked out the property as best we could at first light. Even had a small plane do an aerial. By now I'm starting to think your husband's long gone. Backtracked up the creek or hiked out to a place where he could hitch a ride with someone. But we did find your father."

"Where's my dad? Is he all right? Did he—?" She couldn't bring herself to ask if he'd encountered Spence.

"He's fine—in good hands, in fact." Joel's voice sounded ragged, as she had never heard it.

He cleared his throat and barely missed a beat. "He went by to see the old judge, I guess to get his take on things. Hiram kept him talking, whipped up a pitcher of Bloody Marys, and proceeded to knock the edge off your daddy's mad-on. Leo's"—that would be Leo Carver, former owner of the Feed and Seed and another of her father's cronies—"over there now, too, helpin' them get buzzed. I just left the three of them not five minutes ago."

"Thank God," Claire burst out. "I'm so glad—but . . ."

"Yeah, darlin'?"

She told herself the "darlin' " was just Joel, slipping into the good old boy routine that had endeared him to so many of his constituents. But his familiarity made her uneasy.

At her hesitation, he said, "Claire?"

"Sorry—I just wanted to tell you I'm afraid for Spencer. Afraid he'll go off and confront this gang leader in San—"

"We've been through this already. I know what he told you. I know he's whipped up the idea of this grand conspiracy. It's what people do when they can't cope with something terrible they've been caught at. They find someone they can blame. If no one real is handy, they may even make up some mysterious stranger. Of course, we never find this other guy."

"But this one—I told you, his name is Beto Chavez, and he's in San Antonio. If you call SAPD and ask them—"

"I already did, hon. Right after I talked to you this morning."

"Are they looking into it, then? Is there something they can do to prove Spence didn't—"

"The captain assigned to the Gang Task Force informed me they never heard of any Beto Chavez. I'm sorry, Claire, but the officer agreed with me. Your husband's lied to you. Again."

TWELVE

The last thing—the very last thing—Claire wanted was a celebration. Yet the fifteen or so gathered in the filtered shade of a huge live oak seemed intent on giving her one, complete with smiles, cameras, and the inevitable sheet cake laid out beside a jug of fruit punch on someone's folding table.

As Claire's green pickup swung into the crowded parking area, Ellen waved and beamed at the group, which included a couple of dads, a bevy of mothers— several of whom were also members of the board— and four or five of the wheelchair-bound kids Claire worked with. Ellen's daughter, Meg, who had driven over in her mom's Corolla to take care of the morning feeding, was there, too, chattering her head off with a distracted-looking Lenore Briggs-Hadley.

Though Pogo wriggled eagerly in her lap, Claire groaned at the sight. How was she to maintain some semblance of control when all she wanted to do was hide under the covers and cry for a month straight? The one thing standing between her and total meltdown was the fact that only Joel knew how completely she had fallen for Spence's story last night—and she'd told no one at all that she'd been fool enough to make love with her husband.

One last time . . . A shiver overtook her, though it had to be at least seventy degrees out.

Behind the screen of her tissue, Ellen spoke from the corner of her mouth. "The show must go on. Mine had to after Fred's liver failure. I wanted to die, too, but I had three kids counting on me."

She gestured toward Claire's OT patients. Though two of them had to be strapped into their chairs to keep them upright, each one was grinning from ear to ear to see her. "You have even more, not counting the one you're working on. So get your narrow ass out of this car and fake it 'til you make it, sister."

Claire rippled her fingers in answer to the increasingly frenetic waves. With Joel's words still ringing in her ears, her stomach wanted to revolt, but she swallowed back the nausea.

Claire pulled her keys out of the ignition, but she hesitated before opening the door. "What about Coyote, Ellen? We can't have those kids coming across that poor—"

"Don't think another thing about it. I had the body taken care of earlier this morning. Got that broken window boarded up, too, and all the glass swept up."

But the real question troubling her had nothing to do with the dead horse.

"They know, don't they?" she asked the trainer. "About the sheriff looking for—for my husband?"

She was back to avoiding his name, she realized. Not a bad idea. Depersonalize the enemy and he can't hurt you so much. Yet the thought did nothing to bank the flare of her humiliation. How could she present herself as a competent professional when the whole world pitied her?

"They know," Ellen confirmed. "But they want you to understand that no matter what that jerk's pulled, they're behind you a hundred and ten percent. Besides, we've been planning this surprise for weeks, and it's a gorgeous day. Why let him spoil it?"

"Hell. I can't do this." She never should have allowed Ellen to badger her into leaving the house. With nowhere to hide, Claire let the wagging, whining Pogo out, then stepped into the perfect sunshine of a flawless day.

And wished like hell it would be over as soon as possible.

Nearly exploding with snorts and giggles of anticipation, her young patients wheeled themselves—or were rolled—to one side, uncovering the brand new sign their bodies had concealed. In spite of her misery, Claire gaped, her attention transfixed by the beautifully carved hand-painted panel.

WELCOME TO THE MONARCH RANCH, the jewel-bright letters read. WHERE ALL MAY SPREAD THEIR WINGS. Flanking the words, two golden horses faced one another, each carrying a friendly-looking butterfly aboard its back. The butterflies, she noticed, were imperfect. One had a crimped wing, while the other bore a bent antenna. But somehow these small flaws made their smiles mean more. As if whoever painted them truly understood.

She looked from the happy faces of the children to the much more complex blend of hope and strength and sympathy in the expressions of the men and women who had spent hours stringing fence lines, painting new walls, and hammering together stalls.

She thought of the lessons these parents had taught her, of the way their love endured through disappointments, how it flowed around the obstacles set in its path like water bending around rock islands in a stream.

She thought how every one of them had lived through tragedy, with these kids and Lenore's lost son. How day after day the mothers and fathers must have pasted on smiles when they felt like crawling into holes and dying. How they drove to the umpteenth therapy session and celebrated each tiny step toward normalcy as if it were that perfect report card or winning home run that still lay dormant in their dreams.

Claire swallowed past a knot of grief and blinked back a threatening shimmer. She couldn't cry in front of them. She damned well wouldn't do it.

Clearing her throat, she told them quietly, "It looks— it looks like joy. It's—it's perfect. Thank you. Thank you all for coming out today. And for everything you've done."

As Spence peered back at the wormhole cave where he had rested, he realized he could have been crushed out like a cigarette. By the light of the sunset, he saw that the recent collapse of powdery whitish rock had left the entire bluff far more unstable than he'd suspected.

But at the time, he'd been incapable of noticing anything except pain, hunger, and physical exhaustion. Even those had faded against the all-consuming struggle to free-climb one-handedly over the cliff's lip without going ass over teakettle into the broken rock and tree roots that jutted along the edge of the blue-green hole below.

Every muscle quivered and every square inch dripped with sweat when Spence had finally pushed feet-first into a space not much larger—and considerably less comfortable—than an old-fashioned phone booth knocked onto its side. But he hadn't chosen this spot for its plush amenities. Unlike the more spacious caves pockmarking the so-called beehive, this opening lay hidden by a fallen tree. With russet-colored needles still clinging to the cedar's limbs and the lip of rock jutting above the entrance, Spence figured there was a good chance he could eat the food he'd brought and sleep for a few hours without waking on the business end of a county boy's gun barrel.

He hadn't realized that the cave offered its own dangers. But on waking, he had found his hair and clothes full of sand that had sifted down from the low roof. One leg of his jeans was soaked, too, where water had dripped down through a fist-wide fissure above his bed of leaves.

Now, standing beside the fallen tree's trunk, Spence was grateful—and amazed—that the whole bluff hadn't come down on his head while he had slept the day away, courtesy of the pain pill Claire had fed him. Wind and water had eroded the formation over centuries, but the recent heavy rains had left their mark, too, in deep cracks that scored the rock. Besides that, the central collapse had gouged out a section that looked as if it had been the keystone holding up the whole beehive.

The rest could go at any moment, or it might stand until the next big rain sluiced through the fault lines.

Like him, he thought as twilight stained the sky a bloody crimson. Weakened over years by infinitely slow and patient forces, then devastated by the cataclysm that had taken place last autumn. Left on his feet for a while, though any fool with eyes could see what must come with the next challenge.

Collapse was imminent, inevitable, and no force on God's green earth could shore up his buckling walls. Even Claire could see it, he thought bitterly as he remembered her phone call to Joel Shepherd. Even Claire knew when it was time to cut her losses and move on.

"Good for her," he said aloud, then froze, taken aback to hear his own voice sounding like a stranger's: weak, malignant, and ancient beyond reckoning, as if he'd done a Rip van Winkle instead of a day's sleep in a dank and tomblike hole. It was a voice to match the pain that streaked from arm to shoulder with each movement, the shakiness of his steps, and the way his eyes burned like live coals behind the too-thin shelter of his lids.

"That arm's infected, Spence. You need a hospital." Claire's voice sounded in the current rippling over smooth stone, the whispered sibilance of breezes rustling the dry cedar boughs. He saw her rising from the water, gliding toward him on the last rays of the dying sun. It seemed natural to him, right, as if he'd always known she'd sprung up from this place.

Before it reached him, the mirage dissolved into a cloud of mayflies, leaving him to rub his stinging eyes. And reminding him that the real Claire had called the sheriff to come get him, to lock him back in jail where he belonged.

"What the hell do you care?" he snarled at her memory.

The heat of his words launched a mockingbird from its perch on the fallen cedar. It drew his eye, this bird's flight: a graceful swoop toward water, followed by an upward arc. His gaze tracked the movement until the dusk gray feathers disappeared into the dimming sky. . . .

And into the ragged growl of a rough motor—one Spence was almost certain that he recognized. If he was right, it was Claire's father's ATV, the same one stolen from outside the cabin last night.

The buzz swelled, growing louder as it approached the bluff over his head.

Spence froze in place, straining his ears to hear the direction the ATV was moving. But instead of veering away, the roar intensified, and a cascade of falling pebbles gave him a split second's warning—

Barely time enough to duck as the four-wheeler shot out into thin air no more than a dozen feet above him. Barely time to jerk back toward the cave's mouth as the screaming ATV plunged, bounced off the downed cedar's trunk, then smashed into the half-submerged rocks another twenty feet below.

THIRTEEN

About twenty minutes before sunset, Claire noticed Lenore Briggs-Hadley hanging back as the various vans and SUVs were loaded and the families left the property one by one. Lenore's wait had been a long one, even after the hot dogs and burgers had been grilled and the cake long since demolished. The day had been so pleasant and the children so excited that nearly everyone had lingered, strolling—or in some cases rolling—down by the stock pond, feeding treats to the horses, playing fetch with the deliriously happy Pogo, and pointing out the ring where therapy sessions were slated to begin in only a few weeks.

Throughout the whole long day, Claire had not once checked to see if her cell phone had a signal. Neither had she ducked inside the office to call her dad or Joel. Instead she threw herself into distraction, pointing out the ranch's features, talking up the merits of the second therapist, her friend Janine Jaworski, who would come on board in mid-June, and taking out gentle Bushwhack to allow a dozen eager hands to stroke him. But despite her efforts to pretend every-thing was back to normal, every time she glimpsed Lenore, fingers of dread clutched at her chest.

The woman was altogether too quiet, for one thing, too prone to staring off into the distance while her thin arms wound around her waist. Her coloring looked hectic, as if she'd slapped on her cosmetics instead of applying them with her normal care, and the white blouse she wore with her green slacks was badly wrin-kled. More telling still, she kept her distance from Claire, never approaching throughout the whole long afternoon.

Claire hadn't forced the issue, mainly because it was taking every ounce of energy she had to keep a lid on the questions that kept bubbling to the surface. Where on earth had Spence gone once he left the cabin? Was he hurting? Hungry? Sick now? Had she done the right thing, calling Joel? It was all she could manage to go through the motions with the other parents; she had nothing left to chase after a woman who seemed de-termined to avoid her.

Still, Lenore Briggs-Hadley's black Land Rover lin-gered, parked near Ellen's gray Corolla.

Because she knows something about Adam Strick-land's death, Claire suspected. *Something she's trying to muster up the courage to tell me.*

That was exactly what she needed. One more thing to sweat.

Nevertheless, while Meg and Ellen took care of the evening feeding, Claire decided she had put off the conversation long enough. After a brief search, she spotted Mrs. Briggs-Hadley standing alone in front of the stock pond inside the east pasture.

Since her back was turned, Claire was careful to

make noise as she approached, cracking a twig under-foot, then humming a Bach piece that she loved. Pogo aided in the effort by barking at a turtle taking in the afternoon's last rays, until it slid off the bank and disappeared beneath the muddy water.

Claire saw Meg glance their way from the west pasture. The girl tried to wave, but she was carrying feed buckets. Three of the horses trotted behind her and jostled for position. After flashing a grin, the teen continued on her way, her endless chatter trailing in her wake like birdsong.

Lenore neither acknowledged Meg nor turned around, but a subtle shift in her posture assured Claire she had heard them both.

"What is it, Lenore?" she asked without preamble. "Was it—was it horrible for you, finding that man's body?"

Lenore turned, wiping one eye as she did so. An inch-long smudge of mascara angled toward her cheekbone, and her lipstick had long since disappeared. One gold earring was missing, or perhaps she had never put it on in the first place.

Claire glanced away, unsettled. Seeing Lenore this way felt a little like catching Martha Stewart with a messy house—only far less satisfying.

"Certainly, it was bad enough. That poor man."

"I'm sorry," Claire said, but she couldn't escape the feeling that something else was at work. Before she could think of how to ask, however, Lenore spoke again.

"The board has received an offer. A very generous sponsorship offer from the people at Am-Pride-Co."

Claire's attention perked up. There had been a lot of press of late about Am-Pride-Co, a company that used only American materials and workers to make and market its new line of high-tech athletic wear. In a knee-jerk reaction against anti-American protests overseas, the products had received a tidal wave of support—and profits—from patriotic U.S. citizens.

"That's wonderful, isn't it?" Claire asked, confused by Lenore's grim expression. "Haven't we been hoping for another corporate donor?"

Lenore's head shook. "They don't want to be just another donor. They want the program to be all theirs. On their own land, using their own state-of-the art equipment, their own people—and, of course, a brand new name: 'Camp Am-Pride-Co.' I also got the impression that they mean to feature the kids themselves, in equine therapy sessions, in their corporate commercials."

Claire's heart constricted. Am-Pride-Co wanted to hijack her dream—and exploit the children for its own purposes. Her grassroots foundation would be swept away in wave after wave of slick commercialism. And as a woman mired in a distasteful criminal matter with her "bad cop" husband, she would have no place, no place at all, in the future of the program.

"No. We'll tell them no, of course," Claire said, though she was technically an employee of the board with only the power to act as a tiebreaker in its votes. When Lenore didn't immediately respond, she added, "The other board members aren't seriously considering this . . . are they?"

"I don't know, Claire. I'd certainly rather not go this route. But *should* we?" Lenore glared at her, her eyes glittering with moisture.

"Is there—is there something wrong?" Claire stammered, confusion putting her off balance. "Have I done something—?"

"Wrong? You tell me, Claire. My good friend Marjorie Trent-Phillips called first thing this morning." Lenore dabbed at her face with a crumpled tissue. "And I must tell you, I've never been so disappointed—or so damned mad—at anyone in all my life."

Her glare—and the unprecedented use of the curse—left little doubt that Claire herself was the target of this tirade.

"Marjorie who?" It was some double name, like Lenore's. "What in the world are you talking about?"

Tears rained down unchecked. Lenore was evidently one of those women who wept when angry. "Don't make it worse by lying. I know all about your plans for this land. And still you went on pretending with those poor people all day. Pretending you aren't selling out so this can be developed into overpriced lots around some golf course—"

"What?" A flash of anger heated Claire's face. "You're accusing me of—"

Lenore's blue eyes softened. "If you needed money, all you had to do was tell me. But these people—all of us have worked so hard for you and the foundation. I can't believe you'd sell the land right out from under—"

Shaking her head, Claire raised her palms to stop Lenore. "Whoever said that is nuts—or lying. I haven't—I would never sell this place—I swear it."

Lenore stared a hole into her while Claire recalled how she had told Spence she would sell the land to pay his debt to Beto. Though he'd refused her, she felt guilty now about the offer—disloyal to something larger and more important than their personal problems.

During the lull, a whippoorwill's cry heralded the evening, and the scents of pond and cedar drifted on the wind.

"Marjorie's a friend of mine from San Antonio," Lenore explained. "She's huge in real estate. Develops rural resort properties, high-end subdivisions, the sort of places the affluent—"

"I've never heard of her." Claire kept her gaze locked on Lenore and her voice carefully flat. "And I sure as hell don't appreciate her starting ugly rumors. She told you I'd sold this place?"

"She didn't mention you by name, but she said there was a project going in here. She wondered if my husband and I would be interested in getting in on the ground floor, as investors. When she started describing the location—"

"You made an assumption, right? You figured— what? That I must be having financial difficulties because of this mess with my husband? So I'd betrayed the foundation, all those volunteers and donors— including my own father—and the patients? You really believed I'd do that to the kids? To anyone?" Claire was shaking, her conscience making this insult all the more unbearable.

Lenore grimaced. "I didn't want to. But Marjorie called it a distress deal—said the owner had no clue what kind of gold mine the place was."

"Clueless, huh?" A queasy smile cropped up. "So that's what brought me to mind."

"No—I didn't mean that. It was the 'distress' part—" Lenore cut herself off, then looked at Claire and faltered through a nervous laugh.

"Well, I'm distressed enough, but trust me, I will never sell this property out from under the foundation." No matter what it costs me, she swore to herself. "Maybe this Margie—"

"Marjorie Trent-Phillips," Lenore corrected.

"Maybe she's been talking to my neighbor, Randall Hajek. He was into high-end realty himself, in Houston. This sounds like the kind of project he'd try to put together."

But it occurred to Claire that Randall might have something more in mind than simply selling the land he had inherited from his aunt. That he might be trying to muscle her out of here some way. Was the vandalism part of it, as Spence had suggested?

She pictured the small man with his fancy boyfriend—Giovanni Baptiste, who had flounced around with his stinky foreign cigarettes, his stylishly cut suit, and his flare for the dramatic, the one who had made such a scene at Mrs. Hajek's funeral. No doubt Randall had been genuinely upset to think his aunt was "duped" into selling so much land so cheaply to what he termed "a pair of opportunistic vultures." But would a person who talked like that and looked like that really skulk around the property, chancing scorpions, rattlesnakes, and the indignity of chiggers?

It was almost impossible to fathom. But that didn't make it any less imperative for her to talk to the wienie as soon as possible, to rule out the possibility. For the horses' sake, and her own sanity, she needed to get a reading on the man's intentions.

Lenore Briggs-Hadley drew a deep breath, emotion playing across her face. "Claire—can you forgive me? I—I should have come to you right away. It's just—well, several of the board members have expressed concern about your recent difficulties. I've been telling them your dedication is unquestioned. But this morning, I was upset already over that dreadful business at the bridge last night, so when that call came . . . But there's really no excuse. I'm sorry. Deeply sorry that I doubted you even for a minute."

"I don't blame you a bit. What else could you think," Claire asked, "with every bit of evidence pointing to me?"

She thought about how even more damning facts had implicated Spence. Yet even after she'd learned he had lied to her regarding Beto Chavez, something in Claire dragged its feet—looking for a way out, any avenue that would allow her to continue believing in her husband. Why?

She thought again about the parents who had visited today. Thought about how some people might tell them to quit kidding themselves—to face facts and admit their children would never be normal.

At that moment, it dawned on her that denial wasn't just for dummies, the way Joel Shepherd had implied. That in a lot of cases, self-delusion must go hand in hand with love.

She didn't have long, however, to dwell on the revelation. Her thoughts were cut short by the sudden, unmistakable sounds of a collision. Sounds she could swear rose from the direction of the creek.

As Spence half climbed, half slid down the loose scree lining his path to the water, the lone wheel visible above the water's surface spun to a slow stop. Despite his hurry, he felt he was descending in slow motion, his legs weighed down by the weakness gripping him.

Now that the echoes of the crash had faded, the only sounds remaining were those of his own panting and the sloshing as his shins cut furrows through the cold water.

By the time Spence reached the wreckage at the edge of the deep hole, he realized his hurry had been futile. Not because the four-wheeler's driver was too far gone, but because he found no one at all, either broken on the rocks or limp beneath the water.

He could be certain now: Someone had run the ATV off the bluff on purpose. Someone bent on destruction.

Or with a mission to flush him out, Spence realized belatedly. He turned slowly, his hands already rising, his eyes scanning for gun barrels poised above him or across the creek.

The sight of a protruding rod goosed his already pounding heart, but before he could react, he realized it was nothing but a branch jutting from an old snag. He was still alone: no deputies, no gangbangers, not even Claire's old man. Feeling like an idiot, he lowered his arms and stared up at the bluff above his head.

If he were well, he might climb back up in time to catch a glimpse of someone running. Maybe find the person responsible for Coyote's death and Claire's cut fences.

But he might as well have wished for wings as for the strength to climb so quickly. His limbs trembled and sweat poured off him with the effort of his swift descent, while the hole in his arm throbbed in time with his pulse.

Groaning, he managed to refocus on the four-wheeler once more. It lay on its right side, tilted so far over that it was nearly upside down. Heavy plastic pieces, from the fenders to the seat, were cracked, and one of the rear axle mounts was broken. An iridescent sheen was spreading on the water's surface, and the carburetor had been mangled and knocked clean off. One thing was for damned sure: Even if he'd had all three of his motorcycle-loving uncles here, there would be no putting this humpty-dumpty back together and riding out on it.

Nor would there be any way to tell how the throttle had been rigged to send the four-wheeler shooting riderless off the cliff. But, then, considering the way Spence's head was spinning, he wouldn't have figured that out even if the ATV had wafted gently downward with a schematic duct-taped to its seat.

Yet there was one crucial factor Spence didn't need a diagram to understand. In the quiet off this rural road, the splintering of metal and plastic against rock would carry—and anyone who had heard it, from a ranch volunteer to a neighbor to one of the lawmen searching for him or even Claire herself, would be hightailing it out here at any moment.

If he meant to remain free long enough to investigate things in San Antonio, he'd damned well better get out of here right now.

Barking, Pogo rushed in the direction of the sound, pausing every few steps to see if Claire was coming. A city dog at heart, she never ventured far into the woods alone, perhaps because some instinct warned her that a three-legged sissy dog stood little chance against the predators that roamed the area.

"Someone could be badly hurt," Lenore said. "Should we go and check?"

Like Pogo, she seemed hesitant, and with equally good reason. It would be pitch black out before she could pick her way around every stone and ant pile in those thin-soled ballerina flats she was wearing.

"Better head back to the office and call the sheriff," Claire said, though her instincts shouted at her to run toward the creek while the light held. But considering what had happened last night, she couldn't take the risk.

Yet Pogo took off like a shot, racing after Meg as the girl headed toward the trees. Finally, the brown-and-white Lassie look-alike had found someone to follow.

"Wait!" Claire shouted after her, but if the girl heard, it made no difference. She cut among the thin trunks of the mountain laurel bordering the woods.

"I'd better go after her," Claire told Lenore. "We don't know who's back there. Go find Ellen and tell her where we went. Then call the sheriff's office and have them send someone out right away."

Without waiting for an answer, Claire jogged in the direction Meg had taken. She didn't move at top speed. For one thing, she was no sprinter and couldn't hope to eat up Meg's lead. For another, the shadows beneath the live oak trees had deepened, making the ground more treacherous than usual. From long experience, Claire knew leaf litter shrouded armadillo diggings. Dead grasses hid sharp stones, perfectly designed to snag a toe or turn an ankle. Though she'd put on light hiking boots that morning and knew this acreage as well as anyone, Claire didn't like the thought of falling on her face, landing on her vulnerable belly.

Especially without knowing who might slip up on her.

It occurred to her that her caution was probably unwarranted, that whoever had crashed the ATV was likely hurt or even dead. Still, she avoided the occasional patches lit by the last ginger rays of sunlight. She moved as silently as she could manage, her ears straining for the slightest footfall.

But the sound that came to her five minutes later was Pogo. Claire stopped and held her breath to better hear.

The barking bore no resemblance to the excited woofs that meant the little sheepdog had recognized a friend or a potential playmate. Instead it was sharp, aggressive, as Claire had never heard it. The fine hairs lifted along her arms, behind her neck. Had Pogo come across a feral hog, or worse yet, the rumored cougar?

"Hey! Hold on a minute."

The shout—unmistakably Meg's—echoed from somewhere ahead and to the left, from the same direction as the sound of Pogo's even louder barking.

Operating on pure instinct, Claire glanced around, then snatched up the end of a fallen tree limb. Her foot came down on it as she did so, but the strong wood refused to break.

It was too late to find another weapon. Someone was crashing through the underbrush, so close she heard breath rasping—it sounded like a man's. Abruptly, Pogo yelped—and the thought that the approaching runner might have hurt the sheltie shot hot fury through Claire's veins.

"Hold it. Hold it, mister." She used a memory of Spence's voice as her model—of an evening he'd gone into heavy-duty cop mode to break up a fight in a restaurant parking lot. Stepping into the open space she judged as the man's most likely path, she ordered, "Don't move."

She thought she sounded pretty tough, but apparently she wasn't fooling anybody. As he burst out from beneath low overhanging branches, she caught only a glimpse of a slim white man wearing a navy ball cap and faded jeans. Without slowing for an instant, he struck out with the heel of his hand, catching her right shoulder.

The impact jarred her, spinning her around and knocking her off balance. She came down hard, her rear end cracking the stubborn branch when she landed on it.

A split second later, Pogo was all over her with muddy paws and slobbery kisses.

"Get . . . off." Claire pushed aside the trembling furball and struggled to her feet. Her rear hurt on the right side, but she was more pissed than anything. That jerk had plowed her under—her, a pregnant woman—without a second thought. Worse still, she figured him for the one who'd taken off with the four-wheeler. And maybe the one who had sent poor Coyote to his death.

When Meg burst through the leaves, Claire asked, "Are you okay?"

The girl was panting, struggling to speak. "I'm—I'm fine. You see that guy?"

"Yeah, he knocked me over."

"When Pogo got too close, he—he kicked her. I think—I think I know—"

Her words were lost as Claire stooped to snap off the length of branch her fall had broken. Finally she understood what it meant to see red. Any jackass who would who kick a little dog and push a woman . . . "I'm going to find out where that guy's off to. Don't bother trying to keep up."

Forgetting caution, she took off after the intruder.

That son of a bitch had better hope she didn't catch him, or he would be picking his teeth out of this hunk of tree.

FOURTEEN

Claire's feet slipped out from under her as she hit a patch of damp leaves. She went down hard on one knee, but the spongy mass absorbed the impact—along with a portion of her white-hot fury.

Have some sense, she told herself, or at least do like Ellen says and fake it 'til you make it.

Pushing off with her hands, she started off at a far less suicidal pace. The man she was chasing was faster, stronger, and had too great a lead. Getting herself hurt wasn't going to change that.

At the edge of the woods, she paused and scanned the relatively open land ahead. Night had deepened, casting a few bright stars into the eastern sky. Fireflies hovered around her, their flare and fade a dazzling distraction. With no moon and only the faintest ruddy glow to Claire's right, she couldn't make out much more than a few dark shapes that marked the occasional clump of trees.

And there, cresting the rise ahead of her, something

moving. Running on two legs, heading toward the eastern fence line that bordered the Hajek property.

If it was Randall Hajek, Claire hoped he ripped his crotch out trying to get over that rusty old barbed wire.

But the thought didn't sit right with her. As she half walked, half trotted toward the runner, she tried to think why.

The man had burst into view and disappeared so quickly, she hadn't gotten more that the briefest of impressions. A hat, some jeans, a blur of motion, then *bam*—that hard pop to her shoulder.

It hurt to move her right arm, but she refused to let the pain sidetrack her. It would still be there later, when she could deal with it.

Her attacker's height—that was what had been wrong. Randall was on the short side, she remembered, probably only an inch or so taller than her own five-six frame. The guy she'd seen was bigger—but maybe he had only seemed so, since he'd been rushing at her.

As she stopped to catch her breath, the futility of this chase settled over her. She wasn't going to—and probably didn't want to—catch the guy. Besides, she had long since lost sight of him again; the chances of her getting a good enough look at him to identify him had faded with the sunset. Better to change course, to head back for the office. With any luck, Meg and Pogo would already be there.

She veered southward, following the electric glow ahead. Lenore Briggs-Hadley, or more likely Ellen, had thought to turn on the newly installed practice ring lights.

By the time Claire reached the area, she was walking. Her legs ached with exhaustion, and her clothes clung to her damp skin.

"Ellen," she called out. "Mrs. Briggs—uh, Lenore."

She heard voices in the distance. But they weren't coming from the office up the hill, as she had expected. Turning, she looked over her left shoulder and made out the silhouettes of the two women, along with Meg and Pogo, near the pond.

Since Claire was closer to the front of the property, she decided to grab a flashlight out of her truck before she went to meet them. After a brief stop at the office to take a bottle of water from the small fridge, she jogged out toward her pickup—and stopped dead when a rattling sound caught her attention.

Randall Hajek stood before the new sign, his few strands of mousy hair sticking up like horns and his slight frame wrapped in a royal blue robe. Beneath its lower edge, his bare legs stuck out, white and hairless as bleached bones and ending in a pair of expensive-looking slippers.

Yet it was not his attire that caught Claire's attention, but the rattle of the can of spray paint he was shaking.

"What the hell do you think you're doing?" She strode toward him, her hand tightening into a death grip on her water bottle. "Put that thing down right this second."

Hajek's face flushed and his scant brows drew into a deep V. What with the goatee and the horn thing he had going, he looked exactly like the devil tumbled fresh from bed.

But devil that he might be, he was not the same man who had struck her in the woods. He dropped his arm and jammed the can in his robe pocket. Behind him, she noticed the damage he had done already, the huge black letter *G* dripping down onto the left-hand butterfly.

"Goddamned Meadors—think you can buy this land with your sins."

Claire was about to remind him that the currency she'd paid was a fairly daunting mortgage. But it was obvious that reason would be lost on Randall.

"Goddamned Meadors have no business here," he mumbled. "Never brought my family anything but trouble."

Though Claire thought it weird that he kept focusing on her maiden name, she didn't argue. For one thing, Randall had an off look about him, his gray eyes glazed and his face puffy. And could that be alcohol that she smelled on his breath? It went a long way toward explaining the bathrobe, and maybe the paint, too.

"Your aunt Norma thought different," she reminded him. "And so will Sheriff Shepherd, once he hears what you've been doing to my fences. Now get off my—"

"You really want the cops involved? You really want them peeking in your closets?"

She had to step out of the way or he would have rammed into her. What the heck was it—National Mow Down an Occupational Therapist Day?

He stalked toward his own house, his royal blue bathrobe fluttering behind him.

Claire shouted after him, "You're going to pay for killing my horse. Do you know you broke his leg? Do you even care how much he suffered?"

Randall's stride hitched, but only for a moment. With her pulse pounding out the code of anger, she watched until he disappeared from view behind the oleanders overhanging his front fence.

She took a deep breath, then cracked open the water as she walked to the pickup's passenger side, where she kept a flashlight under the front seat.

When she pulled open the unlocked passenger door, it didn't register at first that the dome light wasn't working.

Until a hard hand clamped on her wrist and a harsh voice warned, "Don't move."

FIFTEEN

She stared up into his face, her eyes flaring and her mouth already opening to scream.

The gun shook as he pointed it at her chest. "Quiet, Claire. I mean it. Now get inside the truck. I need you to drive me."

She blinked twice in quick succession, her brain finally catching on that this was not the runner. That her husband had been hiding in the truck, waiting for her. That he was holding her pistol on her as if he meant it, the same pistol she had used last night to draw first blood.

Her heart pounding, full to bursting, she squeezed out only, "Spence?"

Fever burned in his blue eyes, and sweat darkened both his shirt and his hair. Even in the dim light, his pallor stood out, making him look like a specter. The gun was real enough, though, as was the cold fury in his voice.

"Walk around the hood and get inside, Claire. You're not running off this time to give me up to Shepherd."

"No, Spence. I would never . . ." The denial died on her lips as she realized he must have heard her last night. Doubtless the noise had drawn him when she'd smashed out the office window.

"Move."

She obeyed his cop's voice, so scared that she raised her hands as she crossed in front of the hood. He leaned over, opening the driver's side door for her.

Her mind reeled with the thought that this was a Spence she'd never seen before—a Spence she never had believed in, no matter what anyone had told her. On the verge of climbing in, she hesitated, wondering, would he really fire on her if she ran?

"He's already paid a man to shoot you," Joel's voice told her. *"What the hell do you think?"*

"Hurry up," he ordered.

She got in, pulled the door closed, and fumbled for the keys in her right pocket. Pain shot through her shoulder, and she sucked a breath in through clamped teeth.

"My shoulder," she explained, but she managed to drag the keys free and jam the correct one into the ignition.

"Let's get out of here," he told her as the engine started. "Head out toward Wise School Road. Now."

Automatically, she flipped on her headlights and thought how Wise School, an abandoned one-room building, had long since burned to the ground. There was nothing else out that way, hadn't been for years. Nothing except miles of dark road.

The perfect place to leave a body, if one was of a mind.

Claire's gaze touched the rearview mirror; she was half afraid and half hopeful that a sheriff's department vehicle would be approaching. Hopeful because she wanted to get as far away from Spence as possible, and afraid because in her husband's current state, a shootout seemed too likely.

But she didn't see another set of lights. Some other incident must have delayed the deputies on duty—not terribly surprising, with such a small department.

Turning in the opposite direction from her father's house, she passed by the Hajek place. No one stood in the front yard, not that it would have made much difference. With Spence's gun trained on her, she couldn't exactly yell for help. And even if she did, Randall would probably just flip them both off.

"You—you look sick." She was grasping at straws, praying they could somehow reconnect, the way they had last night. "Should we stop somewhere? Pick up some medi—"

"What the hell do you care? You hoping I'll drop dead?"

"You know I don't want that, Spence. You—you know how upset I was that I hurt you."

He said nothing for a while, but several minutes later he groaned, grabbing his left arm when she hit a pothole. "Damn it."

His voice was shaking and far weaker than it had been before.

She reached for the water bottle she had forgotten on the seat. "Here. You need to drink this."

When he took it from her, their hands touched. He jerked away, but not before she felt his heat. Infection, she was certain. Fever was warring to destroy it, if it didn't kill him first.

After he gulped down half the bottle, he told her,

"Take this right here, just ahead. And turn off your headlights. I don't want anyone to follow."

"This road's too dark. We'll have an accident."

"Just do it. There's a little light still. Enough for now."

She did as he asked, panic jolting through her. Who was this desperate stranger—where had he come from?

When she turned, the truck's tires left the asphalt, crunching on the gravel. Claire slowed to compensate for the change in the road's surface. Even so, the jolting caused Spence to slump against the passenger door.

Frightened as she was, she took her foot off the accelerator. "You're going to die, you know. If we don't get you help soon. Let me drive you to the regional hospital. Please."

He straightened, and out of the corner of her eye she saw his head shake.

"Drive, Claire. You aren't making the decisions. I trusted you once, last night. And you turned on me."

Anger rocketed past caution. "You have a hell of a lot of nerve, Spence, accusing me of betrayal. All I was doing last night was trying to stop you from getting yourself killed."

Frightened by her outburst, she held her breath, waiting for his reaction. But the only sound forthcoming was the crackle of the tires on the dirt road.

She decided to keep talking. "You kissed me off, for one thing. Insisted I divorce you. Then you said you meant to go and see him, this gang leader, the one whose name you lied about."

"You checked into that?" Alarm shot through his voice. "Claire, I warned you not to—"

"Not to what? Catch you in another lie? I trusted you, Spence. In spite of everything they showed me, everything you wrote and said, I trusted you enough to make—make . . ." She couldn't stand to think of making love to him last night. After she wiped hot tears from her eyes, she flipped the headlights back on.

"What are you—?"

"I can't. See. The road." The words ricocheted around the space like shots. She was sick of terror, sick of grief, and most of all sick of believing in a long-dead fairy tale. One of them should play it straight, and if it wasn't going to be her husband, it would be her.

"Shoot me if you have to," she said. "I'd rather take a bullet than listen to more lies. But know this. If you kill me, you'll be murdering your kid, too. I'm pregnant, Spence—I'm pregnant. I found out just last week."

With each jolt and every curve, waves of pain made Spence's vision waver. Yet Claire's news hit him still harder.

Part of him wanted to deny it, to believe she was so scared, she would tell him anything to save herself. Yet the edge of anger in her voice convinced him he had pushed her into telling him the truth.

His mind reeling, he couldn't begin to deal with the chaos of his emotions, so he stuck with directions. "There—by that old fence post. You'll need to hang a left."

She did so, then braked so suddenly, the seatbelt harness grabbed him. His pained shout rose like gorge, and darkness overrode his vision.

When things cleared seconds later, he saw a pair of glowing green eyes staring back at him. They belonged to a full-grown cougar crouching in the dirt road, its jaws clamped around the neck of a good-sized gray goat.

The lion snarled, grasped the still-twitching goat more firmly, then dragged it off into the brush.

"My God." Despite her fear, there was awe, too, in Claire's voice. "I've never seen one. Not outside of a zoo. It's beautiful. And terrible."

"Remember it," Spence said. "Ranchers are gonna want it dead now. That's what they do out here when something's inconvenient."

Or someone, he added mentally.

She put the truck in park and turned to look at his face. "I'm sorry I had to slam the brakes . . . sorry that I had to hurt you."

He understood she was referring to her call last night as much as the jolt. But he couldn't think of what to say about either.

"Better get moving," he started, then noticed she was rubbing her right shoulder. Concern bubbled through the cracked crust of his anger, and before he could stop himself, he asked, "What's wrong? Are you hurt?"

She started driving. "It's nothing much. A little while ago, I heard something out toward the creek. It sounded like the ATV—and then there was a crash."

He nodded. "I saw the thing fall—somebody rigged it to shoot right off the bluff. It's history, of course. But I couldn't see who did it."

"I did. I crossed paths with him when he was running out of there. Jackass popped me in the shoulder with the heel of his hand and kept right on going."

"Who did?" he demanded. "Who hit you?"

"You've got me. It happened so fast. One second he was bursting through the trees, and the next I was on my butt and he was gone."

"You must have seen something. You sure it was a male?"

165

"Oh, yeah. White guy, kind of tallish. Jeans, dark cap." She hesitated. "Ummm . . . maybe a blue shirt. Long-sleeved. At first I thought it could be Randall. The guy was running toward his property."

"You don't sound convinced."

Her head shook. "It's definitely not him. Just before I came to the truck, I caught him. He'd started spraying paint on our new sign. He was wearing his slippers and his bathrobe—I think he might've been drunk."

"Was that who you were yelling at? With the windows up, I couldn't make the words out."

"He was talking some trash about my family, about how we think our sins can buy his family's property. I'm not sure what he was driving at—do you think he could have been referring to my mother's accident there? It happened somewhere on the property, somewhere near the creek. Or maybe he's still mad about my father ratting him out over that party he had at his aunt and uncle's. Maybe he got into more trouble over it than I realized."

Spence was less concerned with Randall's teenaged grudge than with the man who'd hit Claire in the woods. Claire might have been hurt badly, even murdered. His skin quivered as fresh chills detonated far beneath the surface.

"What were you doing back there anyway?" His voice came out sharper than he intended. "With everything that's happened, after you heard that motor, you should have called for help."

"Which is it, Spence? Are you madder when I call or when I don't?"

When he didn't answer, she explained, "My first thought was to phone the sheriff's office, but when I saw Meg running out there, I couldn't let her go alone. She's just a kid. I had to keep her safe."

What about *our* kid, he wondered, but he couldn't force the words past his locked jaws.

Our kid . . .

As the shock of it arced through him, he slumped sideways once again, the gun dropping unheeded between the seat and the passenger door. This time, however, Spence was overwhelmed with more than pain.

Claire finessed the brake as she pulled to the road's edge. After unhooking her seatbelt, she reached up with her uninjured arm and fiddled with the dome light he had switched off.

The light clicked on, revealing the sorrow and compassion in his wife's face. "Spence . . ."

She slid across the bench seat and pressed a gentle hand to his forehead.

Her caress nearly undid him. He turned his head toward the side window.

"Just drive." His words shook with the tears trembling behind them.

"I know you won't hurt me," she whispered in a voice as delicate as new leaves. "I know you never would."

The thin shell of his anger shattered, dealt a death blow by her incredible generosity of spirit. Spence pushed himself into her arms, his fingers stroking her hair, his lips grazing her neck, her ear, her face.

"You're a gift," he said, "a gift I don't deserve. I'm so sorry—so sorry I scared you."

She tried to extricate herself from him. "You're burning up, Spence. We have to get you help now."

"And this baby, Claire," he told her. "I'm so sorry I won't get to be its father. So sorry—"

167

His lips found hers, and he put everything he couldn't say into his kiss. Every bit of longing, every fragment of his love. Passion, too, was in the mix, passion that tamped down the pain.

Until she pushed him back, inadvertently touching the swollen flesh above his wound.

He sucked in air through clenched teeth as a jet curtain dropped before his eyes.

Through the roaring in his head, he made out her voice. "Have to . . . get you . . . to an ER."

The curtain parted, barely enough for him to see. "No. No, Claire. We're heading toward Ranch Road 452, taking it to a place I know outside of San Antonio. There's a doctor there. She'll help me, no questions. And no reports to the police. That's why I needed you, to drive me—"

"What kind of doctor would— She could lose her license for that."

A chuckle rumbled in his throat. "Too late, Claire. I think she has already."

"So you'd trust some quack who's already been kicked out of the profession?"

An image flashed through his mind, a nightmare redhead with skin as pale as death. "Hell, no, I don't trust her. Not as far as her next fix. But she's good at digging bullets out of gangbangers—has herself a reputation for it, among other things. She'll do me right, I'm sure of it."

"You have something on her," Claire guessed.

He tried to shrug. "I've got enough to put her out of business. Would have already, except somebody set me up first."

Claire's gaze snapped to meet his before she looked away. It hurt to know that she wasn't taking anything he told her at face value. That as long as they both lived, she never would again.

After turning off the dome light, she buckled up and started driving once more. They turned onto the same road he and Raul Contreras had taken the day before, and Spence tried to imagine himself back there, deciding to go see Claire to explain how things had happened. It had been a selfish act, he realized, one that had compounded her suffering instead of easing it. He should have left her to her healing and handled what he had to on his own.

He remembered promising himself he would only go to her one last time, and that would be enough. And this evening, after the ATV's crash, he had made another vow—he would see her again, only to get a ride from her and let her know how much her calling Shepherd had hurt him.

He wondered, next time, what lie he would tell himself. For loving Claire was an addiction far more potent than any illegal machine in the back room of Joe Reno's.

"I can't go back to jail again." He reached to dig the gun out of its crevice, then laid it on the seat between them. There was no question now of holding it, of pointing it at her. "Not if I'm to fix things for you, and for the baby, too."

"Fix things with whom, Spence? Not with Beto Chavez, since he doesn't exist."

"He's real enough, all right. I just couldn't give you his street name."

"So you made up a fake one—even after I named the truth as my condition for listening."

He thought about it, nodded. "Yeah. I did, and I was right to. That call you made, to ask about him. It could have gotten you killed if word got back to the wrong person."

"How? How's that going to happen?" The question dripped with skepticism. "I only mentioned it to Joel, for heaven's sake."

"And then he called somebody else, right? Someone in SAPD? You think I'm the only cop this guy's got dirt on? If the wrong person heard the name, you'd be as good as dead, Claire. Both of you—good as dead."

After that, they drove along in silence, but they did not ride alone. Claire's disbelief had crowded in, an unwelcome passenger that filled the space between them like the stench of old regret.

Sixteen

Without her inside it, the house felt dead and vacant: a fly's husk on a windowsill, crumbling into dust.

The one left behind felt just as empty, as he had since that hideous day when he had lost the first.

Need gathered in his darkness, a need he had not tended for a bitterly long time. Tired of fighting it off, he double-checked the dead bolts. Moments later, the curtains whispered as he closed out the stars, along with the prying eyes of any who might look.

It was time for The Remembrance.

Time to tally up the costs.

And time to come to grips with what he had done and still must do to keep his secret safe.

Near the city limits, the truck's tires made rhythmic pops against a section of grooved asphalt. Other than that, the cab was quiet. Spence hadn't spoken in a half hour.

Claire glanced over at him to see that his head had tipped to one side and his good shoulder was braced against the locked door. He had his right hand cupped protectively over the wound in his left arm, and once or twice he twitched, as if his sleep was troubled.

Her gaze flicked to the seat between them, and she thought of grabbing the pistol he had placed there and tossing it out through the window. God knew the damned thing hadn't brought the two of them a thing but heartache. And once it was gone, she could drive him to the ER before he woke. . . .

And he would be taken into custody. With armed abduction added to his charges, he could forget about another chance at bail or any prayer that he might beat the charges.

But instead of relief, nausea bubbled up inside her, along with the memory of the terrible things she'd heard went on inside state prisons. How much worse would it be for a man known as a cop?

Her husband was a lean six-footer, tough and strong and street-smart. But he didn't have a prayer against the gangs that all but ran the prisons. Didn't have a chance of getting through his time unscathed.

He held a gun and made you drive him. Lied to you about the man who set him up. Destroyed your future with his gambling because he was too damned proud or foolish to continue his counseling.

But no matter what she told herself, she couldn't get past the images that flashed through her mind in a grisly slide show: Spence beaten, broken . . . raped. Her husband dead and buried in a cheap box in some prison graveyard.

She swung over to the road's dark shoulder, jumped out of the truck, and staggered three steps before heaving the contents of her stomach onto the gravel. Long after everything was gone, she continued retching—until she felt Spence's hand warm on her back.

"Here, use this. You'll feel better." He pressed the water bottle, still half full, into her hand.

She swished and spit, but a clean mouth did nothing to stop the tears from sliding down her cheeks. Her nose was plugging up, too, and she knew from experience her face was turning blotchy. She had never been one of those pretty little made-for-TV weepers.

Spence didn't seem to care. After leading her a few steps from the mess, he wrapped his arms around her and reached beneath the soft curtain of her hair to rub her neck.

Where they leaned into each other, heat radiated through his clothing. She felt him shivering, though the night was mild. In spite of his obvious illness, he whispered to her, "It's all right, honey. I swear to you, I'm going to make things right."

Of all the lies he'd told her, Claire figured that one was the worst. But somehow she couldn't bring herself to hate him for it.

Perhaps because she understood how badly they both needed this oasis in their desert. How badly they both needed a few moments to pretend.

Twenty minutes later, in the pitch-black far end of a defunct commercial area, Spence climbed out of the green truck and walked over to a metal gate. For a full minute, he stood listening, but he heard no sound save the distant rumble of a semi on I-35 and, even farther off, the keening of a siren.

And nothing at all from inside the city of the dead.

Reasonably assured that no one lay in wait behind

the eight-foot fence, he disentangled the rusting chain that held the gate shut. It rattled and clanked when it fell beside a long-broken lock, which had clearly been shot through.

As he leaned against the gate, it occurred to him that Dr. Rachel Little's "clinic" might have been abandoned, that she could have disappeared in the weeks he'd been away. But some instinct told him she was too far gone to move now, that she remained among the rows of burned-out and twisted carcasses that had once been mobile homes, RVs, and travel trailers. As long as they had use for her, the bangers would bring her food and drugs enough to keep her here and breathing.

Spence pushed hard against the heavy gate until his muscles spasmed and the stars above him blurred. But he hung with it, and moments later, the rusted hinges shrieked in protest, offering anyone inside an early warning. Spence stumbled in his hurry to get back in the truck.

"I don't like this, Spence," Claire told him.

"We can turn around," he offered. "Let me drop you somewhere safe. There's a twenty-four-hour burger joint off of—"

She shook her head. "I'm staying with you. You're in no shape to drive yourself."

They had had this argument before, just after she had thrown up on the roadside. She had shot him, she'd insisted, so she would see this through.

"Better turn those lights off," he warned as they rolled past a tilted KEEP OUT sign. Bullet holes pockmarked the hand-painted rectangle. "They like to keep it dark."

174

The half dozen broken security lights they'd already passed stood as proof.

As Claire switched off her headlights, Spence heard her tight sigh.

"We'll be all right," he said in an attempt to reassure her. "Moon's up, anyway."

Nearly full, it flooded the enclosure with milky light, while the razor wire that topped the fence line gleamed a stark threat.

"That's not what worries me," Claire said as she looked around them. "This is no place for us—no place for you to get help."

He had her make a left and then a quick right. They passed one metallic husk after another, laid out in rows as neat as any cemetery.

Claire said, "You know, I never even stopped to wonder where these things went to die. There must be acres of them. What is this place, anyway?"

"Company thought they could make a go of recycling mobile home components. Guess they thought wrong, because they went belly-up a couple years ago," he explained.

A minute later, he pointed out a dented hulk that looked like a travel trailer from the days of *I Love Lucy*. "Park there, but not too close."

"I'm not waiting in the truck," she said.

He nodded. "I wouldn't leave you out here."

Who the hell knew what other reprobates had holed up in this enclosure? His best chance to keep her safe lay in keeping her in sight.

But "safe" was a relative concept, he decided as they threaded their way through the refuse outside Little's front door. Broken liquor bottles vied for space with crushed soda cans, grease-stained fast food bags, and scores of candy wrappers. The beam of the flashlight Claire was holding glittered off several pairs of beady eyes.

Claire grunted as one gray shape detached itself from the mob. The thing zigzagged for the shelter of weeds along a broken chain-link fence. "Unhhh—I hate those things."

Revulsion shuddered through her voice, and for a moment Spence thought she would run back to the truck. Claire could tolerate—even appreciate—wild hogs, coyotes, and all manner of snakes, but she drew the line on rats as big as squirrels.

Yet she didn't budge from his side, leaving him to wonder if she feared the human vermin of this cesspit even more.

A sweep of her flashlight bounced off weather-dulled aluminum. Red rust showed like bloodstains beneath each set of rivets.

As the two of them made their way to the door, Spence turned to tell Claire, "Just let me do the talking."

"You thought maybe I was going to invite this woman to my book club?"

He smiled to himself, remembering why he'd fallen for her. Then he balled his fist and pounded on the door.

"Open up, Doc Rachel. I've got some money for you."

There was no answer, so he started hammering again. "Come on, Doc. I'm not leaving 'til I see you."

This went on for several minutes, long enough for him to wonder if either the crystal meth or her clientele had finally finished her.

"Is she gone?" Claire whispered.

Spence lifted the hand that held the pistol. "Listen."

From inside the trailer, he heard movement. There

was a bang, then the scrape of a heavy object being pushed away from behind the door. There was a rattling that sounded like chains and latches being undone, and finally the door cracked outward.

"Shh. Be quiet!" a woman whispered urgently, her head silhouetted in the light cast by a propane lantern hanging from a hook. "You'll wake'm. Then we're all in trouble."

"Wake who? Who are they?" When she didn't answer, Spence suspected that he knew. Crank heads, often up for days on end, were famous for their paranoid delusions.

She let Spence and Claire inside, her hands beckoning with frantic, uncoordinated movements.

The Rachel Little backing into the trash-strewn trailer bore no resemblance to the pretty young intern Spence had first arrested two years earlier. At that time, the fresh-faced redhead—an Iowan, no less—had looked a more likely candidate for Candy Striper of the Year than addict. But that was exactly what she was, even though the hospital where she had worked had done its damnedest to sweep her theft of amphetamines and opiates under the carpet.

Maybe they didn't want to believe someone so clean-cut and intelligent could become a junkie. Spence had understood the hospital's disbelief, for he still had trouble figuring out how it had happened.

By now, however, the truth was undeniable. When she spoke, he saw black spaces where straight white teeth had been. Her once glossy hair hung in lank strands, and her stained clothes reeked with the sour mildew stench that overwhelmed the trailer. But more than anything, her movements told on her: the way her fingers scuttled along like beetles, first scratching at her face, then picking scabs along her pallid, stick-thin arms; the way her eyes, twin wells of blackness, flicked back and forth from Claire's big flashlight to his gun.

At first he figured she was scared that they would hurt her. Until she asked anxiously, "You didn't bring no hit for me? You didn't bring no bindle?"

He reminded himself of what he'd heard, that once upon a time she'd been near the top of her undergraduate class, majoring in molecular biology. Yet now even the bare basics of grammar had escaped her.

"No drugs, Rachel. Not from me. But I brought a little money. You can get some good food."

She stared at him blankly, as if she had not the faintest idea of why she might need such a thing. Then suddenly those black wells blinked and she leapt behind a built-in table piled high with garbage. "I—I remember you. You're that cop. Get out of here. I don't want trouble. Don't want all your noise to wake'm."

"Now, Rachel," he said soothingly. "It's all right. I'm not here to make a bust. I just need help—and I can pay you."

"Help?"

Her gaze flickered over his face, and he saw a bit more focus sharpen her expression. It offered him some hope that she might cure instead of kill him.

"There's a bullet in my arm here. It's making me sick—can you get it out for me?"

"A cop? Why don't you—"

"I saw the work you did on Light Year." On a tip, he had come here, along with backup, to arrest the twice-convicted Lamont "Light Year" Carlson, who had been shot holding up a mom-and-pop convenience store. "It was good work, Dr. Little. You probably saved the man's life."

Even though said life would now be spent in prison, since the twenty-year-old clerk Light Year shot hadn't been so lucky.

Doc Rachel edged out from behind the table, her head shaking as she did. "I mess with a cop, they'll kill me. They don't like the cops."

He assumed "they" were the criminals who kept her in this palace.

"Who's gonna tell them?" he asked. "Not me, that's for sure. How 'bout you?"

He tossed the question Claire's way. She had navigated between stacks of cardboard boxes—he noticed several overflowing with what looked like filthy rags— to try to force open one of the sliding windows. The stench was clearly getting to her. Even in the lantern light, she looked almost as pale as Rachel, and he wondered if her stomach would hold out.

Even so, she gamely shook her head for the "doctor's" benefit.

"No cops. No, I shouldn't . . ." Rachel told him, yet his need drew her interest the way the earth pulled meteors from the night sky. Her gaze had locked on to his left arm, where dried blood had crusted on the sleeve that covered up his bandage, and she was sidling closer. Almost close enough to touch him.

She made a gesture of impatience. "Take it off—the shirt. I'll look at it. Just look."

He unbuttoned the shirt and then stripped it off, suspecting that he had her.

Turning from the window, Claire blurted, "You can't let her do this. It's ridiculous. This place isn't close to sterile. And she's a train wreck—"

Rachel spun to face her. "I keep my instruments in alcohol. My bandages are in the wrapper, my meds are the real deal—my friends get 'em from a pharmacy in— Never mind that. Just know I'm still a damned good doctor. You see if I'm not."

She sounded indignant, furious, as if she could not imagine why anyone would question her. She picked at her scalp nervously as Claire stared her down.

The air shimmered with their tension, darkened. Spence blinked as he realized it was his vision wavering.

"It's all right," he said quickly. "I trust you, Doc Rachel."

"Stay, then. I can fix you. But that bitch waits outside."

SEVENTEEN

Claire paced around the truck, her hand aching from her death grip on the hated gun. In her other hand, she held the metal-barreled flashlight, which Spence had once told her would make a good club in a pinch. She kept it off, however, both to conserve the batteries and to avoid drawing unwanted attention with its light.

At first she had argued about leaving, then pleaded to stay inside the trailer. But the doctor and Spence had both been adamant.

"You don't need to see this," he had argued. "It'll be okay. Just stay near the door, where I can hear you. And call out if you need me—or if you see anyone at all. I can be there in a hurry."

That had been twenty-two minutes earlier, according to the dashboard clock. She had spent the time walking nervous relays from trailer to truck, where she started at every sound and worried about Ellen and her father. When they couldn't find her, they would doubtless contact the sheriff's department. She thought of

181

calling them to put their minds at ease, but her cell phone was nowhere in the Chevy's extended cab.

She found no purse, either—then recalled she'd left the house that morning with only her driver's license, forty dollars, and a tube of lip balm tucked inside her pocket. The contents of the truck weren't much more helpful.

She came across a tepid can of Coke that had rolled beneath the seat. A wrapped pack of saltine crackers, too, that didn't look too ancient. She drank a little and nibbled at the crackers in the hope of settling her stomach.

Her mind, however, was a whirl of worry. What would she tell her dad and Ellen about where she'd gone this evening? What would she say to Joel if—or when—he questioned her? And what about Spence? Should she leave him somewhere safe—and where would "safe" be, anyway, for him?

One thing she knew for certain: She wasn't staying with him. Her heart might not have fallen out of love yet, but neither had her brains leaked out her ears.

There could be no going back in time, no rekindling of the trust that had once thrived between them. If she wanted any kind of life for herself and the child she carried, her best chance—maybe her only chance—was to put distance between herself and Spence's problems.

With the moonlight to guide her, she walked back toward the trailer once more, ears straining for Spence's voice, or perhaps a cry of pain. Instead she heard the chirping of crickets making merry in the weeds and a rustling from the trash heap that made her think about the rats she'd seen there earlier.

Shuddering, she kept her eyes averted. Once she got

home, she planned to run through a hot water heater's worth of shower. She would use up every scrap of soap and drop of shampoo she could find.

Her steps quickened at the thought of Spence with all those germs inside the trailer. Even if she never saw him again after tonight, she couldn't let that woman make him sicker, couldn't let her husband die in this hellhole.

Without bothering to knock, she flung open the door and stepped inside.

"It's all right," Spence called to her.

He was sitting on the table. It had been cleared and covered with a blue sheet speckled with no more than a couple of teaspoons of fresh blood. Though perspiration dampened his dark hair and pain underscored his blue eyes, his color had improved and he seemed alert.

Doc Rachel was pressing what looked suspiciously like a feminine sanitary napkin to his arm and wrapping gauze around the arm to keep the thing in place.

Spence glanced down at the bandage and tipped up a wry smile. "They're not high fashion, but they're sterile. Did you know a lot of people keep them in their first aid kits?"

She couldn't smile back, for her gaze had found the ashtray and the bloody bullet in it. Her stomach threatened new upheaval, so she looked away.

"That was quick," she told the doctor.

Beneath the oily fringe of red hair, Rachel shrugged a blade-thin shoulder. "I told you, I'm still good—dug it right out with forceps, where it was lodged against the bone. I could work anywhere, in any hospital."

Claire looked around, tried not to smell the background stench of unflushed human waste. "Well, I can certainly see why you picked this one."

Guilt lancing through her, she added quickly, "I'm sorry, Doctor. I didn't need to say that. I appreciate your helping him."

Carefully, she tucked the little gun into her waistband. It felt wrong, thanking someone while holding a weapon in her hand.

Rachel nodded. "Gave him a shot, too, something strong for the infection. But he's a tough one—wouldn't take nothin' but some Tylenol for pain, and I've got some damned good shit here. Use it myself to come down when I have to."

Judging from her slurred speech, she had done exactly that before performing surgery.

"Gotta stay awake to stay alive," Spence told her.

Doc Rachel shrugged again as if she'd heard it all before. But already her eyes were going dull, more evidence that she'd been sampling her wares. Such a terrible waste of human potential, Claire thought.

When Spencer reached for his shirt, she set down the flashlight to help him put it on, then said to Doc Rachel, "There are treatment programs that would help you. I could bring you numbers later, put you in touch with people who can get you out of this place."

"What for?" the woman asked. "I'd just screw things up again, probably end up somewhere even worse."

Before Claire could ask the question, Rachel added, "Jail's worse—and state prison. I won't live in a cage."

Spence stood and dug into the right-hand pocket of his jeans. "Let me pay you for this. I have a little money."

Doc Rachel's eyes drooped to half-mast, and she made a sloppy gesture, waving him off, then sweeping her hand around to take in the whole trailer. "What the hell do I need money for? Got every single thing a girl could want right here."

Outside the trailer, Spence saw Claire look back.

"I don't know how you stood it so long," she said quietly. "Every night and day, watching people destroy themselves. I work with the results sometimes, but they're usually attempting to get better by the time they come to me."

He thought of all the things he'd seen and felt a grimace pull at his mouth. "There's no law against screwing up your own life. It's something you have to learn to deal with, or you can't help anybody."

He put his left hand on her shoulder to guide her back to their truck. But before they'd taken two steps, a sound leaked through a broken back window of the trailer. A sound that rooted them both to the spot.

It was a thin cry, tentative and fragile. The fretting of an infant in the first days of its life.

EIGHTEEN

"We shouldn't have just left it." Claire's thumbs drummed nervously atop the steering wheel, and she thought of turning the truck around, going back to get the baby. What if Doc Rachel OD'd on her pain meds? What if the rats somehow squeezed inside and found it?

Spence was shaking his head. "We'll find a phone and make an anonymous nine-one-one call, ask someone from the PD to do a welfare check. Trust me, they'll get someone from social services out there in a heartbeat. That baby won't sleep there tonight."

"You're sure?"

He nodded solemnly. "I promise. And besides, we don't need to add kidnapping to my list of charges."

Claire wondered if that meant he had assumed she wouldn't file a complaint. Probably she wouldn't, but the thought chafed that he would be so sure of her.

"What about the doctor?" she asked. "Will they take her somewhere safe, too?"

"Jail's safer than where she is. If she stays in that

place, some criminal will feel like killing her one day soon."

"But she's valuable to them. Why would they—"

He shook his head. "You're assuming these people think like we do. That the things they do make sense."

An image shivered through her mind: Spence pointing the gun at her when she had opened the truck door.

"You said *we*—'like *we* do,'" she told him. "You're forgetting I don't understand you, either. Not lately, anyway."

He said nothing as the green truck glided past a mix of businesses offering automotive services, discount flowers, and used books. Their parking lots were empty, and most of the lights were off. One left burning, by the Blue Moon Bookstore, illuminated a shabby-looking sign with many of its letters missing. She tried to decode it, but the meaning fell away as it vanished behind them.

After a time, she broke the silence. "Does your arm hurt much?"

"Remember that time I was on patrol and those gang kids set their pit bull on me?"

She nodded. His left calf still bore the scars of forty stitches.

"Throbs a lot like that did, but it'll be all right."

She thought he sounded better than he had before. But it was still too soon to say for certain whether Doc Rachel had helped him.

Across the intersection ahead, Claire spotted the cheerful orange-and-white glow of an all-night burger joint just as Spence asked, "Why don't you pull in there? There's a pay phone—see it? And we can grab something for the road."

She waited out the light, then pulled in among the few cars in the lot. Some six feet from the truck's hood, a pay phone was attached to the building's outer wall.

"You can't go inside," she told him. "Someone will see the blood on your sleeve and get suspicious. I can get the food if you want to make the call. I need to use the rest room anyway."

He hesitated. "Once we're finished, there's a place I'll have you drop me. Then I'll grab some sleep and go from there."

"Go where? What will you do?"

"I'm going to make things better for everyone involved."

Inside Claire, something quivered, alone and naked as she imagined that baby in the trailer was. But she thought of the other child, her child, along with the children of the Monarch Ranch. Or "Camp Am-Pride-Co," if she didn't get her act together. Nodding to Spence, she told him, "I'll be back in a few minutes."

As she opened the truck door, he grabbed her wrist. Her sore shoulder sent pain jolting through her as she accidentally pulled against his grip.

"You know I wouldn't hurt you," he said. "Don't you?"

She rubbed the shoulder and looked at him. Had he forgotten he'd been hurting her for weeks?

"I won't tell anybody, if that's what you're after. Later on, I'll say to Dad and Ellen that I had to get some things out of the condo."

He nodded, his expression a mélange of pain and grief and what she thought might be love in its most elemental form.

His grasp turned to a caress before he whispered, "I trust you, Claire. With my life."

She willed herself not to cry, not to take him in her

arms and tell him she would never stop believing in him. Because it would only make things harder, once she had to leave him.

Once she had to leave . . .

At the thought, terror shafted through her, and unspoken words rose like hot bile in her throat. Before they spilled free, Spence turned away from her, disappointment written in his face.

"Wait, Spence."

He looked back over his shoulder.

She swallowed, though her throat was dry as ash. "Whatever you need from me, you have it. Anything at all."

Without waiting for his response, she tucked the gun out of sight beneath the driver's seat and left the truck to go inside.

He was still talking on the pay phone, his bad arm angled to the wall, when she returned with two drinks and a bag that smelled of greasy goodness. While ordering, her appetite had arisen with a vengeance. She snagged a couple of French fries and was about to unwrap a grilled chicken sandwich when he climbed back inside.

"Can we park somewhere else to eat?" he asked her.

He didn't say why, but she suspected the police might already be looking for their pickup. She thought wryly that any officer who knew him would remember he had a major jones for Whataburger.

She drove them to an area behind a strip center a couple of blocks away. "Is this all right?"

He smiled grimly. "You'd make a half-decent fugitive."

"You're the expert." She passed him the bag. "When you called, what did they say? Will the cops go get the baby?"

"Yeah. I'm sure they will."

Spence opened up a cheeseburger and peeked under the top bun. "You remembered jalapeños."

He sounded pleased about it, as if he had nothing more to think about than his unhealthy fast-food habit. The comment was a tiny shard of normalcy, a splinter that lodged deep in her heart.

She managed a few bites, but though she chewed and chewed, her throat closed tight around the knowledge that this could well be the last meal they would share. Finally she rewrapped her partially eaten sandwich and shoved it back inside the bag.

Spence glanced up from his burger. "Your stomach hurting you again?"

She shook her head and said, "You know, that doctor might tell them about helping you. The police could put two and two together any time now."

"If they do, they do," he said. "After I talk to—what was it I called him—Beto, it won't matter anyway."

Her heart thumped against her chest wall and, before she could stop herself, she blurted, "Let's get out of here, Spence. We could drive to Mexico and start all over. We could run away from everything and—"

"Shhh." He crumpled up his wrapper and used his napkin. "You know that wouldn't work. You know—"

"I know I don't want you dying—and that's exactly what you're driving at. It's why I called Joel last night. It's why I can't just drop you off and let you see this Beto or whoever the hell he is."

He slid closer, then leaned toward her and cupped her face in his hands. He moved so close, she could see pain gather like a thunderhead behind his eyes.

He kissed her then. A chaste kiss, it was laden with

their history and burdened with the weight of all the things that might have been.

And then it was over, and Spence was opening the door, stepping out of the cab and out of her reach. "This has gone on long enough, Claire—and it's putting you in too much danger. I have to go now. Thanks for taking me this far."

Before she could call out to him, he was already turning from her, breaking into an odd shuffling jog down the pitch-dark alley.

"Get back here." When he didn't answer, she called, "I mean it, Spence."

But by the time she thought to flip on the headlights, he was out of sight. She might have been able to convince herself the whole episode had been no more than a dream if it weren't for the bag of trash and the cell-deep memory of all the places he had touched her.

NINETEEN

Spence didn't run three steps into the darkness before pain and weakness caught up, slamming into him with the force of a tornado ripping through a stand of trees. He barely managed to stagger behind a Dumpster before it felled him.

He lay on his side, cradling his hurt arm, his body curved into a comma. As the roaring in his head built to a crescendo, he barely noticed the flash of headlights in the alleyway and the deep, familiar thrum of the pickup's V-8 engine.

Leaving . . . Though he couldn't see, Spence's mind conjured a series of images: The green pickup driving back to Little BC—or better yet, the San Antonio condo where he and Claire had lived; then Claire phoning her father, telling him not to worry, she would be back in the morning. He saw his wife in a clean bed, her hair damp and sweet-smelling from the shower, all worry erased from her face as her chest gently rose and fell. The vision was so beautiful, so vivid in its details, that he succumbed to its dark flow, his mind manufacturing a whole and guiltless avatar that slipped into bed behind her to spoon his body against hers.

As Spence drifted in the dream, his hand reached around to her breast and his mouth sought that sensitive spot beneath her ear. But just as she turned toward him with a sleepy, sexy smile, someone shook his shoulder—jolting him back into a world of pain.

"Spence. Spence, you have to help me."

It was Claire's voice, as strong as he had ever heard her. But he couldn't bear to open his eyes, to see an empty alley and know she wasn't here. He wanted only to slip back into illusion—to slip inside his wife again, in the only way he might.

A second, more insistent shake prevented him from returning. "You have to help me get you to the truck, Spence. I can't pick you up. It could hurt me, or the baby."

When his eyes opened, she was out of focus. But she was without question real and present. Gratitude flooded through him, though he knew he should tell her to get the hell out of his life, that if he died here, in this alley, her troubles would be over.

Yet the power of the dream made him obey her. Moving slowly, he struggled first to sit and then to stand. She wrapped her arm around his waist and slowly guided him back to the pickup.

It was all he could do to climb up into the cab. He flopped down sideways on the seat, which left her barely enough room to get into the driver's side.

She closed the door and told him firmly, "We're going to the condo. We'll get you cleaned up and into bed."

He wanted home and her more than he had ever wanted anything. But common sense warned him to protect her.

"No, not the condo. They'll check there first. There's another place I know. A motel off Old Highway 90."

She started driving. "I don't have any credit cards—"

"Can't use 'em anyway, or they'll trace us. This place deals in cash, tries to keep under the radar. SAPD cops all know some below-board stuff goes down there, but it's outside both the city and Bexar County limits."

"How much do you have on you? After the food, I'm down to about thirty-three dollars. And we're going to need gas soon."

"I've got enough for a night or two. This motel—it's not the Hilton. Not by a long shot."

"If it has clean sheets and a shower, that'll be enough."

"We'll see if you still think that once we get there."

From her first glimpse of the squat, one-story building, Claire saw that the Trucker's Luck Motel lived up—or down—to Spence's description. Situated along a rural stretch of highway replaced by the more modern Interstate 10, the Trucker's Luck was too far off the beaten track to attract truckers and too run-down to make it any sort of destination of its own. Yet it remained, an area sin pit favored by adulterers of both sexes for its very isolation, and the fact that the parking lot lay out of sight behind the building.

Claire went inside alone to register, and from the knowing smirk of the enormous greasy man behind the counter, she knew he took her nervousness as a flash of cheater's guilt.

"You want the hour or the night, 'Ms. Williams'?" The

way he said the name she'd given let her know he didn't buy it for one minute. But neither had he asked to see ID. Within their folds of fat, his tiny dark eyes kept flicking from her breasts to her lips and back again.

Discomfited by his stare, Claire dropped her gaze— then had to avert it to avoid looking at the disgusting magazine spread on the counter. Some parts of the female anatomy, she was certain, were never meant for close-up flash exposure.

"The whole night," she mumbled as a cockroach made its leisurely way across the peeling vinyl floor. "How much?"

"Depends"—his voice was as greasy as his frizzy gray ponytail—"on what you wanta show me."

When he started around the counter, her chin jerked higher and she stared him down. She had always hated bullies, and tonight she had no patience for this brand of petty bullshit. "You won't like it if I have to bring my friend in. He's got a record longer than this fleapit's list of health code violations."

The clerk lifted fleshy palms and edged back behind the safety of the counter. "Fine. Can't take a joke. I get it. You got the thirty-five bucks or not?"

She plucked the money Spence had given her from her pocket and moved to place it on the counter. His big paw slapped down onto her hand, and one thick finger trailed upward along the inside of her wrist.

Claire struggled in vain to yank her arm free, her mind overflowing with a cinematic image: Jabba the Hut pawing Princess Leia. "Let. Me. Go," she demanded.

The alien eyes locked on to hers as he leaned forward, so close she could feel the heat of fetid breath.

"You go and have your fun, bitch. But you watch who you threaten. Hear me? Hear me, little girl?"

Panicking, she backpedaled when he let go of her. He picked up something behind the counter and threw it at her. She only realized it was a key when she heard its metallic clink against the floor.

"Room fourteen," he told her, his smirk more pronounced than ever.

To grab the key, she squatted, refusing to give him the pleasure of ogling her rear while she bent over. As she hurried back to her truck, she was shaking with relief to find Spence sitting up, running a hand tiredly across the stubble on his chin and yawning.

"Go all right?" he asked her.

"That guy's a creep, a pervert."

"Did he do something?" Spence's voice dropped to a growl. "Do I need to go take care of it?"

She shook her head and put the truck back into gear. The last thing her husband needed was more trouble. "It's nothing. It's just—he had this magazine out, and it was disgusting."

She drove behind the motel and parked near room fourteen. The moment they entered the cramped and dingy space, Claire understood why Jabba had looked so pleased with himself. Love Pit number fourteen had been cursed with a pair of dilapidated twin beds instead of one double.

Laughing, Claire made for the bathroom. She didn't give a damn about the beds now. The only thing she cared about was scrubbing all the Hutt-germs off her hand.

The angry red glow of digital numbers told Spence it was 3:45 A.M. when he shifted his position and the pain of his arm woke him. The warmth against his back informed him that at some point Claire had slipped into his bed. Maybe she had been there all night, for he had conked out right after she had helped him wash up.

For several minutes, he lay very still, savoring the feel of her body against his, the way her arm was draped protectively over his waist. The exact opposite of how the two of them had slept since their first night together, which followed a two-week, ten-date blitz that had convinced him she was the most generous, fascinating, and dedicated woman on the planet. And one of the sexiest as well. Quietly intense, she had thrown herself into loving him with the same single-mindedness she brought to everything she tackled. Though he had kept himself closed tight as a fist since his parents' deaths, he had stretched toward her warmth like a leaf unfurling toward sunlight.

They had married three months later in a small wedding attended by a few close friends and Claire's father, who had fidgeted his way through the ceremony and gripped Spence's hand too firmly when he shook it. Despite Will Meador's doubts, however, Spence and Claire were good together—more than good . . . for the five years leading up to that horrible day last autumn.

Spence sighed and steeled himself, then lifted Claire's hand off him and set it back down carefully as he climbed from the bed. As he dressed in the darkness, he tried not to wish for a fresh set of clothing, struggled not to long for lost possibilities. Wishing didn't change a damned thing. It wouldn't resurrect the dead or erase his troubles, and it couldn't save Claire and their child from the terrible choices he had made.

He felt around until he found her jeans, draped over

the room's one chair, and he slipped his hand into the pocket for her truck keys. Cupping them carefully so they wouldn't jingle, Spence stood over his sleeping wife. His every molecule ached to reach down to her, to pull her close and give her the good-bye she deserved. But his conscience warned him not to wake her, so he settled for standing there a moment and listening to her breathe.

Just remember how, he told her in his mind. Inhale, exhale, until you make it to a day when you can smile again. And remember we had so much more than the bad times. . . . Please, Claire, just remember the man I used to be.

.

TWENTY

Though he looked and looked, the one left behind could not find The Remembrance—could not even be sure where he had seen the thing last. Panic's dark wings beat inside him, thumping at his rib cage, pounding at his temples.

But still he could not find it, and though he had not looked in some time, the loss now yawned before him, a vast black chasm of despair. He went to the cupboard, pulled out a bottle of scotch, and poured the amber liquid into a tall glass over ice.

He had no idea how long he sat listening to the ice cubes clinking in the featureless darkness, his mind conjuring remembrance of another sort. When the phone rang, he had to fumble for a light to find it. His heart quickened with the hope that it might be her.

As soon as he picked up, he realized it wasn't, for the voice shouting at him was deeper and far rougher. Repulsed, he started to hang up before words disentangled themselves from the black snarl.

"You better tell me what to do, man, cause he's back

here. Poking all around the place, asking his damned questions. You need him left alive? That what you still want? Cause if you do, you better say so right now before *los vatos* go ahead and gut the *placa*—"

He broke the connection with a finger, then gently laid the receiver beside it, off the hook. He didn't need to hear what happened later.

He didn't want a call telling him Spence Winslow was dead.

The blade felt cold against Spence's throat, colder than the pearled light that streamed through the privacy window set high above their heads. And harder than the two sets of hands that gripped him from behind.

As he faced *El Tiburón* for the first time, Spence knew he was a dead man. But instead of scaring him, the knowledge—and the scuffle that had taken place in the after-hours nightclub downstairs—had infused him with a fresh burst of adrenaline. After spreading his feet to brace himself, he stared directly into the face of one of the most powerful criminals in the region.

Though he was commonly called The Shark by friends and enemies alike, SAPD knew him as Javier Garcia Alvarez, the savviest leader in a generation to rise from San Antonio's street gangs. And one of the most ruthless when it came to protecting his interests. A small, slightly built Hispanic with crowded, crooked teeth, he sat behind a desk that might have been purloined from a museum, with its gleaming mahogany surface and what looked like a hand-carved lion's head adorning each corner. A simple gold clock atop the desk marked the hour as 5:45 A.M. Behind him, a picture lamp illuminated a framed diploma and leather-bound volumes crowded a matching bookcase, but it was the man himself who commanded Spence's attention.

Despite his unlined face, it was nearly impossible to accept that he was only twenty-five years old. Alvarez wore a corporate haircut with his fine black suit and white shirt. His blue-and-yellow patterned tie was slightly loosened at the throat, his only concession to the late—or early—hour. Yet it was not his clothing so much as his primordial, dark eyes that utterly belied his youth. They stared without blinking, so impassive that Spence guessed that they, and not the over-crowded teeth, had earned him his street name.

Sociopath, Spence decided in an instant. He'd arrested his share in the past. With no empathy for others and no remorse when they caused pain, they frequently ended up in trouble. But most of them were losers, parasites who drifted through life until they hurt the wrong person or were locked up. What made Alvarez so potent—and so rare—was his ability to sniff out any angle that gave him an advantage.

But what advantage had he gained by framing a cop who owed him big-time?

"Are you here with my money?" Alvarez asked in a calm, unaccented voice. "Because normally I don't handle such details personally."

"Like I told your friends, I'm here to see you, Javier." Spence enjoyed the way the man's face darkened at the sound of his first name. "I want to know, you bastard, what you hoped to accomplish when you set me up."

"*No chingues con El Tiburón!*" one of the thugs warned, but it was the punch to Spence's injured arm that hazed his vision and buckled his knees.

The two men kept him from falling, and as waves of pain washed over him, Spence felt heat where the blade's tip bit into his neck; his own blood, warm and sticky as it trickled down his collar.

"Stop," *El Tiburón* said sharply. "Do you think I want this *cabrón*'s blood on my rug? This is an antique Persian, *idiotas!* Now put him in a chair so we can talk."

As Spence's vision cleared, someone pushed a cloth against his neck. He was guided and then shoved down into a leather club chair across from the black-suited gangster, who was leaning forward, his face set like concrete in an unfathomable expression.

"If I wanted you dead, you would already be—"

"That's what I been tryin' to tell you, *jefe*," the thug interrupted. "I made that phone call like you asked me. We don't have to screw around with this guy anymore."

The Shark's eyes flicked to the club's bouncer, an NFL-sized wall of muscle with a shaved head and a black teardrop tattooed below the corner of his deep brown right eye. The human pit bull, who spoke street Spanish and went by the unlikely name of Cal Smith, had been the representative sent to explain to Spence that his marker had been purchased—and that *El Tiburón* expected a certain type of return on his investment. As usual, he wore a well-made jacket over a navy T-shirt and fairly dripped with gold and diamond jewelry, evidence that *El Tiburón* handsomely rewarded those he favored.

His silent partner, a younger, equally beefy white man, fidgeted with the knife. Not from nervousness, Spence sensed, but out of eagerness to use it. There was something familiar about the way the man moved, something that put Spence to mind of the man he'd met along that dark road with the money three weeks earlier, just before the deputies burst out of hiding to arrest him. But clouds had clotted the night sky, making it far too dark to make out faces clearly, and in his desperation, he had struggled until one of the lawmen—he still didn't know who—had dropped him with a Taser. Spence still remembered little from that evening—little enough to make him wonder if he'd been drugged at some point. Maybe if the thug spoke, he'd recognize the voice—for all the good that would do him in this situation.

Spence pressed his fingers against the chair's side in an effort to leave fingerprints. Might as well make things easier for the evidence unit in the unlikely event that the department's investigation into his death got this far.

"We'll get him out of here, boss," said the bouncer. "Take him out to that dry creek where we usually—"

El Tiburón stood, leaning on his hands over his desk. Small as the man was, his presence filled the room. "How many times do I have to tell you? I don't need to know that shit. I don't *want* to know. If you can't grasp the principles of delegation, then maybe I'll have to find someone smart enough to—"

The so-called Cal Smith hauled Spence to his feet. "That won't be necessary, sir. Me and Hammill here, we both know our business."

"Good, then take care of it by leaving me alone."

The bigger men dragged Spence toward the door. But before they made it, *El Tiburón* added, "Alone with him, I mean. You see, I know my business, too, *compadres*. I still remember every aspect. . . ."

Spence could almost smell the muscles' confusion. But they let go of him abruptly, and he fell down onto his knees. The pair left, closing the door behind them with almost reverent care.

As The Shark came out from behind his desk,

Spence saw the Glock semiautomatic in his hand. Using the chair to help support himself, he struggled to his feet.

If he was about to die here, he wasn't going to do so on his knees—and he damned well wouldn't do it without at least trying to get answers to the questions he had risked his life to ask.

Claire woke from a dead sleep, heart thumping in response to a strange metallic rattle at the door.

For a split second she had no idea where she was, but a glance from the twin bed's shabby linens to the peeling dresser brought with it a flood of memory. Light leaked in around the edges of the heavy curtains, and as the door swung open, a brighter glow silhouetted the heavy figure moving toward her.

With a shriek, she vaulted from the bed, her hands clutching the top sheet to hide her half-dressed state. If Jabba the Hotel Clerk thought he could pop in for a peep show—

Except it wasn't Jabba, but a tall, wide-hipped white woman who backpedaled toward the door. Though she wore a black NASCAR T-shirt tucked into elastic-waisted jeans, the folded linens and the roll of toilet paper she carried clearly identified her as the maid. "Sorry, ma'am. Thought you'd checked out, what with your truck gone."

Her broad, smooth face looked florid in the morning sunlight, yet she didn't seem especially alarmed by Claire's reaction. "I'll come back in an hour—or you can hang the 'Do Not Disturb' sign and I can let you sleep 'til noon."

"My truck's gone?" Claire looked down at the empty bed, then saw the dark doorway of the bathroom. Had

Spence left to pick up breakfast, or had he simply left? Her stomach bottomed out, grasping his absence before she did.

The big brunette paused, her head tilting and a lock of shiny hair escaping from her clip. "Is there a problem, ma'am? Do we need t'call the law and report it stolen?"

Though they were nowhere near his jurisdiction, Claire thought immediately of Joel. How in heaven's name could she explain her lack of judgment?

Shaking her head quickly, she told the woman, "Never mind. I'm sure he'll be right back."

The maid shot her a look of empathy—one that indicated she was well acquainted with the ways of worthless men.

"More'n likely, you're right," she reassured Claire before leaving the towels and excusing herself.

But Claire had never been less certain of anything in her life. Had she finally seen the last of Spencer Winslow?

So what now?

The question kept running through her head as she dressed and cleaned up as best she could. She didn't feel up to facing Ellen or her father any more than she did Joel, but she couldn't exactly take up residence in this rat hole.

She settled on calling her friend Janine at the rehab center, where she still worked. It was only quarter after nine, but she should be there.

"Oh, hi, Claire. Janine's not in. She's canceled her appointments for the whole day," said the receptionist. "Some personal matter, I think."

Claire hoped that didn't mean the woman was off with a new boyfriend. Already twice divorced at twenty-nine, Janine had a blind spot the size of Texas when it came to men. Part of the reason Claire had lobbied so desperately to bring her friend on board at Monarch Ranch this summer was to lure Janine further from the loser-magnet honky-tonks she frequented.

As she dialed her friend's cell phone, Claire decided this debacle over Spence disqualified her from any advice on the subject of ill-advised affairs.

"Claire," Janine erupted at the sound of her friend's voice. "I've been running all over looking for you, hon. Your daddy asked me if I'd check out your place, and then some cop called—no, a sheriff—to see if I had any idea where you'd gone. Where *are* you?"

"I—uh—everything was too much. I—I had to get away." Claire twisted at a lock of hair. She hated compounding stupidity with lies, but she couldn't seem to stop herself. "I need your help, Jan, and no questions."

"Are you—have you been with a *man*, Claire?" Shock crept into Janine's voice, probably at the thought that anyone so boringly straitlaced could do something so human.

"Yeah, Jan. Yes, I have. Now can you cover for me, tell everyone I'm all right, that I just need some time?"

"You bet I will. If anyone deserves a little distraction, it's definitely you."

Behind these generous words, Claire detected a hint of relief. Was Janine glad to be the stable, responsible one, for once? Or was she simply pleased to be paying back her friend, who had covered for her late nights more than once at work?

"I may need one more thing." Claire wondered how on earth to explain her need for a ride home. But before she could say another word, the sound of an engine just outside the doorway brought her to her feet.

"Never mind—I'll call you later. And thanks, Janine. I owe you a great big slushy drink at Margarita's."

Before Janine could answer, Claire hung up and rushed toward the door to see who was outside. But the scrape of an old-fashioned key warned her she would not be quick enough.

TWENTY-ONE

Claire launched herself into Spence's arms and squeezed the breath out of him. Though the jostling sent pain careening through his bad arm, something inside him unclenched at her welcome. He'd been scared to death she would be gone by the time he made it back here.

She kissed his face. "I thought you'd left me."

He lofted three bags. Warm and yeasty smells rose from the lone paper sack among them.

"Just went out to pick up a few things. I brought you back some breakfast." He struggled to keep his words light, though even now, almost three hours after leaving *El Tiburón* and his men, Spence was dizzy with the knowledge that he'd made it out alive.

She looked him over, from the bandage taped to his neck to the fresh T-shirt he'd picked up at a discount store along the freeway. The other one had been too conspicuous, with its bloodstains. As it was, he'd had to stammer some story about a lawn mowing accident to the frightened young clerk at the nearly empty Wal-Mart.

He came all the way inside and pushed the door shut with his foot.

"What happened to you?" Claire asked. "How'd you cut your neck?"

He shook his head. "Here. Let's sit down and eat first. I passed a little bakery and got you some kolaches—and I didn't forget the fruit kind you love, either."

Claire fisted a hand against her hip. "Don't try to shut me up with pastry."

He sat down on the bed and pulled out a small link of sausage wrapped in golden-brown dough. "Who's trying to shut you up? I'm starving."

He was, too, though until he had set eyes on Claire, he hadn't had an appetite.

She stared down at him, her quick brown eyes appraising. "Other than the new bandage, you look a lot better than last night—if you don't count those scratches and that scruffy excuse for a beard."

While he bit into the sausage kolache—heaven—his free hand dumped out the plastic Wal-Mart bag. Beside a travel-sized tube of toothpaste and two toothbrushes, a bottle of extra-strength pain reliever and a three-pack of cheap razors slid out onto the bed. If he'd had more money on him, he would have invested in more clothing, but for the time being they would have to make do with what they had.

He swallowed and pointed to the razors. "Now we won't have to worry about you growing thickets under your arms, either."

She swatted at his hand and laughed, sounding almost like the old, carefree Claire, then pulled out an apple-filled kolache. "Bring anything to drink?"

He pointed to the other bag. Earlier today he had faced down a sociopath, but he knew better than to bring Claire kolaches without milk.

As they broke their fast, Spence could almost hear the questions brewing like dark storm clouds behind his wife's silence. His mind churned frantically for some way to explain that the threat he had believed in was no more than a smoke screen—that behind the unpaid debt, Spence had a greater problem lurking.

A problem he could not begin to comprehend.

Before he had eaten his third kolache—or had time to sort through what he should tell her—Claire had finished her meal and returned from brushing her teeth.

She sat near him on the bed and brushed aside a few crumbs. "I'm still waiting to hear where else you went this morning. What happened to your neck, Spence? And please don't insult me with another lie."

He put down the half-eaten pastry. "I got up in the night. You were sound asleep, so I slipped out to go looking for the man who holds my marker."

"Beto?" She stood, her fist smacking into her palm to punctuate the false name. "You went out hunting trouble without a word to me? I'm so sick of this, Spence. Are you trying to get yourself killed? Do you really see that as the best solution?"

He grimaced. "It's not like that."

"Garbage." She stood again and started pacing, a real trick in this cramped space. "You've been committing suicide since the day Dave and that boy died. You're just doing it a little slower than most people."

His instinct was to argue, but he couldn't with her words still resonating deep inside him.

"Both of us have lost people we love." Claire stopped to look at him, and her voice grew feather soft. "I may not remember my mother, but I was sixteen when I lost my sister—the same age as you were when that bad furnace killed your parents. We both know how hard it is—how completely devastating. But bad as it was, I know my sister fought the cancer, and you know your mom and dad would never have chosen to leave you."

He didn't want to talk about his parents, didn't want to think about the dreams he'd had so often in the sixteen years since then. Dreams of coming home in time that night, of opening the windows and dragging them outside to save them. When they were safe, he'd be a hero, his dad clapping a big work-roughened hand on his son's shoulder, his mom embarrassing him by calling up the newspaper and inviting them to come take pictures. The three of them would celebrate, picnicking in Brackenridge Park and talking over their grand plans for his future. . . .

And afterwards Spence would wake up with the taste of ashes on his tongue.

"This isn't about choice, Claire." His words came rougher than he intended, infused by bitter memory. "It's never been about that."

"The hell it's not." Fresh anger flashed over her expression. "You never gambled before, Spence—not more than a lottery ticket here and there and that one time we watched the greyhounds run in Corpus Christi."

"Don't you want to hear what happened? It wasn't Beto, Claire. He says he didn't set me up."

"And you believe him?"

Spence nodded. "Yeah—I'm sort of surprised about it, but I do. He told me he has three strict rules for doing business. Reward loyalty. Make life hell for the competition. And never bring shit down on your own head."

She frowned. "Donald Trump should take notes. But you said before, he wanted favors from you and you wouldn't deliver. He didn't want to hurt you for that?"

"You need to understand. Above all else, Beto prides himself on being an intelligent, educated man of business. According to him, there are far easier—and less dangerous—ways to get a cop's cooperation than plotting to take him down. If Beto becomes a suspect in setting me up—or killing me, for that matter—every law enforcement agency from the locals to the feds would be all over him. They'd never give up."

He thought of the eerie detachment in El Tiburón's eyes as the man had thrown around terms like "negative risk-reward ratio" and "devalued business climate." Spence suppressed a shudder, knowing that if the reckoning had tallied up differently, if there had been any percentage in cop-killing, his body would have been left for the buzzards and coyotes in some dry creek bottom.

"But what about all that money you owe him?"

"He claims it's nothing to him—that it wasn't even his money in the first place he used to buy my marker. Someone paid him off to front the cash for it."

"What? Who would do a thing like that? And why?"

"That's what I'd like to know, but believe me, it was not the time to ask." Spence felt sick, remembering the way the gun's muzzle had been jammed against his temple—as well as the surreal moment El Tiburón had lowered it and whispered, *"Go and sin no more, friend. No more gambling, no more setting foot on my turf. Comprendé?"*

He could still barely believe he had walked away from the encounter—even though he had left with more questions than ever.

"But if he never really owned your marker, why was he pushing you to feed him information?"

Spence shrugged. "Both my bookie and I *thought* he owned it, and I'm guessing he saw that as an advantage—a way to squeeze out a little more return out of the deal."

"So who's to say he won't come back and squeeze some more, try to blackmail you again for department information?"

"He can't," Spence told her, "since I'm no longer a part of the department."

The way Claire stared at him, Spence could tell she was surprised that he'd been fired.

"Yeah," he added. "They made it official late last week."

"They could have at least waited till the trial. Don't officers have the same rights as anyone else? Aren't you presumed innocent until proven guilty?"

Spence shrugged. "The department's taken a lot of heat lately, so they're pretty quick to scrape the dog shit off the SAPD shoe."

Claire made a face. "Nice analogy, Spence. Glad you at least waited until we were finished eating."

He smiled. "Your stomach doing okay?"

"It's all right. I haven't had much morning sickness so far—or maybe I haven't really noticed because I've been so miserable."

He swallowed back the sour taste of guilt. "And what about your shoulder? Where that guy popped you."

"I'm fine—now please stop changing the subject. I'm still trying to understand this Beto thing. If he didn't set you up, who did? This mysterious guy who fronted the money for your marker?"

"I would guess so, but who the hell could it be? I can't imagine why anyone would go to so much trouble, or what they might hope to gain. Altering e-mails, faking audiotapes, sending me that message to show up with the cash: Those are all sophisticated crimes."

"How did that happen, anyway? Joel said they caught you handing over money to someone in Buck County. A man claiming he would shoot me for ten thousand."

The muscles in Spence's shoulders knotted, setting off small bursts of pain on his left side. "I'm tired of hearing you tell me what your good friend Joel said. Joel Shepherd's either in this up to his neck or he's been snowed as much as I was."

"You may be tired of hearing it, but his is the only version I know. What's yours?"

"I was told that if I didn't make a 'good faith' payment on my debt at this blind drop in the woods off Ranch Road 70, they weren't going to bother with my kneecaps. They were going to go to our place—to take it out of your ass."

Claire's lips parted as she stared, comprehension draining the color from her face.

"I couldn't let them hurt you," he said. "I was the one who—"

"My God. And this whole time, I've been thinking . . ." She shook her head, then went on, "This place was in Buck County? Where they told you to bring the money?"

"At the time, I wasn't thinking of it that way, but yeah—the drop was just inside the county line."

He saw emotions warring in her face. Doubt against

loyalty, love struggling to overcome the pain of his betrayals. And terror over all of it—a fear so sharp he smelled it radiating from her flesh.

She crossed her arms across her chest and once more started pacing. "This ten thousand dollars that was supposed to save me—where'd you get it?"

His gaze dropped to the floor. "My bookie loaned it to me. Said he was sorry he sold my marker in the first place—he only did it because he was scared of Beto. But he didn't want anything bad to happen to my wife."

"Was he the one who passed you the message?"

Spence nodded. "And before you ask, I've already tried to track him down to check it out. It took less than half an hour to figure out I wouldn't get anywhere questioning Lou Freemont. The man's been dead two weeks now. They say it was his heart."

"Do you believe that?"

"I'm not sure. Lou was a big guy, loved to eat and drink, and I think he'd had a triple bypass a few years back. But I've never put a lot of store in coincidences. And the fact that he's dead now, of all times, bothers me. He may have been the only link, my only chance to figure out who's really—"

"There has to be some clue," Claire said. "Something, anything else strange going on in your life—or in ours—before you were arrested."

He ran through all the things he had been thinking about these past few hours. "Maybe . . . maybe there was something else besides the gambling. I keep thinking back to the way Randall Hajek acted at his aunt's funeral, and everything that's been going on around the property. It's not just a few cut fences, it's—"

"No, it isn't *just* that. One of those cut fences killed a damned good horse."

215

Spence nodded. "You're right, but still, you have to admit that sneaking around and snipping a few wires is one thing. Stealing that ATV and running it off the bluff's edge is a much bolder move."

"At least I can tell the sheriff I saw Randall standing with the spray paint in front of the sign. . . ." As her words trailed away, she pinched her lower lip between her teeth.

"What, Claire? What is it you're thinking?"

"Randall had painted just one letter. A big capital *G*."

"Beginning of 'God damn you'?" Spence guessed. He had seen his share of graffiti—though more often than not it was in the stylized shorthand of San Antonio's street gangs.

Claire frowned, then shrugged. "Probably. But I was thinking about something else. Mr. and Mrs. Hajek's daughter, Gloria. I think she disappeared around the same time the hunter shot my mom. Gloria was fifteen at the time, and the thinking was she'd run away to Houston or Los Angeles or some other big city. But no one ever heard from her again. Oh, forget about it. That happened years ago, and why would Randall want to call attention to a disappearance that ended up making him his aunt's sole heir?"

Another coincidence? Spence wondered. "Claire, is your family sure about who killed your mother?"

"As far as I've heard, absolutely. My dad told me the hunter who did it cried like a baby when it happened. He'd lived in the city most of his life, and it was his first deer lease. He'd been in the deer stand drinking coffee when he saw the movement. I guess he got overly excited, fired before he was sure what he was seeing."

"So there was an investigation?"

She frowned. "I was only two, Spence, and that was

twenty-eight years ago. I've tried, but I really can't remember any of it—except a room that smelled like flowers, and the sound of my dad crying."

Spence imagined his own grief if he lost Claire in such an accident. God, it was no wonder Will Meador had avoided women since then and spent his time and money restoring the ranch house his great-grandfather had built so many years before. But at least he'd been a decent father to his daughters. Overprotective, maybe, but that was understandable.

Yet Spence still had questions. "And this hunter, he was alone, and he was from San Antonio?"

"I guess. But it could have been Dallas, or maybe Houston. But I don't see what any of this could have to do with Randall or Gloria or, for that matter, whoever the hell bowled me over when he was running from the creek. That certainly wasn't Randall, I can tell you. There is something else, though. Something a whole lot more recent."

Again she sat beside him, then related a strange conversation she had had yesterday afternoon with Mrs. Briggs-Hadley, a volunteer Spence had met on a couple of occasions. He wondered, Had Randall really told developers he owned all that land? And was he trying, by causing a string of small disasters, to coerce Claire into selling out cheap? But something didn't fit there, either. The vandalism might be escalating, but the plot to have Spence arrested was a much more complex scenario.

"The thing is," Claire added as she smoothed the faded bedspread, "Randall's never offered to buy me out. And I don't really think he would. If there's the slightest chance of his attorneys having the sale voided, I can see him trying that, but this other stuff doesn't really wash."

"There's one other person we haven't talked about. That missing biologist—what was his name?"

"Strickland. Adam Strickland. I've heard they—"

Spence snapped his fingers. "That's it. I should remember, as many times as I've been questioned about him."

"They found a body," Claire said. "Or I should say Lenore Briggs-Hadley found it. In that little offshoot of the creek near her place. The water was up again, and they believe it floated—"

"It's him?"

"That's what they're thinking, but they don't have a positive ID yet."

"Can they tell how he died?" Spence asked.

"Joel says the remains are in pretty poor condition. They're having someone do an autopsy. I guess it would be the medical examiner."

Spence thought about it, his mind struggling to weigh the possibilities. But the darkness he had lived with since last autumn swarmed inside him like a host of black flies, their angry buzzing morphing into questions that dampened other thought. *What difference does it make who did it? You're still screwed all the same. Why'd you even come back for her? Why can't you do the decent thing for once and let her get on with her life? Do you want to mess things up for your kid, too? Or are you man enough to—*

"What if," Claire was asking, "what if Adam Strickland came across the vandal on our property? Do you think whoever it was might have killed him? Spence?"

Her voice was warmth itself, a honeyed light that flooded his dark corners. Yet the buzzing persisted, making him turn his face from her.

"I should go," he murmured. "I don't see how we'll

218

ever figure this out. And even if we do, the sheriff's got his proof. The DA's got his charges. They're not going to want to reopen the—"

"I'm with you." She grasped his uninjured arm, her short nails digging shallow crescents into his exposed flesh. But it was the love in her voice that called him back to her. "Do you hear me? You're worth fighting for, Spence—*we're* worth it. And I mean to straighten out this mess, even if you walk out that door and disappear on me forever. I'm going to figure out who did this to us, and I'm going to see that they pay—and I don't give a damn who it is, whether it's some San Antonio gang leader or the governor of Texas."

He looked into her face flushed with emotion, and into dark eyes lit with a fierce fire. That single glance sent fault lines snaking along the walls of his resistance.

"So tell me right now," she said. "Am I doing this alone?"

She opened her mouth as if to say more, then simply pursed her lips and waited, as if she had until the world's end to wait for his decision. As if she had not just put her heart, her pride, and her future on the line with that one question.

This is it, he told himself. With one word, he could irrevocably sever their connection and save the woman he loved from the consequences of his actions.

His mind conjured a fleeting image from his own dreams. Only this time, instead of pulling his parents through the open window, it was his wife and unborn child whom he dragged into the safety of a windswept, starry night.

TWENTY-TWO

When he didn't answer, Claire fought to swallow back her tears of disappointment. This was like swimming for two people—three, if she counted the new life taking root inside her. She couldn't hope to keep them all afloat.

Not unless Spence was willing to fight as hard as she was.

Defeated, she dropped her gaze and told him, "I'm going to take a shower. If you're still here when I come back, we'll talk more. If not . . ."

The words hardened into jagged pebbles in her throat, so she rose from the bed and stepped inside the bathroom. As she stripped off her clothes, she hoped the hiss of the shower and the noisy little exhaust fan would muffle the sounds of his leaving, along with those of her own sobs.

She stepped into the stream—the water pressure was strong for such a dive—and let the warm jets pulse against her face. Yet when her eyes opened a few minutes later, she found her world still dark. At first she thought the power had gone out, but the bathroom fan continued rattling.

Someone had turned off the light, she realized a moment before she heard the sound—and felt the draft—of the shower curtain sliding open.

Her pulse thrummed loudly against her eardrums, as through the soles of her feet, she felt someone step inside the tub behind her. She cried out as the warm hands reached around her—not from fear, but with the joy and relief of sightless recognition.

Spence cupped her breasts and murmured in her ear, "God help me, I can't do it. I can't walk away from the best thing I've ever known, the only person in this whole world that I love—and that loves me back."

She arched her neck, her eyes sliding closed as his thumbs stroked her peaking nipples. "Thank God," she whispered.

One of his hands slid down the length of her side, then cupped and squeezed her buttock.

She rocked back against his body and smiled as a rough groan rose from his throat. In the pitch blackness of this space, her other senses blossomed, making a symphony of his rasping breaths and the sizzling hiss of water, a garden of the mingled scents of their desire. But it was the solid warmth of him behind her and the hard nudge of his erection that set off her own whimper.

He turned her toward him, capturing her mouth in a deep kiss that sent excitement streaking to her toes and hot pleasure coiling deep between her legs. Powerless to bank her passion, she slid her soap-slick hand along his length.

His moan deepened, and before she realized what was happening, he dropped kisses from her neck to

221

her breasts, then slid down until he nuzzled the inside of her thigh.

"You—you'll soak your bandages," she told him, but the weightless protest spun away and disappeared down the unseen drain. And in a darkness that had begun as hell, she leaned her back against the cool tile and allowed his tongue and fingers to carry her to heaven.

Light exploded behind her eyes, and the fireworks kept coming as he kissed his way home to her mouth. She stood on tiptoe to accept him, and as one, the two of them moved toward a new phase in their marriage. . . .

One that defied the powers seeking to destroy them.

Joel grimaced when the phone rang, and he immediately pressed the heel of his hand to his temple. The combination of a few scant hours' sleep and a hangover had spawned a crushing headache.

Eager to stop the skull-splitting noise, he sat up on his sofa—he hadn't been able to sleep in bed without his wife there—and reached for the portable phone he'd left on the coffee table.

"Damn it," he barked as his hand knocked over a half-full glass. The water from his melted ice cubes splashed onto the dark wood, then ran down onto the carpet next to Kylie's favorite blanket, which he'd brought out here last night to—he didn't know what the hell he'd been doing. Smelling it, he guessed, trying to catch a trace of her baby-girl sweetness.

God, he was pathetic. Next thing, he'd be bawling over one of Tyler's action figures and carrying Lori Beth's panties in his pocket.

"Everything all right, Sheriff?"

Nothing registered save that the voice was female.

"Lori Beth? Is that you?" he asked and breathed a silent prayer that she had listened to the heartfelt messages—at least six of them—he'd left on her parents' answering machine over the past day.

"This is Monica Drake," the woman told him. "From the Travis County Medical Examiner's Office. Did I wake you?"

The heat of humiliation flashed over him as he struggled to sit up. Too small to have its own medical examiner, Buck County contracted out the work to larger jurisdictions, whose personnel frequently treated him like an ignorant backwoods rube. And here he was, playing the part like some stock character from *Hee Haw*. "No—not at all. It's just—I was expecting another caller, that's all."

He glanced at the clock hung over the pass-through counter to the kitchen. It was already past nine—with Spencer and Claire Winslow both missing, he should damned well be back in his office.

"I've faxed my preliminary findings to your office, but your deputy Ashford suggested I call to let you know I've positively identified Adam Strickland from the dental records and that I've ruled his death as accidental."

Joel thanked his lucky stars that the indispensable Ashford and not his idiot cousin Earl had taken the call, or he wouldn't have gotten the news until he found it buried on his desk. Which could take days, considering the shape he'd allowed his office to get into.

"Accidental?" Joel wrenched his throbbing brain back on track. "Did he drown, then?"

"I can't be certain of that." The woman's accent

smacked of the snooty side of Boston. "He may have, after his fall, but due to the decomposition I can't be certain."

"You say he fell?" Joel's mind flashed through all the areas he and his deputies and volunteers had searched. "And there's no bullet?"

"I found no evidence of penetrating trauma. But to put it in plain English, there were a number of injuries that supported the conclusion of a fall from a significant height. A C2 fracture—a broken neck, that is—was what most likely killed him. Without immediate medical intervention, he would have died anyway, as the airway appears to have been compromised. But if he landed in the water, death would have been hastened."

Joel pictured the bluffs at the back side of the Winslow property, which had been deeply undermined by flooding these past few years. He recalled the broken rock lying near the shallow edge of the swimming hole there. Was it possible that Strickland had merely stepped in the wrong place at the wrong time, that Spence Winslow knew as little about the man's disappearance as he claimed?

"But he could've been pushed, right?" Joel asked her. "The injuries—they'd look the same."

He didn't miss the small huff of impatience, which she managed to infuse with pure Yankee condescension.

"City or country, you law enforcement types are all the same, always trying to shoehorn the facts to fit your theories," Dr. Drake said. "I see no evidence of defense wounds, but considering the condition of the body, I can't state absolutely that the victim wasn't pushed. All I can tell you is he landed badly. Now if you have any further questions . . ."

She rattled off a number that he didn't bother to write down. He could get it off of the report back in his office.

But he hadn't even made it to the kitchen cabinet for some aspirin when the phone rang once again.

This time, there was no mistaking the woman for his wife.

For one thing, unlike Lori Beth, Janine Jaworski was calling with good news.

"You don't have to worry about Claire Winslow," she was saying. "I heard from her this morning, and she just needed some time. Things have been a little crazy for her, which I'm sure you understand as well as anybody."

"So where is she?" he asked as he harvested a scrap of paper from the litter on his dresser. Had Lori Beth run off with every damned pencil in the house? Finally he found one of Tyler's fat Crayola markers. It was bloodred, the seven-year-old's favorite color.

"I'm not sure. She didn't want to tell me," Janine said. "She called me on my cell phone and asked me to let everybody know she's okay. I spoke to her dad already, and he said I should call you. Uh, actually, he said you'd better get your butt in gear and bring Claire home."

Joel would bet his next paycheck that Will Meador had used stronger language. By now he had doubtless worked himself into a state. Around midnight, his initial call had sounded almost sheepish, and after questioning him, Joel had determined that after his argument with Claire that morning, her father supposed she had gone off to stay with a friend. Though Joel was worried enough about Spence to make finding Claire a priority for the two deputies on duty last night, he had more than half believed she would turn up by morning. But this mysterious call concerned him—and made him kick himself for succumbing to exhaustion instead of going back to work.

"Was she alone, Ms. Jaworski?" he asked. "Did you hear any other voices?"

There was a pause while the woman thought it over. "No . . . I don't remember any background noises. But she told me something—I really shouldn't say this."

Joel skipped straight from good old boy to the fear-of-the-Lord voice he used to bring both witnesses and suspects to the light. "If her husband's taken her, she could be in serious trouble, Ms. Jaworski. And if I have reason to believe you're keeping things from me, I'll see you're charged with obstruction—or maybe accessory to kidnapping."

"Her—her husband?" Janine's voice trembled, and her reticence exploded like a failing dam. "She led me to believe she'd stepped out with a man, but do you really think it could be Spence? Oh, my God—then he might hurt her. He could kill her, even. I already feel bad enough about things—I was the one who introduced them.

"Here," she went on, "let me give you the phone number that she called from. I have it right here, on my caller ID. You can trace it, can't you? I saw that on TV once."

"We'll track her down, I guarantee it. I only hope we find her before things get any worse."

Claire stepped out of the shower first, feeling for the scratchy towel she'd used the night before.

"Watch your eyes." Passion misted her voice, but practicality had her reaching for the lights. They needed to get moving if they didn't want the maid returning to surprise them.

"Want your razor?" she asked.

"Sure," Spence managed. "Thanks."

Hearing his fatigue, she smiled before walking to the bed to get him one of the cheap disposables he'd dumped there.

She was half dressed, with Spence still in the shower, when she heard a quiet staccato rapping at the door. After pulling on her top, she peeked through the narrow gap between the curtain and the window frame and spotted the broad-hipped young woman who had brought the towels earlier. But this time she was glancing furtively over her shoulder, her face even pinker than before.

It was obvious she hadn't come to clean the room.

Claire's pulse quickened as she undid the cheap lock and cracked open the door. "Yes?"

The woman crossed her arms over her NASCAR T-shirt. "Todd—my old man—says I ought to keep my nose out of this. He said you were a stuck-up bitch last night. But I know how he can be, so . . . a little bit ago, he got a phone call asking if you were still here. Or some woman looking like you, anyhow. The fella calling, he wanted to hear about a man, too, maybe the one with you. Todd told what he knew, how you were with this guy—he gave your description and your truck's, too."

A chill raced down the column of Claire's neck, one not entirely explained by the realization that this poor young woman was married to the Hutt. "Who was it? Who called you?"

"Sheriff somebody—not one of the locals. But unless I miss my guess, he'll be sending some of our county boys to pick you up real soon."

Before she could stop herself, Claire flinched. "How long ago did he call?"

The woman pressed unpainted lips together. "Ten minutes, maybe. Something like that. I had to wait till Todd was in the can to run back out here. I think you and your man had better hurry."

Claire nodded. "Thank you so much. But—but why did you come?"

"I don't know—it's just, there was something in your face this morning, something that made me think of the way I used to feel." Her voice dropped to a whisper, and her broad face went even redder. "The way I used to hope that things would—but never mind that, you just get goin'."

Claire reached out to touch her forearm. "Bless you."

The woman darted another glance behind herself, her shoulders hunching forward in a way that hinted she was risking a slap—or worse—to bring this warning. But she looked up and flashed a smile nonetheless, her blue eyes glimmering with what might have been rebellion.

"Good luck," she told Claire, then hurried back toward the motel office, quick on her feet for a big woman.

Claire relocked the door before grabbing Spence's clothes and rushing to the bathroom, where the water had been shut off. As she opened the door, the contents of his pockets slid out, jingling as they struck the threshold.

Spence, a toothbrush in his mouth and a towel over his shoulder, shot her a curious look.

"Hurry up and get dressed," she told him as she bent

to scoop the keys and change off the floor. "We have to get out of here right now—cops are on the way."

He took the clothes and started to pull them on. "What happened?"

She shook her head. "I don't know, but the maid warned me—I think Joel's tracked us down."

Feeling an odd shape, she flicked a glance down at her palm—and saw the bracelet she had found two days before. Its unexpected presence set off a ripple of discord inside her, but she decided she could worry later about how it might have made its way into Spence's pocket.

Spence winced as his arm flexed, then more carefully pushed his head through the T-shirt's neck hole. "Maybe it was our truck. Someone must've seen it."

"If they're putting our license plate number and the pickup's description on the airwaves, they'll find us pretty fast," Claire said.

"We can take care of that, as long as we get out of here in time."

But as they climbed into the truck two minutes later, their first glimpse of flashing red lights warned them they were already too late.

TWENTY-THREE

Spence spotted the red-and-white lights through the branches of some junipers clustered near the road. The driver couldn't yet see them, but would in only seconds.

"Hurry," Claire urged, since this time he had jumped behind the wheel. She snapped her seat belt into place.

He hung a right—heading in the opposite direction from the cruiser. But he drove cautiously, keeping his speed moderate and avoiding the squeal of tires in the hope the deputy would first pull into the motel to check things out.

Besides, Spence had seen the results—and mangled victims—of high-speed chases too many times. As badly as he wanted to stay out of jail to help hunt down the son of a bitch who'd set him up, he wasn't risking his wife and unborn child to do it.

"Can't you go any faster?" Claire urged.

"Relax," he told her. "All I'd do by speeding off is encourage this guy to radio for assistance. And we sure as hell don't want that, do we?"

He turned right once more, onto a road that led them past small wood-frame houses and a "downtown" consisting of a combination gas station/grill/grocery store, a shop whose peeling sign read AUNTIE Q'S OBJETS D'JUNQUE, and an old grain elevator that hugged a railroad spur. To his immense relief, the flashing lights he'd half expected didn't materialize behind him. He only hoped the deputy hadn't caught sight of them as they had disappeared from view.

"Where are you going?" Claire asked.

"Seems to me there's another road up here somewhere—here it is." He turned left onto an unmarked road and immediately saw the land ahead open into farm country. Some kind of young plants had pushed through tilled soil in vast acres of straight rows, while cattle grazed close to a windmill on their right.

"If deputies come looking, they'll be expecting us to head straight over to the freeway instead of winding along back routes. Still have that Texas map in the glove box?"

She dug for it as he pulled over. "It's right here. But I guess you didn't understand my question. Where do we go from here? How can we look into anything while we're on the run?"

She folded the map to show the roads east of San Antonio, then handed it to him.

He hissed a breath out through his nostrils in a quiet sigh. She wasn't going to like what he had in mind. "First thing we have to do is ditch this truck. Otherwise we're dead in the water."

She blinked, her mouth tightening. They'd picked

out the new green Chevy two years ago, in the knowledge that she would need a larger vehicle to trailer
horses. After years of driving used compact cars, she
loved the four-wheel-drive gas guzzler's powerful engine and commanding view. "Ditch my truck?" she repeated. "Then how will we get around?"

He figured she'd like this idea even less, but there
was no help for it. "I know a guy who'll take care of it."

Her eyes narrowed. "A criminal?"

He shrugged in answer, not wanting to get into it.

"So you trust this person?" she asked.

Spence thought of how he'd looked the other way
on what would have been the car thief's third arrest in
order to get the goods on the ringleader of a chop
shop operation funneling parts from stolen vehicles
out of the country. He thought of the promise, "on the
life of *mi madre*, on the blood of *Cristo*," to repay his
generosity. Yet Spence shook his head. "Of course not.
Not enough to take you within a mile of him."

"I'm not going home until we come up with some
answers." Claire's voice was a strand of barbed wire,
surprisingly strong and with as many cutting edges.

"You're right," he said. "You're not. I'll need you to
help figure this out. And I'm going to need you to keep
me from—from slipping back into the wrong kind of
thinking."

And to remind me what I have to live for, he added
mentally.

"But I won't take you to my car man," he continued.
"It's too dangerous, for one thing, and you can't be an
accessory to— Never mind that. You'll just have to trust
me, Claire. I'm going to leave you somewhere safe and
public, but I'll come back for you. I promise."

He looked down at the map, half his mind scouting

an alternate route back to the city, the other half bracing for Claire to ask how he dared speak of trust.

"I don't want to be dropped off somewhere," she argued. "I don't think I can stand it."

Once again Spence felt the blade against his throat that morning, the gun's muzzle pressed hard into his temple. "You're going to have to—and I'm not arguing about it. These people, whoever's behind this—they've already used you once to get to me. If they see me with you, if they have any idea how much you mean to me . . ."

He gave her time to remember the threat against her, when he'd been conned into the money drop. She crossed her arms in front of her chest, then stared out at the Texas longhorns that glanced up as the truck rolled past them.

For the next ten minutes, they drove in silence, their anxiety thick as cotton batting in the space around them. But after a time, she asked, "You'll take my father's gun, right? For protection."

He shook his head. "It's gone. I'm sorry. A couple of bouncers got the jump on me this morning."

She sighed, then told him, "Hope they have better luck with it than I did."

"I hope they don't," he said. "You hit everything you aimed for, right?"

A smile leapt from one to the other, then disappeared before he could figure out which one of them had sparked it.

A moment later, her back arched as she snaked a hand into the front pocket of her blue jeans. When he glanced over, she was fingering the tarnished silver hearts of the bracelet in her hand. "Where did you find this?"

"Out in the cabin," he said. "Did you take it there?"

Out of the corner of his eye, he caught the movement of her nod. "Yeah, I came across it back at the house, stuffed in between some linens. I'd meant to ask my dad about it, but he was too busy trying to talk me into getting an abortion."

Spence's stomach dropped down to the floorboard. "He what? You wouldn't—?"

"Of course not, Spence. I swear to you, I'd never— don't even think about it."

"But how could he suggest—?"

"Because he loves me more than he loves his own life," she was quick to answer. "Because he doesn't want any reminders around to hurt me in the future, or any ties to— He just means to protect me, that's all. But he doesn't understand. He can't know that even if I went through with—with what he suggested, I couldn't forget you. Ever."

Spence should not have been surprised by the man's reaction, but it hurt nonetheless to think her father would want the new life torn from her, obliterated, so the two of them could pretend they'd never met a man named Spencer Winslow. He thought that if he ever got to be a dad, maybe he would someday comprehend Will Meador's desire to protect Claire. But at the moment, Spence's mood had curled and blackened like charred paper, and he couldn't imagine how he ever would forgive the man.

A conversation came back to him, the last real talk he'd had with his father-in-law.

"You know," Spence said, "I was the one who found that bracelet in the first place. Out near the bluff, back when I was poking around the caves last month."

"Why would you put it in the guest room cupboard?" Claire asked.

"Your father must've done that. He snatched it away from me as soon as I showed it to him. He thought it was your mother's, and I guess it was another one of those reminders he can't bear to have around." *Like my kid*. Though Spence tried to tamp down his bitterness, he failed miserably.

But Claire was shaking her head. "This doesn't look like my mom's. I might not remember her, but I have photos, and Dad gave me her jewelry after Karen died. He told me he was saving it to split between us, but he put it off too long. It's always been so hard for him.

"But what I was getting at," she continued as she fingered first one heart and then the next, "was Mom's stuff. You've seen me wear it once in a while when I dress up. She didn't have a lot of jewelry, but what she had was simple, classic. That gold necklace with the three pearls, for example, and those nice diamond posts. I can't picture her wearing jangly silver heart charms. I'd figured this was Karen's. I can't remember having one like—"

He heard her sharp intake of breath.

"What is it, Claire?"

"I think— Pull over, Spence. I need to get out and see this in the light."

Spence checked the mirrors, spotted no other cars, then did as she asked. He had barely stopped when Claire got out of the truck. He joined her and found her tilting one of the hearts in sunlight softly filtered by thin clouds.

"There," she said. "That's what I thought I saw."

Spence squinted at the spot where she was pointing.

235

He couldn't imagine how Claire had made it out before, but now that he looked at it, he saw it, too. A stylized capital G, barely discernable beneath the metal's grime and weathering.

"There's something else engraved here, too," she said. "An—is that an *L?*"

He pointed to another squiggle. "I think so—and here's an *H.* Claire, this wasn't Karen's or your mother's. This bracelet belonged to Gloria Hajek."

She looked up at him. "Then my dad must've been mistaken. He probably didn't look at it closely enough to see the markings—and you know he hardly ever wears his glasses."

"Maybe he did recognize it," Spence said, recalling how quickly Claire's father had snatched the thing away. The man had barely glanced at the bracelet before stuffing it inside his pocket.

"What are you trying to say?"

There was no mistaking the defensiveness in her tone. It was a sore point between them, that she had always been that way about her father. Once, on their way home from a day spent at her dad's place, Spence had complained that she and her father had excluded him from every conversation by steering their talk toward people and events he didn't know. Claire had thoughtlessly shot back that someone with no parents couldn't possibly understand—a remark that hurt Spence whenever he recalled it. But that was the way of marriages: the geologically slow accretion of little slights and the occasional wounding barb balanced alongside acts of kindness and moments of perfect understanding. Life with Claire had been heavily weighted on the plus side—until his emotional nose-dive, and some sick bastard's setup, had completely screwed it up.

Yet here she was beside him, an unexpected gift. If he meant to keep her there, he must tread carefully. "I'm not sure what I'm saying. I'm just remembering how quickly he seemed to want that bracelet out of sight."

"He obviously leapt to the wrong conclusion, that's all," Claire said. "When it comes to Karen and my mother, he's always been like that. Sometimes it drives me crazy, the way he shuts the conversation down when I mention some story about Karen and me when we were little, or ask him something simple, like how he met my mom."

"I know," Spence said as, by unspoken consent, the two of them climbed back inside the truck. On any number of occasions, he had witnessed her father's reticence about the wife and daughter he had lost. If Will Meador couldn't change the subject, he would simply excuse himself, his brown eyes clouding with such pain that Spence had once or twice pressed Claire to leave the poor man be.

Spence put the truck back into drive, and they started off again. In the distance, he saw that they were nearing a clutch of weathered buildings hunkered around an intersection with a Texas farm-to-market road. More of a town than the spot with the grain elevator, he decided, though this, too, appeared smaller than Little BC with its eleven hundred residents.

"Do you realize," Claire asked, "that nearly everything I know about my mother, I heard from Karen? She was about six at the time of the accident, poor thing. It was horrible for her, but at least she had some memories. You're lucky that way, Spence, that you were old enough to really remember both your parents."

Spence wasn't sure he'd count it as a blessing. As far as he knew, Claire wasn't plagued with nightmares about her mother's death, didn't dream of throwing herself before the fateful bullet. Yet when he thought about it, he knew he wouldn't trade away those hard nights. Not if, in doing so, he would have to forget his dad, a plumber who loved ice cream and told eye-rollingly lame jokes, and his mom, a plump blonde with an outsized laugh and an even bigger heart.

"I guess you're right," he told Claire, the tautness of his own voice taking him by surprise.

They passed the town and continued along a stretch of road lined with scrubby water-starved trees far smaller than those growing on their Hill Country property. In this flat region, the sky seemed to stretch into eternity, with the clouds queued up in strange rows that reminded him of the young crops they'd passed earlier.

As he drove, his mind played tricks on him, making him wonder if he was sleeping, dreaming in his cell at the Buck County lockup. Making him wonder how he could make this drive last the length and breadth of this immense sky so he would never have to part from the woman he loved again.

In a fraction of a second, both illusion and wish shattered with Claire's cry—and a white-and-blue flash streaking toward them from a spot just off the road, hidden behind a thin screen of mesquite trees. The patrol car had its lights on, and the siren whooped out a demand that they pull over.

But the interceptor hadn't yet reached asphalt, and one of its rear tires sent flying a rooster's tail of loose sand, which slowed the deputy for a few more precious seconds.

"Go, go, go," Claire urged him, but Spence was flooring it as it was. The truck, already traveling at highway speed, accelerated, its big engine roaring and the speedometer jumping up to seventy, then seventy-five, then eighty.

"Rookie mistake," Spence muttered, watching the deputy's car fishtail as its two left tires caught the asphalt. If Spence had been behind the wheel, he would have eased onto the hard surface before spooking the suspect with his lights and siren.

But he was happy to take advantage of the deputy's mistake, which would give him precious seconds to decide what he would do. To his surprise, Claire was already one step ahead of him, her finger moving over the road map as she read.

"Looks to me like there's gonna be a dirt road a couple of miles farther on the right," she said over the road noise and the faint sound of the siren, now several hundred yards behind them. "If we can make it that far, the car might not be able to hang with us."

Her idea had merit, since their high-clearance four-wheel-drive could easily handle the rutted cow tracks that often passed for unimproved roads. Such a route would also make it harder for other deputies from the department—assuming there was more than one car within range—to either intercept them or lay down spike strips to blow out their tires.

On the other hand, an isolated route could make it easier to spot them from the air. But since Spence's circuitous path had taken them into the rural—and famously underfunded—Sissel County, air support was unlikely and interdepartment cooperation rare, especially on short notice. If Claire was willing, he felt inclined to take the risk.

"You sure you don't want out of this?" he asked her.

In the rearview mirror, he saw their pursuit slipping farther behind—but not far enough for comfort. Could the deputy have backup here in time to cut them off?

"Don't even think you're leaving me on the side of this road like some unwanted puppy," Claire told him. "There's the turn already. Watch out, it's sharper than it looked on the ma—"

Her voice rose to a shriek when Spence took the dirt track—which veed into the road they were traveling—at far too great a speed. He fought to wrestle the Chevy around the angle, his arm screaming in pain but his attention focused on his own pursuit training. The pickup's rear end began sliding toward a ditch to his left, but in a split second, the big tires grabbed the rutted dirt, shooting out great gouts of earth behind them.

The truck swerved slightly, then jounced along. Sweat poured off Spence, rolling down his back and stinging his eyes.

"You okay?" he asked Claire.

Nodding, she turned to look behind them. "He's going to try to follow. Spence—he's not gonna make it."

Sure enough, when Spence glanced in the mirror, the interceptor's left wheels dropped into the ditch, and the car rolled once, then twice in a moment that seemed to stretch into eternity—like an obscene parody of the timeless sky above.

TWENTY-FOUR

Hot tears blurred Claire's vision by the time the Sissel County patrol car came to rest, lying on its partially collapsed roof with its tires spinning to a stop. She cried out at the sight of smoke, then quickly realized the rising cloud was merely dust kicked up by the sedan's roll.

Yet even without fire, things were bad enough.

Spence had thrown the truck into reverse and was backing quickly toward it, saying, "I never should've tried to run. Never should've risked anybody's safety. Jesus."

The deputy was crawling out the window, talking into a radio transmitter held in a clearly female hand. Her tawny hair had fallen loose, and the broad-brimmed hat Claire had spotted earlier was missing, but otherwise the woman looked unharmed.

Seeing them, the deputy pulled herself free of the car, and started reaching—eyes wide with panic—for the gun still in her holster.

As she drew on them, Spence hit the gas once more.

Claire's head swiveled just in time to see the muzzle flash in their wake. At what seemed like the same moment, there was a splintering crack, and Spence shouted, "Get down, get down," his hand pushing at her and the truck jerking as it took another bump.

She folded forward, her forehead grazing the dashboard. But within a minute, Spence said, "It's okay, Claire. You can sit up now."

"What was that—" Claire was stopped by the sight of a hole in the headliner between them, just above the windshield. Turning, she saw what could only be a bullet hole, surrounded by a spider's web of cracks, in the center of the back glass. "She tried to *kill* us. Why on earth would—"

"She was scared to death—didn't you see her face?" Spence asked. "I think she was afraid we were coming back to hurt her."

"But we wanted to help her."

"Did you see how young she was? She probably didn't have the experience she needed to—aw, hell, I hope the poor kid's all right."

Claire couldn't stop staring at the hole in the headliner. How many inches had there been between the bullet's path and her head, or Spence's, for that matter? She swallowed hard, then forced words past the tight knot in her throat. "She looked pretty damned healthy when she was pointing that gun at us. She'll be fine until her friends get here. But what about us? Will we be blamed for her wreck now, too?"

The truck rolled along, occasionally shuddering over rough spots.

"I was the one who chose to run," Spence said. "You warned me not to—you told me someone could get hurt, but I wouldn't listen."

"What are you talking about?" she demanded. "I'm the one who kept telling you to hurry."

He shook his head. "I'm already in a shitload of trouble. Let's keep the blame off you. One of us needs to be around to raise that baby."

Though she took his meaning, she refused to accept it. "We're going to get this all fixed. You're going to be there holding my hand and putting up with my shrieking when this baby's born. And you're going to be around to change your share of diapers. I'm saving all the poopy ones for you."

A smile tugged at his mouth, and he faked a shudder. "Maybe prison wouldn't be so terrible after all."

She laughed in response, though part of her wondered what on earth was wrong with them that they could find anything remotely funny in their situation. Maybe it was the relief cascading through her system. Relief to find she hadn't imagined what the two of them had, that she hadn't been a fool to love this man. Or maybe it was giddiness that they had escaped both capture and a bullet. Compared to that miracle, a future didn't seem such a hard thing to believe in.

At least it didn't until Spence said, "Let's hope this county's interdepartment communication is as crummy as I've always heard. Otherwise we can expect more company any minute."

Yet in spite of his concern, they reached the outskirts of San Antonio within the hour. To Claire's immense relief, they hadn't seen a single law enforcement vehicle by the time they joined the flow of traffic along secondary roads.

Spence drove them past subdivisions crowded with newer, beautifully landscaped two-stories, banks of upscale condos and apartments, and any number of businesses that catered to their inhabitants. On opposite corners, two chain drugstores vied for supremacy. Shoppers pushed loaded baskets around the parking lot of a discount shopping center, and gas station marquees advertised eye-popping prices with evident pride. Despite their recent crises, Claire decided it was good to see that in this corner of the city, life went on as usual.

But her relief died when Spence pulled into a grocery store parking lot behind a stop for VIA, San Antonio's bus system.

"What are you doing?" she asked, though the knot of fear inside her guessed already.

He claimed a space three rows deep in the lot.

"You'll need to take the bus to the central library on Soledad," Spence said. "You know, the big red building? Remember, we went there before when you were looking up stuff for your refresher course."

She knew perfectly well where the main library was located, but that wasn't her concern. "I thought we'd settled this earlier. I'm with you, Spence. All the way. Please don't shut me out again."

His head shook, and he frowned. "There's a difference between shutting you out and risking your life. I told you before, I won't take you where I have to go now. And I meant it."

"But Spence—"

He touched the bullet hole above them. "You think this is some game, Claire? You think that deputy was playing, or other cops will be if they catch up with me again?"

"She never should have fired. There was no reason—"

"In the heat of the moment, things get crazy."

"You're defending her? She might've killed us."

"I'm not defending anything. I'm just trying to make you understand that when you're running, people get hurt. And I couldn't live with myself if you—" His head drooped forward, and the strength seemed to drain out of him. "I'm taking enough of a chance being with you at all, a bigger gamble than any of the eight-liners in Joe Reno's or the lamest of the horses at Retama. But I will come back, Claire. I'll meet you at the library before it closes."

Claire's stomach tightened, and she fought back tears. "You don't know what it is, waiting. Listening to all the voices unravel everything you've told me, saying you won't be back—that I have to figure out how to live some kind of life without you."

He picked up her hand and used his thumb to stroke the skin across her knuckles as his gaze held hers. "Whose voices, Claire? Joel Shepherd's? Your father's? You ever stop to think that they might have their own agendas?"

She jerked her hand free. "*Everyone* tells me those things—how I'm still young, I can start over, how I should keep busy to forget. But I was talking about the voices in my own head, the ones I can't walk away from."

He ran his fingertips along her jawline. "Were they right before? Haven't I come back for you twice already? And as long as I'm still breathing, I promise I'll keep coming back to you."

She leaned forward as if to kiss him, but stopped a hairs breadth from his lips. "I'm trusting you," she murmured, returning an echo of the words he had given her the night before. "With my life."

Their kiss, too, was a whisper, a ghost of kisses past

and a promise of those that would sustain them through the future.

They had barely finished when she opened her eyes to ask him, "How long will you be?"

"I can't say for certain. It could take a while to find this—this friend of mine. He doesn't exactly have a fixed address."

"What if it you're not back before the library closes?"

"If I'm delayed past dark, I want you to call someone, get a ride back to your father's. Report the truck as stolen, and I'll meet you on the property as soon as I can. You can meet me later, after it's dark."

"Will you go back to the cabin?"

"If it's safe enough. Otherwise check for a message in the cave behind a fallen cedar, but be really careful around that bluff, okay?"

"So what am I supposed to do in the library?"

From some unimagined reservoir, Spence dredged up a smartass smile. "You're always complaining about how you can't find time to read the new bestsellers."

When she shot him The Look, he sobered quickly. "Why not put their public-access computers to good use? See what you can dredge up on Randall Hajek. Maybe there's something that can help us."

"And I'll look up that realtor woman Lenore talked about, too. What was her name? Marjorie something-Phillips, I think. Bet I can get a number online, then use one of the library pay phones to give her a call. Maybe she'll know something we can use."

She dug into the glove box until she found her spare change hoard. Dumping the quarters into her hand, she said, "Hope that wasn't your lunch money."

He smiled. "I'll be fine. Do you have enough to grab a bite to eat later?"

She nodded. "I'll manage."

"Where should I look for you?" he asked.

She took his point. San Antonio's Central Library was enormous, with at least five stories, maybe more.

"Gosh, I don't know. If I'm not at the computers or the phones, why don't you check for me in the genealogy section. I think it's on the top floor, and it's usually pretty quiet."

His forehead crinkling, he hesitated a moment before asking, "Isn't that where they keep the microfilmed copies of old newspapers? Or is it microfiche? I can never remember."

She shook her head. "I don't know, Spence. Why?"

"Because I was thinking that while you're there, you might as well look up any news accounts you can find about—"

"You mean articles on Randall? Or a planned golf course development?"

"Neither of those are bad ideas, but that's not what I had in mind."

"What, then?" Claire asked him.

His blue eyes looked as grim as a funeral procession. "I was thinking of much older stories, ones that might mention Gloria Hajek's disappearance . . . and your mother's death."

TWENTY-FIVE

As Spence drove, he was so distracted that he sailed straight past an SAPD patrol car. It was only dumb luck that the cruiser was parked and the officer absent, perhaps inside the nearby Mexican restaurant on either a lunch break or a call.

Spence let his lapse serve as a warning. He had to keep his mind on finding Skel instead of allowing his thoughts to drift back to the way Claire's face had iced over when he'd brought up her mother.

"Why bother worrying about all that? What could it possibly have to do with anything? It's been almost twenty-eight years."

He thought of the rivers that drained the Hill Country, the Colorado snaking through the Grand Canyon, and all the places he'd explored and read about in college. In every one of them, the modern flow of wind and water had been shaped by ancient forces. In his experience, people weren't much different. Every shooting he had responded to on duty, each domestic call or neighborhood squabble had its larger context. Unless someone dealt with the root cause—a rare luxury in law enforcement—the problem would never really go away.

But instead of saying that to Claire, he'd asked, "If it's not important, why is it such a big deal to read the articles? What exactly is it you're afraid that you'll find out?"

She hadn't responded. Instead she'd glanced out through the truck's window and announced that her bus was coming and she had to go. She'd kissed him on the cheek in a distracted, offhand way, and then she'd left without another word.

He'd watched her for a long time, even after the bus pulled away with her in it. But she never had glanced back once to see him looking.

It took Claire a long time to settle into her work at the library computer. Her skin felt two sizes too small to hold the impulses jittering through her, and every time she laid her hands across the keyboard, images burst out like mice darting from dark spaces.

She saw Doc Rachel in her trailer, picking at the scabs that marred her arms; heard the crying of an infant born to squalor and addiction. Watched the sheriff's department car come shooting toward them, its siren howling furiously, and stared in horror as it rolled, clouds of dust billowing around it.

Claire had a vision of herself poking her fingers into the tunnels bored by bullets. First the one on Coyote's forehead, then the one she'd put in Spence's arm, and finally that bloodless one that had passed through the back window of the pickup and into the headliner between the two of them.

A ragged gasp pulled her into the present. It was the broken sound of her own long inhalation, what could only be the prelude to a round of tears.

She bit down on the inside of her lip hard enough to taste blood, and let the pain wash away emotions. Later there would be time enough to deal with what she had been through and time enough to wonder why Spence's suggestion had upset her, but there was only now to do something that might help put her family back together.

Her fingers fluttered into wakefulness, typing Randall Hajek's name into the search engine. Immediately she hit on a link that took her to a Houston realty site that still listed Randall as an agent. His self-aggrandizing personal page boasted of his ten years of experience serving "Houston's finest families" alongside such honors as "Top Producer in Memorial Area," "Named by *Texas Monthly* as 'Super Agent,'" and any number of awards that Claire suspected might be store-bought. Hardest to believe was his photograph, which showed him suited, smiling—something she hadn't seen in recent memory—and at least fifty pounds heavier than when he had arrived in Little BC for his aunt's funeral.

Come to think of it, Randall had looked thinner still when she had caught him with the can of spray paint—had it only been last night? She thought about his skinny white legs, the puffiness of his face, his unfocused gaze, which seemed so at odds with the angry words he had been hurling.

At the time she suspected he'd been drinking, but now she wondered, Could the man be sick instead?

She grabbed one of the scraps of paper and a stubby pencil she had found beside the computer and

jotted down the phone number of the realty outfit.
Once she had it noted, she hit the browser's "back"
button to return to the listings of Web sites containing
Randall's name.

She found a handful. A couple concerned another
Randall Hajek, a Ford dealer who lived in California,
and the rest took her to various online listings of Houston real estate agents.

Claire frowned. She had been hoping to find something more interesting: perhaps a news article linking
Randall to some misconduct—or better yet, a notice
stating that his real estate license had been yanked.

Next she tried typing in "Marjorie Trent-Phillips." The
name gave her many more hits than Randall's. Aside
from a Web page trumpeting her countless awards,
personalized service, and "unsurpassed knowledge of
San Antonio's luxury market," numerous online articles referenced Trent-Phillips's involvement with chari-
table endeavors funded by the wealthy. Her name
popped up on both the donors' and organizers' rosters
of various events, and Claire found her listed among
the city's best dressed.

It was a fitting honor, Claire decided when she
looked at a photo, for the trim blonde was the very
picture of well-heeled elegance. Though she appeared to be in her thirties, Claire suspected she was
a couple of decades older. Behind the outsized,
vaguely equine smile, her face had the tight air-
brushed perfection of a woman who had spent a fortune and suffered heaven only knew what torments to
turn back the hands of time.

The more she read about Trent-Phillips, the more
Claire realized she wasn't about to find any dirt on San
Antonio's self-proclaimed "Realtor to the Stars" in a

simple Internet search. If Trent-Phillips was into anything questionable, she would have the good sense—
and the pull—to bury it so deep that it would take a
squadron of kamikaze reporters to unearth it.

Claire was beginning to wonder if Lenore had simply gotten her wires crossed about the planned location of the new development. After copying the phone
number of Trent-Phillips's real estate agency, she decided that the only place to go for answers was straight
to the horse's mouth.

Spence expected trouble tracking down Skel—short
for "Skeleton Key," in honor of his proficiency in
hotwiring vehicles. Like the clandestine operations
that employed him, the car thief moved around a lot,
and he was always looking warily over his shoulder. In
the past, Spence had been able to locate him through
his woman, a part-time stripper and full-time prostitute
who went by the name of Betty Blue.

But the tiny crinkled woman standing behind the
chained door of Betty's apartment peered at Spence
through the three-inch gap, clutched a stained, equally
wrinkled robe at her neck, and started screeching,
"That whore daughter of mine's in jail, so don't you
think you're getting no sugar from me, by Jesus. I've
had enough 'a men slobberin' all over my beanbags to
last me three dozen lifetimes."

She gestured toward a pair of breasts that had mi-
grated past her waistline. Even as the door slammed in
his face, Spence shuddered and muttered, "Courage,"
before pounding once again.

It didn't do him much good. From the opposite side
of the locked door, the old lady hurled obscenities.

Unfortunately she was too deaf to hear any of his attempted explanations.

Spence tried two other known associates before a burn-scarred black kid by the street name of Mask gave him an address that supposedly belonged to Skel's mother. "He stayin' there while his old lady's in the joint. 'Til he get him some new bitch, anyways."

Such was the romance of the streets.

It took Spence another half hour to track the place down, a peeling yellow bungalow in a crowded South Side neighborhood. Instead of parking immediately, he circled the block, his gaze touching on the shadowy porches, the numerous parked cars—many of them junkers—and a jumble of little kids, white, brown, and black, out playing, though on a Monday in mid-April he would expect them to be in school.

Must be a teachers' conference day or one of those minor holidays he had trouble keeping up with. Whatever the case, he hadn't spotted any faces that gave him cause for concern. But it wasn't even noon yet. The neighborhood troublemakers—Skel included— were probably fast asleep.

Spence pulled into the driveway behind a van with rust holes the size of dinner plates. It was parked in front of a doorless detached garage piled so high with refuse, there could have been another car hidden underneath the mess. He walked toward the side door in the hope that Skel's mother might take him for a friend and not a cop.

But he didn't make it three steps before trouble stepped out from behind the shrubbery. Trouble with a face he knew—and a hand that pointed a Smith & Wesson at the center of his chest.

* * *

According to the woman's assistant, Marjorie Trent-Phillips was out doing a market analysis when Claire first called her office. Instead of leaving a message, Claire decided to phone Randall's former real estate office instead.

Before dialing, she walked around the Blue Room at the entrance to the library. Coolly beautiful, its neon artwork soothed her jumbled thoughts until she was able to cobble together a story that might get her the information she needed.

A few minutes later she was on the phone again.

"Marlton-Davis Real Estate Associates, where we match quality people with quality properties. Amber Rowling speaking. How may I be of assistance?"

The receptionist had the silken Southern hostess routine down pat, but Claire detected a note of boredom, one she hoped to use.

"Hi, Amber," she said cheerfully. "I'm calling for Randy Hajek. Could you tell him this is Mary Higgenbottom, from the class reunion committee?"

It made Claire want to gag to call Randall "Randy," but she thought it might add a convincing touch.

"I'm really sorry," the receptionist replied, "but Mr. Hajek's no longer with Marlton-Davis."

"Oh, poo," Claire said. "I reeeealllly need to get those invitations from him. He promised to have them to me three weeks ago. Me and Rhonda and Wanda—we're the mail-out posse—absolutely *have* to get them posted by . . ."

Rhonda and Wanda? What was she thinking, to make up rhyming names? And Higgenbottom? Claire winced, thinking how lame her story sounded.

But Amber didn't seem to notice. "I'm really sorry,

Miss Higgenbottom. I wish I could give you his home number, but we're absolutely not allowed to—" Her voice dropped to a whisper. "But you might try the Buck County residential pages."

"Oh." Claire feigned surprise. "He didn't tell us he was moving back here. I can't imagine why not."

Still whispering, the receptionist said, "You're aware of his illness, right?"

Aha, Claire thought.

"His . . . illness? Oh, my," she started, then dropped her own voice to levels favored by gossips and conspirators. "It's not—well, I know he has a special *friend*, not that I'm one to judge. But it's not AIDS, is it?"

"That's what we all thought around here, too, at first," Amber said, "when he was losing so much weight. But it turns out it's cancer, poor man. It started in his colon, I think, but it's gone and spread all over—even in his bones."

"Oh, no." Claire might be lying about everything else, but her dismay was genuine. She wouldn't wish such a thing on anybody, turd or not. "Then Randy's . . . dying?"

"I'm afraid so."

Randall's appearance made more sense now. The puffy face, the lack of focus, even his bizarre behavior. If he was taking heavy-duty pain meds, no wonder he'd acted as if he had been drinking.

"I'd feel awful, bothering him about a couple hundred invitations when he's so very ill."

"Why don't you call Giovanni, then?" asked Amber. "He's turned into a regular guardian angel, taking care of all of Randall's business. I think he even has power of attorney."

"Giovanni . . ." Claire couldn't recall the man's last

name for the life of her, but she could clearly see him. Tall, blond, muscular. Of a size and shape that precisely matched her memory of the man who had run into her in the woods near the creek.

"Giovanni Baptiste," Amber provided helpfully. "And let me give you that phone number, while everyone here's out to lunch."

"That would be great. Thanks, Amber."

"No problem. I was on my high school class reunion committee just last year—our fifteenth. I know how tough it can be trying to pull together these things."

Claire was shaking with excitement as she hung up the telephone. She couldn't wait to tell Spence about Giovanni and his power of attorney—a document that would allow him to make real estate decisions.

But in spite of her elation, worry pinched inside her. Shouldn't Spence have come by now?

She checked her watch, but knowing he'd been gone for an hour and a half was no help whatsoever. He had told her it might take time to find this person he hoped would help him. How much time, he couldn't say, but he had sworn he would come back.

So why, then, was apprehension crowding into her chest and making it so hard for her to breathe? Why couldn't she get past the terrible suspicion that he needed her with him right now?

TWENTY-SIX

Spence forced himself to breathe as he took in the hard gaze of a man he'd once called his friend.

"For what it's worth, I'm sorry," he told his former sergeant. "I know I put you in an awkward spot, maybe caused you a lot of trouble with the job, too."

Though Raul Contreras held his service weapon on Spence, he was wearing jeans and an old Spurs T-shirt. The lack of uniform could mean he hadn't come here to arrest Spence, that he wasn't here officially at all. Yet that was hardly cause for celebration, since Raul looked pissed enough to pistol-whip him into intensive care—or perforate him with the Smith & Wesson. At the thought of taking another bullet, Spence felt his stomach drop into his shoes.

"Get the fuck inside the car." With his pistol, the sergeant gestured toward a dented blue Taurus parked in front of the bungalow.

"But I can't leave my truck here," Spence said, though he had come with the intention of getting rid of it.

257

"Just shut up and get inside." Raul hid the gun behind his back as a pair of little Hispanic girls rode past on a single bicycle with pink streamers flowing from its handles. A stream of giggles glistened like soap bubbles in their wake.

Spence thought of using the distraction to make a run, but he couldn't chance it. Not with all these children playing on the street. Instead he climbed into the passenger side of the old Ford before Raul could slap on the cuffs he'd taken out.

Noticing his old friend's hesitation, Spence leaned back against the velour headrest and closed his eyes, allowing weariness to wash over him. Apparently Raul took his movement as acquiescence, for he got into the driver's seat and started up the car.

"So what happened to the Datsun?" Spence asked.

"What the hell do you care?" Raul shifted into drive and pulled onto the street.

After opening his eyes, Spence tried a second question. "How'd you find me?"

"Clutch and the alternator both went out—after your gas station buddy soaked me for a tire. Anyway, that piece of shit is history," Raul said of his last car.

The sergeant's death grip on the steering wheel and the perspiration gleaming at his temple warned Spence to hold his tongue. Whatever Contreras needed to work out, Spence sensed that any attempt at persuasion was doomed to backfire.

As they wound through the older residential area, something at last unlocked the sergeant's jaw to answer Spence's second question. "I followed you from Betty Blue's place. Figured you might come looking for Skel. And that's the last question I'm answering until you tell me what the hell you've done with Claire."

At the harshness in Raul's voice, Spence opened his eyes. "I told you, I'd never hurt her. She's at the Central Library, the one over on Soledad. You want to come and see her with me? She's fine, Raul. I swear it. We'll both talk to her."

Would Raul believe him? In the lull that followed, Spence sensed his entire future balancing on a knife's edge.

"Yeah?" The sergeant's voice—and the obvious relief in his sigh—formed twin chinks in the brick wall of his anger.

Room enough for hope, Spence thought. "She just found out she's pregnant. Can you beat that? I'm going to be a dad."

He struggled to tamp down a smile, unsuccessfully. Every time he thought of it, a shot of optimism— wildly unfounded—streaked like a meteor across his darkness.

The jutting salt-and-pepper brows rose. "No kidding?"

This time there was no mistaking the friendly note that had crept into Raul's voice. Spence wasn't certain what he'd said to change the man's mind, but given his run of bad luck, he wasn't about to look a gift horse in the mouth.

Instead he nodded. "No kidding."

"That's good news, then, right?" Raul asked as a wry smile tugged at his mouth. "You look like the goddamn cat that swallowed the canary."

Spence shook his head. "Stupid, huh? But yeah, I'm glad about it. I'll be happier still if I can figure out who set me up."

He held his breath, bracing himself for Contreras to scoff at the suggestion. When it didn't happen, Spence thought, *the hell with it*, and dropped the macho suffer-in-silence act that had already cost him so much. "Maybe it's too late, but I want my life back. I want it worse than I've ever wanted anything. You and Claire—and even that damned department shrink— were right. After Dave and—and the kid got killed, I went a little crazy, did whatever I could think of to punish myself for living through it. And it wasn't just that. Dave's death brought back other memories, from when my mom and dad died and I didn't. It was too much, surviving twice by dumb luck. I just couldn't see how I deserved to live when—when they didn't."

Raul was quiet for so long that Spence felt humiliation searing his face. Did the sergeant see him as just another loser with a sob story excuse?

But when Contreras finally spoke, his voice was somber. "I—uh—I don't know where you stand on God and the universe and all that, but did you ever think that maybe you were spared for a reason? That maybe you have stuff you're supposed to do on this earth?"

"Like blowing every dime I could borrow and screwing up Claire's life? Like wrecking my career and getting some nutcase so pissed, he'd try to ruin me?" Try though he might, Spence couldn't keep the bitterness from his voice. "You figure that's what the Almighty had in mind for me?"

"You want to think like that, I might as well run your ass straight to jail now. Seriously, Winslow, what if you're here instead to take care of that little one and make a decent husband for your wife?"

"Claire deserves better, but if there's any way of coming back from this, any possibility of making it up to her, I'll spend a lifetime—two lifetimes, if that's what it takes." Spence cut himself short. He could scarcely believe he was having this conversation with Contreras, who, like most every cop Spence had known, was about as in touch with his feelings as the average cholla cactus.

As they left the neighborhood, the sergeant had to stop the car to wait out the passage of a freight train. As the cars rattled by, he gestured toward the bulky bandage on Spence's arm. "What happened there?"

"A bullet."

Raul's forehead creased. "Who did it? Who the hell shot you?"

Spence wasn't entirely surprised by the vehemence in his voice. Contreras had always been protective of the men and women on his shift.

"Never mind," Spence said. "It was an accident, and I'll be all right." The damned thing still throbbed, but he felt far better than he had yesterday.

The bushy eyebrows rose once more as Raul guessed, "Claire? *Claire* shot you?"

"Now, if I were to answer that for the record, I'd have to say it was a drive-by."

"Aw, hell, Winslow. You must've figured by now this has nothing to do with the job. I—uh—I filled out the paperwork already. I'm retiring from the force."

"Was it because of me?" Spence asked. Had he wrecked two careers? "Did the lieutenant think you let me—?"

His head shaking, Raul said, "Screw that asswipe and screw Internal Affairs, too, for that matter. If they'd done right by you in the first place, investigated the way they should have—but never mind that."

Raul shrugged before continuing. "This has been coming for a long time. I got a buddy, Mark Lyons, who's been talking to me about some security consulting firm he's setting up. Not a rent-a-cop deal, but something where he'll send out experienced guys to analyze companies' security needs. Helps 'em reduce their liability and keep their employees, tenants, and customers safer. He's looking for a couple of partners to help get the whole thing off the ground. It'll be a risk—I'll have to cash in part of my retirement funds to do it—but I've gone over the numbers, and I think it looks rock solid."

"Sounds pretty plush, Sarge," Spence said, though he still suspected his own problems had hastened Contreras's departure.

At the very least, he owed the man the truth. "It *was* Claire who shot me, but it really was an accident. I surprised her out at the ranch—stepped out of some trees and scared her half to death."

Raul's dark eyes blinked. "No shit? I never would've thought she had it in her. She responsible for the scratches, too?"

After Spence shook his head, Raul said, "Even if she did, it's nothing more than you deserve after what you've put her through."

Spence couldn't argue. "And I got the bullet taken care of, so it really will be fine."

Head shaking, Raul held up a palm. "I don't even want to know how you managed that without the doctor filing a report."

"Okay, so I won't tell you," Spence said, understanding that officially Raul couldn't know. "But I was wondering, did you happen to hear anything about a child welfare call over in the old mobile home recycling center near I-35?"

"Infant taken into custody by Child Protective Services?" Raul asked carefully. "Yeah, I heard something about it. Kid was in good shape, considering the circumstances. Now that the system's got a bead on him, they'll make sure he's taken care of."

Spence wondered if Doc Rachel would even try to get him back, or if she would add her child to the mounting costs of her addiction.

The final train cars slipped past, and the railroad-crossing arms rose.

As Raul continued driving, he said, "I guess you and Claire worked things out, from what you said a minute ago."

"I'm not sure. I thought so, after we talked. I gave her plenty of chances, but she didn't walk away. She swears she means to figure out who faked the evidence against me."

"So what's she doing at the library?"

Spence smiled. "Mainly staying away from quality citizens like Skel and Betty Blue. But she's looking up stuff, too. There's this neighbor out at the ranch who's made some threats against us—"

"That'd be Randall Hajek, right?"

Spence let the question sink in before asking, "You've been looking into this on your own, haven't you? Tell me, what have you found out?"

They had passed some invisible boundary and entered a strictly Hispanic neighborhood. Signs were in Spanish, including those advertising an herb shop, a *panadería*—a Mexican bakery—and a farmer's market, which was closed today.

"Hajek has a lover with a history. One Vincenti 'Vinnie' Scarlatti, alias Giorgio Delmonico, alias Theodore DiSantos, alias Giovanni Baptiste. Hard to believe it with a face like his, but Pretty Boy's a two-time loser.

He's done time for fraud, extortion, and embezzlement, all crimes against older, wealthier men he was involved with."

"They screwed him, he screwed them," Spence mused, remembering the twitchy blond Adonis with his affected accent and his clove cigarettes.

"You've got the idea."

As he looked at his sergeant, Spence shook his head. "I'm surprised you checked into it. I thought—I was sure you'd written me off."

Raul gave a terse nod. "I'm sorry, man. You're right. At first, I did think you'd—well, forget it. But when you talked to me about Claire, I heard something in your voice. The more I thought about it, the more I understood it for something so real—hell, maybe Carla didn't suck the last drop of romance out of my veins after all."

Rumor had it that Raul had caught his then-wife in bed and sliding down a firefighter's pole one day after lunch, when the sergeant had gone home with what turned out to be food poisoning. Snippets of the story had leaked out around the station, but no one—Spence included—had ever had the guts to ask for details.

"I need you to know," Raul said, "I had to report it when you took off on me. I couldn't—couldn't be absolutely sure you wouldn't light out after Claire and do something crazy. I mean, you've done some screwed-up stuff of late, and—"

"Point taken," Spence said. "I understand—and I'm grateful you're here now."

"So what's the deal with Baptiste—or Scarlatti?" Spence asked. "You think he's helping Hajek try to run us off?"

"Hajek turns up clean, so I'd guess the boy toy might be running an end play around him somehow. That would certainly fit his MO."

Spence thought about it, but he still couldn't make the pieces fit. A stranger to Buck County, Baptiste couldn't have gotten far on his own. "There's been a lot of vandalism at the property. Cut fences, a wrecked ATV, that sort of thing. And a friend of Claire's told her something to indicate there's a big-money golf course development in the planning stages that might just involve the ranch.

"Still," he continued, "I can see this Giovanni possibly trying to push Claire into selling out cheap, but that doesn't explain how the hell he could have gotten hold of my laptop. Maybe—maybe someone got into Claire's dad's house the last time we stayed over, while we were working on the fences. He never locks the place up. But there's still the audiotape to think about. It was my voice, all right, but like I told my lawyer, the words were all taken out of context, as if somebody edited a bunch of recordings."

"I suppose somebody could've planted bugs." As they passed a run-down elementary school, Raul frowned. "Yet the Buck County DA's office claims the tape was recorded by someone from the sheriff's department."

"You've talked to the DA?"

Raul's smile was both tight and fleeting. "I'm sort of seeing this woman whose sister's a secretary there."

"Quite a coincidence," Spence mused.

Raul laughed. "Not exactly, but she's a nice gal all the same. Teaching me to line dance, if you can believe it."

"This I've gotta see."

"Back to the e-mails and the tapes, Spence. You

know as well as I do, anything is possible when enough money changes hands. With evidence tampering and the possibility of the Podunk Patrol's involvement—" Raul had a city cop's disdain for the rural Buck County's sheriff's department—"this business stinks of organized crime."

"Organized crime? In Little BC?" In spite of his earlier suspicions involving *El Tiburón*, Spence couldn't wrap his brain around the concept. Could a *Godfather*-like conspiracy really take place in a community dominated by wool production, goat ranching, and the occasional bed-and-breakfast? "How are we going to convince the state police, the Texas Rangers, or any outside agency it's possible?"

"I might be retiring, but I can still access SAPD's computers," Raul told him. "Could be I'll turn up something that would interest any number of law enforcement agencies."

"Like what?" Spence asked. "What is it you hope for?"

Looking away from the road, Raul shrugged, a smile pulling at the corner of his mouth. "I think it's altogether possible that behind his elegant Italian name, we'll find that pretty Vinnie Scarlatti has an ugly Sicilian family."

TWENTY-SEVEN

Few people consciously set out to do evil. Ask almost anyone in prison, and you'll hear of fine, often downright altruistic motives. Money to pay for groceries. A decent car to drive to work. A fresh start in a new city, in a neighborhood where children can feel safe playing on a front lawn beneath the sheltering arms of huge grandfather oak trees.

So it was that the man who paid an acquaintance to discreetly procure some explosives figured that he was really doing a good deed. Sure, he might be solving his own problems, but by bringing down an unstable bluff along the banks of Little Bee Creek, wasn't he in fact destroying a known danger? After all, look at what had happened to that poor biologist, killed when a section of the honeycombed rock gave way beneath his feet.

The man with the dynamite—purchased from one who had a friend who had another friend who knew the disgruntled employee of a quarry almost a hundred miles distant—wouldn't want that to happen to any of the people who would soon be flocking to

Monarch Ranch. He thought about the families and especially the children, who would be everywhere, walking, running, or wheeling over the whole property. Exploring, as kids would. Poking into all sorts of secrets that were none of their business.

Secrets that could hurt or maim or even kill. Secrets that must be sealed away forever, not only for the good of all involved, but to keep safe the innocent.

Yes, he thought as he rechecked the detonator caps and the wiring as he'd been shown, then put fresh batteries inside the cheap alarm clock and set it for exactly midnight. Tucking it reverently beside the dusty blue tarp–covered bundle, he told himself he wasn't blowing up the bluffs, along with the caves holding his secret, for strictly selfish reasons.

He was doing it for the children, for all the children who would suffer otherwise.

When Claire finally reached the "realtor to the stars," Marjorie Trent-Phillips was all that is gracious—for the first two minutes, anyway. But as soon as she determined that her caller wasn't interested in buying or listing an upscale property, she slipped out of her Southern gentility like a rattlesnake casting off a borrowed skin. And when Claire asked about the Little BC golf course development Lenore had mentioned, the woman's fangs came out.

"I don't know who you think you're playing, sister," Trent-Phillips fairly hissed, "but I don't give out information on my clients or my pending deals—particularly to some random nobody calling from a pay phone."

"I'm not some nobody," Claire shot back. "I'm the *somebody* who owns the—"

"Please. The only reason I answered at all is to keep you from hounding my assistant, calling here all afternoon."

"But I *own* Monarch Ranch."

"Big fucking deal," the realtor shot back. "I own a condo in Hawaii, a big house on Cape Cod, and more San Antonio properties than you can shake a stick at. Now don't bother me again."

Claire winced, then rubbed her ear after the woman slammed her phone down in its cradle. Was Trent-Phillips really only angry because of Claire's repeated calls? Or did Monarch Ranch mean something to her, something she did not wish to discuss?

One thing was for certain. She could get no further digging into the connection between Randall Hajek, Giovanni Baptiste, and Marjorie Trent-Phillips on her own. She needed Spence to help her determine her next move.

She checked her watch. It had been two hours and forty minutes since he had dropped her off here. Though she knew she should grab something to eat, she was far too anxious. She needed a distraction, something to keep her from obsessing over when—or whether—he was coming back for her.

She thought of Spence's suggestion about checking through the microfilm on old news stories. *"I was thinking of much older stories, ones that might mention Gloria Hajek's disappearance . . . and your mother's death."*

Convinced such a search would prove a waste of time, she hadn't meant to bother. But now, she wondered, was there something else that had provoked her to snap at Spence when he had mentioned the idea?

At the thought, apprehension coiled around her, the

same nervousness she felt whenever her father criticized her husband or Spence made some remark about her dad. That same feeling of being swallowed up by the secret patch of quicksand that lay between the two men she loved best in the world.

More than those involving Gloria Hajek, Spence's questions about her mother's death disturbed Claire. A few frames of distant memory flickered like a newsreel across the span of years: a tiny version of herself burrowing beneath couch cushions in an attempt to muffle her father's terrifying sobs.

Claire covered her own gasp with a hand, an act that drew the curious stare of an older man who was walking toward the pay phones. He stopped short, obviously uncertain about the wisdom of approaching, so she turned and walked back toward the elevators.

Sharp as the recollection seemed, Claire wasn't sure it had ever happened. But even if it hadn't, the image brought with it the gift of comprehension. She was afraid to upset her father by dredging up the memories of the senseless accident that had killed a woman he loved deeply and had cast him, devastated, onto the uncharted waters of single parenthood. In some way, she was still that frightened toddler who couldn't bear her surviving parent's pain.

But the more she thought about the black hole in her memory, the more curious she grew. Why shouldn't she read the articles describing the tragedy that shaped her whole life? As long as she didn't do it with her father present, what possible difference could it make to view this bit of family history, other than to keep her occupied while she was waiting?

Yet she hesitated before going to the fifth floor, her mind churning up the challenges that she and Spence still faced. After thinking for another moment, she turned and hurried back to the pay phone she'd been using. She had one more call to make. Once she reached Janine again, Claire asked her for another favor—one that might just keep Spence free long enough for the two of them to prove that Hajek's "guardian angel," Giovanni Baptiste, was at the root of all their troubles.

But after she hung up, Claire realized that she now had one more worry: the dangerous possibility that Janine might see Spence here when she came to bring the money.

At first, Spence wasn't alarmed when Raul Contreras pulled into the lot of an automotive parts store to take the incoming call on his cell phone. Like a lot of cops, the sergeant often bitched that drivers with phones glued to their ears were at least as dangerous as those who sucked their beers down on the road.

For the first minute or so, Raul mostly listened, only once interjecting, "Sure, I can do that." But Spence's first clue of real trouble came when Contreras asked the speaker, "You have any indication that Winslow's in the library with her? Or that he might be carrying a weapon?"

Throughout the remainder of the call, Spence felt as if fire ants were racing up his arms and legs, stinging as they went. Though it didn't sound as if Raul was giving him away, it was all Spence could manage not to leap out of the car and race toward the library to get Claire out before it was too late.

But that was the adrenaline talking. They were miles from the library, for one thing, and from what little he had gleaned from Raul's conversation, it was already too late.

God help him, he was going to have to break his promise to go back for her.

Raul said into the cell phone, "I'll get there as soon as I can—no more than twenty minutes. But tell me, who else did you call?"

After a pause, he added, "I wish you hadn't done that, Sheriff. If I could have talked to them myself, out of uniform, I think things would go smoother. But never mind that now. I'll come right over."

As soon as he broke off the connection, Raul looked up, his dark gaze intense beneath the salt-and-pepper ridge of his brows. "It seems Claire called a friend, told her she'd dropped the truck off for service and was hanging out waiting in the library. Said she'd forgotten her purse in Little BC and asked if her friend could bring by some cash to pay off the mechanic."

Spence was impressed. It wasn't a half-bad story for someone unused to spinning lies. "So what happened?"

"Sheriff Shepherd had already leaned on the friend, scared her into calling him if Claire made contact. He can't be sure, but he believes you're with your wife, maybe abducting her—possibly with the intention of doing her harm."

Spence swore in frustration. "So he called SAPD and asked them to head straight for the library, right? He'll probably have them braced for a hostage situation."

Especially if the Sissel County Sheriff's Department turned out to be more efficient than he'd heard and the San Antonio police thought they were after a fugitive who'd already caused one accident by fleeing . . .

"They'll scare Claire half to death if they burst in like commandos," he added.

"I'm sure they'll try to do it discreetly," Raul assured

him. "It's a public building, lots of people. They won't want a scene if they can help it."

Spence knew Raul was right, but he couldn't help worrying. Not that Claire would be harmed by the police or charged with some crime, but that she would think he had intentionally abandoned her.

"So what now?" he asked his sergeant. "I heard you say you were going over there."

Raul nodded before putting the Taurus into drive. "I am," he said, "and I'll see if I can find a way to talk to Claire in private."

"So what about me? You have anything in mind?"

"I'll drop you by my apartment, let you lie low until I find out what's going on with your wife. It's on the way to the library anyhow."

Inside Spence, tension knotted at the thought of hiding somewhere while Claire was ambushed and then questioned. Would she lie to the police, and to Joel Shepherd and her dad, too?

Was he even right to expect her to deceive them? Or was he like a drowning man, grasping at a slender— yet ultimately futile—thread of hope?

Claire wrapped her arms around her middle in an attempt to hide her trembling as she stared at the negative-style image set within the white-on-black text.

"Is she the one?" the research librarian asked her. Slender and stylish in a short-skirted pink suit, funky outsized jewelry and a feathery blond hairstyle, the young woman defied the stereotype of the dowdy spinster librarian. But fashionable or not, she was both knowledgeable and helpful as she assisted Claire in finding the archived issues of the *Buck County Express-*

Sentinel from the year Claire's mother had been killed. With no one else waiting for assistance, the librarian not only refreshed Claire on the machine's use but helped her load brittle rolls of dark film on the reader and advance through months of small-town news.

Since Claire couldn't remember the exact date of her mother's death, she started with September. After all, didn't hunting season start some time in the fall?

True to its modern incarnation, the old *Express-Sentinel* had liked to accentuate the positives of life in Little Bee Creek, May's Crossing, and the even smaller—and incredibly misnamed, to Claire's way of thinking—village of Bliss Falls. Accomplishments took center stage: a schoolgirl's essay taking first place in a state contest, FFA and 4-H members posing with the young animals they were raising for next year's county fair, a high school senior who had been accepted to attend the Air Force Academy.

But every so often, tragedy punctuated the idyll. A young couple killed in a one-car accident on Wise School Road. A house burned, with an elderly man in it, before the volunteer fire department could get there. And finally, on the second reel, her mother's eerily reversed face stared back at Claire across the years.

"It's her," she whispered, feeling emotions crackling around her like Saint Elmo's fire playing around a steeple.

Perhaps the librarian, too, felt it, for she touched Claire's shoulder gently before leaving her to read.

DEER HUNTER SHOOTS LITTLE BC WOMAN, blared the headline, while below it, the subheads added, WIFE, MOTHER OF TWO, KILLED IN ACCIDENT. SAN ANTONIO HUNTER QUESTIONED.

Claire looked away, blinking back tears and telling herself, "It was a long time ago."

She forced herself to continue reading, confirming that the mythology of her childhood was as real and solid as an epitaph carved into stone.

> *On Wednesday, Linda Barstow Meador, 36, of Little Bee Creek, was found dead, the apparent victim of what sheriff's department officials are describing as "a tragic hunting accident."*
>
> *According to her husband, attorney William Meador, 41, his wife was taking a late afternoon walk, as was her habit, when she wandered onto the property of Albert and Norma Hajek, also of Little Bee Creek.*
>
> *First-time hunter Felix Navarro, 25, who had taken a deer lease on the Hajek property, shot at what he believed to be a buck located on a bluff overlooking the western branch of Little Bee Creek. As he approached what he reportedly thought to be a mule deer, Navarro instead found Meador, who had stopped breathing and was bleeding from a head wound.*

Claire closed her eyes and whispered to herself, "At least she didn't suffer."

She found herself hoping that her mother had never seen the hunter, either. That she had been simply blown out, without fear or warning, like a lit match extinguished by a breath.

The rest of the article offered few more details. The accident was still under investigation and, pending its results, charges against the "visibly distraught" Navarro would be considered. There was information on her mother, who had come from Austin to work as a licensed nurse in a Little BC clinic before marrying Will Meador. The last paragraph offered details on the funeral services and listed both Claire and her sister among the survivors.

Claire took a deep breath and thought, Well, that was unbelievably depressing. What was it Spence had hoped she'd find here? The only thing unclear to her was the report that Navarro, a twenty-five-year-old first-time hunter, was alone. She understood that for a lot of Texas men, hunting was a social activity, and a lease was usually taken with friends or family members. Had someone gotten sick leaving the eager novice to go alone, or had his partner or partners merely returned to a truck or the cabin for supplies? But she couldn't think of anyone to ask, or why such a thing should matter in the first place. Her mother would still be dead, regardless of why Navarro had been left to hunt on his own.

Since Janine had said she wouldn't be able to meet her in the lobby for another half hour, Claire advanced through several more issues of the weekly paper. She found no further mention of her mother's accident, not even any reference to whether charges had been filed against Navarro. What she did come across was a small article, tucked away on the third page, in which the Hajek family asked for anyone having information on the whereabouts of their fifteen-year-old daughter, Gloria, to please contact the Buck County Sheriff's Department as soon as possible. Apparently the girl had twice run away to Houston during the previous school year, and local authorities were working with law enforcement in that area in an attempt to track her down.

Claire found no further mention of the disappearance in upcoming issues—at least not until she loaded another roll of microfilm. In an issue that came out in January, a half-page boxed ad had been taken out.

HAVE YOU SEEN ME? the top line read. Beneath it was another photograph with its blacks and whites reversed. This one was of a girl with long center-parted hair, perhaps blond, considering its dark tones in this version. Claire couldn't tell much else from the picture, for this particular film was blurred worse than the others. She strained her eyes to read about the still-missing Gloria Lee Hajek, who had disappeared on—

Claire straightened in her seat. The fifteen-year-old Gloria had vanished from the face of God's green earth on the very day her mother had been shot.

So what in the world could that mean?

With her attention so focused on the viewer, she started at the sound of a throat being cleared, very close. And looked up into the blue wall formed by a trio of San Antonio police officers.

TWENTY-EIGHT

Spence nearly jumped out of his skin when the phone rang at Raul's apartment. For the past forty-five minutes, he had alternated between pacing the one-bedroom unit and sitting on the sofa while zapping mindlessly through TV channels.

As he stood, he banged a shin against the coffee table and knocked over the Coke he had been drinking. Swearing as he grabbed the can, he made it by the third ring past the flickering TV screen to the kitchen counter.

There was no caller ID, so he muttered impatiently, "Come on," until the answering machine picked up. Before the sergeant got out his first full word, Spence snatched up the receiver and asked, "What's happening? Where's Claire?"

"By the time I got here, they'd already taken her back to the station to answer some questions," Raul said. "I made a few calls and found out Sheriff Shepherd's driving here to take her home."

And pick her brain the whole way, Spence added

mentally. Once more, he fought the uneasy sense that Joel Shepherd's personal involvement with the Meador family had colored every aspect of his investigation. But could it be worse than simple prejudice? Could the sheriff of Buck County be the person who had tampered with the evidence?

Spence wondered, too, whether Claire would face questions from either SAPD or Shepherd about this morning's accident in Sissel County. Clearly Raul hadn't heard about it, or he would be demanding to know what the hell Spence had been thinking, trying to outrun law enforcement. Rather than bring it up—and risk losing his former sergeant's help—Spence decided to focus on his more immediate concern.

"You think you can get her a message from me?" he asked.

Raul sighed. "I can't see how, man. Not without raising suspicions. Seems to me the best thing to do is wait this out."

"I'll call her tonight, then, as soon as—"

"You might want to think that through," Raul said. "After the way she disappeared last night, her daddy's likely to be screening her calls."

Spence grimaced, then said, "He'd let her take a call from you, right? Probably he'll be hoping you're calling her to say I'm back in custody."

"Or better yet, shot dead," Raul added cheerfully.

Spence meant to laugh, but the mirthless croak that came out sounded more like someone choking. But already his thoughts were running through what he would say to Claire—and how he could possibly find his way back to her.

As if Raul had read his mind, he said, "You know, it's possible the sheriff's gonna feel sufficiently suspicious to monitor the activities around your father-in-law's place, and maybe the telephones as well."

"But he can't bug the phones there. Not without a judge's—"

"Who's to say he couldn't get permission? Or that the sheriff and your father-in-law haven't agreed to put an unofficial tap together for Claire's protection? Stranger things have happened, especially when you've got both a small department and personal involvement."

Raul was right. The normal rules of law enforcement didn't necessarily apply.

The question was, Spence thought, how the hell could he get around the possible surveillance to investigate any of the potential players in this plot? And even more important, how could he get word to Claire that he hadn't skipped town on her?

Again, the sergeant seemed to read the direction of Spence's thoughts. He heard the sound of Raul's car starting just ahead of the gruff threat, "You better be right there waiting when I get home in ten minutes, Winslow. Otherwise, I swear to you, I'll hunt down your lily-white ass and turn you in myself."

"You can put that pack of lies to bed now, darlin'," Joel Shepherd told Claire soon after guiding his department SUV onto the highway that would take them back to Little BC. "They might've fooled those boys from SAPD, but that dog won't hunt with me."

The right front tire bumped over a preflattened armadillo, the official state roadkill of Texas.

"How 'bout you put that 'darlin'' bit to bed, then, too," Claire asked him, "and answer a few questions for me first?"

Joel's gaze jerked toward her, surprise written in his

handsome features. Maybe he'd expected her to cry again, as she had for the San Antonio police. The tears hadn't been a sham; when the officers appeared in the library, she'd been genuinely upset, mainly out of fear that they might spot Spence returning as they left the building. She'd worried, too, that if he came back for her later, he would believe she'd given up on him.

The two middle-aged officers who spoke to her had been solicitous, offering her tissues, soft drinks, and even lunch, and listening sympathetically as she'd explained how she had needed time alone to "get her head together." There had been no accusations, not even a mention of this morning's car chase with the Sissel County deputy. On the contrary, both men had acted not only uncomfortable but embarrassed over the situation with Spence, and neither had pressed her for a more detailed explanation. Maybe they were wondering how their own wives would respond to such an unthinkable betrayal or wondering if it could have been police work that had made Spence go so wrong.

But clearly Joel knew her too well to fall for a few tears and the lame story she'd concocted, as well as her claim that her pickup had been stolen from a side street near the library, where she'd left it parked. He looked haggard today, his eyes shadowed and his color oddly pasty, as if fatigue was weighing heavily on him. Though he was well known as a first-class workaholic, he'd been unusually curt since picking her up: a hint, perhaps, that both his endurance and his temper had their limits.

"You don't get to ask the questions," Joel said. "Not until you tell me where Spence went with your truck."

She shook her head. "I told you, I haven't seen him. I

parked the pickup early this morning when I went inside the library. When I came out, it was gone."

"So let's see your keys."

Damn it. She hadn't thought about that. After dipping her hand into her pocket, she said, "I—I can't find them. Oh, shoot. I must have left them in the truck. No wonder someone took it."

Even to her ears, the lie sounded pathetic.

Joel shook his head, disgust written in the glance he gave her. "Sure, Claire—fine. We'll put that question on the back burner for the moment. How 'bout you tell me instead where you've really been—and why the hell you took off without so much as your wallet or a word to anyone?"

Claire offered him what truth she could. "I was so upset, I just had to get out of there. I had a couple of pretty nasty run-ins on the Monarch property, one after another. I went to investigate what sounded like a crash back by the creek, and this man came running at me—".

"Your father's ATV, that was what you heard," Joel interrupted. "Whoever stole it ran the damned thing off the bluff and smashed it. I responded to a call and talked to both your trainer and her daughter. The girl—Megan Martin, I think her name is—told me how that fella knocked you down. He hurt you?"

She shook her head. "Nothing worth mentioning."

"I understand you didn't recognize him."

"At the time, I didn't, but the more I think about it, the more I believe it could have been that tall blond guy, the one who lives with Randall Hajek. Giovanni Baptiste—"

"That Eye-talian rent-a-faggot—"

"*Joel.*"

He cut his eyes in her direction, his expression sheepish. "Sorry. I've just never cottoned to those kind of—even if he was a female gold digger, I'd still—but you're right—I'll watch my mouth."

She could almost hear him mentally adding, *In front of ladies, anyway.*

"What makes you think he's a gold digger?" she asked, though she'd come to the same conclusion.

He shrugged his shoulders. "Stands to reason, doesn't it? With Hajek sick as he is—"

"So you know about that?"

He nodded. "I knew there was bad blood over the old lady selling to you, so I went to talk to him about your vandalism trouble. He looked a lot thinner than he used to be, and that kitchen of his has medicines laid out from hell to breakfast. I figure, fellow of his persuasion, he's come down with the AIDS. Funny thing. He was a few years ahead, but I knew him back in school a little. Never would've figured him for a—a *ho-mosexual.*"

He drew the word out as if it didn't fit right in his mouth. The man really needed to get out of Buck County for a while, maybe absorb a little of the twenty-first century.

"Randall has cancer," she informed him. "Gay people get that, too."

"That what he told you?" Joel sounded skeptical, but after a moment he shrugged. "I suppose it's possible. But I'm surprised he talks to you."

Since she'd gotten the information under false pretenses, Claire didn't correct his assumption that Randall had told her about his illness. "My second run-in last evening was with him. I caught him spray-painting the ranch's sign—that beautiful brand-new sign my volunteers had just surprised me with."

"Randall did that?" Joel brightened visibly. "Well, then, at least I can charge him with, say, trespassing and criminal mischief, probably get you a restraining order, too. Guess when a fellow's dyin', he tends to hold fast to his grudges."

"It may be more than that," she said, then told him what little she knew about the new golf course resort—and Lenore's assumption that it was to be built at least in part on Monarch Ranch land.

Joel gave a low whistle. "Sounds like quite a motive we've got cooking, if I can prove it's more than rumors. Could be that ol' Randall hopes to push you into sellin' so he can set up his Eye-talian friend in style."

"I can't help wondering . . ." Claire started.

"About what?"

"What if Randall or Giovanni or both of them had something to do with the charges against Spence—"

"Please, Claire." Irritation pounded through Joel's words like silver nails. "Let's not climb back on that tired old horse again."

"Why can't you even consider that Spence might be telling you the truth? What would it hurt to—"

"I know you've been talking to him, letting him fill your head with more of his bull—"

She shook her head, lying as reflexively as an eye blinking to avoid a finger. "No, Joel."

"Then tell me where you really went last night. And don't give me that cock-and-bull about staying with Janine Jaworski, either. I've already talked to her, and she's as worried about you as the rest of us."

Claire bit back a curse at her own stupidity. "She called you, didn't she? I thought she was my friend."

"She is. That's why she clued me in—after I reminded her you were the intended victim in a murder-for-hire scheme and that the man charged is out there on the loose. She also gave me the story you told her, about needing money to pay off some mechanic working on your truck."

Claire's mind raced for an explanation, but she decided not to bother, since Joel clearly wasn't going to buy it. But as bad as it was to be caught in the lie about the pickup, she understood why her friend had betrayed her confidence. Of course Janine was worried about her, just as Joel was. But neither one understood the facts as Claire did. And neither really knew the man Spence was.

Frustrated that Joel wouldn't listen, she turned away from him to look out the passenger-side window. Here, the city had begun its encroachment, sending out exploratory tendrils of suburbia into what had once been a mix of farm and hardwoods nestling along creek bottoms. The outposts were unmistakable, signs advertising "Exclusive Country Living: Five- to Ten-Acre Restricted Homesites." Yuppie farms, which would soon drag with them the home hardware stores and Super Wal-Marts, the Starbucks and the traffic signals, and replace the lazy drone of insects with the gas-powered thrum of lawn equipment. Soon the "pioneers" would be overtaken by the very civilization they yearned to escape.

How long would it be before the inroads cut all the way into the heart of Buck County? How many years before Little Bee Creek's natural beauty was paved over? Not enough, if what Lenore had said about the golf course development proved true.

"I'm waiting." Joel's words were shot through with impatience.

"I have other friends besides Janine. Let's just say I

was with one of them and leave it at that." Claire settled on vagueness, figuring that he would soon prove false any detailed story.

Instead of pressing further, he circled back to his first question. "Where's Spence?"

Relief spread its gossamer wings, for in this as least she could be truthful. "I have no idea."

"You really expect me to believe that?"

"Do you really expect me to care what you believe?" she snapped back, heedless of the fact that she did care, and deeply.

He drove along for several minutes before speaking in quiet tones. "Once upon a time the two of us lived through hell together. Guess I was a damned fool to think that counted for something."

He kept his gaze glued to the road, which had narrowed to two lanes bordered by a pair of fresh green hayfields. But she didn't need to look at his face to read his pain, the old grief struggling like a reanimated corpse to claw its way back to the surface.

Claire braced one hand against the dash, as if to keep herself from sinking beneath the bittersweet slipstream of memories of her sister. She couldn't afford to drown in the past—not if she were going to have a future.

"We both loved Karen, but she's gone." She whispered the statement, as if that would somehow soften its blow. "She's been gone for a long time. It's been fourteen years now."

Joel pulled over on the shoulder, put the SUV in park in the shade of some trees growing at the far edge of the hayfield. His hands knotted around the steering wheel, the skin stretched tight across the knuckles.

"You're telling me we should forget her." Bitterness,

even anger, hammered the words flat. "You sound like Lori Beth. But how can I, Claire, when every time I see you, I wonder how life would have been, how things might have turned out if—if Karen had gotten her cancer now? The treatments today, they're so much better. I've kept up with it. The survival rate for the kind she had is—"

"Stop it. Please," Claire begged him. "This isn't helping anyone."

He gazed at her, looking every bit as wounded as she had seen him at her sister's funeral. Claire felt a pang of sympathy. Would he ever move past that day? Would he ever pass her on the street or see her at the grocery store without the name *Karen* slashing like a switchblade through his consciousness?

She picked her way among her words, stepping as carefully as if her path were strewn with jagged rock and cacti. "You have a family now, Joel. A family and a wife that need you."

He flinched, and moisture filmed his eyes, reflecting the pale blue of a clear sky. "Maybe," he said quietly. "Maybe I still have them."

She didn't understand what he meant, so she kept struggling to find her way. "It's not that I've forgotten Karen. Almost every day, I remember some funny thing we did when we were little, or I think of something I should tell her, some situation I would love to get her take on. But I have a family now, too. A family who needs me as much as yours needs you."

He glanced up at her sharply, pity written in his expression. "God, Claire. You're living in every bit as much of a fantasy world as I am if that's what you believe."

"I'm pregnant, Joel. And before you say another word, I mean to keep this baby."

Joel stared at her, his eyes flared and his mouth slightly open. When he finally recovered, he looked out the window and swore softly.

"And that's not all of it," she said. "I mean to clear my husband's name, give my child its father."

"You're being flat-out ridiculous. Spence Winslow tried to have you—"

"It isn't true," she argued. "And if you'll look at this case—*really* dig into it instead of settling for the ugly little story you've been spoon-fed—you're going to see it, too. I swear to you, you will."

He looked away from her, a deep flush coloring his neck and jawline. "So you think I'm just another stupid yokel duped by a couple of faggots—excuse me—*gay men* from the city?" His voice dropped to a growl. "You think I'm Barney-goddamn-Fife out here, and I don't know my job?"

"Of course I don't," she told him, alarmed by the sudden stiffness in his shoulders and the rough way he dropped the SUV back into gear. "That isn't what I meant at all."

He stepped on the accelerator so hard that pebbles shot out behind them. Though he said nothing, Claire's heart pushed into her throat as their speed increased to forty, fifty, sixty, then well beyond the posted limit.

"Pull over, Joel," she said. "You need to calm down."

He flipped on his lights and siren, prompting a slower-moving pickup to glide to the shoulder so that he could pass it. He rocketed by, his speed now well past eighty, then turned off the emergency signals.

When a yellow road sign warned of a sharp upcoming curve, Claire begged him, "Slow down—please."

Even as she wondered how on earth the two of them would make it to her father's house alive.

TWENTY-NINE

Forty minutes later, Claire sighed in relief at the familiar sight of the old stone-and-cedar house behind its shroud of azaleas dotted with white blossoms. The moment the sheriff's department SUV came to a stop, she unbuckled her seat belt and bailed out, grateful beyond measure when her feet touched down on the semicircular front driveway. She was about to light into Joel over his failure to control his temper, when Pogo burst out the front door, barking wildly and leaping to greet Claire. Her father was right behind the sheltie, hurrying toward her with his arms opening wide and his forehead crinkling.

"Claire. You're—you're safe." His voice broke, sounding as if he had aged decades. He looked older, too, his face deeply lined and his shoulders slumped with worry.

As she met him halfway up the walk, he squeezed her in an embrace so tight that she had trouble catching her breath.

"I was afraid I'd lost you, baby," he told her. "You'll

never know how—how scared I was and how sorry for the crazy way we argued yesterday. I said some things—I could never live with myself if my words caused you to—to go off and get yourself hurt, or maybe even . . ."

Guilt ricocheted through Claire, pinging like a pinball off her heart. How terrible a person she was, to cause those who loved her so much grief and worry. She'd known damned well what a strain her problems had been on her father—and with his health hanging in the balance . . .

"Forgive me." Tears burned her eyes and blurred the open doorway. "Please, Dad. Say you'll forgive me for frightening you so badly."

Behind her, Joel Shepherd said flatly, "Hell of a reception, but I have to get back to my office. I'll be by in the mornin', though, to talk to you some more. And this time, Claire, I expect you're gonna answer me in detail."

To her father, he added, "Maybe you can talk some sense into that daughter of yours, keep her from runnin' off all on her own again. And while you're at it, why don't you fill her in about how Adam Strickland got himself killed."

"What are you talking about?" Claire asked as she turned toward him. Did Joel still imagine Spence had murdered the biologist?

Instead of answering, the sheriff of Buck County merely tipped his dark brown hat to them and climbed back inside the dusty Expedition. Without sparing either another glance, he drove away. Now that he'd rid himself of the aggravation of his passenger, Claire noticed he was moving at a more civilized rate of speed.

The big moron. He could have gotten them both

killed over—what *had* it been, exactly? Wounded pride, that he believed she thought him incompetent? Or was it something more, perhaps even her confession that she was pregnant?

Claire's father frowned after the receding vehicle. "He doesn't seem too happy with you."

She nodded. "I've been making a lot of trouble for him lately, a lot of extra work."

"Might be more than that. Word around town is, Lori Beth took their kids and went back to her folks' place out in Comfort."

She followed her father toward the front door without bothering to ask him how he'd heard. Little BC's rumor mill went after a juicy bit of gossip like a swarm of fire ants stripping the flesh off a fallen nestling.

"So that's what's wrong with Joel," she said. But still she wondered if the feelings evoked by her return home were to blame, or if his long hours were the culprit. Either way, she felt partially responsible.

Uncomfortable with the thought, she changed the subject. "What did he mean about Adam Strickland? I know they found a body, but have they figured out what happened to him?"

The two of them went inside, her father locking the front door behind him while Claire prayed silently. *Please don't let it be a bullet from Spence's gun that killed him.*

Her father turned toward her, his expression somber. "It was a bad fall. Joel figures he was standing on the bluff—your bluff—when part of it gave way. We'd had all that rain, and it's been—"

"So his death was accidental?" Claire asked him. "He wasn't murdered?"

"That's what the medical examiner from the Travis

County coroner's office ruled. Strickland broke his neck—could have died instantly or drowned when he hit the water. Probably didn't suffer long, at least."

Claire remembered the untidy red hair, the mud-spattered glasses, and the shyness of Adam Strickland's smile when he had asked her out. Though she'd only spoken to him the one time, she felt horrible to think he'd died violently and alone after an accident on her land, in a spot she loved above all others.

"God rest the poor man's soul," Claire offered, even as she silently gave thanks that nothing appeared to link his death to Spence. "But what makes Joel so sure he died on Monarch property? The body wasn't found anywhere near there."

"But he was washed downstream from it. And what with the collapse and the fact that a few of his collection tubes were found in the vicinity . . ." Her father shrugged, his expression souring. "That bluff's more dangerous than ever. You need to post signs or have the access fenced off before anybody else gets hurt. And whatever you do, stay off it—I know how you always liked to go out there, look out at the creek. I've been trying to keep you away from that spot since you were a tiny thing."

A line from the article she'd read jolted through her, and before Claire knew what she was doing, her words slipped free, like hot-air balloons loosed from their tethers. "Because my mother died there . . ."

Her father sank down onto the chair closest to the huge stone fireplace. It was a big rocker padded in cowhide bearing both the splotches and the hair of a Texas longhorn. Resting his elbows on his knees, he steepled his fingers and glanced up at the antique rifle above the fireplace.

Claire wondered if he even saw it, or if instead he was picturing the gun that had taken his wife from him. Whatever he was seeing, tears shone in his eyes, and the color had drained out of his face.

"I'm sorry." Her head shook back and forth. "I didn't mean to upset—"

"Where did you go when you went away?" he interrupted, "and why wouldn't you tell Joel?"

She shouldn't be surprised that he had changed the subject. But this time, with her mother's ghostly image hovering in her mind, Claire dared to push a little harder. "I know it's tough for you, Dad," she said gently, "but sometime I'd like to talk about her. You've been a wonderful parent, but I—I need to know my mother. Who she was and why you loved her. What she hoped for me."

He looked up. "Why are you avoiding answering me?"

As she perched on the edge of the leather sofa, Claire tried to ignore Pogo, who rolled over by her feet and began pawing her leg in the clear hope of a belly rub.

Looking into her father's face, Claire nearly threw his question back at him. But once more the memory of his ancient sobs floated like a bit of chaff across the intervening years. And she relented, as she had so often, because she couldn't bear to hurt him.

"You were with your husband, weren't you?" he asked, his voice so quiet, she heard the cuckoo clock call out the half hour from the kitchen.

Was it already four-thirty, or an hour later? She had lost all sense of time.

When she didn't answer, he said, "You're guaranteeing his bail will be revoked, Claire. By violating the terms of his release, you're putting Spencer back in jail until the trial."

Her father's form wavered in her vision until she wiped her eyes. "He didn't do it, Dad. I don't know how or why, but someone made it look like he did."

"Claire . . ." His disappointment wreathed her name like smoke surrounding the wreckage of his dreams. "You were always such a stubborn girl, such a little fighter in your quiet way. Once you grabbed hold of an idea, you latched on to it like a snapping turtle—like that time you stuffed all your pretty dresses in the trash can."

Claire's hand went on autopilot, stroking the sheltie while she remembered her childish act of retaliation against the umpteenth frilly confection Grandma Barstow had sent her on her birthday. It was Karen who loved frills and ruffles. Perfect Karen, not her. To this day Claire hated pink.

But how could her father compare her faith in her husband to a seven-year-old's fit of pique?

"I'm thirty." She felt herself flushing at his insult. "I haven't been a child for a long ti—"

A noise stopped her, made her head turn. Had that been a closing door she'd heard—the door that led outside from the kitchen?

The sound must have reached her dad, too, for he was already rising from his chair, his hands balling into tight fists as he stared toward the opening that led into the kitchen.

He was expecting trouble, she guessed. But was it trouble in the form of Spence?

"Wait, Dad." She sprang to her feet and made a bee-line for the doorway, with Pogo bounding just ahead of her. If it was Spence, she had to get between them before her father reached for the kitchen telephone—or, worse yet, for a weapon. Heaven only knew where he had one squirreled away—or maybe, unnerved as he'd been, he was carrying a pistol.

But the head that popped into the doorway was a blond one, with long hair swinging down to frame her pretty face. "Hey—Will—you—"

Megan Martin, Ellen's daughter, froze as her gaze met Claire's, and her bright blue eyes went as round and as wide as the perfect O formed by her mouth.

"You're back," the teen said as the sheltie wagged her tail furiously and planted her single front paw on Meg's knee. "Thank goodness! My mom will be so glad to see you."

Claire's head canted, as she sought a new perspective—one that would make sense. "What are you doing here, Meg?"

"Oh, um. My—my mom sent me. She wanted to find out if you'd called home. And—and see if your father wanted her to bring over some chili and fresh cornbread." Words poured out of the seventeen-year-old like rice spilling from a torn bag. Her hands jingled, blurs of motion that touched her hair, then fiddled with the hem of her striped T-shirt or scratched a transient itch. Though she usually adored Pogo, she paid the little dog no heed. "She made way too much, you know? Because my brothers are both out for the evening. John's over at his girlfriend's—*again*—I think sixteen's way too young to be so serious, don't you? And Matthew's finally off his butt—he has an actual job interview over in Bliss Falls—"

"Where did you get that?" Claire moved nearer as she pointed toward something glittering near Meg's hand. "Hold still, will you? I want to see it."

Her tone was sharp, demanding. In response, Meg froze again, except for her worried eyes, which looked toward Claire's father as if searching for an explanation.

What the hell is going on? Claire moved in on Megan, nearly close enough to touch her left wrist, which was encircled by a silver bracelet. A bracelet made of hearts.

"Where did you get that?" Claire repeated, nearly overwhelmed by the desire to reach into her pocket and pull out the tarnished piece of jewelry, the one bearing the initials *G.L.H.*

The girl jerked back, clearly frightened. With her head shaking emphatically, Meg cried out, "It's mine. I didn't take it—I would *never.*"

"It's all right, Meg." Claire's father spoke in the tones he used to calm hysterical clients. "No one's accusing you of stealing anything. What is it, Claire? What's upset you? Don't you see you're scaring this poor girl half to—"

"The bracelet was a present," Meg blurted. "It was a gift. To me."

Claire had known her trainer's daughter for nearly two years, since she had become reacquainted with her old riding instructor and they had started talking about an equine therapy program. In all that time, Claire had never seen the normally bubbly teen so nervous. Not over an upcoming final or a big competition for her debate team. Not over with whom—or whether—she would attend the high school's junior-senior prom.

Taking a deep breath, Claire struggled to hide the thumping of her own heart and the sweating of her palms. She feigned a calmness that she didn't feel as she asked, "Who gave you that bracelet? Was it your mother?"

Meg shook her head, as Claire had known she would. Ellen was the soul of practicality. She'd presented Claire with a doormat on her birthday, to keep the new office clean. To her three kids, Ellen gave presents such as school backpacks or gift cards, or to her eldest son—a great houseplant of a nineteen-year-old who'd been rooted to the couch since graduation—a set of luggage and an open one-way Greyhound ticket. Apparently the job interview was proof the kid could take a hint.

"I got it from a boy," Meg whispered, her gaze fixed on a rug made from the spotted buff skin of an axis deer.

But to Claire, the explanation didn't sit right. "Your mother knows about it?"

Once more Meg shook her head. "She thinks I bought the bracelet with my babysitting money—and please, Miss Claire, don't tell her. Mom doesn't like this guy at all. He's a little older, twenty—a sophomore over at the junior college. He's a *really* nice guy, but Mom's made up her mind that he's only after one thing."

Claire didn't know what to believe. Meg's explanation sounded so plausible, and so like one of the typical dramas of a teenaged girl. It would be so easy to accept her explanation, to push past the horrible sinking feeling that something far less natural was in play. Something so hideous, Claire couldn't bear to look it in its ill-formed eye—or to pull the older piece of jewelry from her pocket.

As Claire considered, there was a tinkling at Meg's wrist as she pushed her long blond hair behind her shoulders. Her long, blond, center-parted hair that looked so much like Gloria Hajek's.

* * *

Einstein had it right. All things, in fact, *are* relative.

For example, to a man already indicted for conspiracy to commit the capital murder of his wife, an additional charge of grand theft auto seemed inconsequential—even though Spence knew it could earn him years more in the penitentiary.

And even though Spence knew that it was a rotten thing to do to the one friend who'd stuck by him.

Spence had waited through the meal of Chinese takeout Raul brought home with him and bided his time through lecture after lecture about staying out of sight while the sergeant spent his final set of days off before retirement unraveling this tangle.

But in spite of Raul's assumptions about his silence on the issue, Spence thought the plan sucked wind. For one thing, it left Claire out of the loop—and Spence couldn't see much point of clearing his name if he lost her in the process. He was concerned, too, that by helping him, Raul was leaving himself open to be charged with accessory after the fact—harboring a fugitive and God only knew what other crimes.

So without even a short note of apology—Spence couldn't risk leaving written evidence—he waited for Raul to conk out, then took his car keys off the dresser and liberated the old Taurus a little after eleven. Once he left the apartment parking lot, he thought about his options.

In a few short hours, he could be in Mexico, where he could send for Claire—and spend the rest of his days looking over his shoulder for bounty hunters or fighting extradition. He couldn't do that to her, couldn't make her or their child share a fugitive's lot. And neither could he take Claire from her work or the friends and father whom she loved so deeply.

The only possible solution was in honoring his promise to meet Claire on the property—but not before he made an unscheduled visit to the man they both knew as Giovanni Baptiste.

Because compared to the charge of arranging to have Claire murdered, the idea of intimidating—or maybe even pounding—a known criminal into a confession didn't trouble Spence Winslow in the least.

THIRTY

Even now, hours after he had left her, it pissed Joel Shepherd off to no end that Claire Meador—make that Claire *Winslow*—had accused him of falling for a lie. It ate at him so badly that Lori Beth sensed something wrong within five minutes of the time he finally reached her on the phone, not long after eleven.

"What's wrong, Joel?" she asked him once they'd finished talking over how Kylie and Tyler were taking the extended visit with their grandparents. They hadn't yet been told that their stay might be permanent. Fortunately they hadn't started asking questions, thanks to the exciting distraction of an orphaned litter of beagle pups that Lori Beth's dad, a retired veterinarian, was hand raising.

Taking his feet off his crowded desktop, Joel leaned an elbow on his knee and rubbed the knotted muscles between his neck and shoulder. The office lay in darkness, save for the tight spotlight of his desk lamp and the light leaking through the closed blinds that covered the door's window.

"Everything," he answered. "Everything's wrong since you left."

Silence stretched between them, like the long glass filaments that had become the last remaining link connecting them. When she finally spoke, her voice splintered into fine shards. "You're still at work, aren't you?"

He puffed out a long sigh. True or not, it was the same old accusation. "Beats the hell out of going back to an empty house."

"That's funny. You never seemed too anxious to get back to it when we all lived there, either," she reminded him.

Joel didn't want to argue, so instead he explained, "I was going through a file, thinking maybe I've missed something. On this case with Spencer Winslow."

"That again." Lori Beth sounded as exhausted as he felt, though she'd taken the week off from her teaching at the preschool. "Lord, Joel, you told me this one was a shoo-in, any prosecutor's dream come true. What else do you want?"

"Claire accused me of settling for someone else's story. She thinks I'm just another redneck lawman—"

"Why, Joel? Why does it matter so much what that woman thinks? Ever since she's come back to Little BC—She's Karen's *sister*, for God's sake, not Karen. Not that memory you keep taking out and polishing. Tell me, what's even left after all these years? A reflection of the man you used to be?"

Joel wished he were home with a drink in his hand and a bottle at his side. Antivenin against the bite she'd just inflicted.

Or was his resurrected pain the poison?

"I—I want you to come home, Lori Beth. Please. We can go to counseling like you wanted."

"Seriously?" She sounded cautious, reluctant to believe in the carrot he'd so often dangled, only to scoff at once her threats subsided.

As far as he was concerned, counselors and shrinks were crutches made for weaklings. Real men took care of their own problems—and besides, a lot of his constituents wouldn't like hearing that the sheriff they'd elected couldn't handle his own shit.

But what the hell did it matter what they liked, if he had to live his life without his kids or his wife—a sweet-natured, smart, and loving woman who'd put up with one hell of a lot more than she had coming?

"I swear to you, I'll do it," Joel said. "I don't care if they print it on the front page of the paper. I don't care if I end up toting sacks of deer corn at the Feed and Seed for a living."

Her throaty chuckle made him want to reach through the phone line and take her in his arms. How was it he'd forgotten the way her laughter could arouse him?

"Now you're talking foolishness," she told him, but warmth had displaced the earlier irritation in her voice. "You were born to that job, sugar. All you've got to do is learn to balance it a little better."

"I need to see you," he begged, but it was the scent and feel and taste of her that filled his imagination. The thought of Lori Beth's soft curves and sweet chocolate-colored curls had him hard and ready right here at his damned desk, where he couldn't do a thing about it.

"It's the middle of the night, Joel. I'm not about to wake up Mama and Daddy to tell 'em that I'm off like a bride's pajamas just because you snapped your fingers."

"That's not what I meant," he said quickly. "I'll drive

over there. I'll be out the door as soon as I get through this file."

Another brittle silence told him he'd stepped in it again.

"Sure you will." Sarcasm froze the statement with the bitter chill of too many disappointments. "You can call again tomorrow. Or maybe it would be better if you waited a few days."

"But I'm coming out tonight," he told the dial tone. "I swear to you, I'm coming."

He laid the phone down in its cradle, then slapped the case file shut. He was a damned fool—as blinded by the life he might have lived as Claire was by her faith in Spencer. There was no arguing this evidence. The best, most conscientious deputy on the payroll had engineered the sting off a telephone tip. Frank had brought in the informant, a bar owner from May's Crossing, just north of the Buck County line, and Joel had interviewed him personally. Though he looked as if he'd been weaned on steroids, the man had acted as squeamish as a Girl Scout at a urinal over a drunken SAPD cop mouthing off in his establishment, wanting to get rid of his wife.

"It's shit like this that gives respectable businessmen like myself a bad name." The man seemed unduly concerned about respectability, considering his shaved head and the black teardrop tattooed below his right eye, something he'd shrugged off with the explanation, *"Crazy, ain't it? The stuff a kid'll do, tryin' to act tough and fit in. I'm gonna have the thing removed as soon as I can save the five grand."*

But tattooed or not, Cal Smith had checked out just fine, with nothing more than a four-year-old speeding ticket on his record, and he'd been more than willing to wear the wire when Joel had brought it up.

Ashford had overseen the sting, aided by Joel's cousin Earl, who'd reportedly handled himself well. Which probably meant, correcting for Frank Ashford's natural tact, that the damned fool had mostly kept his yap shut and stayed out of the way.

The tapes were perfect, the clearest Joel had ever heard, with Spence's own words as irrefutable as they were damning. So what else *could* he want, Joel wondered. Why would he be troubled by the accusations of a woman in obvious denial?

As he switched off his desk lamp, the faces of Randall Hajek and his *friend* rose like a pair of ghosts. Unnatural as Joel found the men's relationship, there was nothing unfamiliar in its underlying themes. Lust, affection—maybe even love, at least on Randall's part. And greed, which Joel found at the root of far too many crimes. Just as he figured it had to be at the root of those committed on Claire's ranch. But however disconcerting they had been, Joel would never persuade the county prosecutor that a few selfish property crimes added up to some grand conspiracy to frame Spence Winslow.

After closing his office door behind him, Joel dug into his pocket for his keys. From down the hall, he saw the light on in the office belonging to Peg, the night dispatcher, who was most likely keeping herself awake reading one of the torrid romances the guys always kidded her about. Both of the deputies on duty were out patrolling, or possibly—since one of them was Earl—parked over by the cemetery "resting up" for the next call. So whose light was on in the third office to the right, the one commonly used by deputies as they filled out their reports?

Probably some toad-brained dimwit—again, Earl sprang to mind—had forgotten the last memo about conserving energy. Frowning at the thought of the budget woes that had turned him into Buck County's "kilowatt cop," Joel reached toward the half-open door.

And froze, his hand halfway to the light switch just inside, at the sound of Frank Ashford's voice. He wasn't so surprised to find Frank here beyond his work hours, since Ashford, who was both divorced and apparently devoid of outside interests, rivaled Joel himself in his reputation as a workaholic. It was something in Frank's tone that stopped Joel, a quiet furtiveness that sounded entirely out of place.

He stood there listening for several minutes, minutes that entirely pushed his wife's curves and curls out of his mind.

Though Claire brushed her teeth and washed her face as she always did before her bedtime, there was no question of sleeping. She purposely let her father see her go to the kitchen in her bathrobe for a glass of water, but she had no intention of climbing into bed.

She couldn't rest until she learned whether Spence had made good on his promise to come meet her, couldn't bear to close her eyes until she slipped out of the house to check the cabin. If he wasn't there, she would have to search the cave, in spite of both her father's and Joel's warnings about the bluff's instability. Otherwise she would lie awake the whole night worrying that Spence might fall and break his neck like Adam Strickland—a fear that had long since overshadowed her concerns about Megan Martin and her bracelet.

Halfway through the ten o'clock newscast, her father at last rose stiffly from his chair and stretched.

"Might as well head off to bed," he said, "unless you have something more to say to me."

She shook her head, hating the thought that both he and Joel would start in on her again tomorrow about Spence's whereabouts. She had spent most of the past few hours deflecting her dad's questions about her disappearance and her missing truck—mostly with concerns about the exhaustion etched so clearly on his face.

He had obviously worked himself into a state over her disappearance, and he looked near collapse in his relief since she'd returned. After Meg left for home, Claire had insisted on phoning his cardiologist's office in San Antonio. The nurse put her on hold to consult with Dr. Cohen, then came back on the line to suggest a good night's sleep followed by an office visit in the morning. Her dad put up a token fuss, but Claire wasn't having any of it.

"I'll get you up bright and early, Dad, so I can fix us a decent breakfast before we drive to town." In spite of the anxieties circling her mind like vultures, she forced her best impression of a smile. "After all, we could both benefit from a decent meal to start our day."

This evening, she'd thrown together a quick stir-fry, with chicken tenders, onions, and red and green bell peppers to go along with rice and a prepackaged salad. But neither of them had made much of a dent. For her part, each time Claire tried to swallow, pain jagged through her throat, as if she were choking down the silver charms on both Meg's and Gloria Hajek's bracelets.

On his way into his bedroom, her father gave her a quick hug and bussed her cheek. "I'm so glad you're home."

Again she struggled to arrange her face into a smile, but she couldn't manage the right words to go with it.

"Don't you worry about me," he reassured her, as if he'd noticed her disquiet. "I was up all last night, that's it. I'm fine—or I will be, with a good night's sleep. But if you hear any strange noises, anything at all, you're to wake me straight off. I'll have my shotgun by my bed, just in case we need it."

She felt a grimace make a wreckage of her carefully arranged expression. *Just in case Spence dares to show up,* he might as well have said.

"We may be in the country, but this is *not* the Wild West," she told him. "You leave that shotgun locked up, where I won't have to worry about you blasting Pogo if she tries to sneak up on your bed."

He mumbled an indistinct reply, which she took to mean her orders didn't stand a chance against his protective instincts.

She spent the next twenty minutes making an anxious circuit from the hallway to the kitchen and back again, with Pogo hopping behind her and tangling her feet at every turn.

"Would you stay out from under me?" she whispered furiously. But when the little dog looked up at her with sad brown eyes, her tail fanning, Claire knelt to wrap her arms around the furry neck.

"I'm sorry, sweetie," she said, rubbing the silky ears in apology. Whenever Pogo sensed she was upset, the sheltie did her best to stay close. Now she tilted her narrow muzzle upward to lick Claire's chin.

Claire gave a long exhalation of relief, not at the wet

kisses, but at the sound of her father's snores rumbling through his bedroom door. Thank goodness. She was counting on that deep, exhausted sleep to let her slip out, then come back into the house without getting herself shot.

After hurrying to her room, she peeled off the bathrobe and rolled down the pant legs of the jeans she still wore beneath it. She took time to pull on a long-sleeved dark blue T-shirt, thick socks, and her hiking boots. Since she couldn't risk leading anyone straight to the ranch by "borrowing" her father's Caddy, and it was too dangerous to ride the bicycle when it was so dark, her best option was walking. A lot of walking—she probably wouldn't reach the cabin for another forty minutes.

She only hoped that by the time she made it, Spence would be there.

Please let him be waiting for me in the cabin, she prayed, and nowhere near those damned bluffs.

As quietly as possible, she pulled the kitchen's outside door shut behind her. Then she turned and tried to shush Pogo, who was scratching and crying to get out.

Cursing under her breath, she let out the sheltie before she started barking loud enough to raise the dead. Clearly Pogo had concluded that the hiking boots meant Claire was going for a walk without her.

"You can come," Claire grumbled as the three-legged dog danced happily around her and filled the night with the excited whines her owners had dubbed "talking."

"But cool it with the noise, girl"—Claire shook the flashlight as she warned—"or this is going to be the shortest walk in history."

THIRTY-ONE

It was the glowing tip of a cigarette that drew Spence through the darkness to the man who called himself Giovanni Baptiste.

He was smoking on the new deck built onto the back of the historic Hajek house, a native stone-and-cedar structure even larger than Claire's dad's ranch house. Giovanni—Spence still thought of him by this name—was alone and standing at the railing beneath the overarching bough of a pecan tree. Though the moonlight did little to mitigate the darkness, the Italian appeared to be staring off in the direction of the creek.

Behind Giovanni, weak illumination streamed through a pair of windows. Spence studied them briefly to assure himself that no one was watching from inside. The hood light had been left on above the stove, but otherwise the house appeared completely dark.

It was a stroke of luck, for Spence would find it easier handling one man instead of two. If he didn't like the answers Giovanni gave him, he could always tie

him up before moving through the house in search of
Randall. Spence dared to hope the man was sound
asleep.

He drew nearer to his quarry, near enough to catch
the foreign odor of sweet cloves burning with tobacco.
Though the night was cool, Giovanni was half naked,
wearing the bottoms of a pair of silk pajamas and nothing more. Probably the working uniform for a fellow in
his line of business, Spence thought with disgust.

Since the man showed no sign he'd noticed an unin-
vited guest, Spence edged around to try to get a bead
on what he was studying so intently. The way he held
himself, shoulders and elbows sharply angled, neck
straight and chin high, he didn't look like a man enjoying the music of the insects and the cool, fresh air. Instead his posture spoke of expectation, though his face
remained unclear in the dim light.

Spence wondered if he was imagining scores of
shoulder-to-shoulder McMansions around an emerald
golf course and the way the bucks would flow into his
and Randall's pockets. Considering Baptiste's record,
however, he probably had some scheme to cut his
lover out of the bonanza.

Maybe even murder, if it came down to it.

Still looking in the direction Baptiste was staring,
Spence caught sight of a distant flicker—a thin beam
moving through the trees on Monarch property. The light
quickly disappeared, leaving Spence to wonder if Claire
was going toward the cabin, a flashlight in her hand. He
wondered, too, if Giovanni had also spotted the light.

Impatient to get out there before he missed her,
Spence took a step closer to the deck. An empty pecan
shell left by the squirrels cracked beneath his footfall.

Giovanni glanced down toward the sound, looking

more curious than alarmed. Probably he thought it was an armadillo or opossum. Definitely, he was not expecting what he found instead.

As he recognized a man's shape closing in on him, Baptiste choked on the lungful of smoke he sucked up in his surprise. But in spite of this—perhaps because his reflexes had been honed by the time he'd spent in prison—when the tall blond man reacted, he moved far faster than Spence had bargained for.

The trouble was, Claire's walk was too long, for it gave her time to finger the piece of jewelry in her pocket—and wonder what the hell was going on with Meg. As much as Claire wanted to believe in the girl's story, something about it felt fundamentally wrong.

For one thing, Ellen believed in riding herd on her three teenagers' hormones. She'd tossed their computer when she couldn't keep the boys away from Internet pornography, and she was always griping that the youngest, John, was moving too fast with his girlfriend. So Claire knew she would have heard plenty about it if Ellen was upset over a college kid who'd come into her daughter's life.

Meg's behavior troubled Claire as well. She remembered the situation with the man running through the woods yesterday, recalled how Meg had been telling her, *"I think I know—"* before Claire had broken off a branch and run after the intruder who had just knocked her down.

Not for the first time, she regretted her temper. Why hadn't she waited a few more seconds to hear the girl out? But if Meg had known, or even suspected, the identity of the man running toward the fence line, shouldn't she have mentioned it to Joel?

And if asked about it now, would Meg agree with her that the man who'd smashed the ATV had been Randall Hajek's lover? Or would she name someone else, perhaps even the person who had really given her that bracelet?

As Claire cut around behind the Monarch Ranch's office/stable, darkness forced her to switch on her flashlight. Pogo wasted a little energy hopscotching after the strong beam before she settled back to trotting happily a few steps ahead of her mistress.

Claire passed the fenced pastures at a quick but steady pace until a sharp twinge in her right side stopped her in her tracks.

Panic careened through her system, leaving her heart racing and her body drenched in cold sweat. *This isn't happening—not now, please.*

But her plea was powerless to erase the recognition that had struck with the force and fury of an onrushing train. The pain had started like this once before—the day she'd ended up in surgery, hemorrhaging internally with a ruptured fallopian tube.

Why hadn't she made an appointment with the doctor when she'd first suspected she was pregnant? She knew her past history, knew how close she'd come to bleeding out before Spence had gotten her to the ER. But in spite of all the stress over Spence's arrest, she wanted this child, this one tiny ray of hope for the future, so desperately that she had put off making the appointment with her ob-gyn.

You're being ridiculous, she told herself. This twinge was only a shadow compared to the tearing agony she'd felt that terrible day last year. She was under such strain and she'd been covering ground so quickly—no wonder she had felt a little cramp.

The question was, would she let fear keep her from doing what she must, or would she turn back now, perhaps even ask her father to drive her all the way to the hospital only to find out this was nothing but a case of late-night jitters?

Pogo circled back for her and whined, obviously eager to resume this strange nighttime adventure—and just as clearly afraid to venture far into the dark alone. Like a miniature Lassie leading one of her people to rescue the disaster-prone Timmy, the sheltie trotted forward once again.

Tentatively Claire followed, this time at a slower pace. When she didn't feel another pain, the tight fist of her anxiety eased a little.

It was going to be all right, she assured herself. As soon as she reconnected with her husband, she would feel so much better about everything.

THIRTY-TWO

The best thing about alarm clocks is that one can find them nearly everywhere. Just about any store selling hardware, household items, or even groceries will stock them. They're generally as cheap as they are ubiquitous, and since they're so unremarkable, no one pays much attention when someone brings one to the checkout counter.

But the worst thing about them is they're often unreliable, especially the least expensive models. Even new, the damned things often fail to keep good time. . . .

So an alarm clock set for, say, exactly midnight might easily go off up to an hour later.

Or as much as an hour earlier as well.

Giovanni was halfway through the door leading into the kitchen when Spence caught him in a flying tackle. The two of them crashed down, Spence's elbow banging the doorframe and sending bolts of pain up his bad arm. But judging from his sharp, truncated cry, Giovanni got the worst of it.

"Get off—get off me. Oh, my God. You're breaking all my ribs, you fucking lunatic!" In Giovanni's fear and pain, the Italian accent had evaporated into something innocuously Midwestern.

Spence rose, dragging the taller blond man outside and shutting the door behind them. If Randall had heard his lover's outcry, he would either be dialing the sheriff's office or coming to the rescue. With the latter possibility in mind, Spence kept Giovanni's back to the door.

"Shut the hell up," Spence said. "I've got some questions for you, and I don't have much time."

Giovanni's gaze latched onto his face like a vampire, sucking in each detail.

"You're that wretched *criminal*, aren't you—that awful man who tried to have his wife killed." The pseudo-European accent had already snapped back into place, an amazingly quick recovery. "What in God's name do you want with *me?*"

"I want to know what the hell you think you've been doing. I know about the ATV. I know about the fence lines. And I know about your little real estate project, too."

"Wha—what on earth are you implying?"

Spence shifted his grasp from the man's shoulder to his throat. "I'm not *implying* anything, you sorry shit. I know you've made some kind of deal already, some kind of commitment for a golf course project—and I know you need my wife to sell you her land to make this happen."

"I don't know what you're talking abo—"

A name Claire had mentioned popped into Spence's consciousness. "Marjorie's told me all about it, so you can save the bullshit."

At least he *hoped* that Marjorie was her name.

Giovanni jerked back as if he had been struck. His head shaking, he said, "The bitch lied to you, I swear it. I would never—"

"I know about your past, *Vincenti*. I know all about your prison time and the reasons for it. So tell me, is Randall in this with you, or are you ripping him off, too? Do you tell him that you love him? Do you tell all those men anything you need to gain their trust—"

"No!"

The shout of pain to Spence's left made him spin in that direction. That was when he spotted Randall Hajek, thin and trembling in his bathrobe, clutching the railing of the deck with one pale hand.

The other held an enormous pistol, which gleamed darkly in the light streaming through the kitchen window.

In the sudden silence following Randall's outcry, Spence heard only one sound. The clicking of the weapon as the little man forced back the hammer.

There was no sign of Spence inside the cabin, no sign that anyone had been there since the terrible night Claire had shot him.

Disturbed by the touch of the flashlight's bright beam, a scorpion scuttled across the dusty floor. Claire grabbed Pogo by the collar as the sheltie barked once and bolted toward the movement.

"Have you already forgotten your last sting on the nose?" Claire dragged the dog back outside and shut the door behind her. Though Pogo shied away from anything larger than a field mouse, when it came to scorpions and spiders, she apparently felt honor-bound to defend her owners to the death.

Outside the cabin, Claire squatted to pet her for a moment, but a yawn interrupted her praise of the dog's war on arachnids. It had been a long day, crammed with at least a year's worth of emotion, and fatigue was closing in. But Claire knew she wouldn't sleep until she checked the bluff for Spence, in the cave that he had mentioned.

"Let him be there, please," she whispered to the darkness.

Rising, she cupped her hand over her abdomen. Had that been another twinge?

She waited for a minute before deciding she was so tired she hardly knew what she was feeling. Then she turned and started trudging in the direction of the creek.

The muzzle of Randall Hajek's oversized gun swung back and forth like a pendulum between Spence and Giovanni. His thin, light brown hair stuck up as if he had been sleeping, and in his rumpled blue robe he looked far thinner than Spence remembered. Was the man seriously ill?

Of course he was, Spence thought, with a flash of comprehension. A man like Giovanni would seek out the most vulnerable older man he could. But the un-derstanding took a backseat to Spence's worry over Randall's trembling hand.

"Put that down before somebody gets hurt." Spence spoke with a firm confidence he didn't feel. He recog-nized the pistol—a .44 Magnum of the type popular back when Clint Eastwood had been terrorizing bad guys as Dirty Harry. Randall could barely hold up the heavy revolver, and like most of the movie buffs who'd bought the damned things, he probably had nothing in the way of firearms experience.

But that wouldn't stop him from blowing a melon-sized hole through anything he accidentally hit.

Ignoring Spence, Randall begged his partner, "Say he's lying,'Vanni. You tell me this son of a bitch is lying and I'll kill him for you now. For *us.*"

Giovanni began stammering a denial, but Spence talked over him.

"Don't be a fool, Randall. This guy's been to prison twice already, and God only knows how many times he's gotten away with it. Fraud, extortion, blackmail—always involving an older, wealthy man he'd been seeing."

Randall scowled at him. "How would you know that? How could you know anything about him?"

"I'm a cop, remember. And I've got cop friends who've been real curious about my recent problems. They've been looking into who might stand to profit from my troubles if they forced my wife to sell the land we bought from your aunt. Your buddy here popped up because of all those men he—"

"I swear, darling, they meant nothing to me." Staring at Randall, Giovanni pressed his palms together in an attitude of prayer. "Not a single thing. You're the one who's special. You're the only one I've ever—"

"You—you told me you loved me." Tears shook Randall's voice, and the Magnum trembled worse than ever. "You said you've waited your—your whole life to—to meet someone like—like me."

With the gun trained on him now, Giovanni dropped to his knees. Spence thought dryly that the man had a good strategy going, sticking with the position he knew best.

"I *did* fall in love with you, Rand," Giovanni pleaded. "I swore I'd stay by your side for as long as you had, no matter what. And that's what I've been doing, isn't it? Who's been doling out your medication, meeting with the hospice nurse, changing those bags filled with your—with your shit, cooking meals for—"

As the pistol's barrel drifted toward Spence, he cut in, saying, "What he's been doing, Randall, is chatting up a big-time San Antonio realtor. They're already gathering investors for this development they've dreamed up—and they need Claire's ranch to make it work."

"That's a lie, an utter lie," Giovanni shouted. "We can fit the whole development in the land we have alread—"

This time he interrupted himself, his eyes rounding as he realized the admission in his statement. Clambering back to his feet, he clasped his hands once more, giving the prayer routine another workout. "We're planning it as a lasting *tribute* to you, Randall, something to honor you once you're gone. We're going to call it 'Randall's Way.' "

"Imagine it," Spence said sarcastically, "a big-ass golf course ringed with starter castles. Conservative families at their conservative country club, holding memorial services for the gay man whose 'generosity' saddled them with fat mortgages. Come on, Randall. . . . You know better. You know in your heart a guy who looks like Giovanni has more in mind than playing nursemaid to some middle-aged man with—"

"But—but I *love* him." Randall's voice broke, crumbling beneath the weight of anguish and denial. "And I understood from the start, or at least part of me knew, that the money was always part of the package. But what successful businessman doesn't, whether he's marrying a trophy blonde twenty years his junior or finding a gorgeous specimen like Giovanni here to share his final days?"

"It isn't even *Giovanni*," Spence said, keeping his voice low and as calm as he could manage. "His real name is Vincenti, but he's used others, too. A different one with every man he's taken."

As Spence spoke, he edged nearer to Randall in the hope of leaping off the deck onto the frailer man if it came down to it.

"Don't you move—not one step closer," Randall warned. "I'll shoot. I swear I will. You and that Meador girl all but stole half my land, and now you're trying to steal whatever little peace I have left. Interfering assholes, always screwing up my life. Always messing with my family."

In spite of his threat, the muzzle of the gun was drooping as fatigue took its toll on the sick man. Giovanni moved forward, too, clearly anticipating that Spence would make a move.

"I found her letters—Gloria's," said Randall. "She'd slipped them into a pocket behind some loose wallpaper. I understand now why she ran off. And I have half a mind to tell everyone abo—"

As Giovanni took a bolder step, all three men erupted: Spence demanding both men keep still, Giovanni screaming for Randall to shoot Spence, and Randall merely screaming.

When Randall started to bring up the Magnum, Spence had no choice but to jump before Giovanni closed the distance between them. All three men went down, Spence knocking Randall over just as the taller but leaner Giovanni struck him from behind. The revolver flew a few feet away, kicking up a pile of old pecan leaves.

Spence should have reached the gun first. Of the three, he was the strongest and his experience as a street cop gave him the advantage when it came to gaining control of a weapon in a scramble.

But his attention was diverted by the sound of a loud explosion—it sounded like an airplane crashing—from the direction of the creek. In an instant, his thoughts flashed to the beam of light he had seen flicker through the dark trees, and his mind overflowed with a memory of Claire promising to meet him there if they were separated.

And that split second of distraction was all that Giovanni needed. With his longer reach, he snatched the fallen gun and swung its muzzle toward the disgraced cop who had just given him away.

THIRTY-THREE

It was her own choking that shook Claire back to wakefulness, her body's desperate struggle to clear her lungs of smoke and grit and suffocating darkness.

With awareness came the pain, the crushing pressure of something hard and heavy across her lower right leg. *Get it off,* her mind screamed, and suddenly her hands came back to life, fumbling around her sprawling body. She heard a rattling rain of sand and pebbles that echoed all around her, as if the sounds were closed off in a rocky chamber. . . .

As if *she* were.

Panic arced through every muscle as snatches of memory sparked. The cave—she'd found the rope and harness tied securely to a stout tree that overhung the bluff. Spence's work, she was certain, since she remembered him talking about using it when he'd begun his exploration weeks before.

Had she been brave enough to climb down it? She remembered using her belt to tie Pogo to a tree a safe distance from the bluff's edge, but following that, there was nothing but the echo of—what? Something huge, like a thunderbolt exploding in her ears. She didn't recall either rain or wind, but could she have been struck by lightning?

Her leg hurt too badly to ignore. In her struggle to sit up, she dislodged a cascade of dust that restarted her coughing, and she sucked in a mouthful of what smelled and tasted like burnt air. Still, she straightened—until the top of her head banged against something so hard that tears sprang to her eyes.

"Spence," she whimpered, her voice a tattered croak. "Please come get me."

Prompted by the painful weight across her ankle, she stretched sideways, then reached toward her right leg. Her unseeing fingers stubbed against stones, some fist-sized and others that crumbled into powder. But the largest, a rock larger and far heavier than Pogo, stubbornly refused to budge from its place atop her lower leg, no matter how she tried to push or roll it.

Dear God, it was so black here, as if an obsidian wall had dropped down before her eyes. She panicked at the thought that another rock besides the one she'd bumped must have slammed against her head. Certainly it hurt, and something had knocked her unconscious.

Could the injury have blinded her as well?

She craned her neck in desperation, looking above, below, from side to side while still fighting to pull her injured leg free. Was that—wait. She stared at what seemed to be a lighter spot—and there, another, or at least a thinner patch of darkness. She squinted, then guessed the nearer "bright spot" to be some twenty feet ahead of her, perhaps ten feet higher than where she lay curled on the rubble. So she was seeing, at least a little, but how could she crawl or climb toward what might be the night sky with her leg trapped? How could she possibly get out of this rocky hole without help?

"Spence," she called out, wondering if he had been there—if he could have been hurt or even killed by the . . . memory returned, and with it the word *cave-in*.

As the thought took form, her mind dredged up the imagery of terror. She saw herself poking behind the fallen tree Spence had described, entering the cave to search for some sign of him. When she hadn't found it, she'd shone her flashlight into others.

And then . . . had this been the collapse she had been warned of? What about the noise, the blast whose memory still had her head ringing, and the strange burnt smell inside her nostrils?

And what the devil had happened to that flashlight?

She began to feel around her, burrowing beneath the rubble where she could, stopping periodically to retry her strength against the rock that held her captive. The pinned leg throbbed horribly, eclipsing the pounding of her head and the stinging of a host of small abrasions. She suspected a crush fracture in her ankle. Yet she couldn't feel her toes or foot at all, as if the rock had compressed a nerve—or the foot was simply . . . *gone*.

Swallowing back the taste of bile, she tamped down the horrifying thought. She couldn't think about the damage, didn't want to focus on anything but finding that damned flashlight. With light, she could assess her situation. She could look for a way out—and possibly something to help her move this chunk of stone. And most important, she could shine it out through what she prayed were holes, so Spence would find her here.

If he's still alive, a small voice whispered deep inside

her. *And if he's not the person who brought half this bluff down on me.*

At that thought, the space around her heart hardened into concrete, making it almost impossible to breathe. Another memory teased, just beyond the fringe of comprehension. . . .

The memory of soft ticking. A flash of something blue and the image of the bundle of cylinders her flashlight's beam had touched when she'd investigated.

A wail tore loose from her throat, a cry of horror that came with the certain knowledge this had been no act of nature. No lightning strike, and no cave-in triggered by long years of erosion.

This had been one thing and nothing other.

A bomb set up to kill her at a time when only her husband could know that she was coming. . . .

THIRTY-FOUR

If you happen to be a predator in Texas, the midnight hour is yours. Whether you are a cougar looking for an easy meal—say, a small dog tethered to a tree far from any sign of humans—or a man listening for an explosion that will forever bury the evidence of his shame, the darkness is your ally.

Or so you might believe.

But from time to time the light prevails, no matter what the hour. Clouds part, and the moonlight gives away your movement. Some small sound alerts the creatures of the daylight and puts them on their guard.

Or one of them is willing to venture out into the blackness, to challenge you on your own turf. Leaving you no choice except to kill while you can.

Though Giovanni Baptiste sat less than an arm's length away, pointing the powerful Magnum toward him, Spence pushed off from his knees, then ducked his shoulder and charged toward him, aiming a body blow at the slender blond man's rib cage.

Before he made it, the pistol went off with an obscenely loud crack, rendering Spence deaf in his left ear. The cicadas, too, went silent, and the smell of burnt gunpowder filled the air.

The bullet must have just missed the side of his head, but Spence didn't stop to count his blessings. Instead he slammed the lighter Giovanni onto his back and struggled for control of the big gun.

A blow glanced off Spence's shoulder. He thought Randall was hitting him with a stick, but the sick man was too weak to do any real damage. Giovanni, however, made his efforts felt, raking Spence's neck with a set of nails that felt like talons, slamming his knee into a thighbone—the dirty little shit had been going for the gonads—and sinking his teeth into Spence's wrist when he clamped a hand atop the still-warm barrel.

Spence felt as if he'd been tossed into a cage with a live tiger. It was obvious Giovanni had picked up a thing or two surviving prison. In spite of the pain in his hand, Spence tightened his grip on the Magnum and kicked the hell out of Giovanni's legs until he unclamped his jaws to scream and loosened his hold on the gun's butt.

Snatching away the weapon, Spence rolled free and stood. He shot a glare at Randall, who was struggling to raise his stick again, and warned, "Drop it right now. You're both under arrest."

Spence doubted a fired fugitive had the power to arrest anyone, but neither man appeared inclined to argue with the huge, intimidating Magnum. Maybe Dirty Harry had been right about its power after all.

Aiming the gun toward Giovanni, Spence said, "Tell me what you know about that noise by the creek. And keep your goddamned hands up until I tell you different."

Randall was trying, but he seemed to be at the end of his rope physically.

"You," Spence told him. "Sit down on that deck chair. You can put your hands on your thighs, palms down, but other than that, don't move a muscle or I swear I'll take it out on Goldilocks here."

"I—I won't do anything." Randall struggled to climb back onto the deck—Spence let Giovanni help him as all three of them stepped up—then the sick man sank with a pained sigh into the floral cushions of a deck chair.

"Now answer me," Spence ordered Giovanni, who had paused to rub his kicked knee. "And get those damned hands up."

"I have no idea what that noise was." Giovanni complied but manufactured a supremely bored look. "No idea whatsoever."

The Italian accent had thickened, making Spence wonder if the guy had spent his teen years in the heartland working in a pizza parlor. Either that or taking acting lessons to capitalize on the pretty face he had been born with. Too bad he'd turned his modest talents to fleecing marks like Randall.

"Bullshit," Spence said. "I saw you staring that way. You looked like you were expecting something. What the hell was it? It sounded like some kind of an explosion."

Giovanni shrugged. "Your guess is as good as mine. I was looking at the light—I thought I saw someone moving that way. Perhaps someone with a flashlight."

Apprehension squeezed the breath from Spence's lungs at this confirmation of his own fears. *Claire.*

Suddenly he didn't give a damn about Giovanni's petty mischief, his plans to make the area into a crowded haven for young up-and-comers, or Randall's blind desire to pretend away the truth. Spence didn't care about anything but finding Claire and pulling her into his arms.

But he couldn't simply leave these two free to hunt him down—or to call Joel Shepherd, who would hotfoot it out here with the cavalry in a New York minute. So Spence swung the revolver's muzzle back toward Randall, who was slumping sideways in his seat and gasping with pain or exhaustion.

Spence struggled to tamp down his instinct for mercy; at the moment, he could not afford its price.

"Tell me, tell me right now," he demanded. "Where do you keep rope?"

There comes a point when a person goes beyond tears, a point when fear and even pain fall by the wayside as the mind blunts all extraneous emotion.

Claire had passed this boundary, had pushed aside all other thoughts except her survival. And the survival of the child that grew inside her.

At the moment, she needed the whole of her concentration, the same strength and focus she had demonstrated during her two-year uphill battle to plan, organize, and fund her equine rehab dream—a dream she damned well wasn't planning to give up on. She drew from that experience, drew on every ounce of stubbornness and the special inner confidence born of the knowledge she'd been loved. Of a certainty, by her friends and father. And as surely, by the man she'd married—once upon a time, before the incomprehensible madness of his grief consumed him.

But she didn't dare to think about that now, couldn't do anything but stretch as far as she could bend and reach in all directions. If she couldn't find the flashlight, maybe she'd find something she could use to make a lever to lift the damned rock off her leg. After all, the rock wasn't so huge, simply flat and heavy. And making a fulcrum was no problem, not with all these smaller stones.

She was thankful she had stayed awake in high school physics while half her friends slept through the unit about simple machines. She'd been a grades nerd, she'd admit it, worrying over her GPA to keep from thinking too much about her sister's illness.

"Thank you, Karen," Claire said softly—just as her fingertips grazed the last things she expected: first the tatters of what felt like plastic, and then a soft, dry clump that separated at her touch.

Claire felt it carefully, at first thinking she had found fur from some animal's nest, or perhaps the pelt of some unfortunate long-gone creature that had holed up in the cave to die. But the individual strands were far too long for any animal she could think of.

"Hair?" she guessed aloud, not liking the suspicion that was creeping up on her. Could it be human?

Whatever it was, it couldn't help her, so she thrust it from her mind. Dropping the fuzzy clump, she swallowed dust and wished in vain that she'd thought to carry water with her. A foolish mistake, and possibly one that would prove fatal if no one looked here for her.

She shoved aside her doubts, then reached out with her free foot to rake something long and clublike toward her. Something, she realized as her left hand grasped it, that might work as an arm for the lever she needed.

The thing was smooth and cool and lighter than she would expect of rock, but it was hard enough to work. Propping herself up on an elbow, Claire grunted with the pain that flashed up from her ankle at the sudden movement; then she waited for the tiny yellow fireworks to clear from her nearly nonexistent vision.

"Just breathe through it," she told herself, gritting her teeth.

A minute later, she recovered enough to reach around and push her designated lever's knobby end beneath the large rock, then position the smaller stone she'd found as close as possible for the best mechanical advantage.

Now all she had to do was push down to lift the rock. Push down, then pull back her injured leg as fast as possible.

Claire began to shiver in the darkness, not so much from the cool night air, but at the thought of the agony that would rip through her when she shifted the weight that pinned her lower leg.

What if she passed out, then dropped the rock back on her ankle? Nausea roiled at the thought, and she barely kept down her gorge. Or what if her foot, which she still couldn't feel, had not only been mashed, but partially—or even completely—severed, and the compression was the only thing keeping her from bleeding to death?

Fear had come back on her, circling around like a once-discouraged predator to take her from behind. And this time there was only one way to combat it.

Cold fury at the man who had tricked her into coming here, so cunningly she had almost believed it to be her own idea. The man who needed her dead for some reason.

Insurance, maybe—or he could be as crazy as everyone she knew was saying. One thing was for certain: He was nothing like the loving, vulnerable, and sexy facade he'd hidden behind during the time they'd spent together in the wake of his arrest.

Spence Winslow was a predator, and she'd be good and damned if she would simply lie here and die quietly.

No matter how much pain it cost her, she could never let the bastard win.

Spence cursed as he tripped over a snarl of dry weeds and fell, his left hand striking the ground to send pain shooting up his healing arm. Even with the oversized flashlight he'd liberated from Randall Hajek's mudroom, it was rough going cutting across both the pasture and the woods that sloped down toward the creek.

But nothing was rougher than the fear that gripped him, so Spence picked himself up and climbed through the strands of barbed wire separating the Hajek ranch from his property . . . or, he should say, Claire's.

In his darkest moment, he had relinquished his claim to it, just as he had given up on her. But that time was gone forever, he swore to himself.

Claire's faith in him—her belief regardless of all "proof" to the contrary—had given him the strength to throw off the black blinders he had worn for too long. If there was any way—any way at all—to love his wife as she deserved and heal in the love she offered, he was damned well going to take it. He was going to soak up life and love and family as greedily as a parched land soaking up the rain. . . .

If Claire were only safe now, if she were sleeping soundly in her old bedroom or waiting for him at the cabin. If he didn't learn that the boom he'd heard had taken her away.

Dust hazed out the starlight as he approached the creek. It clogged his throat and made him cough—what the hell was in the air?

The illumination from his flashlight melted into what appeared to be a brownish yellow fogbank. He saw nothing else ahead of him, not a single glimmer of light. Certainly nothing to indicate the presence of another human being. Only this eerie thick cloud and the unnatural silence of the insects.

"Claire?" he called out softly.

Something answered from a spot ahead and to his left, whimpering and whining. Could it be Claire, badly hurt?

Cautiously, he stepped into the dust. He sneezed, then called Claire's name once more.

This time two sounds came back out of the darkness: one an anxious yip he recognized as Pogo's, and the other an agitated, throaty growl that could only come from a big cat.

THIRTY-FIVE

The failure wasn't Claire's.

She didn't faint from the pain, though it would have been a mercy. Instead she cried out when the arm of her lever gave a splintering crack, then snapped in two, and the tilting bulk rolled back atop her injured ankle.

The rock hadn't moved far before the lever broke. Perhaps two inches, maybe three, but it was enough that Claire lay sobbing, digging her fingers into the pressure points below her knee in an attempt to block her nerves' impulses. If the effort made a difference, she didn't notice. She straddled a raft of agony tossed by a raging storm. There was no telling how long it took her to regain some semblance of control. In this darkness, time meant less than nothing. . . .

Except that time was growing short.

She felt her mind's attempt to separate, like the sole of an old shoe. Recognized it for the shock it was—shock that would keep her from fighting, from even trying to break free.

But how could she? How could she risk such pain again?

"Because I have to," she told herself, drawing on a memory of Ellen's take-no-prisoners approach to life. Drawing on the memories of the parents who kept going for the sake of their physically frail children.

Claire dragged in a deep breath to steady herself, then groped until she found the broken handle of her makeshift lever. She couldn't afford to trust its strength again, so instead she used it as an extension of her own arm and started dragging rubble toward her.

She stirred up more dust, then coughed before she finally had her first stroke of good fortune. As her fingers wrapped around the metal flashlight, she whispered, "Thank God, thank God, thank God."

Flipping the switch with frantic speed, she cried out in relief as a beam cut through a dirty haze. Though it swam with swirling dust, the light felt like a miracle. She quickly shone it around her, looking for some way out of her prison.

Her first realization was that the explosion hadn't brought down the whole bluff face. Above her, as she had earlier learned the hard way, was a knob of rock, along with a ceiling creased with thick black cracks. The rubble all around her—the tan stones ranged from pea-small to the size of a grown mule deer—appeared to be the crumbled walls dividing several of the caves. Certainly this space was longer and deeper than any individual cave she remembered.

But the difference was that this new grotto had no exit, for the largest rocks were stacked above and ahead of her, where she had earlier made out what she'd thought of as two "light spots." She thought she saw them now, several slim gaps between the rocks that might, if she was lucky, lead to an escape.

Yet seeing a possible way out meant nothing if she couldn't reach it. She swung her light's beam downward to the small boulder that trapped her lower leg. Twisting around, she spotted the toe of her boot sticking out to one side. Though she still couldn't move the foot, she now felt it aching.

And she thanked God for that pain, which she took to mean that her foot and toes were still living parts of her own body. So barring any internal injuries, she shouldn't bleed to death.

Which, in the long run, wouldn't make a bit of difference if she couldn't find a way to free herself.

The long metal flashlight's beam yellowed, and she panicked at the thought that, sooner or later, the batteries would fail her. Moving quickly, she began a survey of the space around her, focusing most carefully on every item in her reach.

She started with the thing she'd been using for a lever arm before it broke. Her eyes shot wide with the realization that she'd been wrong about it all along.

It was no arm, but a leg bone. A femur, to be exact, dirty tan and splintered where it had broken near the middle.

It was a thighbone, something she had learned to recognize in her anatomy classes back in college. And if she had doubted for a moment that it was human, the clump of hair beside her left hand set her straight.

Once long and straight, it was dry and powdery and somewhat matted. But the flashlight's beam was strong enough for Claire to say for certain that its owner had been blond.

More disturbing still was the rounded shape beyond

the gold mass, lying near what looked like the remnants of an old blue tarp. She reached out toward it, using the flashlight's length to pull the thing toward her. But when it rolled to face her, she wished to God she'd let it be.

Claire whimpered as she took it all in, from the quarter-sized, perfectly circular hole near the top to the sheath of desiccated leathery flesh that still clung in ragged shreds. She'd found a skull, a human skull, that had come to rest on its side and now lay staring at her.

As she stared back mutely, she recognized the accusation in the shadows of its dark and hollow eyes.

"Here, girl. Pogo." Spence deliberately raised his voice and then whistled in the hope that the sounds of a grown man would scare away what he feared might be a cougar.

He prayed that he was wrong, that what he'd heard was a bobcat or coyote, or perhaps even a figment of his overwrought imagination. For nothing smaller than a cougar would dare attack a human being.

Even those attacks were rare, but he had read accounts of mountain lions going after a lone person. Often someone smaller, such as a woman. Such as Claire, who must have come here with no one but the dog for company.

Fearing the worst, Spence raised Randall's Magnum and crept forward, toward the sound of Pogo's now-agitated barking.

The flashlight's beam caught something tawny, something that turned toward him and snarled—sounding for all the world like a Mercury commercial from a bygone day. Before Spence could react, the animal leapt away from him and took off at a dead run.

Some fifteen feet beyond the spot where the cat had stood, Pogo strained against whatever tied her to a young tree, her tail wagging with such fervor, Spence thought she might take flight. The sheltie tossed a few more halfhearted barks in the lion's wake, then gave herself over to wriggling in delight to see her long-absent master.

"What a good girl," Spence said as he knelt down, then set aside both gun and flashlight while he untied her. "Where's your mama? Where's Claire?"

Pogo was far too busy trying to lick Spence's face off to give an answer, even if she could. Spence pushed her away, not because he wasn't glad to see the little fur-ball, but because he was trying to get a look at what she had been tied with.

He recognized the braided leather belt, a brown one Claire often wore because she liked its silver buckle. The sheltie had stretched it and gnawed through several strands, a fact that convinced Spence she'd been left here for some time. Probably because Claire had wanted to keep the three-legged dog from attempting to follow as she climbed down the treacherous bluff face in the dark.

"Claire," he called, not bothering to keep his voice down. For one thing, he didn't want the cougar to think about returning. And if he were worried about pursuers, he'd already made enough noise to draw them here.

Pogo at last fell silent, as if she were listening for an answer, too. But Spence heard nothing, save the thin cry of a distant night bird.

A cool breeze had cleared the air of dust, making it easier to see where he was going. Still, he moved cautiously, a memory of the boom he'd heard warning him of danger while a vision of Claire, hurt and lying in the shallow water near the bluff's base, urged him forward. . . .

Until the land dropped off abruptly several yards short of where its edge had once been. Remembering the instability he'd noticed earlier, he wondered if a collapse could have made the noise he'd heard from Randall Hajek's back deck—and if Claire had been standing on the bluff's edge when it fell.

The thought was like a gut punch, a fear so visceral it nearly dropped him to his knees. And kept him from noticing the light coming up behind him until he heard the voice.

"Where is she? Where is Claire, you bastard?"

Spence spun around, his right hand clutching the Magnum and his brain telling him to stop. Pogo's tail thwapped against a low bush as she wagged it in greeting, but the sound was nearly drowned out by the new arrival's heavy breathing.

Claire's father held a flashlight in one hand and a shotgun in the other. As Spence looked down the double barrel, he framed his answer carefully.

"I think she's nearby. I'm looking for her. I was—I was talking to Randall Hajek and his buddy when I heard this loud noise. And then I came out looking because she said she'd meet me here." Alarmed by Meador's deepening scowl, Spence quickly added, "I'd never hurt Claire, Will. I love her—love her more than I can tell you. And I'm scared now, scared as hell that she's been hurt."

The shotgun's muzzle dropped, and the older man said, "We have to find her. I wasn't feeling too good, so I got up to take one of my pills. That's when I heard the blast, and something—something warned me—I ran to check on Claire and found her gone."

Spence heard pure terror in the man's voice, saw it written in a face drained of all color.

"I—I drove my car straight to Claire's office." Meador's words trembled; he sounded weak with fear. "She wasn't there or in the stable either. And somehow I knew then—I knew that she'd come back here, where someone smashed my ATV."

Spence nodded. "I found Pogo tied here, so I figure Claire must have climbed down."

"I took my car as far as I could—I left it back there by the practice ring. Then I ran—well, mostly walked—the rest of the way out here. I have to find her, Winslow. She's all—Claire's all I have left."

Spence heard the desperation in the man's voice, as well as the exhaustion. If Claire's father didn't calm down, he'd end up needing a rescue of his own.

Very slowly, Spence squatted down, his heart pounding with the risk that he was taking. Laying the Magnum in the leaf litter near his feet, he looked up into Will Meador's eyes.

"I'm leaving the gun right here. I'd just end up shooting myself if I tried to climb down with it. It's going to be hard enough scrambling down the bluff without a rope."

He stood, never taking his gaze off Claire's father for a second. Figuring that if the man was going to shoot him, some shift in his expression would give Spence an instant's warning of the bullet that was about to finish him.

THIRTY-SIX

"Gloria," Claire whispered. As her mind tried to pull free from her horror, the name began spelling itself out over and over, a Van Morrison rock classic turned into the stuff of nightmares.

Gloria herself lay silent, long past singing the old lyrics. And even if she felt inclined, her lower jaw was gone.

G-L-O-R-I-A. The pain pulsed out the letters in Claire's ankle and their meaning in her head. A meaning that had taken shape in a single look that passed between two people, and in a pair of silver bracelets.

A meaning she'd refused to see—a refusal that might have formed the substance of her deadliest denial.

A faint noise caught her attention, the muffled sound of shouts. Blinking back her tears, Claire strained to listen, then gasped with relief at the most welcome thing she'd ever heard.

Her own name, in a male voice she recognized as Spence's.

341

As certain as she was of her devastating realization, she was equally convinced that she'd been wrong to doubt her husband, wrong to believe, even for a second, that the desperation she heard in his voice was that of a murderer, coming back to be sure he'd killed his victim. And just as certainly, answers to other questions followed, pinging into place one after another. And suddenly she realized who had access to his e-mails, who could have taped her husband's voice, and why it might have seemed so crucial to take Spence out of her life.

So she began to call out to him, to guide him to the unholy tomb she had almost shared.

"I hear someone," Spence shouted up at the man standing above him. "I think it's Claire. She's back in here, in a cave behind this pile of rocks."

"Let me climb down to help you," her father called, his own flashlight winking downward from the bluff's edge.

A loose rock tumbled past Spence's head and set off a clattering below him.

"Get back from there," Spence called up. He worried not only about being buried in a slide as the rest of the bluff gave way, but also the very real possibility that Will Meador would end up falling to his death. "Stay up there. You may have to go for help."

Spence wondered if the man would make it if he did go, as shaken and exhausted as he looked. But at least his concern for Claire had prevented Meador from blowing off his son-in-law's head. So far, at any rate.

"I can make it," Meador called back, clearly too distraught to listen. "I'm coming right down. Have to— have to save my Claire."

It would be a hell of a lot easier if his father-in-law obeyed Spence's "sit and stay" command as well as Pogo did.

"No, Will." Spence used his cop voice, unmistakably an order. "Wait and let me see how Claire is. If she's hurt badly, she could need help fast. Do you want to risk delaying it?"

"All—all right," Meador answered, and his light disappeared from the bluff's lip. "Just get her out of there fast—please."

With that question settled, Spence began climbing over a jumble of rocks, edging toward the spot where he'd heard Claire's voice.

Trying to orient himself, he shouted her name again—and heard the muffled thump of rock on rock, followed by the marrow-freezing sound of his wife's scream.

The bead of perspiration tickled as it rolled down Claire's temple. But the sensations that followed were not nearly so innocuous.

I must have passed out when I used the flashlight for a lever, she thought as her eyes opened to darkness. She dug her fingers into her leg again in an attempt that once more failed to block the agony radiating from her ankle. An ankle finally free of the boulder's crushing weight.

Thank God, the thing had moved.

Then she remembered. *Spence*—she'd heard his voice from outside. After she'd lost consciousness, had he given up on finding her and left? Or had he only been a wish—an auditory hallucination brought on by the stress of discovering the bones she felt so sure were Gloria Hajek's?

"Spence," she called, again and again until her throat felt shredded with the effort.

Fumbling around, she found the flashlight, but this time nothing happened when she clicked its switch. Her heart contracted at the realization that she'd left it on, that the battery must had died after she'd passed out.

Would she suffer the same fate here in the empty darkness? Tears burned, dripping down her face and clogging her nose—and then she heard the clatter, a stony banging that was followed by her first glimpse of the strong beam of another flashlight, from outside the cave.

"It's all right, Claire. I'm almost through," Spence said.

A real and solid Spence, she was sure of it.

"Hurry," she answered.

There was a rumble, then a clatter as stones of all sizes rolled down toward her. She held up an arm to ward them off, but only the tiniest of pebbles reached her.

"You all right?" Spence called down.

She could see him now as he squeezed through the opening and started crawling toward her over the rubble.

"I will be, now that you're here."

As he narrowed the gap between them, he had to stop twice to move stones, while working carefully to avoid sending an avalanche down on her.

"Can you move toward me, or are you hurt?" he asked her.

"I'll try, but I think my ankle's broken. I've already passed out a couple times while I was getting that damned rock off it."

He shone the flashlight toward her. "You're trapped?"

"Not anymore. But, Spence, there's something in here—it's a body. Part of one, at any rate."

Spence's flashlight beam found the skull. "Indians lived here for a long time. Maybe it's one of—"

"It's Gloria—Gloria Hajek. See that blue stuff? It's an old tarp, and there's this long blond hair—"

From outside the opening, they heard a cracking sound as something—perhaps a rock or tree—went crashing down the bluff face.

"Later—tell me later," Spence said. "We've got to get you out of here before what's left of this bluff comes down on us."

He was almost close enough to reach now. Bracing herself for the pain, she dragged her body the last few inches, then grasped his hand with every bit of strength she had remaining.

In the near darkness, an unspoken promise flowed between them. *Never will I leave you. Never again will I doubt what we have.*

"I love you, Spence," she told him.

Though his own injury must have been throbbing, he dragged himself forward on his elbow and pressed his mouth against hers in a fierce kiss that captured and redoubled all her emotion. One hand slipped through her hair, caressing her scalp much too briefly.

"There's more where that came from," he promised, "as soon as we get you to safety."

"There *will* be more," she told him, "because I know who did this. To her. To you. To us. He couldn't let you find her—couldn't let you keep poking around this place."

But much of what she'd said was lost in the grind and rattle of small stones as he pulled her toward him in the direction of the slender opening he'd dug. Her breath hissed as she sucked in air through clamped teeth in response to the fresh flair of pain.

"I wish we had the time to try to splint your leg," he said. "I'm so sorry, Claire, but this is gonna hurt like hell."

It already did hurt. Not just her ankle, but the deeper pain of a betrayal every bit as shocking as the one she had faced weeks before.

Mercifully, Claire passed out again when Spence began to move her. She lost track of time as she faded in and out of consciousness. At one point she heard Spence shouting up to the top of the bluff for someone to tie off the end of the rope he'd found. At another she was dimly aware of being hoisted from above while Spence, who climbed at her side, struggled to support and guide her.

By the time she fully came back to herself, she was lying on her back, blinking at a patch of stars that peered down through a gap in the tree branches above her. Something furry—it could only be Pogo—was snuggled close beside her, offering her warmth while occasionally licking her limp arm and whining softly.

"We need to get her to a hospital," Spence was saying from somewhere at her left. "We can either rig up a makeshift splint and try carrying her out ourselves, or you can go back to your car, then run up to the office and call for help."

"I'll—I'll be damned if I'm leaving Claire here alone with you for one minute."

Shocked to hear her father's voice, she swiveled her head toward the light.

Spence stood in front of him, his arms outstretched and his hands empty save for the flashlight he still held. "Put that gun down," he told her father. "You aren't going to need it. It's Claire now that's important. The rest of this can wait."

"The hell it can," Claire interjected, propping herself up on an elbow.

Both men turned to look at her as one. But Claire was staring only at her father.

"It was *you*," she told him. "It's been you all along. I should have guessed it earlier when Megan walked into your house this evening and called you by your first name. You've been—you've been *grooming* her— or maybe—maybe it's already gone past that."

The end of her father's rifle dipped as his face twisted, becoming something, or some*one*, unfamiliar. Or perhaps she was only now seeing that part of him she'd pretended away for far too long.

Stepping nearer, he said, "What in God's name are you saying? You're still out of it—you're talking crazy. Did one of those rocks hit your head?"

"I *know*," she insisted, her lips curling back from the ugliness of the things she had to say. "I know you murdered Gloria Hajek all those years ago, back around the time my mother died. And I know why you did it. Your interest in teenaged girls is nothing new, is it?"

Claire felt sick, remembering all those framed photos in his home office, pictures of the high school debate team students he had helped coach after school. Why had she never noticed that nearly all of them were girls? Blond girls, in particular—as blond as Gloria . . . and Meg.

He dropped to his knees by her side, with Pogo quivering in the space between them.

"Why are you saying these things, Claire? How could you? I can't imagine what this lying sonofabitch"—he glared in Spence's direction—"has put into your head."

"You were sure he'd find out, weren't you?" She felt her heart tearing a little more with every syllable, felt its pain eclipsing what now seemed the negligible discomfort of her ankle. But she couldn't stop now, couldn't afford to let her lawyer father argue her back into disbelief. "When Spence told us about exploring the caves, and when he brought you back her bracelet—the one you'd given Gloria—that's when you knew you had to take him out of our lives. And you had to make it something so bad I'd never want to hear his name again."

Her father tried to interrupt, but she talked over him.

"You were the one who had access to our laptop when we came to visit. You were the person with the opportunity—and the sound system—to record enough of Spence's conversations to splice together those incriminating words. What I want to know is how you managed, who you bribed in the sheriff's office—or did you get help from one of your San Antonio defendants?"

"*El Tiburón.*" Shock resonated in Spence's voice as he spoke the gang leader's street name. "You used him and his men, didn't you? And *you* put up the money for my marker, after it got back to you how much I'd lost, to keep Claire from losing the Monarch."

But Claire was far from finished. Still staring holes into her father, she said, "And I want to know what the hell you're going say to Ellen when I tell her you've been using her to get your damned hands on her daughter."

"I never touched Meg," he exploded. "I never touched any of them after—"

"After what?" Spence prompted. "After the accident with Gloria?"

Claire's father nodded eagerly, like a condemned man offered a reprieve. "Yes," he said quickly. "It *was* an accident. A terrible mistake."

"I understand they happen," Spence said with surprising gentleness. "Can you explain it to us, to Claire?"

"The girl—the damned girl *made* me do it."

Sounding shell-shocked and unfocused, her father swayed on his knees like tall grass in the wind. Blinking back tears, Claire hardened her heart against his pain. She couldn't offer comfort now, couldn't even imagine reaching out to the man who'd raised her.

Surprisingly, it was her husband who found it in his heart to do so. Coming up behind the man, Spence laid his big hand on her father's trembling shoulder.

"Sometimes it happens that way," Spence murmured. "I've seen a lot of it, and I know things sometimes turn out in ways a man would never imagine."

Claire supposed he was attempting to draw out her father's explanation: she didn't know if she could bear to hear it.

Her father nodded, staring vacantly. As she drew the sheltie even closer, she had to look away while he spoke.

"It was never love, Claire. Never. I only loved your mother—your mother and you girls. But a man—well, I was weak and foolish, there's no other way to say it. She—she was so young and pretty, and she did everything but run out in the woods and wave that fanny in my face any time she saw me go out hunting. Every time she saw me going anywhere alone—"

"Spare me," Claire said. She'd rather have another

rock dropped on her ankle than hear one more word about how some fifteen-year-old girl had "seduced" him.

Her father went on as though he hadn't heard her, his voice as flat and colorless as a pane of window glass. "And then one day—this one day, she said she had to meet me. Out here by the bluffs. She told me she was—oh, God, she told me she was pregnant, and now I'd have to leave my wife to marry her."

Claire pressed her face into Pogo's soft back, but that didn't stop the tears from flowing. "Please. No more. I can't stand this—"

"Of course I couldn't do that," her father continued, as if she hadn't spoken. "I could hardly give up Linda, throw away the family and the home I'd worked so hard for just to marry some child."

But you could sleep *with her?* Claire's mind demanded, though she was powerless to speak the question.

"She became enraged," her father said. "She called me names—such horrible things. She swore she would tell Linda—she would tell everybody, even you and Karen, as little as you were. She turned to leave me then, and that was when it happened. I was so upset—so upset I must have squeezed the trigger. I never meant to, but I must have. Because I saw her falling—and there was so much blood. . . ."

"You—you killed to keep her quiet." Claire forced herself to look into his face. She couldn't hide from this truth—not if she wanted to be able to live with herself. "You took your gun out with you, and you killed her to stop her from screwing up your life."

"*All* our lives." His eyes beseeched her. "Don't you see that, baby? I did it for the children—you and Karen."

Throwing up a hand, she said, "Then why not Spence, too, Daddy? Why'd you bother going to the trouble to set him up instead of killing him, too? Still plenty of caves left empty in that bluff you wanted to seal off."

He shook his head emphatically, dropping the shotgun to lay his hand over his heart. "I'm not a murderer, Claire. I'm *not*. Gloria was an accident, and it was so long ago. Since then, I've built my life around caring for you—and Karen, while she lived. So how could you think I'd hurt you that way, by murdering the man you loved? How could I do that when—"

"When ruining my fucking life would be enough?" Spence squatted down and snatched away her father's gun. No trace of compassion lingered in his voice. "You'd have been kinder killing me than doing what you did."

"Please don't hurt him, Spence," Claire pleaded, terror ripping through her as she began to struggle to all fours. "I'll turn him in myself, I swear it. We'll get this whole mess sorted out."

There was a rustling from the brush, and then a deep shout: "Drop it right there, Winslow. Drop it or I'll shoot."

Sheriff Joel Shepherd pushed his way past branches, leading with his own drawn weapon.

"Stop, Joel. This isn't what you think," Claire started. But in her panic, she unthinkingly put weight on her bad ankle—

And passed out cold before she knew whether he would fire.

THIRTY-SEVEN

Spence nearly jumped out of his skin at the sound of a harsh clatter only inches from his ear. Blinking in the near darkness, he rolled off the narrow jail bunk and onto the hard floor.

Good move, he realized when he saw the deputy who stood outside the cell, the idiot whom Spence remembered hearing earlier was some kind of relation to Joel Shepherd. Earl Branson's hammy fist still clutched the baton he'd banged along the bars above Spence's head.

Across the corridor, a big-bellied man rolled over and bellowed a stream of profanity over the noise, ending his tirade with, "Tryin' to sleep over here, for chrissakes. You wake me up again, it damned well better be to buy another round."

But Branson's little pig eyes never looked away from Spence. A huge grin spread across the deputy's wide face, but instinct warned Spence it could only mean bad news.

He stood slowly, the spit drying in his mouth and his

heart smashing against his ribs like a sledgehammer. As worried as he'd been, he was amazed he'd slept at all, but his fatigue, coupled with the wait for news, must have conspired to pull him under.

Yet as he studied the deputy, dread settled over Spence. Had Earl come to tell him Claire was worse off than he'd thought? Or was he being blamed for her father's collapse, within minutes of Joel Shepherd's arrival near the bluffs? Or perhaps—but it was no use torturing himself with questions he couldn't answer.

Instead he raked his fingers through his hair and faked a stretch to hide his shaking. If Earl Branson smelled Spence's desperation, the sorry bastard would doubtless string him out all night long.

Pouring everything he had into disguising his panic, Spence asked, "So, what can I do for you?"

"Put your hands back here so's I can cuff 'em. Cousin Joel—I mean, Sheriff Shepherd—wants to see you in the interview room."

"Is my attorney here?" Spence asked over his shoulder as Earl reached through the bars to snap on the cuffs. Spence had understood his lawyer wouldn't be arriving until morning. But maybe it *was* morning. With this floor's dearth of natural light, who could tell?

"No lawyer for this meeting," Earl said. "I 'spect Joel wants to tell you 'bout the trouble with your wife."

Spence jerked toward him. "Claire? Tell me, you asshole, or I swear I'll find a way to—"

The baton rang against the bars once more, provoking another round of shut-the-hell-ups from the drunk across the way.

"Hey, now. You gonna play nice, or am I gonna have to leave you here a few more hours?" Earl asked, once more ignoring the other prisoner's outburst to point with the stick.

Spence clenched his jaw and reminded himself that threatening a deputy would only cause more trouble. As soon as he could manage it, he ground out an apology.

"Just so you behave right," Earl said before unlocking the cell door and marching Spence down the corridor. The deputy punched a code into a keypad to unlock another exit, then escorted Spence to a door with dingy, puke green paint and a metal sign so faded it now read, IN RV EW.

Along the hallway's opposite side, a narrow window near the ceiling glowed with pinkish light. Morning, Spence thought. The dawn had finally come.

Earl put his hand on the doorknob before hesitating. A moment later he turned to look Spence in the eye, a flush of discomfort reddening his round face. "Sorry if I was a little rough before, wakin' you like that. But I been thinkin'. I want'cha to know I had no idea that Deputy Ashford'd been bought off. No idea at all. If I'd had any inklin'—"

"What?" Spence asked. He found Earl's show of remorse as stunning as his comment about Ashford. So the veteran deputy had been the one bought off by Meador?

"Sheriff's having him brought up on charges. Frank's tellin' it like Mr. Meador talked him into helpin'. The old man told him you were gamblin'—gonna lose everything for your missus just the way Mr. Meador's daddy lost his ranch back in the old days. But me and the other deputies figure that's bunk. Frank really sold out so he could run for sheriff hisself and put Cousin Joel out of a job. That Mr. Meador knows everybody who's anybody here in Buck County, and he could talk up Frank like—"

Spence couldn't listen to the man's blather one more second. "All I care about is my wife. What's happening with her? *Please.*"

Earl lowered his voice. "My other cousin, Ray Lee, volunteers on the ambulance. He told me your lady started bleedin', said she's like to lose that little one she's carryin'."

Spence squeezed his eyes shut. *Oh, Claire. Not now. Not again.*

But the baby's loss was not his only worry. Had she fainted not from pain, but because she'd been bleeding internally from another ectopic pregnancy? Was he going to lose her, too?

"What—what else do you know?" he managed, almost fearing to ask.

"The fellows on the other ambulance, they had to shock her daddy's heart twice. They had to bag him, too, to keep him breathin' when they got him off the ambulance."

So Meador had happened upon another way out of paying for his sins—including the horrendous crime he'd copped to after Claire passed out.

The green door opened from the inside. "What the hell have you been doing, Earl?" Joel demanded, his words snapping with impatience. He looked as rough as Spence felt, his hair ruffled and his face unshaven.

Earl cringed. "Nothing, Sheriff. I was just lettin' him know about his wife and her daddy."

A look of regret shadowed the glance Joel Shepherd gave Spence. Nodding, the sheriff told his cousin, "Unlock his handcuffs, Earl. We won't be needing those now."

Less than a minute later, Spence found himself sitting across the table from the sheriff with a cup of much-needed black coffee in his unbound hands. At Shepherd's bidding, Earl had left the two of them alone.

As the lawman took a long pull from his own cup, Spence said, "Your deputy told me Claire was bleeding. Have you heard something more about her? Please, Sheriff—I need to know how she is."

As they peered over the rim of his foam cup, Joel Shepherd's eyes looked sad. But a split second later, the expression recast itself into pure frustration. "I've been calling that damned hospital off and on the last few hours, and all they'd give was me some crap about privacy laws. I had to threaten to drive over personally and start shaking things up to even find out she was stable. She'll make it, anyway."

"And the baby?"

Shepherd shook his head. "I don't know any more than you about that, but I finally wormed it out of someone that Claire's gonna need surgery to set that ankle."

Spence downed half the cup of coffee without caring that it was too hot. It tasted bitter, too, as bitter as the grief that had come of a nearly thirty-year-old murder.

Two of them, in fact.

"What about Claire's father?"

Shepherd grimaced, shook his head once more. "Deader than a hammer. Good thing for you he confessed before he kicked off."

Spence rubbed his forehead in a vain attempt to soothe his mind. "About that confession, Joel. It's going to be hard enough for Claire, losing her father and learning he murdered that poor girl, then went to such lengths to keep me from finding out about it. And it'll be hell for Claire if it turns out she loses this baby. But if she finds out now about what really happened to her mother— God. I'm afraid it's going to kill her. *If* she hears."

A long pause lodged itself into the space between them. Spence choked down more coffee, both his mind and his stomach roiling with the thought of the things Meador had told them. How his wife had grown suspicious of him, suspicious enough to leave her daughters playing at a neighbor's home while she followed the man she loved into the woods. And caught up with him in time to see Gloria Hajek die.

When Linda Meador started screaming, Will had turned and shot her, too, in his panic. But unlike Gloria, who had earlier run away on two occasions, he knew his own wife's disappearance would be investigated seriously. So he'd made a terrified call to one of his clients, a part-time house burglar named Felix Navarro, and paid the man six thousand dollars to claim he'd accidentally killed her.

And afterwards, Will Meador, respected attorney and new widower, had quietly resumed life in the family home he had begun restoring. Raising his daughters on his own and struggling against the longings that drew him like a crippled moth to the bright flame of Little BC's teenaged girls. Until he had lost consciousness, he'd continued to swear that he'd touched none of them since Gloria.

Spence hoped to hell it was the truth. Just as he hoped that Joel had understood what he was suggesting—and that he cared enough for Claire to seriously consider it.

At last the sheriff shrugged. "I don't see why Claire—or anybody—needs to hear about that last confession. No one's alive to substantiate it—I checked on that

Navarro character. He died in prison on an unrelated robbery charge just a couple of years ago. And no one's alive to punish, either, except the innocent."

Spence exhaled. "When Claire's ready—when she starts to ask the questions—I'll tell her then. I'll have to. But for now . . . I owe you."

He put out his hand and waited until Shepherd shook it.

"You're wrong," the sheriff said. "I'm the one who owes *you*. I should've listened to Claire earlier. And I should've understood how pissed my deputy was after he was passed over by the county Republicans when they decided to support my run for sheriff. He had worked here longer, and the fellow who'd retired apparently said some things that more or less promised Ashford he was next in line. He'd made the work his life—a mistake I understand well."

Spence nodded an acknowledgment. Though neither of them would speak of it, he understood that last night's events and this morning's conversation had shifted their relationship into something like a friendship. Something requiring an admission of his own.

"I know I looked plenty guilty. And I was—of being a damned idiot after that shooting last October. It hit me really hard—"

"Back when I was still a greenhorn deputy, I had to kill a man in the line of duty," Joel said. "Drunken bastard was coming at me with a knife—would've gutted me just like a catfish. But I still had dreams about it every night for weeks. And with you havin' to shoot a kid and watching your best friend die . . ."

Spence swallowed back a knee-jerk impulse to bury his pain in a macho shrug or offhand comment. Instead he sucked in a deep breath and thought about how closing himself off had worked out for him so far. "I wasn't wrong to take it so hard. I was wrong in shutting out help. And especially in closing myself off to Claire so I could hide out gambling. I swear I'll never make that mistake again."

Instead of scoffing, as Spence half expected, Shepherd sat in silence a few seconds before saying, "Probably take your lawyer and the DA a couple days to sort the legal stuff out. I'll talk to the prosecutor, see what he can do to speed things up . . . and maybe smooth some ruffled feathers."

"Uh, there was this incident, out east of San Antonio—" Though his lawyer would go crazy if he knew what his client was saying, Spence had an inkling that Joel Shepherd was willing to pull a few strings if he could do it off the record. "It was purely accidental. Involved a deputy and a chase and—"

"You mean that thing that happened *after* Claire's truck was stolen near the central library?" Shepherd prompted.

Spence hesitated, then breathed a sigh at the invisible door the Buck County sheriff had just opened. Thank God for long-standing family ties and small communities.

"Yeah," Spence finally answered. "It's a damned shame the kind of stunts car thieves will pull."

Another thought occurred to him, and he added, "But what about Randall Hajek and Giovanni? Are they going to press charges?"

"Nah, they want to keep things quiet, keep Randall's final days as peaceful as they can. And I don't think his buddy's too eager to have any more dealings with the law." Shepherd flashed a grin. "Especially after I mentioned we'd found his prints on the wrecked ATV."

"Did you?" Spence asked.

Joel shrugged. "A good bluff comes in handy for somethin' besides poker. And it put a stop to all the squawkin' they were doing when I showed up and untied 'em. Lucky break for you that Randall had already called me before he went out to rescue Giovanni from your clutches. He actually said that. 'Clutches.' "

The sheriff chuckled, head shaking in amusement. But he sobered soon enough. "You know, if I hadn't gone looking for you, I never would have heard Meador's confession. Then you'd have been up shit creek."

"Once I get out, I'll have to thank Hajek personally for his help," Spence said.

Shepherd made a face. "I don't think I'd push it that far. 'Specially if he has any more guns like that Magnum I picked up."

But Spence could not resist the urge to try his luck on a far more important issue. "Can you take me to the hospital? You can cuff me, shackle me, I don't give a damn what. Just let me see Claire. I need to go to my wife. I have to tell her—I have to make things up to—"

Joel Shepherd shook his head. "I'm really sorry, man. Wish I could, but I can't do it till you're cleared of conspiring to kill her. I'd be in violation of the judge's orders on your bail conditions, for one thing."

Spence saw in the lawman's eyes the futility of arguing.

After finishing his coffee, the sheriff stood up, adding, "And for another, it's high time I finally went to see *my* wife. Seems I've got some grovelin' of my own to do before this morning's done."

EPILOGUE

Seven months later

Spence sprinted down the hospital corridor, heedless of the nurses, lab techs, and other visitors whose heads turned to watch his progress.

If he'd had any inkling Claire would need him, he would have skipped this trip. His partners, Raul Contreras and Mark Lyons, had both told him they'd be happy to cover his duties in their shared security consulting business while he took all the time off that he needed.

But it was Claire herself, weary of his hovering, who'd all but pushed him out the door of the house where she had been raised. *"Go ahead, Spence. Make the trip to Lufkin,"* she'd urged. *"I'm feeling better, really. Talking things through with you and the counselor, and Ellen telling me how well Meg is doing—it's all helped me so much. The only thing you'll be missing is a few more days of hanging around here watching me get bigger."*

Spence would have been happy doing just that, sitting beside her nest of pillows. It didn't matter whether the two of them were smiling over the way Randall Hajek, dead six weeks now, had fooled everyone by leaving his property to a nature conservancy group and his former lover high and dry, or going through floor and countertop samples for the new house they were building on the Monarch property. Spence was content simply playing witness to the growing miracle that had confined his wife to bed rest these past few months.

After what they'd been through, being with Claire at all had taken on the aspect of a miracle to him.

But what if somehow, before he reached her, the miracle slipped through his fingers? When Ellen had called him hours earlier, as he'd been driving home, the normally levelheaded woman sounded flustered, telling him little more than, "Sorry, Spence. This can't wait. Lenore and I have to get her to the hospital right now if we don't want to end up taking care of business on the side of the road somewhere."

Two weeks, Spence kept thinking. We were supposed to have two more weeks until this happened. What if something's wrong?

He took a right turn where a sign pointed to BIRTHING SUITES. And banged into a man whose charts went flying across the corridor.

Spence stopped, mainly because he recognized Claire's obstetrician, a doctor with silver-streaked red hair and kind eyes that crinkled at the corners when he smiled.

"Sorry, Dr. Baker," Spence said, taking in the blue scrubs beneath his white coat. "But why aren't you in with my wife?"

As Spence helped him pick up the charts, Dr. Baker said, "Because my job's already over, Mr. Winslow— whole thing happened so fast, I hardly had time to put on my catcher's mitt."

Spence blinked. That couldn't be right. They'd been practicing Lamaze breathing for weeks. He was going to be there, holding Claire's hand and coaching her through every last contraction.

The doctor's blue eyes sparkled. "Why don't you come and take a look at how we did . . . *Dad?*"

Later Spence would not remember Dr. Baker escorting him those final few steps, nor would he recall both Ellen and Lenore stepping out of the room, offering hugs of congratulation before allowing him to go in on his own.

The only thing he knew was Claire, who smiled at him sleepily, a pink bundle cradled in her arms. Though her wavy hair was pulled straight back and her face was as pale as milk behind its freckles, her brown eyes glowed like the harvest moon outside the window.

"Claire," he breathed before he gazed down for the first time at the perfect rosebud of a face that peeped out from the swaddling. The newborn's eyes were closed, but her mouth worked at dream-time feeding.

"This is Sophie Hannah," Claire whispered, her eyes gleaming. Then she gazed down at the bassinet by her side, where an identical pink bundle raised a tiny, perfectly formed fist. "And this—this is Olivia Marie. Look at what we made, Spence—oh, just look at them."

Hearing her voice break with emotion, Spence felt his own throat clog with tears. Not caring when one broke free to wash down his face, he wrapped his arm around Claire and leaned to kiss her sweetly, his heart breaking into pieces and re-forming itself into something far more expansive than the organ that had beat in him before.

And then, one by one, he held each of them in turn: his beautiful twin daughters, and then their mother, the woman whose faith and love had carried him from hell itself into a heaven he meant to spend his whole life striving to deserve.

When the nights are steamy and
everything can change in a flash,
take cover from the...

Heat
Lightning

COLLEEN THOMPSON

a special preview

Coming November 2006!

CHAPTER ONE

Beneath the vapor lights past moonrise, all color is corrupted. From the humid, summer night sky to the paint of cars in a parking lot to the ski mask worn by the single, sweating man there, nothing appears natural. Nothing appears real.

But the man inside the ski mask doesn't notice, absorbed as he is by the small, square SUV whose lights have just winked out. His full attention is commanded by the slender figure emerging from the vehicle and by his own, vise-like grip on the steel shopping cart he has maneuvered into prime position.

That focus is his gift, the blessing left to him in place of the fool's burden of a conscience. Tonight it serves him well—or would, except he fails to note the other vehicle that slips into the lot, its headlights dark despite the dim illumination. The movement is peripheral, no more important than the stirring of hot breezes or the first pulse of distant thunder . . .

Or the question of what color blood will gleam beneath these eerie lights.

* * *

If anyone in Houston should avoid a poorly lit grocery store parking lot after sunset, it was Luz Maria Montoya, who had spent the past three years pissing off people for a living. Not that she lost much sleep worrying about it. Her job, as spokesperson for the Voice of Poverty, charged her with speaking out for those who couldn't afford the fancy lawyers of the select citizens she offended during her frequent appearances on the evening news.

The trouble was, the business leaders, politicians, and prominent sports figures she went after could afford more than just attorneys. And some of the "help" they hired didn't hesitate to color outside of the lines. Besides that, a number of public figures, especially the sports icons, had unbalanced fans, who wrote her equally unbalanced letters. And then there were Luz Maria's own "admirers," men—and the occasional woman—caught up in the drama of a fresh-faced twenty-six-year-old battling against the system. With her wavy, waist-length hair, her flowing skirts and tinkling bracelets, Luz Maria had apparently become a gypsy warrior goddess in the pantheon of the slightly off. So far this summer, along with the usual hate mail, she had received twenty-seven letters of admiration, eight marriage proposals, and a good many more less traditional invitations—the kind that would have her mama insisting she give up tilting at windmills, or at least cut her black hair short and dress *en ropa profesional*. Luz Maria sighed, thinking how Mama's version of business attire would likely involve a suit of armor bristling with padlocks.

But as she hustled through the scattered parked cars at 10:37 on a suffocatingly humid August night, Luz

Maria Montoya wasn't thinking of the nasty phone messages or the even uglier e-mails and letters she had received in recent days. Her work attracted such things, as naturally as her exhalations drew mosquitoes angling for a late-night snack.

Thoughtlessly, she swatted at a small cloud of the insects as thunder murmured in the distance, then teased her with a half-hearted breeze that stirred the heavy air. Heat lightning licked at the horizon, and Luz Maria thought of turning back for her umbrella. Instead, she flipped her single braid over her shoulder and picked up her pace, eager to escape to the air-conditioned store and grab the only necessities she would be desperate enough to stop for on her way home from a late meeting: Chicken Nibblets canned cat food and a box of tampons.

The nibblets were for *Borracho*, the battle-scarred old tom cat who had wandered into her life—and the open window of her apartment—about six months earlier. The yellow-eyed tabby, with his torn ears, scruffy black-and-silver fur, and broken-off fang, had been so put out after she had had him neutered that ever afterward, he yowled with outrage if she dared present His Majesty with anything less than the most expensive cat food known to man.

Neutered or not, *Borracho*—Spanish for "drunkard"—had no use for the tampons. But as crampy as she felt, Luz Maria figured she would need them any time now. And a pint of vanilla Blue Bell ice cream, too, since *Borracho* wasn't the only one known to compensate with a little pampering.

Heaven only knew that she could use some TLC after this evening's meeting with the board of Tex-Rid, a company planning to build an industrial incinerator a

369

couple of hundred yards upwind from the only low-income daycare center in a rural corner of the county. She'd even put on *pantyhose*—in this heat—for those *idiotas*, yet neither her sacrifice nor the half-dozen adorable toddlers she'd rounded up had dented their resistance.

"Certainly, we would have considered other locations"—Not bothering to hide his sneer, their pompous *piojo* of an attorney had paused to clean his half-moon glasses with a linen handkerchief—*"had there been any* licensed *childcare facilities in the vicinity."*

She would see how smug the louse was when she took reporters to film the sweet-faced grandmother hugging her little charges and serving homemade soups and *tortas*—irresistible Mexican sandwiches. That, in addition to the air quality reports her assistant had unearthed from other areas where Tex-Rid ran incinerators, ought to poke some anthills.

With her thoughts wandering toward a petition demanding a public hearing, Luz Maria was slow to see the movement out of the corner of her eye. Slow to recognize—was that a shopping cart pushed forward by the breeze? Reflexively pulling her shoulder bag beneath her elbow, she jerked her head toward the dull gleam—

And cried out at the sight of the steel cart rushing toward her, or more accurately, the man running behind it, his face obscured by a ski mask.

With a grace born of years of Latin dancing, Luz Maria whirled out of the cart's path. Letting go of the handle, the man leapt at her.

Their collision abruptly cut off Luz Maria's scream.

She found herself pitching forward, her body twisting in mid-fall to land hard on her side.

A fraction of a second later, her attacker hurled himself onto her, slamming her rib cage against the asphalt and bumping her head painfully. There was a metallic bang—the cart striking a parked car. The shrill blast from its alarm cut through the buzzing in Luz Maria's ears and the terror ripping through her.

Now straddling her, her attacker had his hands around her throat, the fingers digging painfully into the soft tissue. She struggled to scream again, but her lungs refused to fill. Fighting to pull his hands away, she ripped nails digging into what felt like gloves. Too late, she remembered the self-defense lessons her sister-in-law had taught her and slashed at her attacker's face in a desperate struggle to reach the dark mask's eyeholes.

Luz Maria's world exploded into shards of sound: the buzzing in her skull, the wailing of the car alarm, an angry snarl of thunder and a distant voice—all overlaid with a torrent of profanity as her assailant shook her by the throat like a pit bull throttling a stray cat.

Behind her eyelids, heat lightning strobed, and there was a series of pops a moment before the cacophony inside her head rose to a crescendo . . .

But in the end, a deathly silence reigned.

"The way I see it," Grant Holcomb's newly-promoted partner, Billy Devlin, went on, "there's not an honest man within a hundred-mile radius who's got a ski mask in his closet. If we could get Wal-Mart and the like to track sales, we could just go ahead and bust the guys before they did any harm."

Grant knew his young partner was deadly earnest, but if Grant laughed at him, the red-headed rookie investigator would simply stare back in confusion. Sucked the joy right out of teasing Howdy Doody.

"Interesting concept, Billy." As Grant turned the corner, the unmarked Crown Victoria's balding tires squealed, and it rent the thick night air with a greasy-sounding backfire. Unlike the "real" investigators in Homicide, those assigned to the Major Assaults Unit's night shift always drew the shittiest heaps. "But what about all those guys preparing for their ski trips?"

"In August?"

Grant shrugged, then decided to screw with the kid despite his cluelessness. Grant told himself he was doing it to keep his skills sharp for the day he'd finally be assigned another partner savvy enough to appreciate his sense of humor, another partner who would get him the way John Zeman had. Besides, jerking chains was just as good as a fresh jolt of caffeine when it came to revving Grant up—or getting him through what promised to be one of the toughest victim interviews he'd ever done.

"Oh, yeah," he said with a mock seriousness that would put the veterans in his unit on alert. "Most of 'em are headed somewhere south of the Equator. Probably the Andes Mountains, down in Chile."

"Don't tell me they got skiing down there, too?" Billy's blue eyes widened, looking lonesome in their nakedness, since his pale blonde brows and lashes were almost invisible. The effect was to make him look younger than his twenty-eight years and somewhat dim, too, which Grant figured could come in handy in their line of work.

Provided that Billy turned out to be smarter than he

seemed. After a week together, the jury was still out on that question. If it proved to be the case, though, Grant thought they could get a lot of mileage out of the Good Cop-Dumb Cop routine.

"Oh, yeah. It's a well-known defense among criminals in this part of the city," Grant said as they rolled up to a red light on Fannin. "Just before popping on their ski masks to commit a violent crime, they book Chilean ski trip packages on the Internet. Then if they don't get caught, they cancel."

During the pause that followed, Grant could've sworn he actually heard gears grinding inside his partner's head. As Grant wondered who the hell had given the kid the answers to the investigators' test, Billy burst out with, "I've been warned about you, Holcomb. By more than one of your ex-partners. You like to fuck with people. Well, I'm here to tell you to save it for the suspects."

Billy shot him an intense stare and Grant flipped on the dome light. Amazing. Though he was clearly pissed, without visible eyebrows, the kid couldn't muster a facial expression if his very life depended on it.

"What the hell are you looking at?" asked Billy as he switched off the light.

"An edge," Grant told him seriously. "And I can damned well guarantee we're going to need one to get through an investigation involving this particular victim."

"Luz Maria Montoya? I saw her on the news last week, demanding that somebody tear down those crack houses off of Navigation. Sure, she stirs up her fair share of shit now and then, but what's the big deal? It's the city she goes after, and rich schmucks who can't think past their wallets. Not regular guys like us."

After crossing the light rail tracks, Grant pulled into the hospital parking lot, swung into a space reserved for a day-shift administrator, and jammed the brakes on hard. His gaze locked front and center, he said, "The Z-man was a guy like us. A guy *better* than us—or me at any rate."

Billy gripped the door handle, then hesitated before saying, "Aw, hell. I forgot about that. I—uh—I'm sorry, Grant. I heard he was your partner, but I completely forgot *she* was involved. I was still with the Northwest Patrol then, and I'd only been with the department for a few . . . Listen, you think you can handle this tonight? You don't want to get in trouble your last shift before vacation. Let's call the lieutenant to see if somebody else can take this—"

Grant popped the steering wheel with the heel of his hand, then ripped his shaking fingers through his short-cropped, wavy hair. "Lieutenant Mouton's out on leave—and I can do my job. I just have to remember that *this* time, it's Luz Maria Montoya who's the victim, and looking into it's my duty."

If he was going to get through this investigation, he needed to keep focused on those two facts, instead of his regret.

The regret that Montoya's assailant had fallen short in his attempt to kill her.

FADE *the* HEAT
COLLEEN THOMPSON

Someone is setting fires in the Houston *barrio,* and Dr. Jack Montoya is the first intended victim. Is there some connection between the torching of his apartment and the gorgeous blonde from his past who appears at his clinic on the same day? For sure, Reagan Hurley turns up the flames of his libido, but these days the beautiful firefighter is more interested in putting out conflagrations than fanning old sparks. Yet when a hotly contested mayoral race turns ugly, when Reagan's life is threatened and Jack's career almost destroyed, when desire sizzles uncontrollably between them, it seems that no one will be able to . . . *Fade the Heat.*
